'Fabulous – an utter trea...

'So clever. I stopped trying to outguess Andrew Wilson and just enjoyed the ride' **Elly Griffiths**

'Fiendishly well-plotted, hugely entertaining – one feels Agatha Christie would have been delighted' **Lucy Foley**

'A heart of darkness beats within this sparkling series. Fizzy with charm yet edged with menace' **A. J. Finn**

'Beautifully written . . . I felt as though I was walking by Agatha Christie's side' **Jane Corry**

'A must for connoisseurs of Golden Age crime fiction' **Sean O'Connor**

'So damn clever – brilliant!' **Kate Weinberg**

'Brilliantly plotted, stylishly written' **Amanda Craig**

'The queen of crime is the central character in this audacious mystery . . . thrilling' *Guardian*

'A brilliant idea to turn a "lady novelist" into a sleuth . . . a fascinating blend of biography, intrigue and melodrama' *Evening Standard*

'This clever whodunit is a fitting tribute to Christie' *The Lady*

'The plot takes multiple unexpected turns before a neat solution that pays homage to Christie's own best fiction. Golden age fans will hope for more' *Publishers Weekly*

Andrew Wilson is the highly acclaimed author of biographies of Patricia Highsmith, Sylvia Plath and Alexander McQueen. His journalism has appeared in the *Guardian*, the *Daily Telegraph*, the *Observer* and the *Sunday Times*. This is his fifth novel.

Also by Andrew Wilson

FICTION

The Lying Tongue

A Talent For Murder

A Different Kind of Evil

Death in a Desert Land

NON-FICTION

Alexander McQueen: Blood Beneath the Skin

Mad Girl's Love Song: Sylvia Plath and Life Before Ted

Shadow of the Titanic:
The Extraordinary Stories of Those Who Survived

Harold Robbins: The Man Who Invented Sex

Beautiful Shadow: A Life of Patricia Highsmith

ANDREW WILSON

I SAW HIM DIE

I Saw Him Die is not authorised by Agatha Christie Ltd

SIMON &
SCHUSTER

London · New York · Sydney · Toronto · New Delhi

First published in Great Britain by Simon & Schuster UK Ltd, 2020
This paperback edition published 2021

Copyright © Andrew Wilson, 2020

The right of Andrew Wilson to be identified as author of this work has been
asserted in accordance with the Copyright, Designs and Patents Act, 1988.

1 3 5 7 9 10 8 6 4 2

Simon & Schuster UK Ltd
1st Floor
222 Gray's Inn Road
London WC1X 8HB

Simon & Schuster Australia, Sydney

Simon & Schuster India, New Delhi

www.simonandschuster.co.uk
www.simonandschuster.com.au
www.simonandschuster.co.in

A CIP catalogue record for this book
is available from the British Library

Paperback ISBN: 978-1-4711-7354-7
eBook ISBN: 978-1-4711-7353-0

Typeset in the UK by M Rules
Printed and bound in Great Britain by CPI Group (UK) Ltd, Croydon, CR0 4YY

MIX
Paper from
responsible sources
FSC® C020471

To M. F.

Chapter One

I made my way down the grand central staircase, preparing myself to meet a murderer and his – or her – potential victim. The borrowed jewels and a beautiful emerald-green evening gown, a gift from my sister, gave me a false, hollow confidence. I forced a smile in the direction of my friend John Davison, a smile which masked not only a raft of uncertainties and doubts, but a deep sense of dissatisfaction, if not anger.

After all, I was supposed to be having a few relaxing weeks on the Isle of Skye before my wedding to my dear Max the following month. My plan was to travel to this romantic island in the Scottish Highlands with my daughter, Rosalind, my secretary, Carlo, and her sister, Mary. The holiday would give me the chance to rest after a rather hectic year. I would go on some lovely, long rambles across the moors, perhaps even lose a few pounds. The fresh air would do me good and I would walk down the aisle of the chapel in Edinburgh with a clear head, a slightly better figure and a peach-like complexion. The last thing I wanted to think about was murder.

But that wasn't how it had turned out. The week before I was due to travel to Scotland, Davison had sent me a note, asking me to meet him at his London flat in Albany. After the preliminaries and polite small talk my friend, who worked for the Secret Intelligence Service, got down to business.

'I know the timing could be better,' he said, clearing his throat. 'But there's something that we would like you to do.'

'What is it?' I asked, taking a sip of soda water.

'I wouldn't ask you, but as I know you're going to Scotland, to Skye in particular, it seemed you were the ideal person for the job.'

I was so taken aback at his suggestion that I give up my precious holiday that I was at a loss for words.

'One of our former agents, Robin Kinmuir, who lives on Skye, believes that he is in danger. He's received a series of threatening letters informing him that his life will be taken from him.'

The situation intrigued me and, despite myself, I wanted to know more. 'I'm not saying I will agree to anything, but tell me a little more about Robin Kinmuir.'

'He's a friend of Hartford's, or was at one point,' said Davison. 'The head of the Service regarded Kinmuir as one of the best agents we ever had. He had a great brain, a photographic memory, and was incredibly brave and fearless. Then he experienced a run of bad luck. His only son, Timothy, was killed in the war, a loss which hit him hard. He took to drink. His wife Catherine, who was younger than him, left him – or rather, it seems she simply walked out of their house and disappeared.'

That word always made my heart miss a beat because of

those 'missing' days in 1926 when the press reported that I had disappeared.

'And then . . . well, in 1916, Kinmuir made a terrible error of judgement out in Maastricht, which resulted in the deaths of eleven of our men,' Davison continued. 'Although he managed to make it back to Britain, he never forgave himself and his drinking became worse. In fact, I'm sure he would have died had it not been for Hartford, who sent him off to a place in the country.'

'And the letters? What do they say?'

Davison reached for his inside jacket pocket. 'I've got a copy of one of them here,' he said. 'Typed on what looks like an old machine, it warns Kinmuir that his time is up. Here, listen to this.' He unfolded a square of paper. '"I know what you did. Soon you will pay for your crimes with your life. Look over your shoulder – death will come when you least expect it."'

'Sounds a bit melodramatic,' I said. 'How do you know it's not from some crackpot? What makes you think there's any substance behind these threats?'

'One could easily dismiss it if we were dealing with an ordinary member of the public,' said Davison. 'It's Kinmuir's work for the agency that sets him apart. Of course, there may be nothing to it, but I said to Hartford that we – or I, at least – would investigate. Although Kinmuir lives in this country, it's not strictly within the remit of the Secret Intelligence Service – as you know, the SIS is a primarily a foreign intelligence service. But what happened abroad may well have a bearing on the case.'

'I see. And are there any suspects?'

'One line of enquiry is that it's something to do with the failed mission in Maastricht. Either that or ... well, let's just say that Kinmuir has hardly led a blameless life.'

'In what respect?'

Davison paused as he considered how best to express himself. 'He had a certain reputation with the ladies. Several affairs and indiscretions, particularly during the time he was drinking heavily. There are also a number of suspect or failed business deals that we're looking into.'

'And who would benefit from his death?'

'Ah, the perennial question! Kinmuir has a substantial estate. Although it goes by the name of Dallach Lodge it's actually a huge old pile and sits in hundreds of acres of land. On his death that would all pass to his next of kin, his nephew, James, his late brother's son.'

'Well, he's the obvious suspect,' I said, standing up. 'There, you've heard what I've got to say on the matter. Now, I must go and finish packing for my trip.'

'You mean, that's it?' said Davison, barely able to disguise the disappointment in his voice. 'You're not prepared to help?'

'Davison, I don't know if you heard, but I'm getting married,' I said, rather more impatiently than I meant to. 'I really haven't got time for this at the moment.'

'So you're prepared to let a man die?'

'Oh, stop,' I said, reaching for my coat. 'Don't try to black-mail me into this.'

'Listen – if it's any comfort, I would come with you. Kinmuir now runs his country house, Dallach Lodge, as a hotel. Of course, he would never call it that – his guests are supposed to feel like old friends who have just come to stay for a few days. Although the estate is a quite valuable one, recently Kinmuir has suffered from a lack of funds. It seems he can't afford the upkeep of the house without taking in paying guests. A number of people are about to arrive at the lodge and we suspect that one of them may want to kill Kinmuir.'

'Why doesn't he simply cancel their stay? That would be the easiest thing, surely?'

'That's what he wanted to do, but we pointed out to him that the best way to catch his murderer – if he or she does exist – would be to act normally and open his hotel as usual.'

'Yes, I can see that,' I said. 'But why can't you just go on your own – or get someone else to accompany you?'

'We've been through all the different possibilities. You're the best person suited for the job. What with your sharp mind and your ability to get to the—'

I cut him off. 'I don't need to hear your flattery, Davison. The truth of the matter is you've got no one else. I'm right, aren't I? Inform Hartford from me that he really needs to sort out his recruitment, especially of the fairer sex.' I paused. 'Tell me this – and I want you to answer honestly, or with as much honesty as you can muster: what would happen if I didn't choose to help you?'

A grave expression crossed Davison's face. 'I'll be frank,' he said. 'Yes, you are the only woman we have free at the moment. If I were to go by myself, or take another man with me, the murderer might suspect that we were from the police, if not the agency.' He hesitated for a moment. 'But if we were to register *together*, you and I, well, it would give us quite a good cover, don't you think?'

'Are you really suggesting that we turn up there as ...' I could hardly get the words out. 'As a *couple* ... when I'm preparing to get married next month?'

Davison must have seen the horrified expression on my face because the lines of seriousness around his mouth melted away and he burst out laughing.

'Sorry – but your face was a picture!'

'How could you be so—'

'I know – it was beastly of me. I couldn't help myself.'

'Look – if you want me to assist you then the least you can do is show me a little respect.' The words made me sound like a prig, and even though I was beginning to see the funny side of Davison's teasing, I wasn't going to let him off the hook that easily. 'Really, it's quite uncalled for.'

'I apologise,' he said, trying to compose himself. 'No, of course I realise that would be quite an unsuitable arrangement. What I propose is for the two of us to turn up at Dallach Lodge as cousins. You register as yourself – and tell the truth about your forthcoming marriage to Mr Max Mallowan. You'll have to do this anyway because you want to register the banns in Scotland. And it will be easy for me to be plain old John Davison, a middle-ranking civil servant. I am here to be your chaperone in the weeks leading up to your nuptials. So what do you say?'

He looked at me with a mischievous glint in his eyes. 'You never know, you might help save an innocent man's life,' he said. 'Surely that's worth sacrificing a little of your holiday?'

'Oh, very well,' I sighed. 'But on condition that it's for a short amount of time only. I won't do anything that puts the date of my wedding at risk. That wouldn't be fair on Max.'

Of course, the man I was due to marry could never know. Max – who himself was seeing various friends in the south of England – thought that I was simply taking a holiday in Skye with my daughter, my secretary and her sister. But what could I tell my travel companions? It was too late to cancel the trip and they were so looking forward to journeying north with me.

It was no surprise to learn that Davison had already thought of this. The four of us would check into the hotel in Broadford, on Skye, as arranged, and after a day or so, I would receive a telegram from my literary agent Edmund Cork requesting my presence back in London. I would say that there were serious problems with the script of my forthcoming play *Black Coffee*, which was due to open in December. The director was on the point of quitting the production. My return to London was a matter of urgency: there was too much work to do from such a distance. Although I was sure that Carlo and Mary would offer to accompany me, I would persuade them to stay on in Skye so that they could give Rosalind the holiday she deserved. I would travel back to Scotland as soon as I could.

What Davison had not counted on in his plan was the sense of guilt I felt at abandoning Rosalind. No doubt this was made worse by the fact it was not the first time. I had left her in 1922 during my ten-month-long trip around the world with Archie, who was then my husband. There was the unfortunate episode of my disappearance in 1926 and then the separation when I travelled to Ur, in southern Iraq, in 1928. During that time in the desert there were times when I doubted I would ever see my daughter again.

The few days we had spent in Broadford with Carlo and her sister, Mary, were a delight. We had enjoyed a picnic in a field overlooking the bay and played endless games of cards and cat's cradle. As I watched my daughter explore the beach I had to keep telling myself that she was a resilient child. After all, she was now eleven years old, away at boarding school, and her headmistress told me she was a happy and self-sufficient girl. Yet I knew that my separation from her would leave me feeling wretched. I could not allow Rosalind to see my distress and so, when the day of our parting arrived, I had to steel myself as best I could. As the taxi pulled away from the hotel in Broadford, I pretended to myself that I was just popping to the shops and I would see her in a couple of hours. However, instead of taking me to the ferry and then to the railway station, the car drove me across the island to a deserted spot to pick up Davison.

Once we had collected Davison, we travelled towards the south-eastern side of Skye, past a number of abandoned cottages, moors covered in purple heather and long stretches of bogland. The drama of the island was on an epic scale: here was a true example of the sublime that I had only previously seen in paintings or photographs.

Since arriving on the island I had been transfixed by the sky. The atmosphere was constantly changing: one moment the clouds were black and ominous, the next the sun would cast its light down and transform the harsh landscape into a sight of savage beauty. Before I journeyed to Scotland, friends had told me to expect four seasons in one day and they had not been wrong. During the course of twenty-four hours one could experience rain, wind and mist but also the most beautiful pure sunlight I think I had ever seen.

Eventually, we turned off the road and down a lane until we reached a set of gates leading to a drive lined with rowan and birch trees to Dallach Lodge. It was a handsome, gabled, three-storey baronial house, built from red sandstone, standing on the banks of a sea loch, set within a lush garden with monkey puzzle and red cedar trees. Above it, on a higher ridge that dominated the bleak landscape, was a ruined castle. In the distance, across the Sound of Sleat, one could see the rocky peaks of the Knoydart Peninsula on the mainland stretching up into the clouds.

'It's all very *Castle of Otranto*,' whispered Davison as we stepped out of the car. 'In fact, it looks the perfect place for a murder.'

*

All that had happened in the whirlwind of the preceding few days. And now here I was on my first night at Dallach Lodge. The drawing room was ablaze with candles and the sparkle of diamonds. The ladies wore elegant evening gowns and the men sported dinner jackets.

A deep voice – upper-class English but with a light Scottish lilt – boomed across the room, followed by the appearance of a huge bear of a man with a ruddy face and enormous whiskers. I knew from Davison that Kinmuir was sixty-seven years old.

'Here are our two new arrivals. Hello – I'm Robin Kinmuir. Welcome. You must be Mrs Christie and Mr Davison?'

'Yes, that's right,' said Davison, shaking Kinmuir's large hand.

The owner of Dallach Lodge knew of our purpose at the hotel, but he had been instructed to treat us as ordinary guests. At the earliest opportunity we would question Kinmuir about the letters he had received and try to learn more about the other guests who were staying there.

'Now what would you like to drink?' A sickly-looking butler approached with glasses of champagne. I noticed that his hands were shaking as he held the tray. I didn't want to appear to be rude and so after Davison took one I did the same, even though I had no intention of drinking it. 'Let me introduce you to everybody,' said Kinmuir.

Kinmuir had lost most of the hair from the top and back of his head. The little that was left had been combed across his bare scalp to give the impression that he had more hair than he possessed. It also looked as though he had taken refuge in the bottle, dyeing his few remaining strands a garish reddish-brown. 'First of all, the ladies. Mrs Buchanan, please, you must meet the new guests.'

He placed a friendly, if not proprietorial, hand on the lower back of a slim, birdlike woman who could have been aged anywhere between forty-five and sixty. She had not lost her beauty and there was something strangely familiar about her. She wore a long, black silk dress and around her throat a diamond necklace cast a vibrant light onto her face. She had blonde hair of a shade a little too bright, which made me suspect that she, too, had sought the help of a chemical agent. She held herself with a poise and an elegance that made me guess that she had been a dancer, or had trained as one when she was younger.

'Mrs Agatha Christie, Mr John Davison – this is Mrs Eliza Buchanan,' said Kinmuir. 'To me she is an old friend, but you may know her from the world of the theatre.'

'Of course,' I said, realising where I had seen her before. I knew that even though her stage name was Mrs Eliza Buchanan, she had never married. 'I thought your Lady Macbeth one of the very best I have ever seen.'

She beamed at the compliment. '*Out, damned spot! out, I say! One: two: why, then, 'tis time to do't,*' she intoned in a breathy, theatrical manner. 'But I mustn't steal the show,' she added, bowing her head and stepping back to allow Kinmuir to introduce the other guests.

'This is Miss Vivienne Passerini,' said Kinmuir. 'I'm told she is a very brilliant botanist and has just returned from her travels.'

'Oh, I wouldn't quite put it like that,' she said, laughing.

Miss Passerini was a beautiful young woman with emerald-green eyes, jet-black hair cut into a neat bob and an olive complexion.

'Where did you visit?' asked Davison, taking a sip of his champagne.

'I've just come back from Berlin,' she said. 'I've been following the trail of the naturalist and explorer Alexander von Humboldt, or at least part of his travels, for a book I'm working on. He was born there, you see.'

'How intriguing,' Davison replied. 'Am I right in thinking that he stopped on the island of Tenerife on his way to Venezuela?'

'Yes, he did,' Miss Passerini said. The two of them started to talk about the history of exploration, plant classification and the fauna and flora of various far-flung parts of the world.

My memories of Tenerife were not pleasant and as I turned away, Kinmuir introduced me to two handsome men in their twenties.

'Mrs Christie, may I present my nephew Mr James Kinmuir, and his friend from Oxford, Mr Rufus Phillips.'

If Robin Kinmuir were to be murdered, here was – by my own reckoning at least – the prime suspect for the crime. I would see what I could find out about James Kinmuir.

'Do you live here on Skye, Mr Kinmuir?'

'Please, call me James,' the young man said, flashing a smile. He was tall and broad-shouldered, with a strong nose and a fringe of blond hair that gave him the look of an overgrown schoolboy. 'At the moment, only during the summer months. The rest of the time I teach – at Flytes, a school just outside Edinburgh. I try to interest the boys in the Greats. Not that I get much thanks from the little brutes.'

This interested me. The implication was that he had to work, that he didn't have an independent income. Perhaps his intention was to get his hands on his uncle's estate. But if so, why would he alert Robin Kinmuir by sending him threatening letters?

I turned to his friend. 'And you, Mr Phillips, are you on holiday here?'

'Yes and no,' he said. Rufus Phillips was a little shorter than his friend, with dark brown curly hair and exceptionally long eyelashes that gave his face a rather girlish look. 'I've just left the Slade art school in London. I'm doing a spot of travelling and supporting myself by doing the odd painting, such as they are.'

'Rufus is being terribly modest,' said James. 'He's a wonderful portraitist – in fact, he's working on an oil of my uncle. Of course, Rufus insists he doesn't want to be paid for it. My uncle hasn't seen it yet, but when he does I think he'll find that it really captures his—'

'My what?' said Kinmuir, slapping his nephew and his friend on the shoulders. 'No doubt you'll show me as the decrepit old fool I am. *Sans teeth, sans eyes, sans taste, sans everything,* like auntie upstairs.' He turned to me to explain. 'I'm talking about Mrs Veronica Kinmuir, I forget how old she is, she's the wife of my father's late brother. She is nearly blind from cataracts, hasn't left the house in years and talks mostly gibberish, childish nonsense. For a long time, she didn't want anything to do with me – treated me something rotten – but when she started to lose her marbles I thought it only right to bring her here.' He addressed Rufus Phillips again. 'I hope you don't paint me as nothing more than a mess of jagged lines and crooked angles. The truth is, I'm not sure I have an eye for art at all – the house is full of paintings, but I've barely given any of them a second glance. Yes, I'm a terrible philistine.'

Kinmuir scratched what looked like an insect bite on his throat.

'As for the avant garde – don't get me started on that! Once I stood in front of a Picasso for a good ten minutes, shifting my position, walking around to take it in from different perspectives, but I couldn't make head or tail of it – and I'm

ANDREW WILSON

talking quite literally. If ladies weren't present,' he said, nodding in my direction, 'I think I would express myself rather more forcefully, if you get my drift.' He took a sip from his glass of soda water. 'But you're not here to listen to my gripes about the state of art today. Let's leave these two scoundrels and I'll introduce you to the group over there.'

He pointed to a trio of people standing in the far corner of the room, which comprised the local doctor, Jeremy Fitzpatrick, a man in his sixties who was completely bald, and two middle-aged sisters, May and Isabella Frith-Stratton. The pair of rather odd-looking women were complaining about the midges – they were simply terrible, such a pest, they said – and were pleading with the doctor to tell them how to prevent being attacked by the beastly creatures.

'Sorry to interrupt,' said Kinmuir, addressing the Frith-Strattons. 'I thought you'd like to meet a fellow author.' Their faces lit up for a moment, before Kinmuir added, 'And Mrs Christie is about to get married. I'm right in saying that the wedding is going to be in Edinburgh next month?'

'Yes, it is,' I said. 'I'm here with my cousin, Mr John Davison, to have a few days' holiday before the ceremony.'

The sisters looked at me with an indifference that bordered on hostility.

Robin Kinmuir cleared his throat and changed the subject. 'As I was saying, Mrs Christie here is a writer of detective stories. May and Isabella, who are twin sisters, write romance novels, under – what name was it again?'

'Maybella Acton,' said May, pronouncing the name as if she were reading it from a catalogue. 'A *Heart United, Force of Destiny*?'

I was none the wiser. And although I smiled with enthusiasm, no doubt my ignorance was quite obvious to the sisters.

'Perhaps the best known is *Bonds of Blood* and its sequel *Bonds of Love*,' added Isabella, in a more natural manner. 'But they've all proved very popular, particularly in the lending libraries. We find that people want to read something that takes them out of themselves, books that offer escape and romance. They don't want to be reminded of the general awfulness of life, of brutality – of death.'

The Frith-Stratton sisters had obviously taken a dislike to me. An awkward silence descended on our little group, one that was broken by the doctor.

'Living out here and covering such a wide area, I don't get much time to read at all,' said Dr Fitzpatrick in his thick Scottish accent. 'I'm afraid my reading material is confined to my patients' notes and the occasional page of the *Lancet*.' I noticed that he had kind eyes and a warm smile. He had, it seemed, the perfect bedside manner of the country doctor, not like some of the more sinister medical men I had come across in the past.

'How did you and Mr Kinmuir become friends?' I asked him, after the two sisters broke away from the group and accompanied Kinmuir across the room.

'Now that's a funny story,' he said, his eyes glinting with delight. 'I'm not sure Kinmuir would thank me for telling you this, but he's out of earshot . . .'

As I listened to the anecdote – which involved a drunken Kinmuir, a bolting horse and a nasty bog – I noticed that there was a solitary figure standing by the window with his back to the room. From him there emanated an air of mystery.

The doctor continued to talk of his friend. 'Of course, Kinmuir drank a good deal back then. But he managed to cut back – not like me, I'm afraid, drinking whisky as if there's no tomorrow – and now he's as fit as a fiddle, as they say. I examined him only a few weeks back and he's as strong as an ox. I told him he'll outlive the lot of us.'

But my attention had wandered to the enigmatic man whose face I could not see.

'That is amusing,' I said. 'Now, tell me, Dr Fitzpatrick, who is that man over by the window?'

The doctor followed my gaze. 'The dark-haired one? I believe he is called – let me see if I remember – Mr Simon Peterson. Seems a decent enough chap. Keeps himself very much to himself, though, as you can see. Not one for small talk.'

'Do you know anything more about him?'

'Only that he's been here for a few days. Works in shipping, I believe. Very popular with the ladies. Sorry, that's all I know. Why?' Dr Fitzpatrick took another swig from his tumbler of whisky and said in a conspiratorial manner, 'You don't think he's about to commit a ... a *murder*, do you?'

'My imagination does run away with me at times,' I said, humouring him.

He lowered his voice. 'And, by the way, don't worry about the Miss Frith-Strattons. I think they took against you a little because of the news of your forthcoming nuptials. My impression is that they write about romance precisely because they don't ... well, because they don't have very much of it in their own lives.'

'That is very sad,' I said.

'Rather like you and murder,' he said, laughing. 'You write about it because you've never experienced it yourself. Or rather – I hope that's the case.'

'Indeed,' I said, trying to smile.

I recalled the words Davison had spoken to me when we first arrived at Dallach Lodge. Did someone really intend to commit a murder here? And if so, what could we do to prevent it?

Due to the death threats against Kinmuir, Davison had arranged to sleep in his dressing room on a camp bed. The next morning my friend reported that despite the older man's awful snores, the night had passed peacefully. He said that he would continue to watch Kinmuir throughout the day, and it was my job to try to make a few gentle enquiries into the guests.

First I intended to explore the kitchens. I knew that one of the easiest ways to kill someone was by poisoning. I had tried to talk to the cook, Mrs Baillie, the previous night – I said I was interested in seeing how she prepared certain Scottish recipes – but she was too busy to see me. Then she sent word that she had a few minutes to spare after breakfast.

Breakfast was a lavish affair with a sideboard full of silver dishes of kedgeree, bacon, sausage, black pudding and eggs: poached, scrambled and fried. Everyone was there apart from Mr Peterson, who apparently preferred to take his breakfast in his room, and Dr Fitzpatrick, who had stayed at the house overnight but left early to attend a sick child in a nearby village.

I took a minute or so to study those gathered around the long table. Mrs Buchanan, the actress, seemed to radiate light, but how much of her character was real, how much a self-conscious performance? Vivienne Passerini, the striking botanist, was like none of the stuffy English girls I had met – there was a spirit of adventure about her that I liked and admired. Then there was the boyish pair James Kinmuir and Rufus Phillips, the young painter; they seemed as close as friends could be. And what was I to make of the Frith-Stratton sisters, Isabella and May? I noticed that May followed Isabella around like her shadow, walking to the sideboard behind her, picking up the same dishes, eating at the same time. The effect was like watching a strange and unsettling mime act.

My eyes came to settle on Robin Kinmuir, dressed in his tweeds, looking the part of laird of the land. As he tucked into a hearty breakfast, no one would ever guess that he had received a threat to his life. Perhaps the presence of Davison was doing something to soothe his nerves.

Davison watched Robin Kinmuir carefully – as he had at dinner the night before – making sure that no one leant over him to put something into his food or swapped his water glass or coffee cup for another. If a killer was present in the house, and if they chose to use poisoning as their preferred method of murder, it seemed unlikely that they would risk corrupting a whole dish. And there was only so much Davison could do. For instance, he could hardly examine everything placed in front of Kinmuir, neither did it seem fair – or prudent – to test what he was about to eat on the two black Labradors that had the run of the house. Everything Davison and I did had to be done with the greatest subtlety; we could not risk our cover being exposed.

After finishing his breakfast, Robin Kinmuir started to tell the table about the history of the ruined castle that sat on the ridge above Dallach Lodge. Although it looked medieval, in fact the family seat of the Kinmuirs dated only to the nineteenth century. The original mansion house, built in the seventeenth century, was extended by the famous Scottish architect James Gillespie Graham in the early nineteenth century. Thirty years later, a fire destroyed a good deal of that building and a new mock-Gothic wing was added. By the end of the nineteenth century, when yet another fire consumed the building, the Kinmuirs decided to abandon the castle for the baronial lodge which had also been designed and extended by Gillespie Graham.

'What with all the fires, it seems somewhat ironic that the family motto is *Resurgere ex cineribus*,' Robin Kinmuir observed. 'To rise again out of the ashes.'

As the polite laughter died down, Mrs Buchanan looked along the table. 'It looks rather murky outside,' she said. 'What are our plans for the day? Oh, there's no point asking you, Robin – no doubt you'll begin your day by taking the dogs for a walk. But what about the rest of you?'

James Kinmuir was the first to answer. 'Rufus was keen to go riding, but tragically we don't have any horses – they all succumbed to some terrible infection and they haven't been replaced yet,' he told us. 'So instead it's going to be a spot of shooting. We thought we might try for grouse since it's the first day of the season.'

'Well, don't think you're going to take the dogs,' said Robin Kinmuir.

'Don't worry, Uncle, I won't spoil your morning routine,' said James in a good-natured manner.

'I've always thought the grouse such a curious-looking bird,' said Rufus Phillips. 'What with that bright red comb over its eye which looks almost like a wound. Of course, I've only seen them in paintings and in books, never in real life.' He looked at Robin Kinmuir, who was buttering a piece of toast. 'Do you think we'll be in luck?'

'I would think so,' Robin Kinmuir replied. 'There will be plenty hiding in heather on the moor. James will show you. You should bag a few for supper, that's for sure.'

'I disapprove of shooting, as Mr Kinmuir well knows,' said Mrs Buchanan. 'It's barbaric. I can't stand the sight, or the taste, of meat. Like my dear friend George Bernard Shaw, I'm a vegetarian. If any of you are interested, I'd be more than happy to explain the reasoning and I believe I have a few pamphlets upstairs. We can all lead perfectly healthy lives without eating animals.' As James bit into a piece of sausage, Mrs Buchanan cast him a hostile look before turning to me and asking, 'And, Mrs Christie, what does the day have in store for you?'

'I thought I might take a walk down to the loch or up to the ruined castle,' I said. 'I'm intrigued to see it for myself after hearing its history from Mr Kinmuir.'

'I might join you,' she said. 'I once took part in a performance of *Hamlet* in a ruined castle in Denmark. Absolutely thrilling, quite uncanny. One could almost feel Prince Hamlet's ghost reach out and touch the back of one's neck.'

'It must have been a wonderful experience,' said Miss Passerini. 'Gertrude is such a fascinating part.'

Mrs Buchanan expressed her displeasure with a quick flash of the eyes. 'I played Ophelia, my dear,' she said with a thin, withering smile.

'Oh, I didn't mean to imply that . . .' said Miss Passerini. 'It was just . . .'

I excused myself from the table and made my way through the hall towards the servants' steps to the kitchens below. Mrs Baillie was sitting at a well-scrubbed table enjoying a welcome cup of tea, while a couple of girls busied themselves clearing up the breakfast pots and pans. I introduced myself and told the cook that the dinner and breakfast were quite superb. I informed her of my forthcoming wedding and the fact that I wanted to extend my repertoire in the kitchen.

'You know what they say, the way to a man's heart and all that.' Mrs Baillie spoke with such a heavy Scottish accent that at first I didn't understand her. She must have been used to seeing the rather blank, stupid look that crossed my face because she repeated the sentence, enunciating her words as she did so.

My real purpose was to ask about the arrangements of the kitchen, who handled the ingredients and prepared the food, and how it was transported to the dining room. Then I hoped to find out a little more about the guests staying at Dallach Lodge. But first I needed to gain her trust. I suspected that the way to Mrs Baillie's heart was through her cooking and I was right. As soon as she started to talk about the cuisine of

Scotland and the Highlands she could not stop. She described recipes passed down from her mother and grandmother and how she made her own sausages, of which Mr James seemed particularly fond.

'So much so that he's recently taken to nabbing them at breakfast,' she said, laughing. 'I've told him the next time I find him stealing he'll feel the back of my hand on his behind. I don't care how old he is.'

She went on to describe a range of dishes that I had never heard of, including Cullen skink, clapshot, cabbie-claw, potted hough and stovies.

'Stovies?' I asked.

'Tatties – potatoes that are slow-cooked in a kind of stew with meat, anything you've got left over from the night before,' she explained. 'It's a good use of the leftovers when it's only the master and—'

Just then we heard a loud scream from upstairs. At the sound of the noise, one of the servant girls standing by the sink dropped the ceramic bowl that she had been cleaning and it smashed into pieces on the flagstone floor. Mrs Baillie's monologue came to an abrupt end and her mouth gaped open like one of the dead fish I had spotted on the cold slab, gutted and ready to be cooked for lunch. I stood up, quickly thanked her and ran up the back stairs and into the hall. In front of the door stood Mrs Buchanan, who was in a state of shock. Her face was pale and her lips had almost turned blue. Her eyes seemed empty and hollow. I took her arm.

'What on earth has happened?' I wanted to ask about Robin Kinmuir, but knew that I couldn't mention his name in case the killer was watching; I had to pretend I had no advance knowledge that a crime might be committed. Where was Davison? Wasn't he supposed to have been looking after Kinmuir. 'Mrs Buchanan?'

She tried to speak, but no words came out of her mouth.

By this point the others had started to gather.

'What's wrong?' asked Isabella Frith-Stratton.

'We heard a scream,' added her frightened sister, just behind her on the stairs.

Through the front door came Vivienne Passerini, an unusual flush to her sallow complexion. 'I heard a gunshot,' she said. 'But I didn't think anything of it because of the grouse shoot.'

At this Mrs Buchanan started to wail again. She put her hands on her ears so as to drown out the noise of her own screams.

'Mrs Buchanan – you must tell me what you've seen,' I said, grabbing one of her hands.

Simon Peterson appeared at the top of the stairs, still in his dressing gown. He had an athletic, muscular body and his face and moustache bore traces of shaving cream, which only seemed to accentuate his handsome features. 'What the hell is going on?' he demanded.

As I started to explain that we weren't quite sure, another figure entered the house. Rufus Phillips looked like he had aged a good ten years. Dirt, and something else, something that looked like blood, were smeared across his smart tweeds. As he opened his mouth to speak, James Kinmuir appeared in the doorway. Tears ran down his face and his blond hair was ruffled and full of mud. His white shirt and tweed jacket were soaked through with blood.

'I didn't mean to … I was out shooting with Rufus … I saw a grouse – or thought I did,' he stammered, trying to catch his breath. It was difficult for him to get his words out. 'I fired and …' He placed a hand against the door to support himself, then slumped to his knees. 'He wasn't supposed to be there. He wasn't supposed to …'

'What the hell have you done?' asked Mr Peterson. 'Who was there? Who was it?'

'It was Robin, Uncle Robin – and I've killed him,' said James.

Chapter Two

The confession served as a kind of explosion, sending shards of shock throughout the house. Mrs Buchanan continued to wail, while Rufus Phillips came to comfort his friend. May and Isabella Frith-Stratton appeared pale and dumbfounded and Vivienne Passerini was being comforted by Simon Peterson. Meanwhile, the servants – the butler, whose name I now knew to be Simkins, together with Mrs Baillie and the couple of maids – had descended on the hall like carrion crows after spotting a fresh kill. In particular, there was something about the relish in Simkins's eyes that unsettled me. Either he was one of those ghouls who simply enjoyed hearing about the murder and suffering of others – and I knew there were plenty of those about – or he was pleased to learn of his master's death.

'Are you sure he's dead?' I asked. But James Kinmuir would not answer me. All colour had drained from his face. 'Mr Kinmuir – James!' I touched his shoulder, but again he was unresponsive. I turned to his friend. 'Mr Phillips – is there any chance that Robin Kinmuir might still be alive? What state did you leave him in?'

'He's dead – I saw it happen,' said Rufus Phillips.

'I was a nurse in the war,' I said. 'Will you come with me and show me where to find him?'

He nodded. 'Will James be all right? He's had a terrible shock.'

'Yes, I'm sure he will.' I looked at Simkins and Mrs Baillie. 'Could you get some brandy for the young man? Make sure he stays here. And could someone please locate the doctor and tell him there's been an accident? And please telephone the police, too.'

I retrieved my coat and stepped outside. The gardens in front of the house – the expanse of lawn, the herbaceous borders, the monkey puzzle and majestic red cedars – were covered in a light mist and the loch was swathed in a low-lying cloud, while the castle on the ridge above the lodge could not be seen.

'A terrible morning for shooting,' I said as Rufus Phillips led me up a track that snaked up to the moor.

'It wasn't this bad when we first set out,' Phillips replied. 'It seemed to descend on us the nearer we got to the top.'

'And what about your guns? Where are they?'

'When we ... when we realised what James had done, we dropped them. We couldn't bear to hold them any longer.'

As I hurried through the damp heather I began to get out of breath, but the young and fit Rufus seemed unaffected by the quick pace and the increased gradient.

'How many shots did you fire?' I asked between gasps.

'I'm not sure. It all happened so quickly. I think I said,

"Look, there's one!" There was something that looked like a grouse in the distance. The next moment James fired. There was a scream and that's when we had the first awful realisation that ... that the thing he had hit was not a bird, but something, *someone* else.' He stopped for a moment and looked at me. 'Do you think James will get into trouble?'

The naivety of the question took me by surprise. 'Well, that's for the police to decide, I'm afraid.'

'Yes, I can see that,' said Phillips.

Eventually, we came up to the ridge of moorland where James Kinmuir had shot his uncle, a man in fear for his life who had come to the agency for help. But we had failed him. I recalled that first conversation I had had with Davison about the case and the flippant remark I had made regarding the person I thought most likely to be Kinmuir's potential murderer: his next of kin, the man who stood to benefit most from his death, his nephew. And so it had come to pass. I asked myself again: where was Davison?

I looked across the purple-tinged moor and into the distance. I could see a figure kneeling on the moor next to two black dogs, his head bowed.

'Is that where it happened?' I asked Phillips.

'Yes – but who's that?'

As we ran towards the lonely spot where Kinmuir had died I realised that the kneeling figure was Davison. He had come to the man's help.

'Is he alive?' I shouted as I approached.

'I'm afraid we've lost him,' said Davison, whose hands were covered in blood. 'I did my best to try to save him, but it was too late. Move off, I say!' He shouted at the two

Labrador dogs who were whimpering by their master's side, one of whom was insistent on licking a spot of blood from Kinmuir's face. 'Can you get these blasted dogs away from him?'

Rufus Phillips dragged the dogs away.

I stared down at the corpse. Kinmuir's right hand, in his death throes, had clutched at a piece of heather, which now lay limp in his palm. His face looked contorted with pain, his mouth set in a horrible grimace.

'Where was he hit?' I asked.

'You can see a wound – here in the right leg,' said Davison. 'I tried to stem the flow of blood by ripping off a piece of my shirt and making a tourniquet. But I'm presuming he must have been hit somewhere else too, although I haven't been able to locate the entry point.'

'Oh God,' said Rufus Phillips, as he turned away and fell, retching, to the ground. 'It's all my fault. If I had not cried out that I had seen a grouse and pointed towards the spot, none of this would have happened.'

'Have the people in the house called for Dr Fitzpatrick?' asked Davison.

'Yes,' I said.

'And what about the police?' he added.

'Let's hope they are on their way too,' I said. But before they arrived I needed to have a word with Davison in private. 'Mr Phillips, would you mind going back to the lodge to see that the police and the doctor have been called? We really do need to get the authorities here as soon as possible. And take these dogs back with you.'

Rufus took another look at the gruesome sight on the

ground and turned away. 'Of course, yes, I'll do that,' he said, as he led the dogs back across the moor in the direction of the house.

We waited until Rufus Phillips could no longer hear us before we started to talk. I didn't want to accuse Davison of relinquishing his duties, yet I still needed to know what he had been doing when Kinmuir had been shot.

'Did you see what happened?' I asked.

'From a distance, yes,' he said. 'I was following Kinmuir, but I didn't want him to know. I watched him leave the house with his dogs and make for the moor and I kept a certain distance behind. I could hear shots across the moor, but didn't think anything of it. Then something must have startled one of the dogs – or perhaps it saw a grouse fall – and the damn thing bolted, followed by the other one. Kinmuir took off too. Of course I ran after him, but I didn't want anyone to see that I was shadowing him. I heard another shot, saw Kinmuir fall. The two young men – Kinmuir junior and Phillips – looked distraught and dashed over to him. When they realised what they had done they went straight back to the house. That's when I ran over here to see if I could save him.'

I looked across the bleak moor to locate the spot where the two young men had been standing when James Kinmuir had fired.

'And I presume there was no one else up here with a gun?' I asked.

'Not that I could see,' said Davison. 'What are you suggesting? That it might not have been James's shot which killed him?'

'I'm not sure,' I said. 'But we have to keep an open mind. The shotguns – Phillips said they dropped them on the ground when they realised the awfulness of the situation. Presumably, they are still there.'

'Let's look,' said Davison.

We tramped across the moorland, our eyes fixed to the earth, until we came across the spot where two shotguns were lying discarded on the ground. We bent down, but did not touch anything.

'What's that, there?' asked Davison, pointing towards the base of a clump of heather.

I leant closer to see. 'It looks like . . .'

'Yes, a cartridge. And there's another one here,' he said, taking out his penknife and using it to turn the cartridges over. 'At some point we'll have to give Hartford the bad news. God knows what he's going to say when he hears that we've failed to protect Kinmuir.'

Suddenly, London seemed an awfully long way away. In the distance I heard the screech of a buzzard. I gazed across the desolate moor, at the dark clouds gathering in the distance, and even though I was standing next to Davison, I felt terribly alone. There was something about the landscape here that was brutal, elemental. If only I could be back in my little mews house in Kensington, with Max by my side. I felt such a deep longing for him at that moment that I imagined leaving Davison there on the moor with the dead body, returning to the lodge and taking a car to the hotel in Broadford, from where I would collect Rosalind and Carlo and her sister and travel on the first train. I could turn my back on all of this and be content.

'Is that . . .?' asked Davison.

The question woke me from my dream of escape.

'Yes, I think it's Dr Fitzpatrick's car – he must have returned from visiting that sick child,' he added. 'If I stay up here with Kinmuir,' he said, looking back towards the spot where the dead man lay on the ground, 'would you mind going to fetch the doctor? He's going to take it badly, I fear – the two men were great friends, I believe.'

I did not respond.

'Agatha? Are you all right?'

Despite the temptation to take flight – an almost physical desire to run away from the bloody scene – I knew that I could do no such thing. There was something rotten at Dallach Lodge and it needed to be rooted out.

When I walked into the house Dr Fitzpatrick was calling upon every last ounce of his professional reserve as he tried to make sense of his friend's death. His face, already lined with wrinkles, looked even older, and completely drained. 'But I just don't understand how it could have happened,' he said, swallowing the anger that threatened to unsteady his voice.

James Kinmuir and Rufus Phillips sat before him in the hall, tartan blankets draped around their shoulders, looking like broken men.

'You're quite certain he's dead?' asked the doctor, running his hand over his bald head.

The two young men nodded. James had tears in his blood-shot eyes and nursed a large tumbler of brandy.

'Yes, I'm afraid he is,' I said as gently as I could.

'Well, I'd better see for myself,' said Dr Fitzpatrick. 'Mrs Christie, you say Mr Davison is with him now?'

'Yes,' I said. 'He was up on the moor when it happened and saw something of the accident from a distance. I can take you to the place, the place where . . .'

'Good idea, and you two,' he said, gesturing towards James Kinmuir and Rufus Phillips, 'you need to come with us.'

We walked up to the moor without talking. The purple heather seemed to stretch on forever. There were few distinguishing features – no abandoned cottages, no trees, no stone walls – and if the mist came down it would be easy to lose oneself, to stumble into a bog and never be seen again. As we climbed, the air seemed to get damper. My old brown brogues had started to let in a little water and my feet felt wet and cold. I immediately chastised myself: how could I worry about my own comfort when a man's life had been taken from him?

Finally, we approached the spot where Davison stood waiting by the body of Robin Kinmuir. Dr Fitzpatrick knelt down by his friend and checked his pulse. He held Kinmuir's wrist for longer than normal, perhaps hoping against hope for some sign of life. When the doctor knew for sure that Kinmuir was dead he turned his face away from us to hide his evident emotion.

All of us stood back to give the doctor some time to grieve, before James Kinmuir walked forwards and said, 'You've got to believe it was an accident. I would never have done anything to hurt my uncle.' There was desperation in his voice. 'He only ever showed me kindness. He took me in when my parents died.' He looked at the body on the ground and made

32

a dash towards it, as if in an effort to try to embrace his uncle for one last time, but was held back by Davison.

'Steady now.' Davison's hands still bore traces of the dead man's blood. 'That's right, step away.'

'Davison, is it correct that you saw something of what happened here?' asked Dr Fitzpatrick.

'Well, I saw it from a distance and then, when I got to him, I did everything I could to save his life,' replied Davison.

'Can you tell me exactly what happened?' Dr Fitzpatrick persisted. 'Everything you saw and noticed, even if it seems inconsequential.'

After Davison reiterated what he had already told me, the doctor asked the two friends to repeat their stories. I listened out for any inconsistencies or oddities.

'It had all started so well, the day, I mean,' said James. 'All the guests seemed to be in a good mood, apart from that little misunderstanding that occurred at breakfast between Mrs Buchanan and Miss Passerini. My uncle had set out for his usual walk after breakfast with the dogs. The weather was a bit gloomy, but the mist hadn't come down yet. We went to get our things together and the ... equipment.'

'You mean the guns?' asked the doctor.

'Yes, that's right. The guns. Rufus has done some shooting before, but has never tried his hand at grouse. As we walked up onto the moors I explained a little about the birds. They fly fast, you see, and can be difficult to spot.'

'Yes, I know,' said Dr Fitzpatrick. 'It's something Robin and I like – sorry, used to like to do together.'

James coughed uneasily. 'I talked about ways of flushing them out and about some of the great shoots we have seen on the estate in the past. I remember we laughed because I tried to do a rather bad impersonation of the bird's call, a kind of *chut! chut! chut! chut!* Rufus started to rib me pretty badly.' James tried to smile, but at the memory of this moment of happiness his face contorted into an awful mask of pain. He bit his lip as he tried to prevent himself from crying. 'From the top of the moor we saw ... It was getting more misty, but I think it was Mrs Buchanan, walking on the hill opposite, the one that leads towards the castle behind the house.'

Dr Fitzpatrick looked at the young man with suspicion. 'And then what?'

'We chose our spot on the moor and I flushed out a few birds for Rufus. They flew up from the heather and we started shooting,' he said. 'I held back to begin with as I tried to help Rufus, since some of his early efforts were wide of the mark. Then we had a break for a flask of coffee.'

'Was there anything in the coffee?' the doctor asked. 'Whisky, for instance?'

'Oh yes, but only a dash to keep us warm,' said Rufus Phillips.

'So not enough to impair your senses?' asked Dr Fitzpatrick.

'Certainly not,' said James, clearly offended. It was almost as though, to a gentleman such as he, an accusation of drunkenness was worse than that of murder. 'My hand was as steady as ever. It was my turn to shoot and I got a few brace within the first five minutes or so. Then we had to wait for what seemed like simply ages and we sat there quietly, trying not to speak.'

It was Davison's turn to ask a question. 'So you didn't see the dogs running towards you, followed by your uncle?'

'No, no, we didn't,' said James. 'We must have been looking out over a different area of the moor. That or the mist. Obviously, if we had seen him then . . .' His voice trailed off.

'And what happened next?' continued Dr Fitzpatrick.

'Rufus pointed at something in the distance in the heather and whispered that he thought he had seen a bird,' said James. 'I steadied myself, pointed and, as I thought it was taking flight, shot at it. That's when . . . when we heard that terrible cry and we saw what we – what I – had done.'

'And what were his injuries, do you know?' Dr Fitzpatrick looked from one young man to the other, but James Kinmuir had been silenced again by the shock of the memory.

'There was just so much blood,' said Rufus Phillips, looking down at the nasty stains on his clothes.

Davison gestured towards the visible wound to Kinmuir's leg from where he had lost a great deal of blood. He wondered whether the man may have died from haemorrhaging or perhaps even a heart attack.

'We'll see soon enough,' said Dr Fitzpatrick. 'I'm right in saying that the police have been informed?'

'Yes, they have,' I said. On returning to the house earlier Simkins, the butler, had told me that a policeman was on his way.

'I suspect it will be too big a job for Maclehose,' said the doctor, referring to the local policeman on Skye. 'Not only is he nearly deaf but he's never dealt with anything more serious than a case of poaching or the odd theft in the whole of his career.' He addressed the group once more. 'I wouldn't be surprised if they send someone from the mainland to deal with this.'

James Kinmuir squared his shoulders, lifted up his chin and nodded to himself a couple of times as if to convince himself that what he was about to do was the correct form of behaviour. He presented himself like a naughty school-boy who had willingly delivered himself to his headmaster's office, ready to be punished.

'I don't mind telling you, I'm ready to be locked up for what I've done,' he said.

Rufus Phillips tried to stop him from saying anything else. 'It was an accident, James, you know that,' he said.

But James Kinmuir – proud of the sense of honour he felt ran through to his very marrow – had made up his mind. 'I know I've got to face up to it and take the punishment, whatever that may be, like a man,' he said. In that moment, as the awful realisation sank in, that the sentence for murder was more than a long stretch in prison, he looked petrified. 'When the police arrive, tell them that I'm the guilty one,' he said, bravely. 'I killed my uncle. And if I have to hang for it, then so be it.'

Chapter Three

'So what do you make of it all?' asked Davison when we returned to his room. Although he had spent the first night in a camp bed in Kinmuir's dressing room, his own room was situated at the front of the house, overlooking the loch.

'It has all the appearance of an accident, doesn't it?' I replied. 'We've got the testimony of James Kinmuir himself, admitting to the incident. Then we've got Rufus Phillips as a witness. And we've yet to listen to what Mrs Buchanan has to say; I think she saw something of the aftermath. And then there's you . . .'

'Indeed,' said Davison, walking over to the open window and looking out at the misty waters. 'There's a confession, a dead body, at least one witness. It seems—'

'Almost too neat to be true?'

'Yes, in a way. If Kinmuir had not received those threatening letters warning that he might be murdered then I could accept the evidence of this being an accident. But it's no coincidence that, within a matter of days of the letters, Kinmuir has been killed.' He paused. 'I wish I'd taken greater care of him. I should have insisted on walking with him.'

'John,' I said, conscious that I was taking the unusually intimate step of using his first name, 'you can't blame yourself for this.'

'I know, but I do. Sometimes I wonder if – well, if it's not time I sought out some other kind of work.'

'Such as?'

'Oh, I don't know – some steady bureaucratic job in the Foreign Office.'

I thought back to some of the blows that Davison had received during the course of our friendship. In addition, there was probably a whole raft of awful tragedies that he had endured which he had chosen not to share with me. I walked over and joined him by the open window. A breeze brought the earthy smell of the moors into the room.

'Look – they're carrying Kinmuir down,' I said.

We watched in silence as Dr Fitzpatrick, together with a couple of young men from the estate, bore the body of Robin Kinmuir on a stretcher, through the wild expanses of heather and down the path that led towards the house. Walking alongside them was an elderly-looking man dressed in a police uniform.

'That must be – what was the name Dr Fitzpatrick mentioned? Maclehose?' asked Davison. 'He looks like he should have retired years ago.'

'I wonder who they'll send to lead the investigation?' I asked. 'And what is the official line on our position here?'

'No doubt Hartford – once he gets wind of what's happened – will inform the officer in charge of the true nature of our presence. Not that we – or rather I – have helped much.' Davison gazed down at the sad sight of the stretcher being borne towards the lodge, where a group of servants had gathered. Mrs Baillie was comforting two of the maids. Simkins the butler stood stony-faced, the very symbol of British restraint. James Kinmuir and Rufus Phillips – who had changed into clean clothes – came out to pay their respects, followed by the other guests: Mr Peterson, May and Isabella Frith-Stratton and Miss Passerini. This was not a funeral with its rigid rituals; there was, of course, no etiquette or standardised form of behaviour when one's host had been shot dead. Yet the group seemed to fall into place as if they were being directed by an offstage presence, forming a semi-circle as they took it in turns to say a few quiet words to themselves. As Davison and I went down to join them a figure bolted out of the house and nearly crashed into us. It was Mrs Buchanan, who was clearly in an extremely distressed state.

'Robin, oh my darling,' she wailed as she ran towards the stretcher. Her normally immaculate coiffeured hair was hanging down in unruly strands around her face, which was now wet with tears. She reached out and, with a shaking hand, tried to lower the blanket that covered the dead man's face.

'Please,' said Dr Fitzpatrick, taking her arm as he gently tried to restrain her. As she resisted him, he looked to other members of the group for help. James Kinmuir and Rufus Phillips stepped forwards, but on seeing them Mrs Buchanan looked at the two young men with contempt.

'I know what you did up there, I *saw*,' she shouted.

'It was an accident, Mrs Buchanan,' said Rufus Phillips. 'James didn't mean to do it. He thought it was—'

'I don't believe you,' she responded. 'Robin told me that

he was in fear for his life. I thought he was being paranoid. But how I wish I had listened to him.' She took a step closer to James Kinmuir. 'You know, James, I never trusted you. Even when you were a little boy.'

I was fascinated to learn that the friendship that existed between Robin Kinmuir and Mrs Buchanan dated back many years.

'There was always something, I don't know, rather cold about you, unfeeling,' she continued. 'Of course, you could turn on the charm when you needed to. And your uncle fell for it.' She raised her hand and, with each of the words, jabbed a finger into the lapel of his jacket. 'And – I – know – what – you – are.'

The young man did not say anything in his defence. He stood there with his head bowed, his eyes lowered to the ground like a schoolboy during a particularly vicious telling-off from his housemaster. Rufus Phillips placed a hand on his friend's shoulder in a silent gesture of support, but James Kinmuir brushed it off, as if to say he knew that he did not deserve any sympathy.

As Mrs Buchanan looked at the two young men, her eyes brimmed with fresh tears, but these were, I suspected, tears not of grief but of pure anger. She turned away from the friends, took one last look at the pitiful sight of the corpse on the stretcher, reached out as if to bestow a blessing on the body and then stepped away to retire inside the house.

Davison and I stood next to them in silence for a moment before we moved away. A mixture of emotions ran through me: guilt and more than a little shame at having witnessed such an intimate scene; a burning curiosity to know more about the past relationship between Mrs Buchanan and Robin Kinmuir; and pity for the figure of James Kinmuir, still in shock, who had been so publicly humiliated in front of us all.

'Do you think I should go and talk to Mrs Buchanan?' I whispered.

As we walked away from the group Davison seemed possessed of a renewed energy. 'Yes, and see if you can find out any more about what Robin Kinmuir told her about those threats to his life,' said Davison. 'There's something not right about this whole thing.'

'What do you mean?'

'I can't say just yet, it's nothing more than a feeling at this stage, but let's talk after you've had a conversation with Mrs Buchanan.' He paused for a moment. 'You saw her perform, you said?'

'Yes, only the once, in *Macbeth*, but she gave an extremely convincing performance.'

As I turned to go and talk to Mrs Buchanan, Davison mumbled to himself a line from the play: '*By the pricking of my thumbs/Something wicked this way comes.*'

Chapter Four

I followed Mrs Buchanan back into the house and found her upstairs in the corridor that led towards her bedroom. The passage, which was painted a dark shade of red, was lined with old prints, faded portraits and small dirt-encrusted oil landscapes. She must have seen me cast a slightly disapproving eye over the less-than-clean artworks because she turned to me and made a comment about the lack of staff in the house.

'Robin says – I'm sorry, said,' she began, correcting herself just as Dr Fitzpatrick had done, 'that he couldn't afford to take on any more servants. The house was getting too much for him, even with the money from his paying guests. I worried so about him. I told him to sell up and buy somewhere smaller, but he couldn't imagine not living here, he said. And now he's no longer with us, well, I suppose everything will go to . . .' A darkness clouded her eyes. 'His next of kin – James.'

'I'm afraid I couldn't help but witness what happened just now, at the front of the house,' I said.

'I'm sorry you had to see that, but I feel so angry about

it all,' she said. 'And, of course, I blame myself for what happened.'

'In what way?'

She looked up and down the empty corridor and gestured for me to follow. She led me along the corridor to a door at the end of the east wing. She pushed it open and ushered me into a delightful room, which was painted yellow. There was an antique bureau in one corner of the room while in the other stood a large wardrobe, open a little so I could glimpse the vast array of outfits that the actress had brought with her.

'What a lovely room,' I said. 'Even though it's a little gloomy outside, it seems to capture the morning light.'

'Robin always gave me the nicest room whenever I came to stay,' she said.

She suggested we sit in the two armchairs by the window.

'Would you like some tea? I can ask one of the girls to bring some up.'

I thanked her and declined.

'I can't stomach anything at all,' she said. 'I'm afraid you must forgive me, Mrs Christie, but you must realise I have experienced a terrible shock.'

'Yes, of course,' I said. 'You were friends with Mr Kinmuir for many years?'

She nodded her head, the pain visible on her face. She lowered her voice to a whisper. 'Robin was a complicated man, but I loved him,' she said. The statement was a simple one, but it spoke volumes.

I did not say anything, but waited for her in the hope that she would continue. She took out a handkerchief and dabbed her eyes.

'Yes, I suppose he was the love of my life,' she said.

'How did you meet?' I asked gently.

She looked at me as if to ascertain whether I was the kind of person to whom it was wise to tell her story – was I a woman who would judge her? I must have passed the kind of test because she began to embark on her narrative.

'You've probably guessed already, but I was Robin's mistress,' she said. 'Have I shocked you?'

'No, not at all,' I said with all honesty. Friends had often told me that I was the least shockable person they knew.

'Catherine – that was Robin's wife – was a nice enough woman, but she didn't have the kind of spark that a woman needed to maintain a husband's interest, particularly if that husband happened to be Robin,' she said. 'And then, after their son, Timothy, died, well . . .'

'What happened to Timothy?'

'He died in the war,' she replied. 'The loss was a terrible blow for both of them, but Robin absolutely doted on him. So many people lost loved ones, of course, but that death hit Robin very hard indeed, and I know he still grieved for him even years later.'

'I see. You said Robin was complicated – in what way?'

'Well, so many ways!' She laughed at her statement, but it was the kind of laughter that could melt into tears at any moment.

I could not let her know that I had any prior knowledge of Kinmuir's background, particularly his work for the Secret Intelligence Service. Perhaps Mrs Buchanan knew nothing herself of this aspect of his life.

'And did Catherine know of . . . of you?'

'Yes, yes, she did,' she said. 'I know I should have been racked with guilt – a woman who lures away a husband is not so popular with her own sex – but the truth is I wasn't in the least. Robin told me that – well, certain aspects of his married life were far from satisfactory, non-existent, if you catch my drift.'

I thought back to the sterile stretch in my own first marriage when my husband Archie had withdrawn his affections. I blushed at the thought of Max's healthy appetite and hoped that that side of my next marriage would continue to blossom. I felt a little lightheaded at the prospect, but forced myself to push the thought away; I had to concentrate on what Mrs Buchanan was saying.

'Robin had such energies and was quite unconventional,' she said. 'I loved that in him. That he didn't care what the next man thought of him. Why should he? He was greater than a hundred average men put together! He had thought of divorcing Catherine – he promised it on so many occasions – but I insisted that he shouldn't. In truth, I was fearful that if he divorced her and married me, then he would eventually see me as his wife and not his ... well, not his lover.' She looked at me once more, assessing the way I responded to her. Her eyes were like those of a cat – watchful but somehow unreadable. 'I've become so used to mixing in theatrical circles that sometimes I forget myself. My frankness can be too much for some. Are you sitting in judgement on me?'

'Not at all,' I said. I told her a little about my writing and my detective stories, of how I was interested in the many shades of light and darkness that lay in the human heart.

'Yes, I can see that in you,' she said, eyeing me once more.

'I've come across many writers during the course of my career and they've all had a quite wonderful ability to feel sympathy with others. Like actors, in a way, who have to disappear into their characters. Yes, I feel very comfortable talking to you, my dear.'

I wanted to steer her back to what she had hinted at earlier. 'You said that you blamed yourself for . . . for what happened up there on the moor?'

'I just wish I had done more to stop it from happening,' she said. 'You see, Robin had received a horrid letter, saying that he should be in fear for his life. He didn't tell me about it to begin with, but I knew something was bothering him. He was a robust man – he'd experienced more than his fair share of tragedies and troubles – but when I first arrived a few days ago I could tell that he was upset. I thought, at first, that he had been thinking about Timothy. But when I raised the subject with him, he told me it wasn't anything to do with his grief over his dead son. Finally, after a lot of persuasion, I managed to get it out of him. That he'd received this nasty letter. He wouldn't show it to me – he maintained that he'd burnt it, but I wasn't sure whether he was telling me the truth – but he told me what it had said. I dismissed it as the work of some crank – after all, there are enough of those on this island, people who think a trip to Portree is like travelling halfway round the world. But now I wish I had taken it seriously.'

'So you think that . . . that what happened to Robin this morning wasn't an accident?' I asked.

'Of course it wasn't! It was part of some plan.'

I knew I must test her by going along with the accident theory. 'But James Kinmuir thought he was firing at a grouse.

He didn't mean to kill his uncle. And he's already taken the blame for the accident.'

'Nonsense!'

'You said that you saw what really happened? What did you see, Mrs Buchanan?'

She blinked repeatedly, almost as if to clear the uncertainty from her mind. 'I saw him shoot him—Robin—dead.'

'But weren't you on the other side of the moor? And wasn't it quite misty?' I didn't want to dismiss her story out of hand, but I had to establish if not the truth then at least how her version differed from the accounts given by three different witnesses, including Davison.

'Yes, I was some distance away, but ...' Her voice trailed off.

'Didn't it happen the way that James and Rufus said?'

'I don't know,' she admitted. 'But what about that letter? It's just too much of a coincidence, surely, that Robin received a threat to his life and then gets shot. I can't *prove* anything, you see, but I suspect a great deal.'

'I'm sorry, but I couldn't help but overhear you say to James, "I know what you did up there – I *saw*."'

'I thought if I said that, that I'd seen something, perhaps he – James – would tell the whole story,' she said. 'It was naive of me.'

'So you didn't see anything ... unusual?'

Her face, normally so poised and serene, filled with tension and frustration; lines that had been barely discernible before made themselves visible. 'If you put it in those terms, I suppose not. I know I'm not making sense. And you must think I'm the perfect fool ...'

'Not at all,' I said gently. 'I understand completely. You haven't got the evidence to back up your claims, but you feel with all your being that you're right. Is that what you are saying?'

She seemed to relax. 'That's exactly right, my dear. I couldn't put it any better myself. But what do you think I should do?'

'You should tell the police about your suspicions.'

'Yes, I suppose I must. After all, there's no love lost between us. James knows what I think of him.'

'Which is what exactly, may I ask?'

Mrs Buchanan paused as she considered how best to express herself, or perhaps how much she was going to give away. 'I've told you so much already, I may as well tell you everything,' she said. She took a deep breath and began.

'Robin's younger brother, Crane, married my friend Ada Sinclair. Ada's mother and my mother were the best of friends and Ada and I had grown up together in a village in Hertfordshire. Our lives went off in different directions – I went on the stage at sixteen, well, fifteen, if the truth be told – but all Ada wanted was to be married. She met Crane at a dance and fell deeply in love with him. She had a child, a son, James, and seemed perfectly happy. She wrote the most wonderful letters, telling me of her life in Scotland. I'd write back, sharing details of my career on the stage and something of my adventures in London. Some of the stories you really wouldn't believe!' A mischievous sparkle lit up her face. 'Sorry, I digress. Ada was always asking me to go up to visit, but of course I had my work. That always came first. Nobody could accuse me of not taking my craft seriously. But at the end of a run of an Ibsen play I felt exhausted, absolutely hollow. I had nothing left to give. And then an invitation from Ada came to go up to Scotland for a weekend party. It was a thoroughly delightful weekend and of course – you know what I'm going to say – that's when I met Robin. And yes, he was with Catherine. I suppose one could say that he became smitten with me, infatuated is the word. I dismissed his advances completely – I'm not *that* sort of woman. But then, when he was next in London, he sought me out. I was playing Cleopatra, one of my most powerful roles. The critics were in ecstasies over me. Robin came to my dressing room and insisted on taking me out for supper. He told me about the misery he was enduring, the prison of his marriage. And that's when our affair began.'

She seemed eager to talk more about herself and Robin Kinmuir, but I had to interrupt her.

'That is interesting, but to get back to James.'

'Yes, him. You do know he's murdered before, don't you?'

The statement seemed too melodramatic to be true. She must have sensed my rather alarmed expression because she began to explain.

'Well, it wasn't a case of who, but rather what and how,' she said.

'Please go on,' I said.

'Let me give you the facts. This was back in 1921 when James was – what? – sixteen years old. I was in a long-running play – now what was it? *The Duchess of Malfi*? *Women Beware Women*? Anyway, afterwards I went up to stay with Ada in Scotland. That was when she first fell ill, poor Ada, God rest her soul. One day when she was confined to bed – we just thought it was a bad cold or the influenza – I went for a walk in the woods. I heard the most awful sound, a terrible cry. I ran towards it and saw James crouching down by a trap. He'd caught a fox and the poor thing had its leg caught.'

The memory clearly still upset Mrs Buchanan because she was forced to pause and compose herself.

'I watched as he tortured that dear creature, bringing the trap down and down on it, until I couldn't bear it any more. I ran out from behind the tree, ordered him to stop and he told me to look away as he shot it.'

I wasn't quite sure how to react. I loved animals dearly and would never want to see them come to any harm. But could I count the killing of a fox as a crime of the first order? No, I could not.

'I can see you don't share my love of wild creatures,' said Mrs Buchanan.

'It's not that, but I'm not sure I would use the term "murder" to describe what you saw,' I said.

'You may not, but let me tell you that's not all I witnessed,' she said. 'The look on James's face as he tortured that fox was that of a sadist.' As she took a moment to reflect on what she had said, she nodded at a distant point located somewhere behind my head, a technique that I felt she had used more than once in her illustrious career in the theatre. 'And I've no doubt that it was the same expression that possessed James as he took hold of that shotgun and deliberately blasted his uncle to death.'

Chapter Five

We were instructed by Maclehose, in his rather weak voice, not to leave the house or grounds. James Kinmuir and Rufus Phillips had agreed to go voluntarily with the elderly policeman to Portree, where they would be asked to give detailed statements. A more senior police officer, an inspector by the name of Hawkins, was on his way from the mainland. Meanwhile, Dr Fitzpatrick had to face the distressing task of performing a post-mortem on his good friend.

'It's the one thing in the world I hoped I would never have to do,' he said sadly.

The enforced containment on the estate gave Davison and me plenty of time to discuss the case, but we were careful to do so out of earshot of the other guests. We went for long walks around the banks of the sea loch and up to the ruined castle, where we discussed the suspicions surrounding James Kinmuir and the information provided by Mrs Buchanan. Why was the actress so keen to cast blame on the young man? Did she have another, hidden motive? Was she using her consummate skills as a performer to divert our attention in some way?

On our long rambles past the misty waters of the loch or up on the heather-clad moor we debated these and other questions, as we tried to tease out the implications of what had happened. At the end of each discussion we came back to the same point. We knew nothing more than the fact that Robin Kinmuir was dead, shot by his nephew James who was set to inherit the man's estate. James Kinmuir had confessed to the accidental shooting and he was ready to be punished for it. It seemed quite a simple, straightforward case. But we knew there must be more to it.

Two days after the accident, when everyone had been confined to the lodge due to bad weather, we received notice that Robin Kinmuir's solicitor was due to pay a visit. All members of the household, including the servants, were to be gathered in the drawing room, ready for the arrival of a Mr Glenelg from the Inverness firm of Renfrew, Glenelg, Forrester & Harbetter. I wondered why a lawyer would request the presence of the guests of Dallach Lodge; after all, until recently most of these people, apart from Mrs Buchanan, had been nothing more than strangers to Kinmuir.

As Davison and I stepped into the drawing room, panelled in dark wood and smelling of cigars and cigarettes, I sensed tension, if not fear, in the air. It was the kind of atmosphere I associated with a doctor's or a dentist's waiting room. I looked around me at the assorted guests, some of whom were looking as nervous and unsettled as the servants. Of course, I understood the servants feeling out of place here, among the fine furniture, lush red velvet curtains and expensive Persian carpet, but why did the guests seem so ill at ease?

A few moments later, a distinguished-looking gentleman with a fine grey moustache and an air of seriousness entered the room and introduced himself as Mr Glenelg.

'You may be wondering why you are all here,' he said, looking at the guests sitting ranged around the room in various aged leather armchairs.

Several members of the group started to talk at once, all eager for information, but Mr Glenelg lifted the index finger on his right hand and raised an eyebrow. The gestures, although subtle, were powerful and the room duly fell into silence.

'Indeed, it is a very unusual situation, one that I have not encountered in my many years of practice,' he continued. He opened his leather briefcase, took out a sheaf of papers and talked of how the Scottish system was different to the one in England and Wales. He outlined some details of the role of the procurator fiscal; then it was time to get down to business. 'I have here the last will and testament of my client, the late Mr Robin Kinmuir of Dallach Lodge. I have been acting for him for a number of years and I hereby, as his solicitor, duly stand before you. But, before I detail Mr Kinmuir's final wishes, I have been instructed to . . .' He paused here and looked over his shoulder towards the drawing room door. 'Well, to introduce you to Inspector Hawkins.'

A middle-aged man with a craggy, weather-beaten face stepped into the room, accompanied by a much younger man who stayed by the door. The inspector came to join Mr Glenelg in the middle of the room. He studied us quickly but in depth, giving me the impression that he had, as his name implied, a hawk-like ability to search out potential prey.

'Good morning, I am Inspector Hawkins from Inverness, I have come with my sergeant, Dedham, and I am here to investigate the murder of Robin Kinmuir.'

The word 'murder' prompted a wave of murmurs and exclamations.

'That wicked, wicked boy,' said Mrs Buchanan from her armchair by the fire. 'I knew there was foul play at work here. *Unnatural deeds/Do breed unnatural troubles.*'

'Excuse me?' said Hawkins.

'The play of *Macbeth*,' said the actress rather grandly. 'But I doubt that you would—'

'*Infected minds/To their deaf pillows will discharge their secrets*,' said the inspector, completing the quotation.

Mrs Buchanan looked surprised.

'*Foul whisperings are abroad*,' he added. 'Indeed they are. But we'll come to that soon enough.' Again, he studied the assembled group before him, eyeing each of us with his intelligent blue gaze. 'First of all, I'm going to ask Mr Glenelg to bring our other guests into the drawing room.'

The solicitor nodded his head, walked to the door and, a moment or so later, returned with James Kinmuir and Rufus Phillips. The entrance prompted Davison and me to exchange a look of surprise. The rest of the residents reacted with consternation; the most vocal complaint came from Mrs Buchanan.

'What is the meaning of this?' she demanded of the inspector. But when Hawkins tried to explain, the actress shouted him down. 'Why isn't he locked up? I can't even bring myself to say his name. I don't understand. After all, you've just said that Robin was murdered.' She got up from her chair, walked across the drawing room towards James Kinmuir, her face full of anger. Hawkins, fearful that the actress was about to strike the young man, was ready to restrain her, but she turned away from him at the last minute. 'I wouldn't dignify him by touching him,' she said, under her breath.

Rufus Phillips tried to speak: 'I'm sure the inspector will—' but again Mrs Buchanan shouted him down.

'I can't be in the same room as a murderer and his accomplice,' she said.

'If you could please calm yourself,' said the inspector.

'Calm myself?' shouted Mrs Buchanan. 'How dare you? I've just lost a dear friend, killed at the hands of this . . . I can't bring myself to say it.'

'Excuse me, what is your name?' asked the inspector.

His ignorance of her fame did not please the famous actress. 'Mrs Buchanan. Mrs Eliza Buchanan,' she said.

'Mrs Buchanan, I realise that you may very well be upset,' said Hawkins, 'but the situation is far from what it seems. I've got a great deal I need to explain – and so I'm going to have to ask you to—'

'No, I think the best thing I can do is leave.' She took a deep breath and tried to compose herself. She nodded at each of the other guests in turn and, with as much dignity as she could muster, strode towards the door.

'I must ask you to stay here,' said the inspector. It sounded more of a command than a request. He signalled to the sergeant to prepare to block her exit.

Mrs Buchanan turned and looked at Hawkins with a furious expression.

'If you will please return to your chair I can begin to explain,' he said. He smiled, but his eyes remained steely.

Mrs Buchanan was about to say something, but she stopped herself. She bowed her head and returned to her chair by the fire and although she had been silenced, it seemed unlikely that she would remain quiet for long. Inspector Hawkins gestured for James Kinmuir and Rufus Phillips to take two chairs in the room and then cleared his throat.

'First of all I must thank you for agreeing to remain at Dallach Lodge,' he said. 'I'm sure you all lead very busy lives and would have preferred to have left this place after that rather terrible incident. Thank you too to Mr Kinmuir and Mr Phillips, who have returned from Portree with me. As I suggested, the case is quite complicated – Mr Robin Kinmuir died on the twelfth of August, the so-called Glorious Twelfth, but the circumstances of the death are not at all straightforward. Before I go any further, I'd like Mr Glenelg to read Robin Kinmuir's last will. You may think it is irregular to read it in front of you all, but I think in the circumstances it is appropriate. Mr Glenelg, if you please . . .'

The guests shifted in their seats as the solicitor shuffled his papers. Mr Glenelg coughed lightly and began to read. As he did so, the inspector studied each member of the group gathered together in the drawing room, watching them for any change of expression, however small.

'I, Robin Kinmuir, of Dallach Lodge, the island of Skye, declare this to be my last will and testament, made this day the tenth of February, nineteen hundred and twenty eight.

'First I revoke and make void all former and other wills

I SAW HIM DIE

and testaments by me at any time heretofore made and of this my last will and testament do appoint my nephew James sole Executor. Also I give and bequeath unto each of the servants who have worked at Dallach Lodge for longer than a period of five years the sum of fifty pounds.'

At this news Simkins, the butler, remained dead-eyed, while Mrs Baillie's face lit up with delight, as did that of a servant girl whose name I did not know.

Mr Glenelg continued in his dry, emotionless voice. 'As to all the rest, residue and remainder of my monies, goods, chattels, personal estate and effects whatsoever after payment of my debts, funeral expenses, costs of proving this my will and other incidental charges, I give and bequeath the same and every part thereof unto my said nephew James to and for his own use and benefit—'

'I knew it,' said Eliza Buchanan, sharply. 'He's getting the lot.'

Mr Glenelg silenced her with a quick look in her direction. 'In witness whereof I, Robin Kinmuir, the said testator, have to this my last will and testament set my hand and seal the day and year first above written.'

James Kinmuir's blond head remained bowed, almost as if he were too ashamed to meet the eyes of the rest of the group, particularly Mrs Buchanan.

'You shouldn't feel any guilt,' said Rufus Phillips, placing a hand on his friend's shoulder. 'You know you did nothing wrong.'

'Nothing apart from murdering his own uncle and profiting from his death,' said Mrs Buchanan.

'I don't think that's called for,' said Rufus, a blush

spreading across his cheeks. 'And what you said there about me being an accomplice, well, it's just not on.'

'Really – and what gives you the right to say so?' replied a waspish Mrs Buchanan.

'I was just trying to—'

'Trying to protect your friend, yes, I know,' she said, with more than a note of sarcasm in her voice. 'But you heard what the inspector said. Robin Kinmuir has been murdered. And the person who is to inherit the estate is his nephew. I think all of us can see that there is a strong connection between those two things. In fact, I'm rather surprised that the inspector is here at all. I would have thought that it was blatantly obvious who was responsible for the death of Robin Kinmuir.'

Mrs Buchanan got up from her chair and stood in front of James Kinmuir. She raised a hand of judgement, a finger pointing directly towards his face. 'The one person who is to benefit from his death: none other than his nephew.'

She turned to face her audience, almost as if she had finished delivering a particularly rousing speech at the end of a play and expected a triumphant round of applause. Indeed, according to the expressions on the faces of the assembled group, the majority seemed ready to congratulate Mrs Buchanan on her performance. Then came a note of caution from the inspector.

'As I stated earlier, the situation is far from simple,' he said.

'What do you mean?' asked Vivienne Passerini. She looked from the inspector towards Mr Peterson, waiting for an explanation.

'I must call on the expertise of Robin Kinmuir's

solicitor again,' said Hawkins. 'Please, Mr Glenelg, if you could explain.'

The lawyer placed his pile of papers down on his briefcase and sighed deeply, as if thinking how best to express something that clearly distressed him.

'My client . . . it seems that his monetary position . . . was not what it had been. What I mean to say is that . . . there were so many debts accrued over the years. Even with the fact that he had, of late, taken to running the lodge as a hotel, well . . . his income did not meet his expenditure. And so—'

'You can't mean . . .?' asked a startled Mrs Buchanan.

'I'm afraid to say that Robin Kinmuir died thousands of pounds in debt,' said Mr Glenelg. 'Even after the sale of Dallach Lodge and its contents, it's most likely that Mr Kinmuir's nephew, James Kinmuir, will not inherit a single penny.'

Chapter Six

The gasps of breath came at once and from all corners of the room. A humiliated-looking Mrs Buchanan excused herself and said she was going to her quarters. James Kinmuir tried to keep his composure, but it was difficult for him: I watched as a series of changing emotions passed across his face.

Indeed, at that moment, each of us in the drawing room were like spectators at the climax of a thrilling drama. How awful it must be to be in the position of James Kinmuir. A young man accused of an accident that killed his uncle. And, if that wasn't enough, the allure of a goodly inheritance dangled before him, only for that prospect to be snatched away.

'Did you know about the extent of your uncle's debts, Mr Kinmuir?' asked the inspector.

James raised his head and nodded. 'Yes, yes, I'm afraid I did.'

It was obvious James Kinmuir could not bear people staring at him and so he bent forward and put his head in his hands to shield his face from view. Rufus Phillips knelt beside him and tried to comfort his friend.

'Who would have thought it?' said Simon Peterson to Vivienne Passerini. 'I feel sorry for the chap, I really do.'

'Fancy, not having two pennies to rub together,' said Isabella Frith-Stratton to her sister, with undisguised relish in her voice. 'And after everyone thought he would inherit all of this!' She gestured at the understated splendour of her surroundings. 'It's as we've always said, my dear, fate works in mysterious ways.'

'The wheel of fortune turns once more,' intoned May, as if she were some kind of wise prophet or guru from the east. 'In fact, we could take that as a title, don't you think?'

At this, Isabella's eyes lit up as the two of them started to discuss the intricacies of a heady romance involving an impoverished young woman sent out to India to live with her wealthy cousin, when Inspector Hawkins asked for everyone to please finish their conversations and listen to what he had to say. I caught Davison's eye. Both of us knew what the other was thinking. What had made Inspector Hawkins believe that the death of Robin Kinmuir was not an accident? Why did he now think that the man had been murdered? And if James Kinmuir did not have a motive then who did?

'I can understand that there's been a great deal of distress here,' said the inspector. 'But I'm afraid we have to face some rather brutal facts.' He paused as he asked a servant to call for Mrs Buchanan. As he waited for her he summarised what Mr Glenelg had just told us. It was obvious that he was preparing to address some of the questions that were in my own mind. 'Mrs Buchanan, please come and sit down,' he said, when he saw the actress by the door. She made a suitably dramatic entrance and, with her head held high, she walked across the drawing room and took her seat.

'As you know, we now believe Mr Kinmuir's death to be murder,' he continued. 'As you've all heard, Mr Kinmuir's nephew, James, will only inherit his uncle's debt, not a fortune as some believed. It has also come to light – and further tests are being carried out as we speak – that Robin Kinmuir's death was not due to the gun fired by James Kinmuir. The wound to the leg caused some bleeding, yes, but it was not responsible for his death.'

James Kinmuir's expression remained impassive, suggesting that he had already been informed of this piece of news. However, as the information snaked its way into the minds of the guests, the implication of Inspector Hawkins's statement began to spread its sinister poison through the group. *But if he didn't do it, then who was it? Could it be him? Or her?* Eyes began to flicker with distrust. Heads turned, but so minutely and delicately that the movement was barely noticeable. Suspicion seeped into the air like an invisible but deadly gas. Each of the guests was consumed by fear. Then an ice-cold blast of logic tried to calm their feverish nerves. *But why would a stranger want Kinmuir dead? The whole idea was ludicrous. There must be some reasonable explanation. The inspector must be mistaken. The man must have had a heart attack or some kind of stroke brought on by that gunshot wound.* Then the hot tongue of fear licked the back of the neck and the whispers began again. *Was there a killer in the house? I was sure X was behaving oddly. What has Y got to hide? I will be certain to lock the door to my room tonight. Or would it be possible to leave the house today?*

All this and and more went through the minds of the guests of Dallach Lodge. But none of us was going anywhere.

'And of course,' said the inspector. 'I'm afraid all of you must continue to stay here until the investigation is complete.'

Chapter Seven

Over the course of the next few days, while we waited to hear news of Dr Fitzpatrick's post-mortem examination, Davison and I tried to make some preliminary enquiries into the case. We did not have much to go on and what we did have did not seem to make sense. A man hit by a gunshot, but not killed by it. A next of kin accused of the crime and set to inherit only debt. A mistress with a taste for the dramatic, keen to cast suspicion on a seemingly innocent man.

We approached the mission with stealth and at tangents. There was no point in advertising our real presence at the house. It was easy enough to make light conversation about the subject. After all, each of the guests seemed keen to share their theories about the death of Robin Kinmuir. Once the initial shock had worn off, no one, apart from Mrs Buchanan, seemed to mourn the loss of the laird of the lodge. The actress spent most of the days that followed in her room, occasionally leaving her quarters for a walk by the loch. She dressed in shades of black and grey – selected from her extensive wardrobe – and often sported a pair of very elegant sunglasses. She behaved at all times like the famous actress she was. But how did any of us know what she was really thinking?

Simon Peterson and Vivienne Passerini continued to enjoy a light flirtation. Their conversation, if transcribed, would seem innocuous enough – talk of travel, ports around the world, both the sightseeing and the squalor. The real meaning of the depth of their attraction was signified by a series of looks, gestures and sudden heightened charges of what can only be described as electricity.

Certainly, they made a handsome couple – he with his matinee-idol looks, she with her exotic beauty. However, Isabella Frith-Stratton was not pleased by this development, probably because she had assumed, rather foolishly, that Mr Peterson would be hers. As far as I could make out Mr Peterson had only shown a polite interest in her, nothing more. And so she took it upon herself to be rude to Miss Passerini, cutting her down in mid-conversation and turning her head whenever the young woman started to speak.

When Isabella was not being discourteous to Miss Passerini she could be found gossiping about the crime with her sister. It started innocently enough: perhaps Robin Kinmuir had been killed by an adder? They were sure they had read about the risk of the snakes in Scotland. But then their suspicions became darker. Maybe the butler wanted to do him in? After all, Simkins, they said, looked just the sort of servant who would kill his master. His breath smelt of whisky. He was a good-for-nothing sort of man. They had once caught him complaining about doing duties expected of a housekeeper. And did you see the way he looked when that solicitor announced he was going to be given a sum of fifty pounds in his will? He wasn't at all pleased. He would have liked much more. And would he even get that money now that it had been revealed that Kinmuir had died in debt? How had he frittered away his money? There was a rumour, founded in truth, they said, that Kinmuir used to be a heavy drinker. And no doubt with drink came other vices too – if not gambling then almost certainly women, and women of the worst kind. If there was one expression they used more than any other when discussing the murder it was this: *there was no smoke without fire.* The sisters repeated it enough to establish the fact that they believed that Kinmuir had brought his death upon himself. That he deserved it.

James Kinmuir and Rufus Phillips remained reserved and aloof from the rest of the group, but not in a stand-offish manner. This had more to do with the unspoken traditions of mourning and the quiet dignity that came with a death in the family than anything resembling arrogance. The two of them avoided the moor, the scene of Kinmuir's death, and mostly spent their time indoors, reading, working through the funeral arrangements or looking at some of the dusty paintings that hung on the walls. I remembered Rufus telling me of the portrait that he had been working on of Robin Kinmuir. I mentioned to him my interest in seeing it – I told him that I was thinking of commissioning a portrait of my new husband – and, one drizzly afternoon four days after the murder, Rufus showed me into one of the attic rooms that served as his studio. As I stepped into the bare room I noticed that the air smelt of turpentine. The floorboards were covered in daubs of paint and an easel had been turned to face the wall.

Rufus Phillips hesitated as he followed me into the room, his eyes fixed on an empty comb-back Windsor chair. 'I'm sorry, it's just that ... that's where Mr Kinmuir sat when I was—' He broke off as he fought to control his voice. 'It seems so odd to see it without him sitting there, telling some wild story.'

'I can imagine it must be strange for you,' I said. 'You know, I would have loved to have been a painter.'

'You would?'

'Yes, training oneself to really *see*, not just with the eyes but with the mind too. And then to capture the essence of a person. It must be wonderful.'

'I often think that my work is really just an exercise in failure,' he said.

'What do you mean?'

'Just that I'm always disappointed in what I achieve. I get terribly excited by the planning, the preparation, studying a person's face, working out the dimensions of the portrait, doing the sketches and suchlike. But somehow there's always a gap between what I see in my head and the finished thing.' He considered what he had just said and gave me a sardonic smile. 'I suppose I shouldn't be telling you this. As you might have gathered, I'm hardly a good salesman for my own work.'

'I'm just the same, when it comes to writing, I mean,' I said. 'Sometimes at night I scribble away in my notebook, thinking I've had the most thrilling idea, but the next day when I sit down to write the words on the page they feel leaden and forced.'

'Perhaps it's the nature of the artistic condition,' he said in a mock-pompous voice.

'Oh, I don't see myself in such grand terms,' I said, laughing. 'I'm just a storyteller, nothing more, nothing less.'

'I wouldn't be so self-deprecating,' he said, taking up one of the brushes that stood in a pot of liquid and drying its bristles with an old cloth. 'You need to take more pride in your work.'

'Have you read any of my stories?'

As he blinked I noticed again the length of his eyelashes. I got the impression that he knew the power of his attractive appearance. I was sure that he had already broken more than a few hearts in his short life.

'No, no, I haven't,' he said. 'But I'd like to. I'm sure I'd find them—'

'Don't worry,' I said. 'I know they're not for you.'

'How do you know that? How do you know what I like?' Was there a note of flirtation in his voice or was I imagining it?

'Let's have a look at the portrait,' I said in a matter-of-fact tone. I didn't want him to get the wrong idea. He was beautiful, certainly, but not for me. Besides, soon I would be marrying for the second time.

Rufus Phillips walked over to the far wall and stopped before he turned the easel to face me. 'It's not quite finished. Normally, I wouldn't let anyone see a work that was still in progress. But somehow, well, because of what happened, I feel that this serves as a kind of tribute.'

'Yes, I can understand that,' I said, smiling at the fresh-faced, well-meaning boy. 'Did you know Mr Kinmuir well?'

'Not really,' he said. 'We didn't have long conversations, if that's what you mean. But working on a portrait like this, just spending time with someone, I feel that, I don't know, that I do get a glimpse into ...'

'Into their soul?'

His eyes lit up and he nodded. 'Yes, into their soul.'

'And what did you see?'

'With Mr Kinmuir? Look for yourself.'

He lifted up the easel and slowly turned it around. I stepped closer to view the painting, which at first sight looked like a series of blocks of colour: blacks, reds, beiges and greys. Then I made out the shape of a man, dressed in a pale brown jacket. Here were his hands, his hair, his face. There was his nose, his chin, his cheeks, his jaw. But in the spaces where his eyes should have been there was nothing but the colour of the canvas peeking through.

'As I said, I'm afraid it's not very good, and of course it's unfinished,' said Rufus Phillips.

'I find it fascinating,' I said, grasping for words. Indeed, the portrait was not without its elemental power. The artist had managed to capture something about the personality of Robin Kinmuir, but what? There was an air of decadence, of vague corruption, even degeneration, about it. Here was a man who had loved and who had suffered, perhaps a little too much on both scores. But it was the absence of the eyes that really unsettled me. Was this because Rufus Phillips had not yet put the finishing touches to the portrait? Or was he trying to suggest something else? 'Of course, I'm immediately drawn to the eyes – or the lack of them.'

He started to laugh. 'You mean, you want to know

whether that's a deliberate decision on my part or whether I hadn't got round to painting them?'

'Well, yes, I suppose I do,' I said.

He smiled enigmatically. 'I'm not going to tell you.'

'Well, that's hardly fair.'

'That's as much as you're going to get, I'm afraid,' he said mischievously.

A portrait without eyes. What did that mean? A man who could not see – either literally or metaphorically – what was before him. Was Rufus Phillips trying to capture something in Kinmuir's personality – a certain blindness – or was it something more banal, the simple fact that he hadn't yet completed those parts of the picture? Or was he trying to make some kind of grand statement about the perilous state of modern society? Any of these was possible, and, maddeningly, the painter refused to discuss the issue.

'Do you like it?' he asked.

'Yes, yes, I do, very much so,' I said, not quite telling the truth. 'I think you really managed to capture something of Mr Kinmuir. It must have been a fascinating process. You said he told you some wild stories?'

'Did I?' he said absent-mindedly as he studied the portrait as if seeing it for himself for the first time. 'Oh, a load of nonsense. Stuff about letters written in invisible ink, cryptic clues written on glass with a silver point, which are then made visible with a special solution made up of God knows what. I didn't take him seriously.'

I had to mask my surprise. 'That sounds interesting. I wonder what he was talking about?'

'I honestly couldn't tell you,' Rufus Phillips said, stepping away from the portrait. 'He went on and on about some chaps he knew – now what were they called? – Tinsley and Cameron. One, he said, was a scoundrel who was partial to a bit of blackmail. Actually blackmail on what sounds like a grand scale – he had fleeced two hundred thousand pounds out of some companies in Holland by threatening to put them on a list that said they had dealt with German firms during the war. The other, this Cameron fellow, was locked up after pulling off some fraud involving a pearl necklace. Apparently, he took the blame for it when really it was the fault of his wife, a woman who was addicted to morphine.'

'Gosh, that does sound rather wild,' I said.

'Robin was adamant that all this – and more – would make good material for his memoirs.'

'Really?'

'And that he saw no reason why he shouldn't follow the example set by ... now who was it? ... a chap called Dukes, who had written about his life in a series of articles for the *Tatler*.'

I remembered the pieces written by Sir Paul Dukes, a master of disguise who had been knighted for his services and celebrated for his ability to infiltrate a wide range of Bolshevik and communist organisations. Yet when the features had appeared in the magazine earlier that year they had caused something of a stir. I recalled Davison reacting with horror. Even though Dukes had not given away anything of any particular import and had not placed his colleagues at risk, there was a sense within the Secret Intelligence Service that his actions were unforgivable. There was a code of silence that should never be broken.

As Rufus continued to talk about his sessions with Robin Kinmuir – about how difficult it had been to capture his personality, his choice of colours for the portrait, the size of the canvas and so on – I began to wonder about the manner in which the man had been murdered. If he had not died due to the shotgun wound then how had he been killed? And if James Kinmuir was innocent – as Inspector Hawkins seemed to believe – then who was behind the death? Could someone have heard Kinmuir talking about his exploits to Rufus? What if the Secret Intelligence Service knew that Kinmuir intended to try to write his memoirs? Would they go so far as to try to silence him, perhaps even kill him?

As these questions circled through my mind I began to feel a little dizzy. I walked over to the window and opened it a few inches. The fresh air helped restore me. However, there was one uncomfortable thought that continued to unsettle me. Another person had been up there on the moor when Robin Kinmuir had died. He had slept in the man's dressing room the night before the murder. He had the knowledge and the ability to kill someone using a wide array of methods and techniques. That person was Davison.

Chapter Eight

Davison was, I felt sure, avoiding me. Whenever I tried to catch his eye, his gaze seemed to drift away from me or he would focus on another person in the room, initiating a conversation about the weather, touring in the Highlands and Islands, the various old myths surrounding Skye, in short anything but endure an encounter with me. After dinner, unable to tolerate his resistance any longer, I waited for the house to go to sleep before I stole along the corridors and knocked on the door of his bedroom. There was no answer.

'Davison, it's me – Agatha,' I whispered. 'I need to talk to you.'

I heard footsteps approach the door. 'I was about to get into bed,' he said.

'I'm sorry, but it's important.'

'Can't it wait until tomorrow?'

'No, I'm afraid it can't.'

Davison turned the handle and allowed me into the large room. As I entered he turned his head from me, like a guilty child who knows he has done something wrong. I didn't say anything, hoping that the silence would prompt him into talking to me.

'I thought you said you had something you wanted to say,' he said, turning up the collar of his red silk dressing gown. 'Have you discovered something?'

'Yes,' I said. 'Rufus Phillips showed me the portrait he was painting of Robin Kinmuir.'

'Any good?'

'I'm not sure. It's a little too modernistic for my liking. All blocks of colour. Sharp angles. Fragmented lines.'

'So definitely of the non-realist school, then.'

'Indeed,' I said.

'But I doubt you've come to talk to me about the style of Mr Phillips's art.'

'No,' I said, sighing. 'Rufus told me a little of the conversation that took place between him and Robin Kinmuir during their portrait sessions together.'

'And?'

'It seems as though Robin Kinmuir had rather a loose tongue.'

'Insofar as?'

'His work with the intelligence service.' I let the meaning of the words sink in. 'But presumably you must have known this? That Kinmuir was thinking of writing his memoirs?'

'Ah, that,' he said. 'Yes, Hartford mentioned something along those lines.'

I'd had arguments with Davison before, the most heated of which were about this very issue: how much, or how little, he chose to tell me of a specific case. I knew there was no point in losing my temper. Not only was it late at night, and

I couldn't risk waking up the other guests, but Davison was not the kind of man who responded to a raised voice or a cross word. Instead, I let my silence speak for itself.

'You don't think that—?' He stopped himself as he tried to read my expression. 'Surely, you can't believe that—?'

'I'm afraid I'm not quite sure what to believe,' I replied. 'We know that Robin Kinmuir didn't die of an accidental gunshot wound, inflicted by his nephew. It seems as though James Kinmuir had no motive for wanting his uncle dead as he knew about his enormous debts. But, interestingly, today I learnt that the only other person out there on the moor that day, the same person – you – who was supposedly keeping watch on our potential victim, does have a motive for wanting Robin Kinmuir out of the way. And, significantly, that same person not only had a motive – to silence a man who was on the point of blabbing about his time with the Secret Intelligence Service – but he also had the opportunity.'

'Have you quite finished?' Davison asked, unable to keep a note of sarcasm out of his voice.

'Well, I could go on, but—'

'Yes, I'm sure you could,' he said wryly. 'No wonder you're able to write those fiendish books of yours. Your imagination really is quite something.'

'So you mean to say that you had nothing to do with the death of Robin Kinmuir?'

'Of course I didn't,' said Davison. 'It's a nice theory of yours, and I can see why you put two and two together and got five, but—'

'I don't think that's quite called for.'

'You're right, that was rather below the belt,' he said,

twisting the cord of his dressing gown. There was a sparkle in his eyes now, a sense of mischief that began to melt away my misgivings. 'But you've got every right to question me,' he said, more seriously now. 'And indeed Hartford did express his displeasure at Kinmuir's intention to write his memoirs.'

'Do you know if he's written anything?'

'I'm not sure, but clearly we should search Kinmuir's papers to find out.'

I looked at him, assessing him afresh. 'And neither you nor your associates tried to silence Kinmuir?'

'No, not at all,' he said.

'But I don't understand; if you had nothing to hide, why were you behaving so oddly today?'

'What do you mean?'

'Shifty eyes. Unable to look at me. Acting as if I wasn't there.'

'Oh yes, that,' he said. 'Those awful sisters, the Frith-Strattons, cornered me after lunch and started asking questions about our relationship. They seemed to have got it into their silly, sentimental heads that we are not cousins. Or either that we are cousins, but we are *more* than cousins, if you see what I mean.'

'I see,' I said.

'There's something decidedly odd about them, particularly the one who calls herself May,' he said. 'Anyway, I could feel their eyes watching me, and you, and I had to put them off the track. I couldn't risk them finding out about what we were really doing here.'

'So you gave me the cold shoulder?'

'Yes, if you like.'

'Well, I wish you had told me before embarking on this silent treatment.' I thought it was about time I got my own back. I gave him a flirtatious look and took a step closer. 'Perhaps the Frith-Strattons thought we'd had a lovers' tiff.'

'What do you mean?'

'Well, it's often the way with people in love, isn't it?'

Davison had started to blush a little. 'Is it?'

'All that pent-up passion comes out during an argument and then the pair can't help themselves, which is soon followed by a tremendous sulk.'

He took a few strides around the bedroom. I had clearly worried him. 'Perhaps you're right. Perhaps I have given them the wrong idea. Oh dear. I wonder what I should do?'

The pained expression on Davison's face together with the strain of continuing with the tease proved too much for me and I burst into laughter.

'Is something funny?'

'You, that's all,' I said, clapping my hand over my mouth.

'Well, I'm pleased I've given you a little amusement,' he said rather stiffly.

'I'm only pulling your leg,' I said. 'Anyway, tomorrow I'll have a word with them and talk a little about my real husband-to-be.' I thought of Max and wondered what he was doing. I would write to him, care of his friends, telling him of my relaxing time at the hotel in Broadford. I couldn't let him know what I was really up to.

'Tomorrow I'm due to talk to Inspector Hawkins,' said Davison. 'I'm sure Hartford or someone from the agency must have told him, but it's best to fill him in on our true purpose here. Otherwise he might come up with some extraordinary idea that either I, or—' breaking off to look at me with a mock-horrified stare '—God forbid, perhaps even you, might have been responsible for the murder of Robin Kinmuir.'

I left Davison in good humour and went back to my own room. The night was quiet, the wind nothing but a low murmur outside the house. I settled myself in the chair by the bureau in the corner. From a drawer I took out a sheet of paper and picked up my fountain pen, but just as I was about to start writing a letter to Max, something made me walk over to the window.

I opened the curtains and saw the moon reflected on the surface of the loch. The water was still, but I had heard that it was at least a hundred feet deep. Perhaps it was this – the contrast between the superficial appearance of the water and the reality of its murky depths – that made me think of another quote from a Shakespeare play, from *Hamlet*. Just because Davison was charming, just because he made me laugh, did that necessarily mean he was telling the truth? I knew, perhaps better than most, how even the nicest of people could hide deadly secrets. Was Davison lying to me? And what of Mrs Buchanan? She was an actress, a woman adept at pretending. And what of the other guests? What did I know about them? Practically nothing. The words from the play repeated themselves over and over in my mind. Finally, I took out my notebook and wrote them down at the top of a clean page.

That one may smile, and smile, and be a villain.

Chapter Nine

It had been this very observation – this knowledge that good looks or surface allure could mask something darker – which had made me fearful of embarking on any new love affairs. After what had happened with Archie, who had been both the handsomest and the most selfish of men, I had become nervous. The divorce from him had left me feeling as though I walked about the world bearing an invisible badge of shame.

When I first met Max Mallowan earlier in the year in Ur, in southern Iraq, I did not see him as a potential mate but merely as a nice, quiet, Oxford-educated young man. I never suspected he would look twice at an old maid such as me. I suppose the fourteen-year age difference between us – and my assumption that we were more like aunt and nephew than anything else – meant that from the very beginning I felt relaxed in his company. I was immediately taken by his polite manner and, when he was given the task of showing me some of the sites of the ancient land, he accepted with pleasure.

I remember the lack of embarrassment I felt as we stripped down to our underclothes to bathe in that lake in the desert just outside Ukhaidir. After enjoying that blissful swim we dressed and were ready to continue our journey, but the car had become covered by the desert sands during our time in the water and refused to start. There was no point causing a fuss, I thought, and so I waited for the situation to be resolved, taking shelter in the shadow of the vehicle. Later, Max told me that it was during those few unbearably hot hours, when I endured the uncomfortable circumstances without complaint, that he decided that I was the woman for him. Although I had no awareness of this at the time, it was then that he made up his mind that I would make the perfect wife.

He was considerate, too. There was that awful night at the police post in Kerbala, when I needed to use the lavatory. Max, ever the gentleman, had insisted that if I needed any help during the night that I should call on him. Although I was desperate not to, I had no choice, and the dear thing managed to secure a lamp from a policeman and escorted me in the darkness, waiting outside until I had finished. But he had shown his real strength of character on the journey home. The plan was for the four of us – Leonard and Katharine Woolley, who led the archaeological expedition in Ur, Max, who was Leonard's assistant, and myself – to travel back from Iraq to England via Aleppo, Athens and Delphi. But soon after arriving in Greece I received a batch of telegrams informing me that my daughter, Rosalind, had been taken seriously ill at school with pneumonia. Luckily my sister, Madge, was on hand to care for her at her home, Abney Hall in Cheshire. If that wasn't bad enough I then fell over in the street and managed to tear the ligaments in my ankle, making it impossible for me to put one foot in front of the other.

Max, with that kind, self-effacing manner of his, immediately offered to forgo the delights of sightseeing in Greece and accompany me back to England on the Orient Express. He said he would do everything for me, support me as I hobbled along, bring food from the dining car to my cabin, even bandage my ankle. I was fraught with worry, but he managed to take my mind off my anxieties over Rosalind's condition. He chatted about his family – his father, Frederick, and his mother, Marguerite, and his grandmother who was the famous French opera singer, Marthe Duvivier. He told me too of his school, Lancing College near Brighton, and his time at New College, Oxford.

Was there a chance that Max might have met James Kinmuir and Rufus Phillips at Oxford? Max was born in 1904 – the difference in our ages still brought a blush of shame to my cheek – and the two young men looked roughly the same kind of age. But even if they had been contemporaries there was no possibility of writing to Max to ask for more information. My intelligence work had to remain a secret. I just hoped they didn't know him, or at least speak to me of him. I couldn't bear the repressed sniggers that surely would come when they realised that one of their acquaintances at university was about to marry an older woman.

Indeed, I was astonished by it myself. Max had paid me a few compliments during our friendship. I think he enjoyed my company. Yet, when his proposal came – back in England, after I had learnt that Rosalind had recovered – the approach was an enormous surprise. I considered that we were nothing more than good friends. I thought of every reason why we should not marry and told him so. He was so much younger than me. He was a Roman Catholic. Surely he wouldn't want to burden himself with me.

Then there were the private reasons I didn't want to express. My reluctance to allow a man to get close to me. My fears over what had happened with Archie. There was a line in Psalm 55, its words standing as a warning about the sting of betrayal at the hands not of an enemy but 'my companion: my guide, and mine own familiar friend'. That was what had happened with my first husband. I wasn't sure I could endure it if I was forced to experience such a deception for the second time. My sister too had been against the match with Max. The scenes she had caused when I had first told her about the romance. The tears and the raised voices. But, despite everything, and all the arguments – not least those I had rehearsed in my own mind – I had said 'yes'. In a few weeks' time, on 11 September, we would be man and wife. I smiled at this thought, and enjoyed it for a moment, before a shadow darkened my mind.

I was living in a house with a murderer.

Chapter Ten

The method by which someone commits a murder often serves as a clue in itself: for instance, a poisoner will have a different personality to someone who uses a knife or a gun. The choice of poison – whether it's arsenic or belladonna, cyanide or veronal – can also be indicative. Often the reasoning is banal: what a killer happened to have to hand, such as fly papers from which arsenic can be extracted. However, sometimes this information can help track down the killer. I remembered the 1924 case of the Blue Anchor Hotel murder, which was overseen by William Kenward, the same policeman who investigated my disappearance two years after that.

The case focused around the universal themes of sex and lust. A Frenchman, Jean-Pierre Vaquier, was having an affair with a married woman, Mabel Jones, and he wanted to dispose of her husband, Alfred, of the Blue Anchor Hotel in Byfleet, Surrey. Each morning Alfred, who was a heavy drinker, was partial to take some bromide powders in water to help with his hangover. One day Jean-Pierre added strychnine to the drink and Alfred died an agonising death only hours later. Obviously Jean-Pierre was not that bright a man because when he bought the strychnine at the pharmacy – under a false name – he wrote in the shop's register that he wanted the substance for various wireless experiments. The mistake led Kenward straight to Vaquier, who was by trade ... a wireless operator. I often thought of this case because the method of murder bore a certain similarity to the one I described in my first novel, *The Mysterious Affair at Styles*. I just hoped that Vaquier hadn't got the idea from my book.

It was frustrating to try to begin the investigations into the death of Robin Kinmuir without the knowledge of exactly how he died. Although Davison pressed Inspector Hawkins for details, he refused to give anything away. The detective, however, did accept our presence at the lodge; in addition to the statement provided by Davison outlining his work for the Secret Intelligence Service, it's likely that he'd received news from higher up. Yet the inspector was professional enough to continue to treat us as ordinary guests. In front of the others, he regarded us with the same level of suspicion that he cast upon the rest of the occupants of Dallach Lodge.

Hawkins began the process of investigation by announcing that he was going to interview each of the guests, commandeering the library for the purpose. I would have liked to have hidden behind a door to listen to the testimonies, but I couldn't run the risk of being discovered. Hawkins, however, did promise to share anything of significance with us. Unbeknown to the inspector, Davison and I intended to do a little detective work of our own.

'What do you say to taking advantage of these interviews?'

Davison had asked during our customary stroll after breakfast.

'In what way?'

'Well, it makes sense that while Hawkins is talking to, say, Mr Peterson, we steal into his room to take a look around?'

'Do you think that's wise?' I asked.

'It may prove not to be so, but I don't think we'll get a better chance, do you?'

I considered this for a moment. 'No, I don't suppose we will. But we're going to do this without telling Hawkins?'

'Yes. I don't think he would understand that some of our tactics are different to those employed by the ordinary police.'

'Quite,' I said. 'But aren't you forgetting one important thing?'

'Which is?'

'Some of the guests may have chosen to lock their doors. And to open a door we need a key.'

'Blast it!' cursed Davison, clearly irritated by his momentary lapse into slow-wittedness. 'We'll have to forget that then. What a shame. I thought we were on to a rather good plan there.'

I thought back to something I had seen, something I had heard. 'I think I know of a way,' I said.

'You do?'

'Simkins, the butler. I've seen him around the house carrying a large bunch of keys, which I presume open the doors to the guest rooms. He's also a drunk. Or rather, a drinker. I noticed when we first arrived that his hands were shaking as he held the tray of champagne. And then the Frith-Stratton sisters said that they noticed that his breath smelt of whisky.'

'Is that so?' Davison's eyes brightened. He knew what I was going to suggest. 'So you think that if we leave a little temptation in his way, then perhaps ...?'

'He might take a little too much and forget where he placed the keys to the rooms,' I said. I could easily have added that we could slip a little something into the whisky to make him sleep even more soundly, but I thought it best not to do so at this stage. There was a doctor in the house. And an inspector. And I might need to resort to serious measures such as these at a later date.

'Now, I've got a question for you,' I said. I didn't want Davison to think I knew all the answers. After all, he was a man. And men – even men such as Davison – could only stand so much female superiority. 'How will we know when we should vacate a guest's room?'

'I think it's best to keep the searches brief,' he said, pleased with himself that he was back in charge now. 'A quick in and out to look for anything suspicious. And one person should always stand outside the room, serving as a kind of sentinel. Why don't I do the rooms occupied by the men and you can do the ladies.'

'Very well,' I said. 'And what about Robin Kinmuir's room? When will we get a chance to look around that?'

'That young sergeant who came with Hawkins – Dedham – is still standing guard outside, which is irritating, but understandable.'

'Do we know whom Hawkins is going to interview first?'

'No, not yet, but I've made a plan of the rooms,' Davison said, taking out a scrap of paper from the inside pocket of his jacket.

He had drawn a rough plan of the first floor, divided into sections. Each of the squares was annotated with a set of initials to correspond with the name of the guest. Davison ran his finger along the drawing as he continued to explain the geography of the house.

'If we work anti-clockwise, starting in the east wing, we have Eliza Buchanan, then the room used by the doctor, then James Kinmuir. Next are the quarters of Rufus Phillips which look over the front, as do the rooms of Vivienne Passerini and Simon Peterson. Also at the front there is my room and yours, which is a corner room, and in the west wing we have Robin Kinmuir's. Then a slightly larger room, which is occupied by the Frith-Stratton sisters. I haven't drawn a plan yet of the servants' quarters which are on the floor above. Up there I believe that, in addition to old Mrs Kinmuir, we have the cook, Mrs Baillie, the butler, Simkins, and the two maids. Not only has there been a murder in the house, but they are in need of finding new employment. The inheritances that have come their way will not last forever, that's if they get anything at all.'

'You mean because of Kinmuir's debts?'

'Indeed,' he said.

'How could he have squandered his wealth?' I asked. 'I know that he used to drink, but he was something of a reformed character, wasn't he? Where did all the money go?'

'That's one thing we need to try to find out. Perhaps there's a motive there. An unpaid debt. A deal gone wrong. A man, or men, whom he had crossed and who wanted to carry out some kind of revenge.'

An idea began to form in my mind. There was a great deal to do before I could be more certain that it had substance.

I recalled something Robin Kinmuir had said that first night at drinks. 'And we should of course, if we can, question Kinmuir's aunt, Mrs Kinmuir,' I said.

'From what I've heard, I'm not sure how reliable her statement will be,' said Davison. 'Apparently she is in her dotage and doesn't make much sense any more. So I think we should start with the other guests and see what we can find. I'll ask Hawkins if he has an idea of whom he wants to talk to first. Obviously I can't let him know that we plan to search the guests' rooms. I wouldn't waste your time on Mrs Kinmuir. Or if you do insist on talking to her, I'd leave her until last.'

From my experience of my own grandmothers and their circle, old women were often the very best sources of information. They had years of practice – gossiping, swapping stories, sharing seemingly insignificant changes in a person's appearance. A missing button, a lock of hair out of place, a lost cameo brooch. These were some of the clues that they used to interpret odd or even illicit behaviour. I remembered as a very young girl sitting at the knees of my grandmothers and listening wide-eyed to the tall tales they shared. The experience left me with not only an innate love of storytelling – the unstoppable 'what next?' – but a long-held belief that, as one of my grandmother's worldly friends would say, the good God is in the detail.

Chapter Eleven

The first to be called into the library was Eliza Buchanan. I waited until the last swish of her dress disappeared behind the closing door before rushing upstairs, where I met Davison. He nodded as I went by him, down the corridor and past the landscapes, the portraits of ancestral figures and paintings of saints and Jesus on the cross, towards Mrs Buchanan's room. I stopped for a moment, pretended to brush a speck of dust from my skirt and looked around me, listening for any signs of an approach. As quietly as I could I took out the keys from my handbag.

It had been easy to get them from Simkins. Davison had asked the maid if she could send the butler up to him. He told Simkins that he felt he had drunk too much since first arriving in Scotland and asked him to remove the bottle of whisky that Kinmuir had placed in his room. He would not mind in the least if Simkins were to enjoy the spirit himself, he said. A man needed the odd dram living up here. The main thing was to get the bottle out of his sight. He had his cousin's wedding to prepare for – my forthcoming nuptials in Edinburgh – and he had promised his aged mother that he would turn up for the ceremony looking as fresh-faced as possible.

According to Davison, Simkins had reacted with nonchalance; he had simply bowed his head and retreated with the bottle. After lunch, when the butler had a few hours to himself before his duties started again in the early evening, Davison stole up to the man's room, where he eased open the door and found Simkins sprawled fast asleep on his bed. The keys were sitting on his bedside table next to a Latin primer. If he were to miss them he would, Davison reasoned, hardly broadcast that fact around the house; to do so would risk exposing his fondness for drink. Hopefully, on waking, perhaps Simkins would presume he must have left them somewhere around the house, in the parlour or in one of the bathrooms. After our search of the rooms was over – which Davison estimated would take just over an hour – the keys would be left in a place where Simkins could find them again.

I tried a key, then another, before finding the right one. Taking a deep breath, I stole into the room. The air smelt of orange blossom and musk, the remnants of a heady perfume that Mrs Buchanan must have sprayed over herself before the interview. I moved to the bureau and began my search. The top drawer contained writing paper, envelopes and stamps, nothing out of the ordinary. The drawers beneath were empty. There was a jewel box on the desk, full of diamonds, rubies, sapphires and emeralds, trophies earned by her own efforts and some, I was sure, that were gifts from rich admirers. A perfume box held glass bottles of exotic aromas from Chanel, Lanvin, Coty and Guerlain. Her cosmetics comprised various powders, rouge, lipsticks, eye pencil, together with what looked like a particularly expensive, rose-scented night cream. No wonder Mrs Buchanan looked so youthful.

From there I moved over to the wardrobe. I wondered how long Mrs Buchanan planned on staying because it was bursting with clothes. Dresses, kimonos, scarves, sweaters, skirts, blouses, together with boxes full of every style of boot and shoe. In my tweed skirt, green woollen jumper and sensible brown brogues I felt rather conventional, if not downright shabby, in comparison. If a woman of Mrs Buchanan's age could dress with aplomb and style then why couldn't I? Doubts about Max began to seep into my mind again. He really was too young, wasn't he? I'd make myself look a fool. Women like the Frith-Stratton sisters would talk, if not laugh, at the sight of us together. But who would want to live by the standards set by people like that anyway?

I knelt down and pushed my hand into the bottom of the wardrobe. Again there was nothing out of the ordinary. Then I saw a box that looked too small for shoes. I brought it out and eased off the lid. The first thing I saw was a photograph. Here was Mrs Buchanan, still in costume from one of her productions, smiling at the camera. It looked as though it had been taken in a dressing room; in the background there was a mirror surrounded by lightbulbs and various extravagant displays of flowers in tall vases. The photograph had been torn in half, but in the looking glass one could see what appeared to be the reflection of part of a man's shoulder. Who was the gentleman, I wondered, and why had the image been ripped in this way?

Inside the box there were dozens of letters, written in a near-illegible scrawl. But some phrases jumped out at me – 'my darling', 'my sweetheart', 'the rose of my life' – as well as a few more intimate details. These were clearly letters from a lover. The letters, however, were neither signed nor dated. My assumption was that they were written by Robin Kinmuir to Eliza Buchanan, missives penned at the height of their romance which the actress could not bring to throw away. I was conscious that, at any moment, Mrs Buchanan might be finishing her interview with Inspector Hawkins. I knew that she was a capricious creature and could terminate the meeting on a whim.

I could feel my heart racing, my breathing increasing. I had always been a quick reader, able to gulp down pages of text at a time, but even so I felt overwhelmed by the sea of words that swept over me. The letters spoke of arrangements for future meetings, memories of their time in various hotels in Inverness, Edinburgh and Glasgow, snatches of romantic poetry. Then, as I turned a page, a name stood out: Catherine. The name of Robin Kinmuir's late wife. I squinted to try to make out the words. There was something here about ... yes, about a plan. 'It's the only way,' read a sentence. 'I can't think of anything else,' read another. Then the terrible words became clearer. 'I keep thinking of our life together when she is dead.'

Catherine, I had been told by Davison, had walked out one day and disappeared. But what if Robin's wife had been murdered?

I dropped the incriminating letter and photograph in my handbag, hoping that soon I would be able to sneak back into Mrs Buchanan's room and put them back. I restored the box to its original position and stood up. I straightened my skirt, checked the room for any signs of disturbance and was about to step outside when Davison appeared at the door.

'Mrs Buchanan is on her way up,' he whispered.

I stepped outside, locked the door and placed the keys back in my handbag. We walked quickly down the corridor and came face to face with an angry-looking Mrs Buchanan.

'I warn you both, it's far from a pleasant experience,' she said. 'Such impertinent, vulgar questions.'

'I must admit I'm not looking forward to the interrogation,' I said.

'Well, at least you might be able to use some of it in one of your novels,' she said. 'I had to draw on every last ounce of my considerable experience on the stage just to endure it. So humiliating. And some of the things that inspector was implying.'

'Implying? In what way?' I asked.

'About my relationship with Mr Kinmuir.' Mrs Buchanan lowered her voice and leant a little closer to me. 'You know, my dear, what I'm talking about. But I really don't see it's anyone else's business, do you?' I thought of the letter in my handbag. 'Best to keep one's private life private. I loathe a scandal. Anyway, you'll have to excuse me because talking to Inspector Hawkins has really left me feeling quite wretched.' She nodded first at me and then at Davison and then retreated into her room. At what point might she notice that a photograph and letter had been taken from the box?

'I've got something to tell you,' I whispered, as we walked away from Mrs Buchanan's room and down the corridor. 'But what about the next person to be interviewed by Hawkins?'

ANDREW WILSON

'I'll go and find out,' Davison said and hurried down the stairs.

A minute or two later he was back.

'Hawkins has just called Miss Passerini into the library,' he said. 'So I'm afraid you're doing the dirty work again.'

'Very well,' I said. We checked the corridor for approaching guests and, hoping that the sergeant stationed outside Kinmuir's room was not about to walk around the corner, I took out the keys and entered Miss Passerini's quarters.

It was a small room overlooking the front of the house. Everything looked terribly ordered and in its place, almost as if it were some kind of stage set. I suppose Miss Passerini, with her love of the classification of flora and fauna, must have applied that sense of the strict regulation and organisation of natural systems to her own life. In her wardrobe, the few clothes she had were coordinated by colour, a pleasing blend of greens, greys and blacks. The accessories that she allowed herself – two scarves, two pairs of gloves, two hats and her various undergarments — each occupied their own space within the specific sections and drawers of the wardrobe. Books – about fungi, birds, orchids, mosses, and a tome on Karl Marx – were stacked neatly by her bed. I moved across to the chest of drawers by the window. In the top drawer was a silk-lined box containing a string of pearls. In another, smaller wooden box there was a magnifying glass and a compass. The drawer below contained Miss Passerini's watercolour set and a sketchbook full of meticulously detailed drawings and paintings of flowers, ants, birds, beetles and butterflies. She not only had a real talent for capturing the anatomy of a stem or a leaf or the wing of a bee but clearly possessed a keen artistic sensibility too.

As I began to feel more than a little guilty for rummaging through the young woman's belongings – it seemed that Miss Passerini had nothing to hide – I opened the bottom drawer. There was her passport. I opened it at the photograph of Miss Passerini. Although the image was not a flattering one, it was undoubtedly that of the woman sitting downstairs. I turned through the pages when something jumped out at me. The stamp showed that Miss Passerini's most recent visit had been to Argentina and before then she had travelled to Venezuela and Uruguay. But at the drinks reception that first night at the lodge she had told Davison that she had just come back from Berlin.

Just then there was a sharp knock at the door.

'Agatha, come on,' hissed Davison. 'She's on her way up.'

'What?' I said to myself. I'd only been in the room for a matter of minutes. I quickly shut the drawer, pushing it back as if my fingertips had been licked by fire. I ran to the door and opened it. Panic hardened Davison's eyes.

'Quick, you've only got a few seconds,' he said, before he turned and walked away.

I shut the door as quietly as possible and, with shaking hands, locked the door. The next moment, as I looked up, Miss Passerini appeared at the top of the stairs. Understandably, she seemed startled to see me standing outside her room.

'Oh, there you are,' I said, thinking quickly. 'I just came to knock on your door to ask you a question.'

'A question?'

'Yes, I wanted to see whether you had any books I could borrow. It's so boring being cooped up like this, don't you think? There are only so many walks one can go on and only so many lunches and dinners one can endure. I only brought one novel with me, which I've finished. I wondered if you had anything I could borrow?'

'Yes, of course,' she said, although I detected a hesitancy in her voice. 'But have you looked in the library?'

'I would have done, but I didn't want to disturb Inspector Hawkins.'

The answer seemed to satisfy her. 'Well, I'm not sure whether I've got anything that you'd like,' she said, taking her key out and opening the door. 'But you're very welcome to come in and have a look at what I've got.'

'That would be so kind, thank you,' I said as we stepped into the room.

She walked over to the chest of drawers, almost as if she was drawn there by an invisible force. Her eyes darted back and forth from one drawer to the next, before they came to rest on the one at the bottom that contained her passport. I noticed that it was not quite closed; I had been in such a rush to get out of the room that I had not shut it properly.

'How was the interview?' I said, trying to distract her. 'With Inspector Hawkins? I'm dreading talking to him.'

'Why, do you have something to hide?'

'Oh, no, nothing like that, it's just that—'

'I was joking,' she said. 'Unless you *do* have something to hide?' She gazed at me for a little too long.

'No, not at all,' I said, feeling a slight blush rise to my cheeks.

'I wouldn't concern yourself with the inspector,' she said. 'It's all very straightforward.' She rattled off some of the questions in an officious-sounding voice. '*What were you doing at the time of Robin Kinmuir's death? Did you see or hear anything unusual? Do you think Kinmuir had any enemies? What made you come to Dallach Lodge? How did you hear about it?* Those sort of things. I raced through it all at top speed. And I think the inspector wanted to get on with talking to the men in the house – I think he's got his suspicions regarding some of them. So he let me go.'

'Whom does he suspect?'

'He was asking me all about Mr Peterson, but I can tell you for a fact he had nothing to do with it. As you know, he was in his room when it happened that morning. You saw him with your own eyes, standing at the top of the stairs in his dressing gown.'

'Yes, I remember,' I said. 'But who do you think . . . did it?'

'My money's on Simkins, don't you think? That's what the Frith-Strattons are saying anyway. It's a cliché, I suppose, one that you couldn't use in your novels. But in life, with real crimes, it's so often the butler, don't you find?'

'Perhaps,' I said.

'And he's behaving very oddly if you ask me,' Vivienne Passerini continued. 'I tried to call him earlier and he was nowhere to be seen. In fact, I wouldn't be surprised if he had a just cause to strike out.'

'But why would he want to kill his employer?'

'All those years of having to bow and scrape and do his master's every bidding. I would have thought that's enough to drive a man to murder.'

'But if that were the case wouldn't every servant one comes across be a potential murderer?'

'I'm not going to argue with that. I don't know if you've guessed already, but I'm not a fan of all this,' she said, gesturing at the sublime view of the sea loch framed by the window.

'All this . . .?'

'The aristocracy. The landed gentry. The great and the good. Whatever it is you want to call them. I think they're a dying breed. Inheriting wealth and privilege and connections. It's all got to stop.'

'So you're a socialist?'

'Yes, I am, and I don't mind telling anyone. I'd go further and say I was . . .' She quoted some long, incomprehensible paragraph about Marx, the means of production and the sins of capitalism.

I didn't want to have an argument with her.

'In fact, I've got a splendid idea,' she said. 'You were asking for a book. Why don't you read this?' She picked up the political tract by her bedside and pressed it into my hand.

'Thank you, that does look interesting, but I was thinking of something a little more . . . entertaining.' She looked disappointed in me. 'Something to take my mind off all this terrible business in the house.'

'If it's fiction you want I can't help you there. I don't believe in it,' Vivienne Passerini said, turning her back on me. 'It's nothing but a capitalist venture, an opiate to dull the senses of the populace.'

When I didn't respond she looked back at me.

'Sorry, I didn't mean to insult you. I know that you write novels, but my guess is that they're a great deal better than the romantic dross churned out by those two sisters. At least in your books the colonel or lord of the manor or whoever gets bashed over the head with a piece of lead piping in the library. Serves him right, I'd say. Actually, one could argue that your novels could be read as . . .'

Again she spouted some intellectual theory that completely passed me by, but she seemed to be saying that, on some level at least, she approved of my work.

'I suppose you must have mixed with some very clever people in Berlin?' I asked.

'In Berlin?' For a moment she seemed unsettled, before she composed herself. 'Oh yes, it's full of people who really want to change the system, and not just the awful bright young things you see here. The frivolity of that scene makes me sick. I mean, James and Rufus are all very well, but they're not *serious* people.'

'And what do you make of Mr Peterson?' I had observed the two of them becoming increasingly friendly, but from what she had just told me he did not seem like her type at all.

'Simon? He's an interesting chap. There's more to him than first meets the eye.'

'In what respect?'

'He's very mysterious but awfully good-looking, don't you think?'

'Indeed.'

'He says he wants the same thing as I do. The breakdown of established society. A new order.'

'I see,' I said. 'And what does he do for a living?'

She looked uncertain and didn't answer the question. 'Now, you said you wanted to borrow a book?'

I left Miss Passerini's room with a beautifully illustrated volume by a female botanist by the name of Priscilla Susan Bury, showing lilies and amaryllis and other exotic-looking plants. Davison was waiting for me by the stairs. Apparently, Inspector Hawkins had asked for tea, so we had a few minutes before he was ready to call in the next person. Neither of us talked until we entered Davison's room.

'It's certainly looking as though not everyone is what they seem,' I said. 'First of all, in Mrs Buchanan's room I found a bundle of letters written to her from a male admirer, in which the writer talks of life after the death of Catherine Kinmuir.'

I took out the letter I had taken and showed it to Davison. 'And here's a photograph of Mrs Buchanan, part of which has been removed. But look, you can see the shoulder of a man reflected in the mirror.'

'So do you really think Robin Kinmuir and Mrs Buchanan may have disposed of his wife?'

'It's certainly something to look into. Do you know when and how Catherine disappeared?'

'I think it was in 1916, but I'll check,' Davison said. 'We might be dealing with another case of murder here. After all, it's a classic motive – a man and his lover plotting to get rid of a troublesome wife. Sorry, I—' He realised that, in one respect, this scenario was similar to the one I had endured when, during the days I went missing in 1926, Superintendent William Kenward of the Surrey Police believed that my husband might have disposed of me. It was, of course, a theory that had blinded the superintendent to all other possibilities.

'Not to worry,' I said. 'Perhaps you could ask your office to find out if there were any unidentified bodies found around the same time?'

'Yes, a good idea.' Davison glanced down at his wrist-watch. 'I'm conscious that we don't have much time before Hawkins calls someone else. And what of Miss Passerini?'

'Do you remember that night when she told us she had just come back from Berlin?'

'Yes, yes, I do.'

'I found her passport and according to that, Miss Passerini last visited not Berlin, but South America.'

'So why would she lie about that?'

'Exactly,' I said, pausing for moment. I told him what Vivienne Passerini had said about Simon Peterson's desire for the collapse of the establishment. 'If she and Mr Peterson are lying, as well as Mrs Buchanan, what about the others? I'm beginning to wonder if everybody in this house has something to hide.'

Chapter Twelve

Davison was keen to get into Simon Peterson's room, but it was the Frith-Stratton sisters who were summoned into the library next. I couldn't search their room because it was next to Robin Kinmuir's, outside of which the sergeant was still stationed. And so we waited with the rest of the group – apart from Mrs Buchanan and Miss Passerini who were upstairs in their quarters – in the drawing room, where tea was being served and people were enjoying the warmth of the fire. At least the occasion gave me the opportunity to question the mysterious Mr Peterson.

'More tea, Mr Peterson?' I asked, as I walked over to the tea table.

'No, thank you,' he said.

'A cucumber sandwich? Or perhaps some Dundee cake?'

'No,' he said, somewhat irritably, before his thin lips formed themselves into a false smile. 'No, thank you.'

'It's hardly what I'd call a holiday – being cooped up here, I mean. I'm sure you'd much rather leave and go somewhere else – that, or get on with your business.'

'Yes, indeed,' he said.

'Shipping, isn't it?'

'Yes,' he said, clearly not wishing to elaborate.

There was an awkward pause, during which I took a sip of tea. 'Glorious things, ships,' I said, realising how stupid I sounded. 'Ocean liners, particularly.' I had to think of something to engage him in conversation. 'I went round the world – well, a good deal of it anyway – in 1922 to help provide the British Empire Exhibition tour. I love being up on deck, looking out at the horizon in the distance. There's something so thrilling about it.'

'Fascinating,' he said, taking up the copy of *The Times* that he had been reading earlier.

'Do you feel the same? I mean about being up on deck?' I gave him a warm and friendly smile. Surely there was only so long he could keep up his rudeness.

'I'm afraid I don't get very much opportunity to travel myself,' he replied, letting the newspaper drop down onto his lap. 'I'm very much chained to the office.'

'What aspect of shipping are you involved in, if you don't mind me asking?'

'Finance,' he said.

'Have you always been employed in that area? I mean, worked in shipping?'

He narrowed his eyes as I felt him scrutinising me. I knew what he was thinking: Why was I asking these questions? Was I just a bored, silly, but quite harmless woman who liked nothing better than prying into the lives of other people? Or was there something behind my enquiries? Did I have a hidden agenda? I would have to be careful; I didn't want him to suspect why I had booked a stay at Dallach Lodge.

'Sorry, it's a professional habit of mine – asking too many questions,' I said. 'I'll leave you alone in peace.'

'No, not at all,' he said, smiling with a little more warmth. 'It's just that I woke up with a terrible headache and I haven't been able to shift it all day.'

'Too much whisky last night?' asked James Kinmuir who, with Rufus Phillips, walked up to the tea table at that moment. 'I know that's the only thing that has kept me going the last few days.'

'No, it's not that,' replied Mr Peterson. 'Perhaps it's the strain of . . . what happened.'

'It's certainly a terrible business,' said Rufus Phillips. 'And then there is all that nonsense with Mrs Buchanan. Walking out of rooms when James enters. Making those cutting remarks. No wonder people are on edge.' He turned to James. 'Once this is all over you should think about launching a suit for defamation of character. Some of the things she's said are quite disgraceful.'

As the two young men took their tea and walked away to stand by the large windows framed by a pair of elaborate red velvet curtains, they continued to discuss the issue. I concentrated on what they were saying. James Kinmuir was far from keen to pursue legal action on the grounds that it would be too costly and he did not have any money, but Rufus Phillips was insistent. I noticed a tension between the friends that had not existed previously.

I sat down in an armchair next to Mr Peterson. 'Have you taken any remedies to help your headache?'

'I've got some sal volatile somewhere, I think,' he said.

'Well, if it doesn't go please let me know, I've got some powders and tonics in my room that may help,' I said, smiling. I thought of the collection of little vials hidden in my suitcase upstairs. The colourless liquids that could kill a man in a matter of minutes. A drop of poison that could be added to a cup of tea. The toxic grains that could be stirred into a glass of water. I hoped that I wouldn't need to use them. But, as my mother always said, it was better to be safe rather than sorry.

'Is there anything in the newspaper?' I asked. I hoped this might elicit some information regarding his political views.

'Unemployment rates rising to two million. The Miners' Federation demand for a seven-hour day. The resolutions and encyclical letter of the Lambeth Conference.' Each point was delivered drily, without emotion. Simon Peterson smoothed his hand over the newspaper, fixed me with his small, beady eyes and said, 'And I've got a question for you.'

'Yes, of c-course,' I said, trying not to fluster. I hoped he wasn't going to ask about Davison and me or what I was doing at Dallach Lodge.

'I know you're a writer of detective novels.'

'Yes, that's right,' I said.

'I'm afraid I haven't read any of yours, but you might have a better idea than most who is likely to be responsible for what happened.'

The question came as something of a relief. 'Well, I – I have a theory or two, like everyone here.'

'I don't believe those two sisters – all that nonsense they're spouting about Simkins. He hasn't got the mental capacity to commit a murder like this.'

'Do you think someone clever is behind this?'

'Oh, yes, it has to be, don't you think?' He seemed more animated now. 'I mean, men like Simkins are all very well, but it's unlikely he would have the intellect to plan such a complex scheme, don't you agree?'

'I see what you mean,' I said. 'Because of the way in which Mr Kinmuir was murdered?'

'Well, the fact that we still don't know what actually killed him tells us something,' he said.

'Yes, I wonder when we'll find out,' I said.

It was then that Mr Peterson gave me a queer sort of look that implied a shared understanding or expectation. What did he think I knew? He glanced over at Davison and back at me, then, with an enigmatic smile, he took up *The Times* once more.

Chapter Thirteen

In the end, Davison was unable to search Mr Peterson's room; nor did I get the chance to snoop around the quarters of the Frith-Stratton sisters. We had run out of time. We knew that Simkins would soon be waking up from his alcohol-induced afternoon nap and would go in search of his keys. Davison left them on a washstand in a bathroom used by the butler just off the servants' corridor on the top floor. I kept watch outside the door to make sure neither Simkins nor any of the other servants discovered Davison entering or leaving.

As we were passing down the corridor on the way back to the stairs we heard a faint cry come from behind one of the doors. I stopped Davison, put a finger to my lips and listened. Fragments of speech, none of which made sense, came from the other side of the door. I stepped back, so the occupant of the room could not hear me, and whispered to Davison to leave. It had to be the room of the ancient Mrs Kinmuir. Perhaps now would be a good time to talk to her.

'Are you sure?' he asked.

I nodded. There was, from what I had been told, little

chance that Mrs Kinmuir would add anything to the investigation into her nephew's death. But if I could provide a little companionship, maybe even bring her a few moments of comfort in a life that surely must be desperately lonely, then the day would not have been wasted. I had been brought up on Bible stories, the Good Samaritan, the parable of the Prodigal Son. It was, I reasoned, no less than my duty. And I always relished the company of elderly women; they seemed to enjoy an easy freedom to say anything, often the most shocking and outrageous things, without censure.

I knocked gently on the door and, after hearing a muted, strangled cry, turned the handle and stepped into the room. It was a cramped space with a narrow bed and a low ceiling. In the corner was a wash basin and stand; the air smelt of lavender and coal tar soap.

Sitting in one of two tartan armchairs by the window was a small-framed woman with white hair, a relatively unlined pink face and cloudy blue eyes. She was wearing a brown tweed skirt, a white blouse and a green cardigan. Her head tilted in my direction as she began to speak.

'*There was a crooked man and he walked a crooked mile,*' she mumbled.

'Hello,' I said, smiling. 'I hope you don't mind me calling on you like this.'

Her face lit up and she smiled with all the joy and innocence of a child.

'Could I come and sit by you?' I asked.

'*Cry Baby Bunting, Daddy's gone a-hunting,*' she replied.

Perhaps Davison was right and there was little point in talking to her. But I could hardly back out of the room now.

'My name is Agatha. What is yours?'

'*I had a little hen, the prettiest ever seen, she washed up the dishes and kept the house clean.*'

'You have got the most wonderful view here, you can see for miles around,' I said, looking out of the window. Indeed, the attic room enjoyed lovely vistas of the sea loch and the heather-covered moors. With embarrassment, I remembered Robin saying that the poor old lady's cataracts prevented her from seeing very much. 'I think it must be lovely living out in the wilds of the country like this,' I said, sitting down. 'I grew up in Torquay, so very different from here. Of course, when I was a girl the town was nothing like it is today. And the villa where we lived – Ashfield, it was called – was situated almost in the countryside. I adored living by the sea, watching it change with the light and shade and wind. But you have the loch here.'

There was no response from Mrs Kinmuir. On a side table by her chair was a Bible and a pack of cards. But what was the point of them if she could not see?

'I see you've got the Bible here. And a pack of cards.'

'*The Queen of Hearts she made some tarts all on a summer's day,*' she said. So Mrs Kinmuir did understand something of what I was saying to her.

I finished the couplet for her. '*The Knave of Hearts he stole the tarts and took them all away.*'

At this she giggled like a little girl and her cheeks turned more pink.

'Do you like patience? Should I take the cards and play?'

Again there was no response. I reached for the cards, shuffled them and started to lay them out for a game, placing seven cards face down in a line. I turned up the card on the left, placed six cards on top of the existing number and repeated the sequence until I had one card to put down which I turned over. I began to play, talking her through the cards as I did so.

'Red Queen on black King,' I said. 'Black seven on red eight. Red two on black three.'

The simple sequence seemed to delight her. Indeed, the rhythm of the game was somehow comforting, like the sound of gentle rain on a window pane or the taste of crumpets with butter.

'Do you get much company?' I asked, as I continued to play. 'I'm sure Robin, your nephew, would have come up here a good deal. And I suppose now you must miss his visits.'

At this, her smile seemed to fade away.

'I know when my mother died I missed her enormously,' I said. 'I still do, of course. But grief also drove me a little mad. Some of the silly things I did!' I tried to laugh, but the sound came out as more of a stifled cry. I took a moment to compose myself. 'I wonder, has anyone told you about what happened to your nephew? To Robin?'

Her eyes seemed to mist over and her bottom lip began to tremble.

'I don't want to cause you any upset. I'm sorry,' I said, placing the cards to one side and taking her hand. The skin, despite the liver spots and natural blemishes that came with age, was smooth to the touch. One of her fingers was decorated by a beautiful sapphire and diamond ring.

'That's a lovely ring,' I said. Perhaps the jewel had, at one time, been a talisman of memories. A touchstone to recall happier times. But what of those memories now, where had they gone? Or was it the case that Mrs Kinmuir could indeed remember the past, but could no longer communicate that fact? What were we if not a collection of our memories? The thought of ending up like Mrs Kinmuir unsettled me. This was not how I wanted to spend my last few years on earth. Stuck up in an attic, fed and watered and looked after like a genial pet, but unable to engage or talk to anyone. Yet perhaps it was for the best that Mrs Kinmuir was divorced from reality; at least in this state she seemed protected from the harsh brutalities of life.

'Robin,' she said sadly. A single tear slipped down her cheek.

So she wasn't as lost as I thought. I had managed to reach her. 'Yes, your nephew,' I said. I coughed as I thought how best to phrase it. 'I'm sorry to tell you that Robin had a very bad accident. And I'm afraid he didn't survive.'

She slumped back in her chair and fell silent.

'You see, he was out walking.' I looked out of the window across to the moor. If Mrs Kinmuir had not been disabled by the cataracts in her eyes she would have had a perfect view of the site of the accident. 'I wonder, did you see anything that day? You might have heard shooting. The two young men, Robin's nephew James and his friend Rufus Phillips, were shooting grouse.'

There was no response.

'But the inspector has ruled them out of the enquiry,' I continued. 'James shot Robin by accident, but the wound in the thigh was only superficial. And James did not have a motive. Although he is the beneficiary of the estate, I'm afraid – well, I'm afraid there is nothing left.'

What would happen to poor Mrs Kinmuir? Once the house was sold, and the debts were paid, where would she live? Would some kind soul on Skye take her in? Or would she end up in some home for ladies of reduced means in Portree or Inverness? Even that would require money. I would ask Davison and the doctor to look into it.

'But don't worry, my dear. Everything will be taken care of. *You* will be taken care of.' I gave her hand one last clasp and got up to go. I smiled and said goodbye, and told her that I would pay her another visit soon.

The next time, I decided, I would just come and sit quietly beside her and hold her hand or perhaps I would play another game of patience. I wouldn't talk of Robin Kinmuir or upset her with talk of his death. It had been foolish of me to think that Mrs Kinmuir could give me any insight or information into the mystery of what had happened to her nephew. I walked to the door and turned to give her one last smile.

'*L'ho visto morire*,' she said in a low voice.

I knew some Italian. The words fixed me to the spot and I grasped the door handle forcefully.

'What did you say, Mrs Kinmuir?'

Although she had mumbled the words the meaning was clear; I had not misheard them. I stepped away from the door and came closer to her. I didn't want to put her under any pressure or give her the impression that the words were especially significant; to do so might make her clam up.

'You saw him die?' I asked the question in a way I might when enquiring of a young child what they had done that morning with nanny in the nursery.

'Who *saw him die? I, said the Fly, with my little eye, I saw him die,*' she replied.

Oh dear. She was back on the nursery rhymes again. She recited some fragments I could not quite place before she declaimed, '*Oh, the grand old Duke of York, He had ten thousand men,*' before breaking off and saying, 'Oh yes, it was a grand tour all right,' followed by the rest of the verse, '*He marched them up to the top of the hill, And he marched them down again.*'

I knelt down by her and took her hand once more. She smiled softly at me with the kind of sweetness of nature and compassionate regard that reminded me of a woman in holy orders.

'You said something in Italian, "*L'ho visto morire.*" Can you tell me what you saw?' I asked gently.

She gestured for me to come nearer. I eased myself forwards, so close that I could smell the milkiness of her skin.

Her voice was nothing more than a whisper now. '*Who killed Cock Robin? I, said the Sparrow, with my bow and arrow, I killed Cock Robin.*'

Chapter Fourteen

That evening, as I went down for dinner, I had a sense of a scene being played out for the second time. I was wearing the same emerald-green dress I had worn that first night at Dallach Lodge, the same borrowed jewels. I stepped into the drawing room, beautifully lit by candlelight, to see most of the guests I had met that night. Yet there were now two people missing: Robin Kinmuir, our genial host who had been killed, and Dr Fitzpatrick, who was due to report on the method of his murder.

The inspector had gone for the day. He was staying in a guest house further up the coast. A uniformed officer was still stationed outside Robin Kinmuir's room and he was under strict instructions not to let anyone in. Hawkins had not yet shared with us any of the information that he had gathered during the course of his interviews. But he said that he would do so the next day, when he had finished working up a neat copy of his report. Hawkins told us that this was when the doctor would come to the house to present him with the findings of the post-mortem investigation.

There was a false jollity to the drinks. Everyone was relieved that their interviews were over and the atmosphere was like that of an end-of-term gathering, when pupils had finished their exams. However, unlike schoolchildren, the guests at Dallach Lodge had access to alcohol. Although everyone was polite at the moment, I worried that by the end of the night that façade of respectability would have been stripped bare to reveal something quite ugly underneath. After all, it appeared that there was a murderer among us.

As I talked to Davison, I studied the guests. There was Mrs Buchanan, a beacon of light in a diamond necklace and matching earrings, holding forth about some of the great actors and writers she had known during the course of her glittering career. As she drank her champagne she bandied about famous names – Noel Coward, Gerald du Maurier, even Charlie Chaplin. She had been Robin Kinmuir's mistress and there was an implication that she could have been involved with the disappearance of his first wife, Catherine. At the other end of the room, involved in an intimate tête à tête, were Vivienne Passerini and Simon Peterson. She had told everyone that she had just returned from Berlin, when her passport showed that she had been in South America. Miss Passerini, who held socialist if not downright communistic views, had avoided telling me what Mr Peterson did for a living. And the strange look that Mr Peterson himself had given me, implying some sort of shared knowledge – what did that mean?

I walked around the room with Davison and heard the Frith-Stratton sisters boring poor James Kinmuir and Rufus Phillips to death about their romance novels. The young men were doing a noble job of being polite, nodding their heads and saying appropriate things such as, 'Really?', 'How fascinating' and 'You must tell me more about that'. Whenever they thought the sisters weren't looking both of them nervously glanced over at Miss Passerini, but of course the beautiful young woman did not return their feelings of admiration. What had she called them in that dismissive manner? *Not serious people.* She only seemed to have eyes for Mr Peterson. I looked at him again. What was he hiding?

'Should I rephrase the question to make it more interesting?' asked Davison.

'I'm sorry?'

'I was wondering if you had any inkling about what the doctor might say tomorrow?'

'Oh, I was miles away,' I said.

'Evidently,' said Davison. 'I just hope you're not having second thoughts about your forthcoming nuptials.'

'What are you talking about?' I said rather crossly.

He looked over at Mr Peterson and raised an eyebrow. 'There seems to be a particular man who has become an object of fascination.'

'Don't be ridiculous,' I said, keeping my voice as low as possible. 'You know very well the reasons why I might be studying him.'

He glanced at Mr Peterson, who leant forwards and whispered something in Miss Passerini's ear, an observation that made the young woman laugh out loud. At that moment, Simkins rang the gong for dinner and we proceeded into the dining room. The room was painted the same deep shade of red as the upstairs passages and, like them, its walls were lined with a number of old paintings in gilt frames. The long wooden table was beautifully set, with candles, silverware and sweet-smelling flowers from the gardens.

Normally, I would have been sitting beside Davison, but even though I wasn't that cross with him I felt as though I should signal my annoyance and so I took a seat at the other end of the table. Mrs Buchanan sat by me on one side and Simon Peterson on the other.

Initially, the conversation steered clear of the murder and the prospective findings of Inspector Hawkins and Dr Fitzpatrick. Mrs Buchanan was fascinated by the imminent birth of a new royal baby at Glamis Castle – it seemed she had some inside knowledge of certain aristocratic circles – while Mr Peterson talked about the problems facing the islanders of St Kilda in the Outer Hebrides. Illness, crop failures and contamination of their soil would soon lead to the complete evacuation of the remaining population. As they talked I tried to listen to some of the other discussions around the table. Davison was asking Miss Passerini more about her supposed time in Berlin and the young woman was answering with confidence about the sights on and around Unter den Linden. James Kinmuir and Rufus Phillips had broken free of the Frith-Strattons and, fuelled by wine, were engaged in a debate about some obscure aspect of the Italian Renaissance, while the two sisters were talking about the possibility of setting a book in a remote Scottish castle.

After the soup, Simkins served the meat course, a rich beef stew (which Mrs Buchanan rejected in favour of a plate of creamed potatoes and carrots), and then poured a fine claret for those drinking wine. As I predicted, voices rose and, somewhat inevitably, the conversation turned to the subject we had been ignoring – the inspector's report and the post-mortem results of Dr Fitzpatrick.

'Whatever happens tomorrow we must all remain calm,' said Mr Peterson, giving me that strange look of approbation once again.

'I agree with Simon,' said Miss Passerini, using his Christian name.

'I wonder what the inspector will find,' May Frith-Stratton remarked.

Mrs Buchanan scowled down the table at James Kinmuir; it was obvious that, despite all the evidence to the contrary, she still believed that the young man was responsible for her former lover's death. James, feeling the force of her glare and taking advantage of the momentary silence around the table, blushed a little and pushed his chair back from the table and stood up.

'I've been m-meaning to say something to you all during the last few days, but I never found the right time,' he said somewhat hesitantly. Rufus Phillips nodded as if encouraging him to go on. 'First of all, I want to apologise to you for the inconvenience you've experienced here at Dallach Lodge. Of course, none of you expected any of this . . . trouble and disturbance.' His voice trailed off for a moment, before he began again. 'I know the situation looked terribly bad for me, soon after the accident, and I wouldn't blame you if you thought the very worst of me.' He did not need to look towards Mrs Buchanan to convey the fact that he was referring to her. 'But, as the inspector informed us, my uncle did not die because of a gunshot wound. We will learn the truth tomorrow, when I hope the inspector will be able to release you and we can all try to get on with our lives. I want to thank you for co-operating with Inspector Hawkins. I'm certain the explanation will clarify everything.'

Just as the young man was about to sit down he remembered one last thing. 'And, of course, none of you will have to pay for your stay at the Lodge. It's the least I can do considering the circumstances.'

There were murmurs of assent and approval around the table, apart from Mrs Buchanan who was whispering something to herself.

'But don't you need the money rather desperately?' asked Davison.

'I'm sure I'll manage,' James Kinmuir said. 'Although Glenelg told me my uncle was stony broke, I've got some small savings of my own that I can draw on.'

'That's extremely noble of you,' said Mr Peterson. 'Very generous indeed.'

'And what about the servants?' asked Miss Passerini. 'It would be awful if any of them were to suffer. After all, none of this is their fault.'

James Kinmuir looked around to make sure that neither Simkins nor any of the servant girls were in the room.

'I'm going to honour all my commitments,' he said vaguely, noticing that the dining room door was ajar.

I coughed lightly before I spoke. 'And do you know what will happen to Mrs Kinmuir?'

The mention of the name was met by a certain blankness of expression.

'Your uncle's aunt?' I added.

'Of course,' he said. 'Old Auntie. She'll be looked after, there's no doubt about that.'

'It's just that I went to see her earlier,' I said. 'I know she's nearly blind and . . .' I thought how best to express the state of her mind, or lack of it.

'Yes, I'm afraid the old girl is not what she was,' James Kinmuir said. 'It's a very sad state of affairs. I believe she used to be quite the intellectual and spoke half a dozen different languages.'

I turned to Mrs Buchanan and related something of my visit. 'I do feel quite sorry for her,' I said. 'I wanted to know if she had seen anything of the accident from up in the attic, but of course her cataracts are really quite disabling.' As I said this I noticed that the table had fallen silent. 'My hopes were raised for a moment when she said, in Italian, "*L'ho visto morire*".'

'I saw him die,' said the actress.

'Exactly,' I said. 'But it proved to be nothing but a line from an old nursery rhyme.'

'It's *Who Killed Cock Robin?* isn't it?' said Mr Peterson.

'Yes, that's right,' I said. 'Now I think of it, it was one of my nanny's favourites. Quite gruesome if I remember.'

I repeated the opening of the rhyme to myself.

> *Who killed Cock Robin?*
> *I, said the Sparrow,*
> *With my bow and arrow,*
> *I killed Cock Robin.*

Who saw him die?
I, said the Fly,
With my little eye,
I saw him die.

'Yes, Auntie seems to have retreated to her childhood,' said James Kinmuir. His face had lost its colour now and a certain melancholy expression clouded his features.

'It's extraordinary how ghoulish they are, some of the old nursery rhymes,' said Rufus Phillips, trying to cheer up his friend. 'I remember having nightmares when my mother read *Three Blind Mice* to me before bedtime.'

At this the group erupted into good-humoured laughter, apart from Mrs Buchanan who could not even force a smile. But Mr Phillips was right: there was something definitely unsettling about these rhymes. Just as Simkins began to serve an apple tart with custard I thought of *Sing a Song of Sixpence* and those horrid blackbirds baked in a pie.

'No, thank you,' I said, as the butler came to a stand by me. 'I couldn't eat another thing, I'm afraid.'

'Neither can I,' said Mrs Buchanan, dismissing Simkins with a quick wave of her hand. 'Honestly, to think that Robin is not even in his grave yet and these people think it's all right to laugh and joke as if nothing has happened.' She stared down the table at James Kinmuir and Rufus Phillips. 'It's disgraceful.'

'Do you know Mrs Kinmuir well?' I asked.

'Which one?' she said, without a moment's hesitation.

'Robin Kinmuir's aunt, the lady who lives in the attic.'

'I've met her many times, but I couldn't say I know her well.'

I lowered my voice. 'And she knew of . . . of your friendship with Robin?'

'Yes, of course,' she said. 'But I don't think she approved. She was very fond of Catherine, you see.'

'Would she recognise you now?'

'I doubt it,' she said. 'Although it's difficult to say what she knows and what she doesn't know. Personally, I think her mind has gone to pieces. I popped up to see her the other day and she just spouted gibberish. It's sad to think of her stuck up there, all alone. She used to love travelling. She always said she wanted to spend her last days in Italy. I think at one point in her life she must have been very happy there.'

The observation gave me the opportunity to talk about my love of travel – my trip around the world, my passion for the Orient Express, the journey to southern Iraq – a subject which I knew I could then use to ask Miss Passerini an important question.

'There is one continent that I've always wanted to visit and that's South America,' I said, as the table fell quiet. 'Have you ever been there, Miss Passerini?'

She blinked as if to erase traces of deception from her eyes. 'No, I haven't, but of course I would like to,' she said. 'In fact, I'm going to have to go there, if I want to carry on with my project about Alexander von Humboldt.'

And so she continued to lie. As she talked a little about the work of the famous Prussian explorer and naturalist I took time to study her appearance. She was, as I had noticed before, of an olive complexion. But could her skin colour have been due to exposure to the sun, something that she had encountered in South America, rather than her natural hue? It would be winter in the southern hemisphere at the moment, but surely the sunlight in parts of that continent would still be strong enough to produce a darkening of the skin. She was a bewitching creature and, as she spoke, it was understandable that all the men at the table, even Davison, seemed drawn to her. There were, however, three women who were less than enamoured: Mrs Buchanan and the Frith-Stratton sisters.

'I wouldn't go there, to South America, I wouldn't trust the Latin men,' said Isabella Frith-Stratton. 'Not with their reputation.'

'I quite agree,' said her sister, in a voice that was half-excited, half-terrified. 'Some of the stories I've read about them, you wouldn't believe. All those passionate dances like the tango. One would be lucky to escape with one's reputation intact.'

Simon Peterson and Vivienne Passerini exchanged an amused glance as if to say, *I'm not sure she would be quite so fortunate.*

'And all those spiders and insects and snakes; I couldn't bear it,' continued Isabella. 'It's bad enough here with these midges. Even if I lived here, I don't suppose I would get used to them. The late Mr Kinmuir was a sufferer, I believe.'

At the mention of his dead uncle's name James Kinmuir bowed his head, while Mrs Buchanan blinked back some tears.

'I can't wait to get back to civilisation,' said May. 'Keeping us here like prisoners against our will. Really, it's been unbearable.'

'Not to mention interfering with the muse,' said Isabella, somewhat pompously. 'Romance is a most fragile flower. Its bloom can wither and die if the right conditions aren't met.'

Mr Peterson and Miss Passerini could not look at one another; as if to do so would risk the eruption of involuntary laughter. Instead, Mr Peterson quickly excused himself from the table, while the young woman pretended to drop her white napkin on the floor.

'Talking of romance,' said Mrs Buchanan, turning to me, 'you must be so excited about your forthcoming wedding. I want to hear all about the man you are marrying.'

I squirmed inwardly, as I hated being put on the spot like this. 'Oh, what would you like to know?'

The questions sprang forth with unsuppressed relish. 'What kind of man is he? How did you meet him? What does he look like? Where are you going to live?' She looked along the table at Davison. 'And what does your cousin think of him?'

Did she suspect that Davison and I were not, in fact, related? Where could I begin? I had always been reticent, guarding personal information with a certain possessiveness that at times bordered on an obsession. Since the scandal of the time I went missing in 1926, that instinct had intensified. Yet I knew that if I didn't share something about myself then, in turn, Mrs Buchanan and the other guests gathered at the table were less likely to reveal details about themselves. The question was what kind of information I was prepared to give away and how much.

I took a sip of soda water and told her and the other guests something of how I had met Max Mallowan in Ur, in southern Iraq, and my first impressions of him. I related how we became friends and how the romance blossomed. I talked a little about Max's work as an archaeologist and his fascination for ancient Mesopotamia. I did not, of course, mention anything about my earlier trip to Ur in 1928, when a murderer had stalked the camp.

A glint of mischief sparkled in Mrs Buchanan's eyes. 'I hope you don't mind me asking – are you and your future husband the same age?'

How on earth had she picked up my anxiety about the age difference? 'Well, there is something of a gap between us.'

'How many years?' asked May Frith-Stratton, in a tone of voice that sounded as though she were reading the question from a book.

I could not bear to tell the truth – that the gap was more of a gulf, one of fourteen years. 'I think Max is just a little over ten years younger,' I lied.

Isabella Frith-Stratton appeared to nearly choke on her water biscuit. 'I've known such marriages,' she spluttered, 'and I'm afraid none of them – no, not one – have lasted very long.'

'Don't listen to her,' said Mrs Buchanan. 'I'm friends with some women who have enjoyed very satisfactory partnerships with much, much younger men.'

At this she seemed to beam, as if she was talking from personal experience. I thought again of the damaged photograph showing Mrs Buchanan and the shoulder of an unidentifiable man.

'Women need to find love where they can, and sometimes that can come from the most surprising places,' she said, addressing the Frith-Strattons now. 'I would have thought, as writers of romance novels, you would understand that better than most.'

There was a certain tension in the air. Mrs Buchanan was clearly in the mood for a fight. And although I was not well-disposed towards the Frith-Strattons, I did not want the dinner to end in a nasty dispute.

'I'm sure the gentlemen don't want to hear us ladies discussing the finer points of romance,' I said, standing up. 'So I think we should continue in the other room and leave the men to their port and cigars.'

Mrs Buchanan smiled gracefully and smoothed out her napkin. The Frith-Stratton sisters nodded in sour acquiescence and stood up, shortly followed by Vivienne Passerini. Davison cast a look of admiration in my direction for the way I had defused the delicate situation as Mr Peterson came back into the room and began to pour out glasses of port for the men.

'I think we all need an extra drink or two if we're going to get to sleep tonight,' he said. Before I left the room he glanced over at me, again in that knowing manner. 'Are you sure you won't take a glass? After all, Mrs Christie, tomorrow is judgement day.'

Later on, when I was tucked up in bed, Mr Peterson's words began to trouble me. This continued through the night and I must have enjoyed only one or two hours' sleep. However, 'enjoyed' was not the right word; 'endured' would be more accurate. When I wasn't tossing and turning, thinking over the queer looks Mr Peterson had cast my way, and the manner in which he had turned to me and made that comment about judgement day, I was haunted by visions from the book of Revelation. The pale horse whose rider was Death. An earthquake after which the sun became as black as sackcloth made of hair and the moon like blood. A great red dragon with seven heads and ten horns.

I woke up covered in sweat. As I put on my dressing gown I caught a glimpse of myself in the mirror. What an absolute fright I looked! I washed my face at the basin in the room and then took myself off to bathe. I had always adored the feeling of submersion in water. Lying in water, I felt free, released from the thoughts of work, liberated from regrets surrounding the past and from worries about the future. But as I bathed that morning the memory of Mr Peterson's words continued to disturb me. Could I risk asking him outright? After all, what would I say to him? That he had looked at me oddly and that I was sure I had picked up an underlying implication in the sentences he had addressed to me? No, that would not do. The evidence was as light and insubstantial as gossamer. Another image came to mind: that of a spider and its web. We all knew the identity of the prey; the victim had been Robin Kinmuir, but which of the guests at Dallach Lodge was the spider? At the moment the supporting structure of the web seemed invisible and unknowable.

However, I too could cast myself in the role of the arachnid, quietly weaving its dangerous latticework in a far corner of the room. I would watch, observe and wait until my prey was in sight.

Chapter Fifteen

The atmosphere at breakfast was strained. Each scrape of a butter knife across a piece of toast or the cutting of a crispy strip of bacon on a plate seemed to reverberate around the room. There were the usual requests for the salt or pepper and polite interchanges between the guests and Simkins, but for the most part we remained quiet. Even the normally chatty Frith-Stratton sisters were reserved.

As I quietly ate my poached eggs I felt the eyes of Mr Peterson on me. But when I looked up to catch his gaze he diverted his attention to a coffee pot sitting on the starched white linen tablecloth or looked out of the window at a distant spot across the loch.

Finally, Miss Passerini broke the silence when she turned to me and said, 'I have a feeling that you more than any of us might have an idea of what we might learn today.'

'In what way, my dear?' I asked.

She glanced at Mr Peterson, who gave her an encouraging look. 'Just that ... with the knowledge that you must have picked up from writing your detective stories, you might be in a better position to know what to expect,' she said.

'Oh, I'm not so sure about that,' I said, trying to make light of the matter.

'Come, now, Agatha,' said Davison. 'You shouldn't be so modest. Your novels read like an encyclopaedia of unusual deaths.'

What was he up to?

'I wouldn't quite say that,' I said, feeling all eyes on me. A blush began to burn its way through to my cheeks.

'As her cousin, I know how modest she is,' Davison continued, addressing the rest of the group. 'For instance, when her first novel was published, under the title of *The Mysterious Affair at Styles*, she received a wonderful notice from – what was it? Oh, yes, the *Pharmaceutical Journal*, praising the book for the accuracy with which she wrote about poisons. I think she was more proud of that review than any mention of the book in the newspapers or high-circulation magazines!'

A light ripple of laughter echoed around the breakfast table.

'How do you know so much about the subject?' asked Mr Peterson, looking up from his copy of *The Times*. 'If you don't mind me asking.'

'Well, I suppose it all goes back to the war,' I said. 'I was a VAD, you see. After training as a nurse, I spent time in the dispensary in Torquay. I sat my apothecary examinations and served under a couple of dispensers and picked up some knowledge along the way.'

'How fascinating,' said Mr Peterson, with the trace of a faint smile. 'Yes, I can see how you would be good at it.' There was an air of something left unsaid in his statement.

Again all eyes turned to me for a reaction, but I was at a loss to know how to respond. My mother had always told me that it was bad manners to boast about one's achievements and neither was it in my nature to do so.

'Please tell us more about your time there – at the dispensary,' said Miss Passerini. 'Unless you'd rather not, of course. I find it so terribly interesting. As you know, I'm a botanist and no doubt we've read many of the same books. It always strikes me as so fascinating how many plants have the ability both to heal and to harm.'

'Indeed,' I said. As I chatted about aconite and belladonna, Miss Passerini nodded along in an encouraging manner. Finally, I became so bored of the sound of my own voice that I brought my monologue to a close. 'But you must be the real expert,' I said to her. 'Not on poisons, obviously, but on the world of flora and fauna.'

I listened as she talked of her fascination with plants. 'I don't know where my interest came from,' she said. 'All I know is I was a very lonely girl. I grew up without a mother or father, you see. I'm an orphan and I was brought up by a guardian. I didn't have any brothers or sisters to play with, and so I spent hours in the garden outside.'

'I adored the garden of my childhood home,' I said. I was aware that my experience must have been very different from Miss Passerini's isolated existence so I was careful not to overwhelm her with talk of Ashfield, which had been so full of life with my mother, father, brother and sister, servants, guests and frequent visitors. I wondered what had happened to her parents. I couldn't imagine a childhood without my mother or father. Even though they had both died – my father when I was eleven and my mother only four years ago – I still felt their presence. I was certain that a part of my mother still lived inside me; again I didn't voice this, but just kept the conversation on a friendly level. 'In fact, I'm sure I had actual conversations with some of the trees in the garden. I was a very odd little girl.'

The people around the table, no doubt relieved to think of something other than murder, laughed at this.

'I can't wait to get away from this house,' said Miss Passerini. 'Out of Britain altogether. I've had enough of this country for a while.'

'Where will you go next?' asked Davison.

She addressed her reply not to him, but to me. 'Perhaps I will visit South America after all,' she said. Her lightness of tone disguised a certain mocking quality, as though she were teasing me. 'That's where Mrs Christie urges me to go, isn't it?'

I remembered the stamps in Miss Passerini's passport. Did she know somehow that I had searched her room?

'As I said, I've heard so many interesting things about that continent,' I replied. 'I've never had the opportunity or the time to—'

Before I could finish the sentence there was a knock at the door. Simkins was standing there with Dr Fitzpatrick and Inspector Hawkins; all three wore sombre expressions that made them look like the male equivalent of the Three Fates.

Hawkins cleared his throat and stepped into the room. 'I'm sorry to disturb your breakfast, but we have the results that we were waiting for,' he said. 'About the post-mortem of Mr Kinmuir.'

The reminder of death at close quarters forced everyone to stop eating and place their knives and forks down on their plates. Mrs Buchanan took out a handkerchief and dabbed her eyes. James Kinmuir looked a little green around the gills. Rufus Phillips fiddled with a small sketch book that he had by his plate. The Frith-Stratton sisters' eyes shone with a queer excitement. Miss Passerini gazed down into her lap, her thoughts unknowable. Davison's gaze remain fixed on the inspector and doctor standing at the door. And Mr Peterson studied me once more as if he wanted to gauge my reaction to the news.

'Why don't you finish and join us in the library when you're ready,' said Hawkins, retreating with the doctor.

I placed my napkin on the table and felt a sense of excitement building inside of me, quickly followed by a pang of guilt. This was not the murder of a character in a novel but of a real person, someone who had lived and loved. He had clearly not been an easy, straightforward man – no doubt he had had his fair share of people who did not care for him – but Robin Kinmuir had not deserved to be murdered. I was about to find out the method used to kill him. That knowledge would prove significant, I was sure, as it would give me a clue to the identity of the killer.

The library was a large room painted a light shade of green, with French doors that led out onto the terrace. Ranged around the walls were a number of alcoves in which were set bookcases filled with volumes that looked as though they had not been opened in years. As I took a seat I felt the eyes of Mr Peterson and Miss Passerini on me. I pretended not to notice and unzipped my handbag to look for a handkerchief, but the strength of their gaze was unmistakable. Each of the guests, some still with coffee cups, took their seats in the room, while Hawkins and the doctor remained standing in front of the marble fireplace. Morning sun streamed through the east-facing windows, casting the room in a delicious golden glow. It was the kind of day that should have warmed the body and the spirit. I suspected, however, that the news the inspector and the doctor would soon impart would not be bright or sunny.

'Thank you for your patience over the last few days,' said Hawkins. 'I'm sure it cannot have been easy for you to remain here. But, as I said, it was essential to the investigation, an investigation that has not been without its difficulties. As you know, six days ago, on the twelfth of August, Robin Kinmuir, owner of Dallach Lodge, died while walking his dogs.'

At this point the two black Labradors trotted into the room almost on cue, an appearance that was greeted by a ripple of light laughter, the kind often used to dispel tension.

'As I was saying,' said Hawkins, 'on the twelfth of August, Robin Kinmuir died while taking his customary morning walk. At first it was suspected that Mr Kinmuir was killed as a result of a shot fired by his nephew James Kinmuir. Yet it was subsequently discovered that that injury was merely a surface wound. It produced a great deal of blood, but it was certainly not serious enough to kill him.'

He looked around the room, studying each of our faces. 'So what did kill Mr Kinmuir? At this point I will pass you over to Dr Fitzpatrick, who can tell you a little more about the details of the death.'

The doctor looked pale, his eyes puffy as though he had not slept. 'You know that in addition to acting in a professional capacity as Robin's doctor I was also his good friend. Although some may think that I was therefore not able to carry out the solemn task of examining his body, in fact the opposite was the case. The knowledge that I had known this man who lay before me gave me an added incentive to do the very best for him.'

He took a piece of paper from his inside jacket pocket and glanced down at it with an air of disbelief. He cleared his throat, and his thumb and forefinger rested on his chin for a moment, as he gathered his thoughts and controlled his emotions.

'I have here the post-mortem report I have prepared into the death of Robin Kinmuir. I won't read it to you verbatim – there is a great deal of technical vocabulary and certain details which, well, which you probably don't need to know. But I will give you a summary of my findings. As the inspector said, the shot that hit Kinmuir's thigh resulted in a certain loss of blood, but that was not what killed him.'

The tension in the room was palpable now. Each of us was transfixed on Dr Fitzpatrick and what he was about to reveal. All I could hear was the sound of my own breathing and the chatter of birdsong outside.

'Robin Kinmuir was poisoned, a poison that—'

Dr Fitzpatrick was forced to break off due to the gasps and cries in the room. Both Mrs Buchanan and James Kinmuir looked distraught and broken by the news. I noticed how the inspector was studying each of our reactions in turn. So that was why he had taken this highly unusual step of revealing the details of the post-mortem to us. He wanted to see if he could discern traces of guilt on our faces.

After the group settled back down, Dr Fitzpatrick resumed his statement. 'A poison that, after a number of tests, has turned out to be ... curare.'

The name of the poison was met by blank stares and the odd shake of the head. But I knew my poisons. In particular, I knew curare. It originated in South America, a continent that Vivienne Passerini said she was ignorant of but one which, according to her passport, she had recently visited. I looked over to her and the young, beautiful woman returned my gaze with a proud, almost accusatory, expression in her green eyes.

'It's a poison that originates in South America,' said Dr Fitzpatrick as if reading my thoughts. 'And one that was traditionally used in ... well, the tribes there used it in poison arrows and darts.' As he said this, the doctor realised that the words seemed far-fetched and ridiculous. 'It sounds like the stuff from a novel,' he said, a comment which caused more heads to turn towards me, 'but I am afraid this is all too true.'

'It can't be,' said James Kinmuir.

'I don't understand,' said Mrs Buchanan, wiping a tear from her eye. 'Robin was a very well-travelled man, but as far as I know he never set foot in South America.'

'It seems as though someone must have brought it back with them,' said the inspector. 'Apparently curare is a dark paste and so it could easily be smuggled into the country wrapped in a handkerchief or concealed in a vanity case.'

'Was it in something that he ate?' asked Miss Passerini.

I knew the answer to this, as did the doctor, who went on to explain how a person would suffer no ill effects from ingesting curare; it was only when the poison entered the bloodstream that it caused devastating results.

'A person dies from asphyxiation due to the inability of his respiratory muscles to contract,' said Dr Fitzpatrick.

'So it would have been a painful death?' asked Mrs Buchanan.

Dr Fitzpatrick nodded silently but, quite rightly, he refused to go into any more details.

I remembered the horrible grimace on Robin Kinmuir's face and the way his right hand had been grasping at that sprig of heather. Yes, it must have been very painful indeed. At least the death was not a long and lingering one. My guess was that he had suffered for only a few minutes, but in that time he must have realised that his life was coming to an end. What terror he must have felt. There was something I wanted to know.

'The gunshot wound?' I asked. 'Did that serve as some kind of catalyst to bring about Mr Kinmuir's death? The shock of that impact, being hit in the leg – could that have hastened his demise?'

'It's difficult to say; all we know is that Mr Kinmuir was alive when he was shot.'

'I see,' I said. 'And do you know yet how Mr Kinmuir became exposed to curare?'

The doctor looked at the inspector, who answered the question. 'We do, but it's something we've decided to keep to ourselves, for the time being.'

For the curare to enter Kinmuir's bloodstream, his skin

would have had to have been punctured. What if James Hawkins had dipped the gunshot in curare, which he then fired into his uncle's body?

'But what I can tell you is that there was no trace of curare on the shot that entered Mr Kinmuir's leg,' said the inspector, addressing James Kinmuir and Rufus Phillips. 'The accident that occurred was unfortunate, but no guilt or culpability should henceforth be associated with either of the two young men here.'

The friends nodded their acknowledgement. No doubt they were relieved to know that they were in the clear.

Yet, almost immediately, a nasty air of suspicion descended upon the room. If not James and Rufus ... then who had killed Robin Kinmuir?

'Have you heard of this poison, Mrs Christie?' asked Mr Peterson.

The question took me by surprise. 'Well, yes, I have as a matter of fact.'

'Really?' said the inspector. 'I was led to believe that it's incredibly rare and unusual.'

'Yes, it is,' I replied. 'I came across it when I was in training at the dispensary, during the war.'

'Indeed?' said Mr Peterson.

'It sounds a little hard to believe when I recall it now, but there was a pharmacist who told me he used to carry a lump of curare in his pocket.'

'I can't believe that,' said the doctor.

'That's what I thought,' I replied. 'He said he carried it around with him because it made him feel powerful.'

'Sounds like a most unpleasant man,' said Mrs Buchanan.

'On the surface he appeared respectable,' I said. 'In Torquay he was very well-liked.'

I looked up to see Hawkins eyeing me with suspicion. 'But you've never carried it yourself?' he asked.

'Me? Of course not. Why would I want to do that?'

I thought of my secret selection of poisons locked in my case upstairs. My heart began to race.

'Oh, come now,' said Davison, standing up. 'You can't be seriously suggesting that my cousin here has anything to do with Mr Kinmuir's death?'

The room fell silent before the inspector began to read from a sheet of paper. 'Strychnine, cyanide, morphine, arsenic, veronal, and ... ricin – these are just a few of the poisons that you've used in the plots of your books. Am I right?'

'Well, yes, but—'

'And how did you come to acquire this expert knowledge?' asked Hawkins.

'I think I told you – I was a VAD and then I worked in the dispensary in Torquay.'

Davison cast me a reassuring look from across the room, but it did nothing to settle my nerves.

The answer did not seem to satisfy the inspector. 'You worked under a man who carried a lump of curare in his pocket?'

'Yes, that's correct,' I said. I was conscious that my voice sounded weak.

Hawkins and Dr Fitzpatrick continued to stare at me, as did Mr Peterson and Miss Passerini. There was an air of heavy discomfort in the room now. I didn't know quite what to say, and it was surprising who came to my rescue.

Mr Peterson stood up and declared, 'Look here – just because someone writes books in which these sort of things occur doesn't mean that the author should then be under suspicion. It's preposterous to think that Mrs Christie could have anything to do with the murder.'

Inspector Hawkins did not look convinced, but he obviously decided not to pursue the matter. As he turned from me I felt I could breathe freely for the first time in what seemed like many minutes. The inspector had that admirable quality so rare in many policemen I had come across, an ability to see into the soul of a suspect. I wouldn't want to be cross-examined by Hawkins as he almost made me want to admit my guilt to him, even though I had nothing to confess.

'So now you all know the manner in which Mr Kinmuir died,' said Hawkins. 'Of course, this has consequences, I'm afraid.'

'Consequences?' piped up Isabella Frith-Stratton. 'What kind of consequences?'

'Yes, what do you mean?' echoed May, no doubt emboldened by her sister's question.

'All of you will have to remain here for the near future, I'm afraid,' said Hawkins.

There were immediate sounds of protest – announcements of imminent meetings and visits and travel schedules and claims that what he was suggesting was against the law – but the inspector silenced the group with the subtle raising of an eyebrow and the stern expression on his face.

'I've informed the procurator and the sheriff's office and

all the relevant authorities, and they've agreed,' he said. His voice was quiet, but anger whispered through it like a cold east wind. 'You can stay here until one of you confesses or I can take you all to Portree and lock you away. The choice is yours.'

Chapter Sixteen

I remained dumbfounded as Davison trailed behind Hawkins and Dr Fitzpatrick out of the library, closely followed by a clearly distressed Mrs Buchanan. The rest of us stayed behind in the room.

Surely the inspector was putting on something of an act in front of the other guests. After all, Hawkins knew that I was staying at the lodge with Davison at the behest of the Secret Intelligence Service. He couldn't seriously suspect me of wanting to kill Robin Kinmuir.

'That was a bit harsh, I must say,' said Simon Peterson.

'Thank you so much for coming to my defence,' I said. 'It was very gallant of you.'

'Well, I couldn't let him talk to you like that. Not after . . . well, everything that's happened.' As he lowered his chin his eyes widened and became more intense. Under normal circumstances it was the kind of absurd expression that would make me want to laugh, but now it just sent a horrible shiver through me.

'I'm not sure I understand you,' I said.

'You're a very brave woman,' he said enigmatically.

I was about to ask him what he meant by that, but then he, in turn, put a question to me.

'I say, do you think he really intends for us to stay here until one of us confesses?'

'I suppose so,' I replied. 'He doesn't strike me as the kind of man who makes empty threats.'

Peterson and I were joined by the Frith-Stratton sisters, who proceeded to ask me more about my work at the apothecary, and Miss Passerini who said she wanted to know more about curare. I played along with the requests for information, but as Vivienne Passerini listened to me I kept wondering why she had lied about her visit to South America. I knew from my visit to her room that she had travelled to the continent where the poison originated – and had kept that trip secret. I could not let her know that I was aware of her lie, however. Deception would have to be met with deception.

As I spoke, I couldn't get Mr Peterson's odd behaviour out of my head. I needed to find out what he was thinking.

When the ladies in the group finally left the room I turned to him and asked, 'Mr Peterson, would you mind stepping outside with me for a moment?'

He looked taken aback. 'Of course,' he said.

We walked out of the French doors and onto the terrace that overlooked the sea loch, passing the lawns and the well-stocked herbaceous borders. The morning was a beautiful one. The mist that usually gathered just after dawn had cleared, leaving an expanse of water that seemed to stretch on forever. The air was soft and the sun warmed my cheeks. In the distance I could hear birdsong, but I couldn't identify the call. As I strained my neck to see if I could spot the bird I looked up at the silhouette of the ruined castle that stood above the lodge.

'Have you been up to the castle yet?' asked Mr Peterson. 'I find it a wonderful place to walk.'

'Yes, but only a few times,' I said. 'I would like to get up there more, but either it's been drizzling or something has been happening around the house.'

'Yes, quite,' he said.

I looked at him, trying to pick up clues about his character from his appearance or the way he held himself, but there seemed to be nothing but surface. Was that in itself a clue of sorts? I cleared my throat and, with a slight hesitation, began, 'I'm not quite sure how to ask you this, Mr Peterson ...'

'You don't need to say anything,' he said, looking over his shoulder and lowering his voice. 'I want you to know that we are all behind you.'

'You are?'

'Oh, yes, indeed.'

'Well, as I said, I am very grateful for the way that you spoke up for me back there, in front of Inspector Hawkins.'

'I don't think he has any idea about what's been happening here,' he said.

'You don't?'

'No, he's very much in the dark, I think.'

'Well he certainly believes he knows how the curare got into Mr Kinmuir's system – not that he's telling us about it,' I said.

'It's all bluff and double bluff,' he replied.

'Now, what I wanted to ask you is this. Correct me if I'm

wrong, but it seems to me that you've been ... how can I put this? You've taken a certain interest in me.' I realised how wrong that sounded. 'Oh, I don't mean like that. No, not at all in *that* sort of way.'

Mr Peterson started to blush at the awkwardness of the encounter.

'I'm terribly bad at this,' I said, feeling my cheeks begin to burn too. 'No, I mean to say that I caught you looking over at me on a number of occasions. And, yes, I realise that your interest is purely platonic. You were probably surprised by, I don't know, a certain ill-advised item of clothing I was wearing, a badly chosen blouse or skirt, say, or something silly or foolish that I had said.'

There was still no response from him.

'But then, as time progressed – and please tell me if I'm in the wrong – I seem to have caught you sending me what I can only interpret as messages of encouragement. The odd look here, the nod of the head there. Is that right?'

He puffed out his chest a little and looked immensely pleased with himself. 'I suppose you could say that, yes.'

'But what I don't understand is *why.*'

He looked at me as if the sentence I had just spoken had been in a foreign tongue.

'W-why?'

'Yes, why? No doubt I'm being particularly stupid, but I don't know whether I've said something or given you the impression that I was going to do a certain thing. Whatever it is I'd like you to enlighten me.'

'So you didn't get ... a letter?'

'A letter? What kind of letter?'

At this his handsome face drained of colour and he turned his back to me.

'Mr Peterson? What are you trying to say?'

'Just a terrible misunderstanding, please forgive me,' he mumbled, running his fingers nervously over his moustache.

'Has this got something to do with Mr Kinmuir's death?'

But he refused to look me in the eye. 'Crossed wires on my part,' he said. 'No offence meant. Please forget what I said.'

He started to walk away, back towards the main door that led into the house, but I rushed forwards to try to stop him.

'Please, Mr Peterson, if I could just ask you a few questions,' I said.

His eyes had hardened and he looked through me as if I wasn't there.

'What was it you thought I had done?'

There was no reply.

'And the letter you mentioned? Should I have received a letter?' I reached out to him and took the sleeve of his jacket, but he brushed me off. 'Mr Peterson. I'm just trying to find out what you think I know.'

'Nothing, I thought you knew ... It's nothing,' he said. His voice was curt and cold. 'Now, please, there are certain things I need to attend to.'

There was no point in trying to shift him from his position. I knew that to do so would only lead to greater stubbornness. He turned from me and disappeared into the house.

I would have to find out the answers to my questions by other, less direct means.

Chapter Seventeen

I needed to speak to Davison urgently, but I couldn't find him anywhere. The door to the library was locked now so I presumed he must be in another room with Inspector Hawkins and Dr Fitzpatrick. As I was about to go up to my room I met Miss Passerini coming down the stairs.

'It's a lovely day, isn't it?' I said. 'Shame we can only venture so far as the gardens. I'd much rather be walking around the loch or exploring the moor.'

'I can't understand women who fear the great outdoors, worried that their hair might come out of place or they might dirty a shoe,' she replied. 'I mean, who cares? I'd rather that than haul around a desiccated husk of a body and a dead spirit all through my life, wouldn't you?'

'I think we are of the same opinion on that point,' I said. 'My hand is aching from all the letters I've dashed off. I don't think I've written so many letters in such a short period in the whole of my life! I suppose catching up on one's correspondence is one of the benefits of imposed confinement.'

She smiled. 'Yes, I suppose it is.'

It was time to take a risk. But what should I say?

'Would you mind coming into the drawing room for a moment?' I asked. I knew the room was empty and I needed to ask her something in private. 'Talking of letters, I did receive a very interesting one recently.'

Her green eyes flashed me a look of – what was it, warning, shock, bewilderment, fear, or a mix of all of these?

'Y-you did?' she asked, as we stepped inside the room.

'Yes, really quite fascinating,' I said. 'Telling me of the most, well, the most – how can I put it? – extraordinary things.'

'How unusual,' she said.

'I'm probably talking out of turn here, but you didn't by any chance receive such a letter yourself?'

Miss Passerini stared at me with the most terrible intensity and I could feel her emerald eyes burning into me. She took a step closer, so close that I could smell the musk of her perfume, and whispered, 'I thought we weren't supposed to talk about the letters.'

'Of course,' I said, lowering my voice. 'Yes, I realise that and I know I shouldn't talk, but I just wanted to know what you thought of its content?'

'What did you think of it?'

I was at a loss for words. I felt the heat of her breath on my skin. Her olive complexion was flawless and her fulsome red lips reminded me of an exotic bloom I had seen in Tenerife, a plant that survived by eating insects and flies. My mouth felt full of sawdust.

'I-I wasn't quite sure what to make of it at first,' I said.

'And then? After you had read it once or twice? After you had . . . digested its contents. What did you think of it then?'

There was only so long I could carry on like this. I felt like a blind woman trying to find a needle in a haystack. 'To be honest, I couldn't make head or tail of it,' I said. 'And – and what about you?'

'Me?'

'Yes, I wondered what you thought of your letter, the one that you had received.'

'Well, it was—'

Suddenly a voice boomed from behind us. 'Look at you two – thick as thieves!' It was Simon Peterson. He strode over to us and took hold of Vivienne Passerini's arm. 'May I borrow Miss Passerini for a moment?' he said. The words were gallant and polite, but there was desperate look about him. A line of perspiration had broken out across his forehead.

'Well, Miss Passerini was just about to tell me something very interesting, weren't you?'

'You were?' There was a note of threat in Mr Peterson's voice as he stared at the young woman. 'And what was the nature of the discussion? I hope it wasn't malicious gossip. When women get together they have a tendency to behave like nasty old cats, I find.'

'Yes, just some idle tittle-tattle,' I lied. 'Nothing of any import. But we will be finished soon. It won't take long, will it, Miss Passerini?'

The girl's eyes darted between me and Mr Peterson. 'Mrs Christie was telling me about a letter that she had received.'

'Was she?' said Mr Peterson, turning towards me. 'Now, isn't that a coincidence.'

'What do you mean?' asked Miss Passerini.

Mr Peterson left us for a moment in order to close the doors to the drawing room. As he walked across the floor, back towards us, his footsteps were like those of a hangman making slow progress towards the trap. Fear constricted my throat and I felt my breathing quicken.

'Now, Mrs Christie, why don't you tell us about this letter?'

'It was n-nothing really,' I said. 'Just a practical joke, I'm sure.'

'Why don't you share it with us?' His voice was light, almost amused. He was playing with me now, a cat which had caught his mouse and was going to act out his sadistic game until the very end. 'I'm sure we could do with cheering up. After all, the atmosphere has been quite sour of late, don't you agree?'

'I can't really remember what it said,' I replied.

'That's a shame. I was so looking forward to a little light relief,' he said.

'What's all this about, Simon?' asked Miss Passerini.

'I suggest you ask Mrs Christie, here,' he said, turning to me. 'Do you not have anything you'd like to say?'

I remained silent.

'You know, I'm disappointed in you,' Mr Peterson continued. 'I thought you were a mistress of words, able to command them at will to keep us all enthralled. And now you seemed to have clammed up.'

I moved to step away from him. 'Excuse me, I really must go and see my—'

'Oh yes, your *cousin*,' he said, pronouncing the word as if he knew full well that Davison was not a relation of mine. 'You don't want to neglect Mr Davison. No, that would never do. He's quite a *sensitive* soul, isn't he?' Again he lay emphasis on the word, clearly intending it as a slur on his character.

I suddenly felt anger rise within me. Mr Peterson could threaten me all he liked, and endure it I would, but I could not stand there and let my friend's name be taken in vain.

'Don't you dare say anything against my cousin,' I said. There was fire in my voice. 'Mr Davison is a good and honourable man. And I must warn you, you cross him at your peril.'

Mr Peterson and Miss Passerini were both rather taken aback by the strength of my words.

I took a deep breath and spoke more politely. 'Clearly, there has been a misunderstanding between us and for that I can only apologise,' I said. I chose my next words carefully, echoing those that Mr Peterson had used with me on the terrace outside just a few minutes before. 'Now, please, there are certain things I need to attend to.'

Chapter Eighteen

'Gosh, you look flushed,' said Davison, welcoming me into his room. 'Have you come back from an energetic stomp across the moor?'

'No, I wish I had,' I said, walking over to the window. 'I've just had a strange encounter with Mr Peterson and Miss Passerini.'

'I want to hear all about it,' he said.

'I'll tell you after you fill me in on what happened between you and the inspector,' I said. 'I presume you've been locked away with him and Dr Fitzpatrick in the library. And what was he implying with all that nonsense about the poisons in my novels?'

'I think it was a bit of a show,' he replied. 'To put people off the scent. He has to be seen to treat you like the other guests, a fellow suspect.'

'Well, it was rather too convincing for my liking,' I said. 'Anyway, enough of that. What did he tell you about Kinmuir? How did the curare get into his system?'

'I suggest you sit down.' Davison gestured to a leather

armchair. He took a deep breath and ran his fingers through his blond hair. 'As you know, curare does no harm to a person if it is taken orally, so we can rule out somebody spiking his coffee at breakfast. As you also know, Hawkins took the very sensible step of sealing off Kinmuir's bedroom suite. When Dr Fitzpatrick discovered that the method of death was curare poisoning he looked for possible signs of entry on the body, puncture wounds and suchlike. The injury to his leg was dismissed out of hand because there was no trace of curare on the shot. Dr Fitzpatrick went over every inch of Kinmuir's body and the only other possibility was an inflamed area on the dead man's throat, a piece of skin that looked as though it had been cut recently.'

I thought back to our first night at Dallach Lodge.

'That first night when Kinmuir was talking about his difficulties appreciating modern art he scratched his throat because he had a midge bite,' I said.

'Did he, now?'

My thoughts came quick and fast. 'But surely that insect bite can't have anything to do with it? No, that wouldn't do at all. But could the curare have been on his fingers somehow? Possible, but very unlikely as I'm sure Kinmuir would have noticed – as the inspector said, it often comes in the form of a dark paste – and he would have washed it off his hands. What would he have done that morning?'

Davison knew the answer to the question, of course, but enjoyed watching me try to piece it together for myself.

'Don't tell me,' I said, getting up from the chair. 'I want to work it out.' I walked over first to the window and looked out at the sea loch before making my way over to the wardrobe and then coming to stand by Davison's basin in the corner of the room. There, on the sink, was the answer.

'Of course, his razor!' I exclaimed. 'That's the only thing that makes sense. I'm right, aren't I?'

'Yes, Agatha, you are,' he said, in the patronising manner of a tutor towards his rather dim charge. 'Dr Fitzpatrick found traces of curare on Kinmuir's razor. That morning Kinmuir shaved as usual but must not have noticed anything unusual about his razor. It's most likely he cut himself – Dr Fitzpatrick says the spot or inflamed area was a midge bite that had got infected and then he nicked it with his razor. The poison from the razor entered his bloodstream and, after breakfast, when he went for his routine walk with his dogs, he died as a result of asphyxiation after the shot which hit him was fired.'

'How awful,' I said. 'And we were sent to protect him.'

'Indeed we were, and we failed,' said Davison. 'But we can't dwell on that now. The best we can do is to try to find out who did this. Now, what have you learnt?'

I told him of the odd conversation I had had with Mr Peterson and the awkward scene involving both him and Miss Passerini.

'Let me see if I have this right,' said Davison. 'So the whole business centres around a letter which you think Mr Peterson received. He also believes that you were the recipient of a similar letter. But we don't know what the letter said.'

'I know it doesn't sound like much when you say it like that, but there's something behind it which is extremely odd.'

'I have every trust in your instincts and I don't doubt you for a moment,' he said. As he blinked a couple of times I could almost hear his brain whizzing away. 'I'm just trying to think through the possibilities.'

'Well, we know that Miss Passerini lied about her recent trip to South America,' I said. 'We also know that curare comes from that continent. It seems to me that Mr Peterson suspects me of being the one behind Mr Kinmuir's death. And Mr Peterson and, most likely, Miss Passerini received a letter, a missive that he thought I had received too.' I paused as I tried to make sense of it all. 'Do you think we should tell Hawkins what we know?'

'No, not just yet. We haven't got quite enough yet to go to him.'

'We need to find out what was in that letter,' I said. 'And who else in the house received a similar one.'

'What are you suggesting?' he asked.

'I'm wondering whether there is any connection between the threatening letters that Mr Kinmuir received before his death and the enigmatic letters that Mr Peterson and Miss Passerini received.'

Davison looked alarmed. 'What? I don't understand. Are you saying that Peterson could be a victim? I thought we had him down as a potential murderer, or at least an accomplice to the act.'

'I'm not sure, but I'm certain that there are other people in the house who are in danger.'

'But why?'

It was then that we heard a scream.

Chapter Nineteen

We flung open the door of Davison's room and rushed out into the corridor. The noise – high-pitched, full of terror – seemed to be coming from the very top of the house. Davison ran ahead, taking the stairs three at a time, following the screams. As I trailed behind, up towards the attic rooms, I had a horrible sense of foreboding. *Oh please, please let it not be her.*

I reached the top level of the house and ran as fast as I could. Outside Mrs Kinmuir's room stood a young maid, a hand over her mouth, her skin ashen. At her feet was a tea tray, its contents spilt onto the floor. There was a slice of Victoria sponge on the carpet; jam oozed out of its middle like a fresh wound. Tea leaked out of the broken teapot and spread a nasty bloom across the carpet.

Although my natural reaction was to turn away and run back downstairs, I forced myself to step forward towards the open door. The girl was clearly distressed. I needed to see inside the room, even if it was, as I suspected, some-thing I would find greatly distressing. As I approached, the young maid looked at me with eyes full of fear. She opened her mouth to say something, but she could not form the words.

'Now, now, my dear,' I said. 'You've had a terrible shock.'

She gestured down at the broken tea things and started to apologise. 'I'm sorry, I didn't mean to drop them, but ...'

'What's your name?'

'It's R-Rose. Rose Stewart, ma'am.'

'It's not your fault, my dear. We can get one of the other girls to help clear up the mess.'

'Thank you, ma'am, but I can manage,' said the girl. It was clear she was in shock. 'She always used to like a cup of tea and bit of cake in the middle of the morning. But now she won't be able to enjoy her Victoria sponge.' Her breathing quickened and she looked as though she might start to cry out again.

'You must pull yourself together, Rose,' I said, taking a stern tone with her. 'You have to be brave. All of us must.'

She wiped her tears, saw that I was talking sense and bent down to try to gather the pieces of the broken pot. As she reached out I noticed her hands were trembling.

The inspector and the doctor and other occupants of the house would no doubt arrive at any moment. We did not have long to examine the room. I left the girl to her tidying, took a deep breath and stepped through the open door.

I saw Mrs Kinmuir sitting in the tartan armchair, her head lolling forwards, her arms dangling down by the sides of the chair like an old rag doll. Davison was crouched down next to her, checking the floor for clues. By his feet, spread across the carpet and scattered underneath the armchair, were the playing cards that I had used that day when I had paid Mrs Kinmuir a visit. It looked as though the cards had been knocked from the table in the last moments of the old lady's life.

As I stepped closer I noticed that blood had trickled down the back of Mrs Kinmuir's head, creating a scarlet necklace and staining the collar of her white blouse a bright crimson. Tears pricked my eyes as I contemplated what had been done to the dear old lady. She should have spent her remaining days in a state of blissful ignorance, something akin to a second childhood, her every need met. She did not deserve to die such a death.

Davison gently lifted the hair at the nape of Mrs Kinmuir's head to reveal a small stab wound. There was nothing nearby that looked like it could have been used to kill her. The murderer must have taken the weapon with them when he, or she, fled the scene.

What was it Mrs Kinmuir had said to me that day when I had paid her a visit? *I saw him die.* The words of that nursery rhyme echoed through my thoughts. I began to repeat the words, first to myself and then out loud so Davison could hear.

Who killed Cock Robin?
I, said the Sparrow,
With my bow and arrow,
I killed Cock Robin.

Who saw him die?
I, said the Fly,

With my little eye,
I saw him die.

When I had finished the second verse I saw Davison looking at me as though I had become quite deranged.

'I know it sounds odd,' I said. 'But it makes sense, don't you see?'

'I don't see anything and in case you forget, neither did Mrs Kinmuir,' said Davison. 'She was blind, or close to it. Cataracts.'

'Yes, I know that, and of course when you put it like that, it makes no sense. But Cock Robin, I think that's Robin Kinmuir.'

'He wasn't killed by a bow and arrow, but by curare poison.'

'Yes, but—'

Just then we were interrupted by the appearance of Inspector Hawkins and Dr Fitzpatrick at the door.

'We heard the screams and came running, and then saw the girl outside in a state. What's—' said Hawkins, stopping himself as he saw the body in the armchair. 'Oh my dear God. Is she . . .? Please examine her quickly, doctor.'

Dr Fitzpatrick felt her pulse and pronounced her dead. 'Poor Mrs Kinmuir,' he said. 'I've known her ever since I was a boy. She was as gentle as a newborn lamb. Never had a harsh word to say against anyone. In fact, she was like a second mother to me when my own mother died. I'll never forget her kindness. And in her dotage she was the same. She may have lost her faculties but not her ability to be kind.'

I expected the inspector wanted the doctor's professional opinion of what had happened to her, not his personal reminiscences.

'What do you make of it?' asked Hawkins.

The doctor began to examine the body. He saw the wound at the back of the neck, the blood that soaked into the collar of her blouse, the cards on the floor.

'It seems obvious, doesn't it? There's a deep stab wound here on the neck, as you can see,' he said, pointing to the source of the blood, 'which would have resulted in if not an immediate death then at least a mercifully quick one.'

The inspector examined the room in silence. Then it was his turn to utter his interpretation. 'I would have thought that the old gal was sitting in her chair, perhaps asleep, perhaps pretending to herself that she was playing a card game, when someone came in,' he said. 'That person walked behind her, took out the weapon – a sharp knife or hunting dagger, say – and then attacked the old lady, pressing hard on the spot in the back of the neck. During the attack the cards got displaced from the table. But there would not have been much of a struggle – Mrs Kinmuir looked fragile and could not have been very strong. One must keep an open mind about the murderer.'

'What do you mean?' asked Davison.

'One always assumes that a killer has to be a man,' he said, glancing at the floor, 'but on certain occasions one cannot be entirely sure.'

'What makes you say that?' I asked. I had still not quite forgiven the inspector for the way he had addressed me in front of the other guests, but I couldn't hold my grudge against him for much longer. Also, my curiosity got the better of me.

His eyes shone and, with a triumphant air, he bent down and picked up something from the carpet. 'Voilà!' he exclaimed, brandishing an earring in the palm of his hand.

I stepped forwards and examined the jewel. I knew that I had seen it before.

'Do you recognise it?' asked the inspector.

'Yes, I believe it belongs to Miss Passerini,' I said.

'I see,' said Hawkins, nodding his head, as if this one piece of evidence was enough to convict her.

I knew I had to relate to the inspector the lie Miss Passerini had told about her visit to South America, but I had to be careful what I said. 'Talking of Miss Passerini,' I began, glancing at Davison in the hope that he would agree that now would be an appropriate time to share the information. 'I think it's only right that you should know something that has recently come to light. It seems a little indelicate to discuss it over . . . well, at this particular moment,' I said, looking down at the body of Mrs Kinmuir.

'Yes, of course,' said the inspector, turning to the doctor. 'Sad business, this, but, Dr Fitzpatrick, you know the procedure.'

'Very well,' said the doctor, whose stoic expression concealed the depth of his pain. The poor man had lost first his good friend and now the kind old lady.

We left the doctor behind as we filed out of the room, past the tea-stained carpet and towards the stairs. At the top of the stairs stood a sombre-faced Simkins who, on the inspector's instructions, had taken on the role of serving as a kind of sentinel to stop the curious and the caring – Mr Peterson, Vivienne Passerini, the Frith-Stratton sisters, Mrs Buchanan, James Kinmuir and Rufus Phillips – from entering the attic floor. Even now, in this desperate state of affairs, after everything that had gone on, including the death of his master, the butler was doing his best to try to protect the reputation of the house. Even though his new master, James Kinmuir, was telling him to stand down so he could get past, Simkins remained impermeable.

'This is a disgrace,' shouted Kinmuir. 'I order you to let me pass.'

'I'm sorry, sir,' said the butler. 'But I have my orders directly from the inspector not to let anyone up.'

'What's the meaning of this?' demanded Kinmuir as he saw the inspector. 'What is going on? Who was making all that noise?'

'Yes, I do think you owe us an explanation,' said Mrs Buchanan, who stood behind James Kinmuir.

'You will find out in due course,' said the inspector. 'Simkins, prevent anyone from going up to the attic.'

'Has someone been hurt?' asked a frightened-looking May Frith-Stratton, who had joined the group with her sister. 'Are we in any danger? If we are, we really should be allowed to leave the house.' She stepped towards James Kinmuir and looked up at him with spaniel eyes. 'Oh, Mr Kinmuir, thank goodness you are here to protect us.'

'And yes, at least we have the men to keep us safe,' Isabella said.

As I passed by the little group, Mr Peterson and Miss Passerini remained silent. They looked at me with eyes full of dark suspicion. They knew that I knew something. But did they have any inkling what that was exactly?

The inspector led the way into the library, which had been unlocked again and now had something of the atmosphere of an inquiry room. A desk and two chairs had been commandeered to serve as Hawkins's interrogation space. Papers full of scribble lay scattered across the surface of the antique bureau. The shelves of books no longer spoke of their own stories contained within their leather covers, but seemed to want to whisper the secret accounts of the guests who had sat before the inspector. But which tales were true and which were false?

'Now, Mrs Christie, you had something you wanted to say?' asked Inspector Hawkins.

I looked once more at Davison, who returned my gaze with a bow of the head.

'Yes, there's quite a lot to tell you, so please forgive me,' I said. I checked to see if the door had been shut and the windows were closed. 'As you know, all this started with the death of Mr Kinmuir, Mr *Robin* Kinmuir, who was poisoned by curare, the toxin having been placed on his razor.' The inspector looked surprised. 'Yes, Mr Davison told me all about that,' I explained.

'We are working as equals here,' said Davison.

'I see,' said the inspector with a note of astonishment in his voice. No doubt he was the kind of man who believed a woman was only good for one or two things, activities confined to either the kitchen or the bedroom.

I did not want to alienate him at this stage and so indulged him with a little flattery. 'You were quite right to pick up on Miss Passerini. I've had my suspicions about her for some time.'

'You have?'

'Oh yes, indeed,' I said. 'You see, Miss Passerini lied about her most recent trip. It was not to Berlin but to South America. Her passport, which I have seen – never mind how – says as much. And we all know where curare originates, don't we?'

'South America,' said the inspector, as if he were the one who was near to solving the case.

'Exactly,' I replied.

'The other aspect to this murder is a rhyme, a nursery rhyme,' I said.

Inspector Hawkins looked baffled. As I recited the first two verses of *Who Killed Cock Robin* his look of puzzlement turned to bewilderment. Davison wasn't quite sure where this was leading and so I had to convince him too.

'It's clear that the Robin in the rhyme is Robin Kinmuir. At first it looked as though he was killed by the modern equivalent of a bow and arrow – the shot fired from the gun of James Kinmuir, his nephew – but we now know that to be wrong.'

I took a breath and the two men waited for me to continue. 'Now, to the point of "Who saw him die". In the rhyme it is the Fly. The words go, if you remember, "With my little eye/I saw him die." When I went to speak to Mrs Kinmuir in her attic room she repeated the words to me. But we know that Mrs Kinmuir was as good as blind due to her cataracts.'

'I really can't grasp what it is you're trying to say, Mrs Christie,' said the inspector.

Even Davison looked confused, if not a little embarrassed for me.

'I'm sorry, no doubt I'm explaining it very badly indeed,' I said. 'But I think someone is having a game with the rhyme. Using it as a device, if you will. Presenting something as truth as laid down according to the story of Cock Robin before undermining it.'

'I'm still none the wiser,' said the inspector.

'Why would anyone want to do that?' asked Davison.

'That's something we have to find out,' I said.

'So you don't know?' asked the inspector in an irritated tone. He was clearly losing patience.

'No, no, I don't – not yet,' I replied.

The inspector turned from me to make his way out of the library. 'I can't say this has helped, Mrs Christie,' he said. 'In fact, all it's done is confuse me.'

But I had one last trump card to play, a piece of information which I hoped would change the course of the investigation. 'Do you know what Miss Passerini's name means? Its Latin origin?'

Davison, whose education was vastly superior to mine – he had been to Eton and Cambridge – suddenly realised what I was talking about. His eyes sparkled and his face shone with a renewed energy.

But the inspector remained unmoved. 'No, and I don't see what this has to do with anything. I've got another dead body upstairs. I can't stand around talking about children's rhymes and the Latin origin of people's names. Sorry, Mrs Christie, I think you mean well, but perhaps it's best if you took a step back from the inquiry.' He looked at Davison, hoping that the other man in the room would back him up.

'I think it would be wise of you to listen to what Mrs Christie has to say,' said Davison.

'Do you know anything about birds, inspector?' I asked.

'Really – I've told you already, I don't have time for idle chit-chat,' he said, spitting out his words now. 'Where's that sergeant? Dedham?'

He walked across the room of the library towards the door, turned the handle, and was about to open it and step out when I spoke.

'You see, inspector, a passerine is any bird of the order *Passeriformes*, which accounts for around half of all bird species. That in itself is not much of a help to us. But when I tell you that, as with so many words, the root comes from the Latin, *passer*, which means, of course . . . sparrow.'

The inspector seemed paralysed. His fingers froze around the door handle. He took a moment to compose himself, made sure that the door was closed and moved back towards us. As the various pieces of the puzzle fitted together in his mind he looked at me with a new-found admiration.

Now it was his turn to recite the first verse of the rhyme:

> '*Who killed Cock Robin?*
> *I, said the Sparrow,*
> *With my bow and arrow,*
> *I killed Cock Robin.*'

He took out his notebook and scribbled the verse down. 'So we have her,' he said, working through his thoughts. 'We've got the fact that she lied about her whereabouts, the fact that she recently paid a trip to South America, which, as we know, is the main source of curare. We have the factual evidence in the form of her earring, which I discovered at the scene of Mrs Kinmuir's death. And then we have the incontrovertible truth of her name. Miss Passerini is the Sparrow. She killed Cock Robin.'

Chapter Twenty

'No, but wait . . .' I said, but Inspector Hawkins was already out of the door.

'Dedham?' he called out. 'Where are you, man?'

We followed Hawkins into the hall, where he was met by the sergeant who came rushing down the stairs.

'Have you seen Miss Passerini?' shouted Hawkins.

'Yes, sir, I've left her upstairs, with Mr Peterson,' replied the young sergeant.

'Bring her down at once,' he said.

'What do you intend to do?' asked Davison.

'The only sensible thing I've done since I've arrived,' said the inspector. 'Arrest her, of course.'

'You can't,' I said. 'You see, I suspect it's not as simple as Miss Passerini being the murderer.'

But Hawkins did not want to hear my convoluted – and still far from complete – explanation.

'I'm grateful for the information you gave me, Mrs Christie, really I am. Now the law needs to do its job,' he said.

Listening to this was a shocked-looking Miss Passerini,

who had appeared at the top of the staircase, accompanied by Sergeant Dedham and closely followed by Mr Peterson.

'What information?' asked Mr Peterson.

'You don't need to worry about that, sir,' answered the inspector. 'If you would be so kind as to come down, Miss Passerini.'

What was the phrase that sprang to mind? Lamb to the slaughter? That's what the beautiful young woman looked like as she elegantly descended the stairs towards the inspector.

'Is there something the matter?' she asked as she came face to face with Hawkins.

'Miss Passerini, I'm arresting you for the murder of Mr Robin Kinmuir—'

At this there was a clamour of voices as everyone seemed to speak at once.

'I don't understand,' said Miss Passerini.

'This is absolute nonsense!' exclaimed Mr Peterson.

'It was you?' said an astonished James Kinmuir, who walked into the house with Rufus Phillips just at that moment. 'What did you have against him? What did my uncle ever do to you?'

'If you'll let me speak,' I said. But it was no use.

'Please lower your voices,' said the inspector. 'That's better ... and, Miss Passerini, I'm also arresting you for the murder of Mrs Veronica Kinmuir.'

The statement devastated James Kinmuir. His face looked gaunt, his eyes haunted and he clenched his fists. It was obvious he was doing everything in his power to stop himself from attacking the young woman. Then he seemed to lose all strength in his body like a puppet whose strings had been cut. Had his friend not been there to support him he might have dropped to the floor. All he could do was whisper over and over again one word, 'Why?'

All eyes turned to Miss Passerini for a response.

'Why are you looking at me like that?' she asked. 'I didn't do it. I didn't do it, I tell you!'

As the inspector approached her she panicked and began to look at the main door and then back up the stairs as if searching for a means of escape.

'You can't run from us, my young lady,' said Hawkins. 'It's over for you, I'm afraid. You may as well co-operate, make it easier on yourself.'

'I'm not co-operating because I have nothing to do with this,' she said.

'Yes, what evidence do you have?' demanded Mr Peterson. 'You can't just arrest her without any evidence.'

'All that will be presented to the specific authorities in question,' said the inspector. 'All you need to know, Mr Peterson, is that we have a great deal of very strong evidence that directly points to Miss Passerini as the murderer.'

'And does it have something to do with what Mrs Christie told you?' he asked in an accusatory tone.

Now all eyes turned towards me. I felt myself begin to blush.

'That's confidential, I'm afraid,' replied Hawkins, who took hold of Miss Passerini's arm.

'Simon, please make this stop,' she begged. 'I don't think I can bear it.'

'The law's the law, I'm afraid, and nobody is above it,' said Hawkins. 'Dedham?'

'Yes, sir?' replied the sergeant.

'Go and get the car ready. After that you stay here, at the house. I'll deal with Miss Passerini.'

'But I had nothing to do with it!' said Miss Passerini, her voice rising. 'If you want to arrest someone it should be her!' She lifted her arm and pointed at me. 'She's the one who's been acting queerly.'

'That's right,' said Mr Peterson. 'Both Mrs Christie and her so-called cousin.'

'Really,' said Davison in an exasperated voice.

'Now, now,' said the inspector, trying to calm the situation.

'She's the one who has been asking all sorts of odd questions and putting strange notions into people's heads,' said Miss Passerini. 'I wouldn't be surprised if she's behind this.'

'Yes, I'd suggest reviewing whatever material you may have,' said Mr Peterson to the inspector. 'There's such a thing as fabricated evidence, you know – placed there at the scene of a crime so as to incriminate a person. And she, Mrs Christie, should know. After all, she's a writer of detective fiction.'

'Well, thank you for teaching me how to do my job, Mr Peterson,' said Hawkins. 'Now, Miss Passerini, if you'd be so kind as to accompany me to the police station.'

Chapter Twenty-one

The arrest unsettled the house, but underneath the surface chatter there was something akin to relief. The murderer had been rooted out from among us. The purging had occurred. The poison had been cut out. The sinner had been expelled.

I knew, better than most, that these comforting ideas were tropes from the world of detective fiction. Which is why I felt uneasy about the whole situation. There was something wrong about the arrest of Miss Passerini. Mr Peterson had a point. It felt too neat, too staged.

I had tried to tell Inspector Hawkins, but he had rushed ahead like – what was that phrase of my mother's? – yes, like a bull in a china shop. I admired the inspector in many ways – he was a great deal more intelligent than many policemen I had encountered in the past – but there was nothing subtle about his method.

After driving Miss Passerini to the police station in Portree, the inspector returned to the house. First of all he went to see Dr Fitzpatrick to ask how he was progressing. Apparently, Mrs Kinmuir's body would be taken away soon for the doctor to carry out the post-mortem. The inspector's next task was to find the murder weapon. Hawkins enlisted the services of his sergeant and told us to confine ourselves to the dining room.

When lunch was served at one o'clock, most of the guests enjoyed the food with a relish I had not seen for days.

'This roast beef is delicious,' said Isabella Frith-Stratton.

'Indeed it is,' said May, taking a forkful of flesh up from her plate. 'Quite first-rate. And so rare, just how I like it.'

There was something about the way the two sisters feasted on the nearly raw meat that turned my stomach. I placed my fork down on my plate.

'I don't know how you can eat that,' said Mrs Buchanan. 'I know I've become something of a bore on this subject, but really it's barbaric.' She sighed as she added, 'I can't wait to get back to London. I must start rehearsals on the new play. And what about you, Mr Peterson?'

'I'll stay around here for a while longer,' he said, staring at his plate. Perhaps Mrs Buchanan's words had made him think again about eating the roast beef. 'Vivienne, Miss Passerini, will need all the help she can get.'

'Help? Why would you want to help her?' Mrs Buchanan's voice rose with controlled anger. 'After all, she was responsible for those two murders.'

'Some of us like to believe in the law of innocent until proven guilty,' he said rather pointedly.

Mrs Buchanan turned from him and began talking to the Frith-Strattons.

'And what are your plans, Mrs Christie?' asked James Kinmuir. He had composed himself after the shocking news of his elderly relative's murder. 'You must be looking forward to your forthcoming marriage? It's not long now, I believe.'

'Yes, the eleventh of September,' I replied.

'I'm only sorry you had to witness ... well, all of this,' he said. 'It's been just ghastly.'

'Terrible,' said Rufus Phillips. 'I still can't believe it, though, that Miss Passerini would do such a thing. She seemed quite a lovely girl.'

'Yes, it does seem surprising, and not at all in character,' I said. 'And what about you, Mr Phillips? What are your plans? What of your painting of Mr Kinmuir?'

'I suppose it will remain an unfinished portrait,' he replied. 'Perhaps that's more fitting in a way. To complete it would be to dishonour its subject. As for my plans, I should like to go to Italy, but first I shall stay here and help James clear the house. I doubt we'll have that long before the lodge has to be sold.'

'Yes, I received a letter from Mr Glenelg this morning, telling me what to expect,' said James Kinmuir. 'It all seems very depressing, but of course nothing compared to the dreadful events of recent days.'

'What I don't understand is the motive,' said Rufus Phillips. 'Why would Miss Passerini want to kill your uncle and then old Mrs Kinmuir? It doesn't make any sense to me.'

'I suppose the inspector will uncover all of that, unless you beat him to it,' said James Kinmuir, addressing me.

'Me?' I asked, surprised.

'Yes, Mrs Christie,' he replied. 'What with your reputation, I would have thought you could crack the case.'

I was beginning to feel nervous now. What did he know? I saw Davison glance over in my direction.

'My reputation?'

'As a writer of detective novels,' he replied. 'What did you think I meant?'

I laughed this off.

'So, come on, what are your thoughts on the subject?'

I took a deep breath. 'Well, of course, I don't know too much about the background of the case, but to be honest, I'm rather surprised by the arrest of Miss Passerini.'

'You are? Why?' asked James.

'I don't know,' I said. 'It just doesn't seem right to me. I can't explain it any better than that.'

Mr Peterson heard my comment and, flinging his fork down onto his plate, said, 'That strikes me as a little rich. I believe it was something you told the inspector that got Miss Passerini arrested in the first place.'

The room fell silent.

Mr Peterson continued. 'Inspector Hawkins wouldn't tell me what information you gave him, but perhaps you would care to enlighten me?'

What could I say? If I told the table about the rhyme it would sound nonsensical. And I had a feeling that that information should not be shared for the time being. If I told everybody that Miss Passerini had lied about her trip to South America I would inevitably have to reveal how I had discovered the truth: that I had stolen into the young woman's room and taken a look at her passport.

'What's wrong – the cat got your tongue?' Mr Peterson said, enjoying his new role as a bully. To think he had once come to my aid in front of the inspector and now he was talking to me in this fashion.

There was something about the words that struck me as slightly incongruous coming from the mouth of a man like Mr Peterson. It was the kind of phrase one might use in the nursery, like the *Cock Robin* rhyme. Part of me thought it best to endure the slight, but why should I be silenced?

I wasn't about to let myself be intimidated by a man like Mr Peterson. It was time to take a risk.

'No, not at all,' I said. 'I was just thinking how best to spare your blushes.'

I could tell the comment unsettled him. 'W-what?'

'If you must know I simply told the inspector about the letter,' I said.

The whole atmosphere changed in an instant. Someone around the table – I didn't notice who – dropped a knife or a fork onto their plate. Another person coughed nervously. Mr Peterson glared at me with a fury I hardly thought possible.

'But I thought we—' mumbled May Frith-Stratton.

'Shut up!' exclaimed Mr Peterson. There was a panic in his voice now. It was obvious he had something to hide. 'Don't say another word.'

James Kinmuir looked puzzled and was about to ask for an explanation when the noise of a cough came from the entrance to the dining room.

'I hope I'm not interrupting,' said the inspector.

What had he heard of the heated interchange? How long had he been standing at the door?

'What's all this about?' he asked. 'Why the raised voices?'

Everyone around the table, apart from Mrs Buchanan, looked down.

'Mr Peterson?'

He did not answer.

'I can understand you must all feel a little unnerved, after what has gone on here,' said the inspector, walking around the table. He stopped and placed a hand on James Kinmuir's shoulder. 'It must have been awful, first to lose an uncle and then to be accused of his murder. But as I said, no suspicion should be directed towards you.'

The young man nodded a silent thank you and the inspector continued his tour around the table. 'And then this second murder, which snuffed out an old lady's life.'

I noticed that he was holding something in a white handkerchief.

'I wanted to keep you up to date with the investigation,' he said, coming to stop at the far end of the table. 'I feel it's the least I can do after making you stay at the lodge when I'm sure you'd rather be ... well, anywhere else but here. But now, at last, I believe you will soon be free to leave. You see, I've found one final piece of evidence which suggests beyond a reasonable doubt that the murderer was indeed Miss Passerini.'

'I don't believe you,' said Mr Peterson.

'I think you will when I show you this,' he replied.

He paused as he unfolded the corners of the handkerchief. Inside, I caught a glimpse of a metal object – brass, I think.

'This paper knife was found among Miss Passerini's belongings. It matches exactly the type of murder weapon Dr Fitzpatrick says was used to kill Mrs Kinmuir.' Hawkins pointed to the edge of the knife with his little finger. 'You see this here,' he said, as if he were giving a demonstration of how a tool could be used for everyday tasks in the home or workshop such as drilling a hole or planing a piece of wood. 'This sharp end was used to puncture the back of the neck. And the dimensions of the paper knife match exactly those of the wound.'

'So Miss Passerini is guilty?' asked Mrs Buchanan.

'It seems so,' said the inspector. 'What we need to do now is take her fingerprints, which can be done at the station. And, by the way, as part of the process of elimination, we will need to take everyone else's too.'

'Honestly,' said Mr Peterson under his breath, uttering the word almost as if it was a profanity.

'Do you have something you'd like to say, Mr Peterson?' asked the inspector.

The man shook his head.

'Don't worry, this needn't be done in Portree,' the inspector added. 'I can arrange for the fingerprinting to be carried out here, at the house, so as not to put you to any more inconvenience.'

'That's most kind,' said Mr Peterson, barely bothering to disguise his sarcasm.

'Very well, I'll leave you in peace to enjoy your lunch,' said Hawkins.

The inspector closed the door of the dining room on his way out. But nobody picked up their knives and forks again. Their appetites had now gone and their faces looked pale and worn. And it wasn't only Mr Peterson who was looking at me with contempt.

Chapter Twenty-two

'Peterson, I think it's about time you told me what the hell is going on,' demanded James Kinmuir. 'And don't try to give me any flimflam.'

'I don't know what you mean,' said Simon Peterson.

James Kinmuir slammed his fist hard down on the dining table. 'Both my uncle and my great-aunt have been murdered in this house,' he said, his face flushing. 'If you know anything that might help solve the crimes, you must tell me, even if that means betraying your new girlfriend.'

'Excuse me?' asked Peterson.

'I've seen the way you and Miss Passerini have been carrying on, whispering in corners,' said Kinmuir. 'And I know you've been trying to protect her.' He took a deep breath and adjusted his tone slightly. 'Of course, that's natural. I would probably have done the same if I were in your position. But things have got out of hand now. The police are involved. Miss Passerini is in custody and it looks as though she will be charged with the murders.'

Mr Peterson bowed his head and remained silent.

'I've heard talk about a letter or letters and just now Miss Frith-Stratton confirmed to us, or at least implied, that it was something being kept secret,' continued Kinmuir. He rightly suspected that May Frith-Stratton held certain feelings for him and took advantage of this fact as he addressed her, speaking in a silky manner. 'I think – I hope – that we get on, don't we? We've always enjoyed one another's company?'

May Frith-Stratton blushed and nodded her head like a silly schoolgirl being addressed by the handsome gentleman of her dreams.

'Are you going to tell me what's been going on?' asked Kinmuir. 'I won't be cross with you, I promise. In fact, you'd be doing me the most terrific favour.'

'Well, I . . . it's just that—' she began.

'Miss Frith-Stratton, may I remind you what we talked about?' said Mr Peterson, standing up in a bid to silence her.

'Which was what exactly, Peterson?' asked Kinmuir.

'It's none of your damn business,' snapped Peterson.

'How dare you,' said Kinmuir. With his left hand he grabbed Mr Peterson by his collar while his right formed a fist. 'I'm warning you, if you don't tell me exactly what has been going on, I will strike you.'

Mr Peterson tried to push him away and it looked as though the scene could turn ugly. The rest of the guests reacted with horror. Rufus Phillips tried to prise his friend away from Mr Peterson and when this failed he attempted to use himself as a buffer between the two men. But Kinmuir managed to brush him aside.

'Oh, please stop,' cried May Frith-Stratton. 'It's too much.'

'I think you've proved your point, Kinmuir,' said Davison

as he tried to intervene, or at least made a gesture of doing so. I was sure that he hoped, as I did, that the conflict between the two men would inspire someone in the room to tell the truth.

'Look – he's showing his true nature,' said Mrs Buchanan of James Kinmuir. 'I always knew he was a brute.'

'Don't talk about him in that manner,' said May Frith-Stratton. 'You know he never laid a finger on his uncle.'

Mrs Buchanan stood her ground. 'He may not have killed Robin, but . . . well, you can see what kind of man he is.'

James Kinmuir was readying himself to punch Mr Peterson, when suddenly Isabella Frith-Stratton uttered a cry of despair.

'Stop!' she shouted. 'Don't lay a hand on him. I'll tell you everything you need to know, I promise, as long as you don't hurt him.'

'Miss, please, restrain yourself,' said Mr Peterson. 'You don't know what you're doing.'

'I know very well what I'm doing, sir,' she replied.

'Sister – what are you saying?' asked May. 'Surely you don't . . .'

Isabella looked with such love at Mr Peterson that the expression almost brought tears to my eyes. None of us had had any idea of her true feelings for the handsome young man until this moment. And the revelation silenced the room.

'You're right, Mr Kinmuir, th-there was a letter, or rather a n-number of letters,' she began somewhat hesitantly.

Mr Peterson tried to free himself so that he could stop Isabella Frith-Stratton from continuing, but he was restrained by Kinmuir.

'Go on, miss, please,' James Kinmuir said.

'Isabella, best not say another word!' exclaimed May.

Kinmuir turned to May and again gave her that particular look which no doubt melted her heart. 'If you'd let your sister tell me the truth,' he said gently, 'I'm sure that it would be in everyone's interests.'

May remained silent as Isabella began to speak. 'Yes, the letters. I think, if I'm right, that each of us in this room probably received one before coming here,' she said.

Mrs Buchanan looked bewildered, as did James Kinmuir and Rufus Phillips.

'Or if not all of us, then at least quite a number,' Isabella continued, looking at Davison and then at me. I nodded my head in encouragement.

'What did the letters say?' asked Kinmuir.

'They, well, they were written in the form of an invitation. And that invitation was to come to Dallach Lodge to see someone suffer.'

At this, James Kinmuir stepped away from Mr Peterson as the strength in his body appeared to seep away. He placed a hand on Rufus Phillips's shoulder to support himself.

'Go on,' said James, even though it was obvious that, pale and in shock, he would rather not hear another word. 'And who was that someone you would see suffer?'

'It was Robin Kinmuir,' said Isabella.

Mr Peterson looked broken now. All those strange looks and odd intimidations made sense now. He must have believed that I too had received one of the letters; it had seemed that he had even thought that I had been responsible for the crime.

'Do you still have the letter?' asked James. 'And do you know who it was from?'

'No, I'm afraid not on both counts,' she replied. 'I was told that I should burn it as soon as I had read it. And it was unsigned.'

James blinked repeatedly as he tried to comprehend the awful truth. 'But I don't understand – why would you want to come here to see my uncle suffer?'

'I can't speak for everyone, by any means, but for me it was a way of seeing justice done.'

'Isabella – please, no more!' beseeched May Frith-Stratton.

'Justice?' asked James, pronouncing the words as if he had tasted poison in his mouth.

'Yes, for what he had done . . .' said Isabella. 'In the past.'

I looked around the room and gazed upon the guests with a horrible new fascination, as if seeing them for the first time. They had all been playing their parts, declaring their lines and taking their cues with a grotesque profes-sionalism that rivalled that of Mrs Buchanan.

'And what was it he had done?' I asked. 'What could possibly be so bad that he deserved to die?'

'I must warn you once again, Miss Frith-Stratton,' said Mr Peterson.

'Let her speak!' shouted James Kinmuir.

'I'm sorry, Mr Peterson,' said Isabella. 'I know you're right, we shouldn't be talking like this, but I couldn't bear to see you hurt. Also it's better it's all out in the open, among us at least. After all, we now know who was behind the death of Mr Kinmuir. Now that Miss Passerini is going to be charged with the murder it means, well, surely it means none of us is implicated.'

'Thank you, Miss Frith-Stratton,' said James Kinmuir. 'I know how difficult this must be for you and I can't tell you how much I appreciate your honesty and bravery. I'm sure Mr Peterson, once he has composed himself, will thank you for it, too. Now, can you tell me more about this letter. I ask you again who did it come from?'

That was a clever touch. Isabella, thinking Simon Peterson might show her a little attention or some kindness in the future, immediately became more animated and confident. And of course, there was no love lost between her and Miss Passerini.

'The letter was typewritten and not signed so I don't know who it came from,' said Isabella. 'I realise it was very wrong of me to come here with my sister. But we'd had such a difficult time of it over the years. Our mother, God rest her soul, was always telling us how Robin Kinmuir had ruined our father. You should have heard the way she spoke about him – and she was quite the lady.'

'I know my uncle was no saint and he had his faults, as do we all,' said James. 'But what was he supposed to have done?'

'Although we are quite well-off now, which is due in the main to the success I – or rather, we – have had with our romance novels, that was not always the case,' said Isabella. 'You see, Mr Kinmuir swindled our father out of his fortune. Apparently, we once lived very comfortably, in the country-side, in a big house just outside Reading. Daddy invested a great deal of money in an investment scheme with Mr Kinmuir. They were supposed to share the risk. But when the scheme started to go wrong Mr Kinmuir stepped away.

Our father tried everything, even said he would go as far as taking the case to the courts, but Mr Kinmuir threatened him with certain ruin. He had, it seems, amassed evidence which seemed to show Daddy in a bad way. Blackmail, I'd call it, but apparently our father thought the risk too great. He didn't want a scandal and so he took full responsibility for the failure of the scheme. The house had to be sold. Everything he had worked so hard for disappeared almost overnight. He felt he had let our mother down. He was nothing, worthless, he'd brought shame to the family. What was the point of carrying on? My mother was pregnant at the time. And then, just before she went into labour with us . . . he took his own life.'

'Oh my,' said James. 'I had no idea.'

'Our mother made us promise that if we came across Robin Kinmuir we should exact the most terrible revenge,' added Isabella. 'Obviously, we were never going to do the very worst, but when that invitation arrived it seemed fortuitous. Almost too good to turn down.'

'But of course we didn't realise that it would turn out like it did, that it would actually end with . . . with murder,' said May as she turned to address James Kinmuir. 'And obviously I wouldn't do anything to hurt you. You do know that, don't you?'

'I see,' said James, who was just beginning to comprehend the repercussions of Isabella Frith-Stratton's testimony. He looked at each of the people in the dining room in turn as the realisation sank in.

'Oh, my God,' he whispered. 'Is that what you all came here for? To watch my uncle be murdered?'

Chapter Twenty-three

James Kinmuir fled from the room, closely followed by Rufus Phillips. May Frith-Stratton looked like a broken woman. I caught Davison's eye, nodded my head and, thinking quickly, began to speak. I hoped that if I too 'confessed' then it might lead to some of the guests telling me more about their own backgrounds. I took inspiration from the story I had just heard from the Frith-Stratton sisters.

'I suppose it would be a good idea if we all came clean,' I said. 'And I don't mind going first. I too got a letter, identical to the one that the Miss Frith-Strattons received. I thought at first it was some kind of practical joke. You all know that I'm a novelist and a few years ago my name was in the newspapers when my marriage broke down and I ran away. Since then I've received my fair share of missives from the unhinged and the unbalanced. You see, I didn't recognise the name of Robin Kinmuir – I was certain I hadn't come across him before. But then, I began to think back to my childhood, when my father – like the father of the Miss Frith-Strattons – had lost a great deal of money.'

That fact was true enough, as were the memories of that difficult time which I could draw upon. I told the guests of the fear of losing the family home, Ashfield, and how my elder brother and sister had pleaded with our mother not to sell it. I related tales of servants having to be dismissed and cutbacks in the kitchen. There were no more lavish dinner parties with endless numbers of courses. As a girl I hadn't understood the seriousness of the situation, but as an adult I looked back at the time first with sadness and then with anger.

At this point I had to draw on my imagination. When the mysterious letter arrived, I said, I asked my sister a little more about the circumstances of our father's change in fortune and it was then that she had recalled that it had had something to do with a Mr Kinmuir. I kept the existence of the letter to myself but had enlisted the services of a friend – Mr Davison – who volunteered to accompany me to Skye to find out more. I thought, foolishly, that it would put to rest certain ghosts that had been troubling me. I also believed, again naively, that it might have the beginnings of a good story.

'But when Mr Kinmuir was actually killed I was, like all of you, shocked by the course of events,' I said. 'I also felt guilty, as if I had somehow contributed to the terrible crime.'

'And yet the letter said nothing about poor old Mrs Kinmuir,' said Isabella Frith-Stratton. 'If I had known that she was going to suffer too I certainly wouldn't have come here.'

'I wish we'd never set foot in this place,' said May. 'And why didn't you keep your mouth shut? Did you see the way James looked at me as he left the room?' She looked at Isabella with a peevish expression; she no doubt blamed her sister for extinguishing whatever small flame she had imagined existed between herself and James Kinmuir.

Isabella ignored her. 'I can understand why Miss Passerini would want to do such a thing to Mr Kinmuir – what with all that had happened to her,' she continued. 'But doing *that* to the old lady – no, that was too much.'

I felt I was getting closer to the dark heart of the mystery. But I could not risk asking too many questions in case I was exposed. I saw Mr Peterson studying me closely. I could tell he did not trust me, but I needed him and my fellow guests to believe that I was one of them, that I had received a letter that had brought me to Dallach Lodge in order to – if not to seek revenge exactly – then at least revel in watching it being meted out. And so, even though I was desperate to ask the next natural question – what had happened to Miss Passerini in the past? – I remained quiet.

'I know something of your story, Mr Peterson,' said May Frith-Stratton. 'But perhaps you'd like to tell us a little more?' Her tone was far from sympathetic. Was she out to try to hurt her sister just as, in her eyes, Isabella had hurt her?

'Do you think that's wise?' he replied.

'I think it's only fair, after what we've shared,' said May.

'Very well,' he said. 'In addition to Mr Kinmuir's business interests, which you are aware of, he also served as an agent in the Secret Intelligence Service.'

'A spy?' cried May.

'I don't believe it!' said her sister.

The statement caused Davison to stir in his seat, but years of practising deceit in the name of duty meant that his reaction was so subtle that probably only I was aware of it.

'A secret agent?' responded Mrs Buchanan with scepticism. Her expression shifted from one of doubt and disbelief to thoughtful consideration, to acceptance and understanding. 'I see, it all makes sense now. I wondered why he would often leave me with no explanation. There were long gaps of time with no contact. I thought he was just being ... well, a man, or a certain type of man. Thoughtless and selfish. But now that makes perfect sense, and, if I'm honest, it serves as a source of great consolation.'

May Frith-Stratton looked with frustration at Mrs Buchanan before she addressed Mr Peterson again. 'If we can just get back to the matter in hand,' she said. 'Your connection with Mr Kinmuir.'

'Yes, of course,' said Mr Peterson. 'My father also worked for the SIS. He was everything a boy could want in a father – brave, handsome, with a sense of duty that ran through him like his own blood. He was my hero ...' His voice cracked, but he forced himself to continue. 'Of course, he never talked about his work while ... while he was alive. It was only later, after his death, that I learnt a little of the truth. In 1916 my father was sent on a mission to Maastricht, where he worked with Robin Kinmuir. Kinmuir was behaving somewhat erratically at that time. I believe that had something to do with the death of his son in the war. But even so, it was no excuse for what he did. Kinmuir got rather lazy and relied too much on one route to get his reports out of the country and back to Britain. The Germans took advantage of this, they managed to intercept a batch of reports and, as a result, my father was one of eleven men who was captured and executed at Hasselt that December.'

'I don't mean to sound callous, but isn't it one of the risks of the job?' asked Davison.

'Yes, I'm sure it is, but there was something rotten about the whole affair if you ask me,' replied Mr Peterson. 'It was odd that Kinmuir managed to wheedle his way out of the country, while my father had to sacrifice his life.'

'How do you know all of this?' asked Davison, in as cool a manner as possible.

'Of course there were no written records that I had access to, and so it was information that had been relayed to my mother from various sources.'

'And you trust these sources?' asked Davison.

'Yes, I do,' said Mr Peterson. 'And obviously I must make it clear that, when I came here to Skye, I had no intention of hurting Kinmuir.'

'But you were very happy to watch him get hurt?' asked Mrs Buchanan.

'Yes, I suppose I was,' said Mr Peterson. 'And what about you, Mrs Buchanan? Did your letter say the same thing?'

Mrs Buchanan drew herself upwards with grace and dignity, as if she were stepping on to the stage at one of London's grandest theatres. She declaimed the words slowly, enunciating each consonant and vowel for maximum effect. 'I received no letter, no letter of any kind,' she said.

The revelation silenced the room.

'And I must admit I've been left *shocked* by what I've heard here,' she said, placing great emphasis on the word, which she then repeated. '*Shocked* by you, Mrs Christie. *Shocked* by you, May and Isabella. And *shocked* by you, Mr Peterson.'

The other guests all tried to speak at once, but Mrs Buchanan quietened them with a light rise of her hand.

'And to think I was staying here among a group of people, some of whom I came to regard as my friends,' she continued. 'I feel like I've been living on top of a nest of vipers. I can't bear it a moment longer.' She got up to go. 'I feel it my duty to tell the police of this.' She raised her voice as she headed for the door. 'Inspector!' she shouted. 'Inspector!'

It was Davison, ever the diplomat, who tried to calm the situation. 'Mrs Buchanan, I can understand why you're feeling distressed.'

'Distressed?' she answered. 'I'm not distressed. I'm horrified. I loved that man more than I can say. Do you know how it feels to lose someone you love in that way?'

I knew Davison had experienced such a loss himself when his friend had been killed and had felt the pain keenly. But of course he could never make his feelings public.

'And then to find out that a group of, of . . .' She was going to use a more impolite term, but stopped herself, '. . . *people* had turned up at Robin's home with the express purpose of watching him die. The whole prospect sickens me to my stomach. Even if none of you killed Robin, then at least you should be punished for—'

At this moment, a stern-faced Inspector Hawkins opened the door and entered the dining room followed by James Kinmuir and Rufus Phillips. It seemed the whole thing would come out into the open now. Even though I had lied about my part in the scheme, that I too had received a letter, I was sure that the inspector would understand that I had done so in order to try to expose the guests' nasty little secret.

'What's all this I hear about a letter?' he asked.

The guests stood before him like shame-faced children who had been caught out.

'I have had enough of your lies,' Hawkins declared. There was anger and passion in his voice. 'This man has lost his uncle and his great-aunt, two people who were dear to him. They were murdered here at their home, a place where they should have felt safe. And now Mr Kinmuir tells me that you were all summoned here so you could witness his uncle's suffering, his death.'

'No, not I,' said Mrs Buchanan. 'In fact, I was on my way to talk to you about this exact matter.'

'Well, we'll get to that in due course,' said Hawkins, who clearly did not believe her. 'First of all, I want to hear about these mysterious letters. Who received them? What did they say? What did they look like? Do any of you still have one in your possession? Were there any marks on the envelopes to give a clue as to where the letters were posted? Then I want to know about each of you. Why did you come here? What connected you and the late Mr Kinmuir? And if any of you have started to make any travel plans I suggest that you cancel them immediately. No one is leaving this place.'

Chapter Twenty-four

The protestations flew like bullets across the room. James Kinmuir said he didn't want to share his house with men and women who had travelled to Skye to watch his uncle be murdered. Mrs Buchanan claimed she was not only innocent – she stated again that she had received no such letter – but that she had an important rehearsal for a play to attend in London. Both the Frith-Stratton sisters said they regretted their behaviour and began to apologise. And Mr Peterson demanded some sort of legal representation.

After silencing the guests the inspector sent everyone back to their rooms. He said he would call us one by one to the library to be interviewed once more. I accompanied Davison back to his suite. Neither of us knew how to begin the conversation and we sat in silence in the armchairs by the window while we contemplated what we had just witnessed. There were so many questions that we didn't know where to start.

Finally, it was Davison who spoke. 'The first thing I can do is check Mr Peterson's story about his father. That's easily done by going to Hartford.'

'Had you heard of a Mr Peterson in relation to that failed mission in Maastricht?' I asked.

'No, I never learnt the names of the individual men. I only knew that Kinmuir headed it and that it resulted in the deaths of eleven agents.'

'Do you think that's the kind of thing that Kinmuir wrote about in his memoir?'

'I wouldn't have thought so. He would have known that to expose such a mission in detail would be actionable,' replied Davison. 'But we need to hunt down that manuscript. Now that the sergeant is no longer stationed outside the late Robin Kinmuir's room we should have a better chance of finding it. I doubt the police would have taken it away, to them it's just a boring pile of paper. And what do you think of the Frith-Stratton sisters' story?'

'It strikes me as plausible,' I said.

Davison looked baffled. 'But what I don't understand is why. Why would the murderer send a letter to each of these people inviting them to stay at the lodge to watch Robin Kinmuir suffer?'

'And how did the killer know of the connections between each of the guests and Mr Kinmuir?' I asked.

'Let's presume Miss Passerini is the murderer,' said Davison. 'We don't know what kind of grudge she bears against Mr Kinmuir, but obviously it was something so deep and painful that it drove her to commit a murder and also compelled her to search for other people who had been wronged by him. Then she took the trouble of finding out where each of these people lived and sent an invitation to come to Dallach Lodge.'

'Then there's the issue of the rhyme,' I said. '*Who Killed Cock Robin?* Why would Miss Passerini, by virtue of the Latin root of her name, advertise the fact that she had killed the man?'

'Unless she always knew that she would be caught and she was proud of her revenge.'

'Perhaps,' I said. 'It does seem that all the evidence points to her as the killer. Yes, there's the lie she told, the stamp on her passport showing that she had recently returned from South America, the source of the curare poison. And also the weapon that killed Mrs Kinmuir, the paper knife, was found among her possessions. And yet ... and yet. There's something not right about all of this.'

'What do you mean?'

'I don't know, it feels as though somebody is playing a kind of game. A very wicked game, but a game nonetheless. It's like they are having fun. Enjoying the complexity of it all, almost like setting a particularly fiendish puzzle.'

'Or the plotting of a detective novel?'

The idea troubled me. 'I hope not,' I said. I had come across that kind of person before and I did not relish the thought of encountering it again.

'What do you think of Mrs Buchanan's denial?' asked Davison. 'Her statement that she had never received a letter?'

'I don't trust that woman,' I said. 'She's an actress.'

'Indeed. And there is our suspicion about her possible involvement in the disappearance of Mr Kinmuir's wife, Catherine.'

'Yes, what do you think we should do about that letter?' I asked, referring to the one I had found, together with the torn photograph of Mrs Buchanan with a mystery man, among the actress's belongings. 'Do you think we should hand it over to Inspector Hawkins?'

'I'm not sure,' replied Davison. 'Perhaps we should keep it to ourselves for the time being.'

'I'm wondering about the identity of that man in the photograph,' I said.

'What do you mean?'

'It's best to keep an open mind, that's all,' I said. Another thought crossed my mind. 'What are we going to do about the newspapers? Surely reporters will begin to descend on us like flies when news of the deaths gets out?'

'Don't worry about that,' said Davison. 'The department will issue a notice preventing any reporting of the deaths until a certain date in the future, by which time both of us will have moved on from here.'

Just then a black car drove up outside and a couple of men stepped out. A minute or so later the shrouded body of old Mrs Kinmuir was carried out on a stretcher and placed inside.

The thought of what had happened to the dear old lady with the pink cheeks sickened me. It also made me very angry. 'That was particularly evil,' I said. 'To do that to a defenceless woman who was losing her senses.'

'Do you think there are two different killers at work?'

'It's certainly possible,' I admitted. 'After all, the curare on the razor was a premeditated crime if ever I saw one. That took a great deal of planning. As did the assembly of the various guests at the lodge to witness the murder. But then the stabbing of Mrs Kinmuir in the back of her neck with the paper knife was something more spontaneous, done in a panic to silence her.'

'Because she had seen something out of the window from the attic? The murder of her nephew? She certainly looked out over the moors where Robin Kinmuir died. However, it doesn't make sense because the old lady was not only senile but practically blind as well. She can't have seen anything.'

'Something is being held back from us,' I said. 'How do we know that what we have heard is the truth? After all, so far we've only got the word of Mr Peterson and the Frith-Stratton sisters that they came here to watch a man be punished. That sounds bad enough, but it's not the same as murder. The point is that even when the inspector has finished his interviews, how will he know what is true and what is a lie?' I paused. 'What if *all* of them are lying?'

Chapter Twenty-five

We waited until the house had gone to bed before entering Robin Kinmuir's quarters. Both of us carried a candlestick and as we stepped inside the room the dim golden light from the flame cast a series of strange shadows across the red walls. Looking at the constantly shifting dark shapes, I was reminded of that haunting image told by the Greek philosopher Plato about a cave and a group of prisoners.

I felt like one of those prisoners confined to the cave that was Dallach Lodge and the events I had witnessed – the murder of Robin Kinmuir and his aunt, Mrs Kinmuir – were like the shadows in the story. Although the bodies were very real, there was something fantastical about the murders themselves. In Plato's cave the images were created by objects passing in front of a fire and then projected onto a blank wall. But who was the person at Dallach Lodge who was hidden behind a fire, responsible for the fabrication of these shadows?

And then there was the mystery about the Cock Robin rhyme, the Sparrow, *passer*, and Miss Passerini. Even though the evidence pointed towards the young woman — and the paper knife had been found in her room – I still had my doubts about her guilt. It was almost as if there were *too many clues*.

'Shall I start over here by the desk, while you look in the bureau over there?' asked Davison.

The spell was broken and I was brought back down to earth. There was little point in indulging myself in philosophical allegories or childish nursery rhymes when I had a job to do. The room needed to be searched.

'Yes, very well,' I said, as I placed my candlestick on the top of the mahogany bureau.

I opened the front and immediately noticed a sheaf of papers sticking out of one of the top drawers. Bringing them closer to the light, I saw that they were related to the running of the lodge: household expenses; bills from the people who supplied the house with meat, fish and provisions; and copies of receipts from various guests who had stayed at the lodge in the past. As I continued my search I came across evidence of Kinmuir's perilous financial position. There were a few stern letters from a bank in Inverness and threats of legal action over building work that had not been paid for. It was clear that Robin Kinmuir had been in a great deal of difficulty. Could the real motive for his murder have had something to do with that? Was he killed because of an unpaid debt or series of debts? But, if so, why did old Mrs Kinmuir have to be murdered too?

'I think I've got something,' said Davison. 'Look.'

I turned to see him holding two black notebooks. 'This must be the memoir he was writing,' he said.

'Listen – Kinmuir has called it *My Secret, Secret Life*. Well, as soon as Hartford sees this he will make sure it stays secret and never sees the light of day.'

'Do you think James knows about it?'

'I'm not sure, why?'

'Well, if the estate is in debt, as I'm sure it is—'

Davison finished my sentence. 'Then this might well prove to be a valuable asset. Yes, I can see that James may feel the need to exploit any resource available to him. The first thing we need to do is see what it contains.'

'What's the best way of doing that?' I asked. 'I'm sure Mr Glenelg will be back any day to carry out an inventory of everything in the house.'

'I know it's not ideal, but let's take a notebook each. If we work through the night we might be able to finish it.'

Davison opened one of the journals at random and read a few sentences that I could tell annoyed him. 'How I am going to control my temper is beyond me,' he said. '"Traitor" is too weak a word for this man. Honestly, if Kinmuir had not already been murdered I swear I could have done it myself.'

'I wish I could believe you were joking,' I said. 'If it makes it any easier, why don't we read through them together with a pot of coffee to hand?'

'Yes, that's a good idea. Otherwise I might work myself up into such a frenzy my blood will boil and I'll end up having a seizure.'

'Take the notebooks back into your room and I'll see if I can make some coffee,' I said. 'I'll join you in a few minutes.'

I left Davison and, with the candlestick, made my way down the corridor. I took the stairs one step at a time and as gently as I could, as I did not want to disturb the sleeping guests. With each creak of the steps I winced inwardly, willing my feet to make myself as light as possible. I had put on some weight recently, no doubt the result of my happiness at meeting a man I wanted to spend the rest of my life with. But did Max really want the same? The nagging doubts invaded my mind once more. What would he be doing this minute? I knew he was seeing friends in England, but where was he? Would he still be awake, reading some dusty text about the ancient world? Or would he be lost in sleep, his handsome head resting upon his pillow? I was desperate to talk to him, but I could not risk contacting him. If I did so, he would pick up the timbre of unease at the back of my throat. Also, I could not bring myself to lie to him. If I did, how would that bode at the very beginning of our life together?

Suddenly, I was gripped by a sense of panic. I had to bring this to a halt. What was I doing, creeping down the stairs of a strange house in Scotland in the middle of the night? How could I ever explain my work for Davison to Max? The very idea of uttering the words 'Secret Intelligence Service' seemed impossible and absurd. The notion that I worked for the British secret services would be met by a hearty laugh; something so blatantly ridiculous that Max would assume I was pulling his leg. His amusement would turn to shock and then horror. How could I have kept something like this from him? He would rightly wonder, if I had been lying about this aspect of my life, what else was I hiding from him? And how could I put myself in danger in such a way?

When this was over – whatever 'this' was – I would tell

Davison that it was my last collaboration with him. I could not continue to work for the SIS as a married woman. It would be unseemly, too difficult to incorporate into my new married life. My thrills would be confined to those of my imagination, the ones I managed to tap out on my typewriter, the ones that lay between the covers of a book.

But my sense of duty and obligation meant that I would not let Davison down. As I descended the servants' stairs into the kitchen I resolved to complete what I had begun. The next task in hand was to work through Kinmuir's journals to see what they contained. I was a quick reader but also the kind whose eyes started to close when I took up a book before bedtime.

I began to make the coffee. Even though the kitchen was located in the bowels of the house, far away from the guests' quarters, I tried to be as quiet as possible. I put some water on the range to boil, making sure that I used a saucepan and not the kettle, which had a whistle in its spout. As I waited I walked around the kitchen, examining the gleaming pots and pans, dishes and tins that Mrs Baillie used each day. What would happen to her now? I suppose with her reputation as a wonderful cook she would secure another position very easily. But what about the rest of the servants? No doubt, the young girls would be pleased to leave a house that was now associated not only with death but with murder. I felt sorry for Rose, the poor maid who had discovered the body of Mrs Kinmuir. That image of the old lady, her white collar turned red by blood, would stay with her forever. It would haunt her sleep and pollute her thoughts. The person who had done that – and who had killed Robin Kinmuir – would have to be brought to justice. And if I could help lead the murderer to the gallows, then all the better.

I found a tray and laid it with a cloth, cups, saucers and a small jug of milk. Just as I was pouring the hot water over the coffee in the pot I felt a certain coldness on the back of my neck. I turned to see a figure lurking in the shadows by the door. The shock made my hand shake, and a spot of boiling water splashed onto the inside part of my arm. The pain forced me to drop the pan, which crashed onto the flagstone floor, the remaining water puddling at my feet. The figure stepped forwards – I was relieved to see it was only Simkins.

'I was just trying to make some coffee,' I explained. I grabbed a tea towel, ran it under the cold water tap and pressed the fabric to my skin.

Simkins continued to watch me, looking at me as if he were a reptile gazing out from a cage at the zoo. There was a certain coldness, an indifference, to his stare that frightened me.

'Sorry,' I said. 'I didn't want to disturb anyone.'

'Is there anything I can do to help, ma'am?' he asked. But he uttered the words as if he didn't mean them. 'Let me get a cloth for the spilt water.'

As he walked across the kitchen I noticed that his foot-steps were quite unsteady and as he passed me I caught the distinct peaty whiff of whisky. Perhaps the shock of learning of the death of his master and the murder of the old lady had been too much for him; the refuge of the bottle was one in which many found comfort and although it had never been my choice in times of great distress, I could understand its allure for some.

'Thank you, Simkins,' I said, as he began to mop up the water. 'Very clumsy of me. Fortunately, I didn't spill the coffee in the pot too. In fact, I do believe that there is quite enough, so I don't need to make any more.'

He mopped up the last of the water and steadied himself as he stood up. He narrowed his eyes as he looked at the tray with its two cups. 'Would you like me to carry this up for you . . . and your guest?'

'No, I'm sure I can manage,' I said, feeling a blush spread across my cheeks. I was about to take the tray and leave when I thought it might be a good idea to take advantage of the situation and ask the butler a few questions. Not only were we alone, but Simkins's tongue might be loosened by his recent ingestion of alcohol. 'It's terrible what's happened here, at the lodge,' I said. 'I'm sure you have felt it more deeply than the rest of us.'

'Yes, ma'am, it all came as a sh-shock,' he said, slurring his words.

I noticed that his eyes were bloodshot. 'Can I ask, did you know any of the guests here – I mean, before they arrived at the lodge?'

'Only Mrs Buchanan. She has been a regular visitor over the years. A great friend of the late Mr Kinmuir.'

'And you've seen no correspondence from any of them in the past? Or telegrams?'

'No, nothing like that,' he said.

'What do you make of all this, everything that has gone on here?'

'I'm not sure it's my position to say, ma'am.'

'I just wondered if you'd heard anything. Or sensed

anything. After all, a butler of your standing and experience will have seen many things over the years.'

'If I have learnt one thing from my time in this position, it's that it's best *not* to see things.'

'What do you mean?'

'Discretion. Silence. Blindness. These are the real qualifications for the job.'

I felt my heartbeat quicken. 'So you *have* seen something, then?'

'I didn't say that, ma'am.'

I could see I wasn't getting anywhere with this line of questioning. 'What kind of man was your late master?'

'Mr Kinmuir? He was a real gentleman. Always did right by me. Never a cross word.'

'Did you know anyone who would want to do him harm?'

He hesitated and his eyes looked even more shifty than usual. 'No, ma'am.'

'If you are protecting someone – even someone that you care for – then I beg you to think again.'

Simkins stared at me with his blank eyes. 'I'm afraid I don't know what you are referring to,' he said.

'Very well. Tell me, what will you do when you leave here? Will you try to get another position?'

'I'm not doing this job again, no, not in a month of Sundays,' he said dismissively. 'I've got better things to do.'

I wondered whether he had been listening to Miss Passerini spout her revolutionary politics. Had he been corrupted by her?

'What makes you say that? Don't you need a job?'

'Don't worry about me, ma'am.' There was something

smug about the way he said this. His face seemed to glow, whether from some secret knowledge of future good fortune or from the amount of alcohol he had consumed I did not know.

'Very well,' I said. 'And I'm sorry once more about this mess.'

'Are you sure you don't need any help with that, ma'am?' he asked as I placed the coffee pot and the candlestick on the tray.

'No, but thank you,' I said. I doubted whether he was in any fit state to walk up to the top of the house, never mind carry a heavily laden tray. Or was he just putting on an act for my benefit?

I left Simkins leaning against the range, eyes closed and smiling to himself, and carefully carried the tray up the two flights of stairs to Davison's room. He was already deep into one of Kinmuir's journals, and it looked almost as though he were suffering physical pain from the experience. I thought once more about the light-hearted comment Davison had made about how he could have killed Kinmuir if someone had not already beaten him to it. Although he had meant it as a kind of joke, behind his observation lay a deadly truth which spoke of the loyalty that agents showed to the Secret Intelligence Service, the code of honour that bound them together and the sense of betrayal they felt when one of their ranks stepped out of line.

'Is it that bad?' I asked.

'It is if you know, as I do, some of the characters and scenarios he's writing about,' Davison replied as he poured the coffee. 'Anyway, we're not going to get very far if I carry on like this all night. I suppose we should get down to work.'

I steeled myself to ask a question, but before I could speak Davison said, 'Of course, I know what you're going to say.'

'You do?'

'Yes, you want to ask me again about whether we would go so far as to get rid of someone who was on the point of betraying us.'

'Well, yes, I was wondering about that,' I said.

'It's a good point and a fair one. I'm sure there have been cases where someone high up at the SIS has signed an order to make an agent vanish. But they would have had to have done something pretty abominable, like be a double agent, working for the enemy.'

'Yes, I can see that,' I said, taking a sip of coffee. 'But not someone whom you suspected of breaking the Official Secrets Act?'

'No, that wouldn't be enough. I'm sure that would be pursued by the slow feed of negative and damaging stories about the traitor to the press and then through the courts.'

'So you don't think someone here – one of our fellow guests, for example – could be one of your fellow secret agents who had been given the mission to bump off Kinmuir?'

Davison looked taken aback. 'No, I'm almost certain I would have picked up the signs.'

'But would you? I don't mean to blow my own trumpet, but look how easy it has been for me to work undercover, both in the past and here at the lodge.'

'What are you suggesting?'

'You know what I think about surface appearances and how dangerous it is to trust them, that's all,' I said.

'Do you have anyone in mind?'

'What do you think of Simkins?'

'The *butler*?'

'I know it sounds strange, but he was behaving very oddly in the kitchen just now.'

'In what way?'

'As well as being drunk he didn't seem to care that he was going to be out of a job soon.'

'Perhaps he's got some savings put away?'

'Maybe. Do you remember you told me that when you stole into his room to get those keys you saw that he had a Latin primer by his bed,' I said. 'That might prove significant when it comes to working out the *passer* "sparrow" business.'

'Yes, indeed,' Davison said. 'And what about the others?'

I ran through the other guests at the lodge. 'I don't think the Frith-Strattons are quite as dim-witted as they seem. There's something not right about them.'

'You can't seriously think that those two have what it takes to be undercover agents?' He laughed nervously. 'I can see Peterson carrying it off, or even Miss Passerini, but not those two sisters. Anyway, all this is a distraction. It's time to get reading.'

'Very well,' I said, picking up one of the journals and a sheaf of paper. 'But before I begin I want to check something.'

'What?'

'I want to compare the letter I found in Mrs Buchanan's room with Kinmuir's handwriting.'

I opened my handbag and took out the letter. It was immediately obvious that the journals were written in a neater, more measured hand than the letter that I had taken from Mrs Buchanan.

'So it seems they are written by two different men,' said Davison.

'Yes, it does,' I said. 'Anyway, let's get on with the task in hand. Is there anything I should look out for?'

'Kinmuir is writing about a world I know,' said Davison. 'And so it will be useful to have a view from the outside. In addition to a summary of the main points, write down anything that strikes you as odd or surprising and any passages where you think he might have given away too much information, information that might endanger the lives of other agents.' He looked at his watch. 'And if he gives any hints about the events in Maastricht as related to us by Peterson, and also the allegations of the Frith-Stratton sisters regarding his business dealings. If we start now, we should be able to finish the blasted thing by the morning.'

As I began to read the first journal, I learnt of Kinmuir's childhood growing up in London and Edinburgh, and something of his ancestors, including his father, a rich landowner. He briefly covered his time at school, Fettes College, before detailing his time at Dartmouth Naval College, a place I knew quite well. There he met the man who was to define his professional career – Mansfield Smith-Cumming, four years his senior and later head of the Secret Intelligence Service. Cumming – known by his initial 'C', which he signed in green ink – seemed like quite an extraordinary, if not downright odd individual.

Kinmuir related how, in 1914, while driving his Rolls-Royce in France with his son, Cumming suffered a terrible car accident. Realising that his son was dying and aware that the accident had left him with a badly injured leg,

Cumming amputated his own limb with a pocket knife. Kinmuir also told how later, during the interview process for new recruits, Cumming would take hold of a knife and stab his leg; if aspiring agents (who did not know his new leg was made from wood) so much as flinched the head of the SIS would tell them that they had not got what it took to be an agent.

When Kinmuir lost his own son in 1915, Cumming did everything in his power to console him, and the two men became even closer. Kinmuir, then a businessman, related how he had been called to see Cumming at his office at the top of a building just off Trafalgar Square in London. The British people were worried, as indeed was the government itself, about the number of German spies in the country during the war, and Cumming was recruiting men to help in the effort to root them out. Kinmuir took to the work and led a number of successful operations in France, Rotterdam and the Baltics. There was little mention, at least in the journal that I was reading, of any of the events of Maastricht apart from a veiled reference to 'one particular foreign mission that did not go as planned'. The name of Peterson was entirely absent from the journal. Instead, there was talk of men such as Vernon Kell, Paul Dukes, Augustus Agar, while some were only known by their initials: J.B., W.S.M., and C.M. It was no surprise to learn that women were entirely absent from this notebook, apart from a few references to Kinmuir's 'dear, devoted wife', whom he had met through Cumming's own wife, Leslie Marian Valiant-Cumming, heiress of the Logie estate, in Moray.

Kinmuir told with schoolboy relish of the preparation of

invisible ink: I was surprised to learn that, if a man found himself without his normal supply, a chap could manufacture his own by the means of self-pleasuring. Who would have thought that semen could be put to such a use? The resulting saying, 'Every man his own stylo', became something of an in-joke among the agents.

'What are you smiling at?' asked Davison.

'A reference to invisible ink,' I said.

'Oh, *that*,' he muttered, his face darkening. 'Now, would you like a little more coffee?' he said, standing up and turning his back to me. 'I can go and get some more.'

'No, I'm afraid if I drink any more I will never catch any sleep,' I said. I reflected on all the times Davison had enjoyed teasing me; perhaps now I could get my own back. 'I wonder, did you ever use that particular method?'

'Certainly not,' he said, still refusing to face me. 'I doubt it's even true.'

'I'm trying to work out the chemical composition and how it would work, on a purely technical level, you understand. I don't suppose you would know?'

There was no answer from Davison, who was clearly mortified by the conversation.

'"Every man his own stylo",' I said, quoting from the journal. 'Quite a good line, but I doubt any of that section would get past the editor's pen.'

'Quite right, the whole lot should be confined to the bonfire,' he said. 'Disgusting. In fact, I wish I hadn't asked you to help with the reading of the journals. It was foolish of me. I should never have exposed you to such base material.'

'You should know me better than that,' I said, trying to

lighten the mood. 'I'm not in the least shocked or offended. In fact, I was just trying to pull your leg.'

'Well, I'm afraid I'm not in the mood for it,' he said sourly. 'In fact, I think it's time we called it a night, don't you?'

'But don't you want me to tell you what I've read? And what have you discovered?'

'Sorry, but it's late.'

His words hit me like a punch to the stomach. I had been thoughtless and foolish to embarrass him in this way.

'Davison, I didn't mean to . . .'

But I knew it was pointless to persist with the conversation. It was better to slip away and so I said a quiet goodnight. Back in my room I stood at the window and watched the sun rise. The soft light caressed the surface of mist that rippled over the loch. Beneath lay hundreds of feet of dark, cold water, water that had never seen a chink of sunlight or touch of warmth. As I closed the curtains and got into bed I sank into the darkness. Inside, I felt hollow and empty, and utterly, utterly miserable.

Chapter Twenty-six

When I awoke from a brief sleep my mood was no better. The shadow of my uncomfortable encounter with Davison continued to haunt me. But there was something else, a realisation that I didn't have a clue about what to do next. I felt like I was drowning, thrown into the dark sea loch without a lifeline or a helping hand. If I couldn't talk to Davison about the case then there was little point in me being here. The doubts I had had about working with him and the SIS resurfaced.

I was stupid to think I could help. It was time for me to leave. I was worried that I had been away too long. I would wait until Inspector Hawkins gave me permission, of course, but as soon as he told me I was free to leave I would make sure that I took a car back to Broadford, back to the hotel and the comforting presence of Rosalind, Carlo and her sister. With them I could talk about the delights of Skye and the possibilities of sightseeing, enjoy nice cups of tea, hearty meals and brisk walks by the sea, and finalise the details of my forthcoming wedding in Edinburgh.

I did not belong in this world of espionage and intrigue. I had never really belonged in it. Davison and his boss, Hartford, had flattered me into thinking that I had something to contribute, but in reality I knew that they had manipulated me. In the past I had struck lucky. I had used what little skills I possessed to search out and expose evil. But this case was too much for me. I would have to acknowledge that I had failed. Perhaps Davison would be relieved. I hoped that we could remain friends – after all, we had gone through so much together – but I understood that, once I had made that break, there was little chance that I would ever bump into him again. I would use the knowledge that I had obtained, or at least some of it, in my books. That would be the silver lining that came with this very dark cloud.

As I checked myself in the mirror, I wasn't surprised to see an exhausted face staring back at me. The lines that I normally covered with powder seemed more defined, the shadows under my eyes more pronounced. And the light in my eyes that normally lifted a very plain and mediocre face seemed to have dimmed if not died. I couldn't stomach breakfast or the prospect of sitting across the table from Davison and so I quickly dressed and decided to go for a walk.

I knew from past experience that walking improved my spirits. I remembered the dreadful feeling of hopelessness that had almost engulfed me when I had been at a loss to decide how to finish my first published novel, *The Mysterious Affair at Styles*. My mother had packed me off to a hotel on Dartmoor and each afternoon I would stomp across the moorland, talking to myself about plot points and poisons. The fresh air and exercise, the simple act of placing one foot in front of the other, had done the trick and, after a fort-night, I had returned to Torquay with a nearly-completed manuscript.

I threw on a tweed skirt and a plain blouse, and laced up my old brown brogues, before grabbing a scarf, my notebook and a Burberry gabardine coat from the hook on the back of the door. It was the outfit I always wore to walk my dog, Peter. How I missed him. I told myself that it would not be long before I saw him, before I could pick him up and push my head into his wiry fur.

The house was mostly silent and I was relieved not to meet anyone on the way out. Instead of taking the path that led to the moor where Robin Kinmuir had died, I chose the one that went up to the ruined castle behind the house. The mist had not yet cleared from the sea loch and, even though it was August, the early morning air was still cold. I pushed my hands into the pockets of the coat and, with my head bowed, slowly walked up the hill. Although I took a few deep breaths and tried to clear my head, worries about what I would say to Davison clouded my mind. What reason would I give for leaving? Would I be letting him down? I reasoned that per-haps he would find my absence something of a blessing. He would not be hindered or held back and could make greater progress without me. I thought of Miss Passerini locked away in that jail in Portree. Didn't I owe her anything? Surely the inspector and Davison together would work out whether she was guilty or innocent?

And what of poor old Mrs Kinmuir? The memory of the elderly lady, blind and senile, up in that attic room reciting nursery rhymes to herself, brought tears to my eyes. Yes, the nursery rhymes. What was I to make of those? Or that one in particular, *Who Killed Cock Robin?* I told myself that there was little point wasting mental energy on the case as I would no longer be working on it. I would soon be a married woman. I would be on my honeymoon. I was about to begin a new life.

Yet my thoughts kept returning to the murders at Dallach Lodge. Surely, it couldn't have been a coincidence that the victim was called Robin and his killer, according to the rhyme, was the sparrow, Miss Passerini? And then there was the line quoted by Mrs Kinmuir – *I saw him die* – before she herself was murdered. The words from the rhyme echoed through my brain in a seemingly never-ending cycle. But I couldn't make sense of them. *Sparrow, bow and arrow, die, fly, blood, fish, dish, shroud, beetle, needle, grave, owl, shovel, parson, rook, book, clerk, lark, dark, link, linnet, minute, mourner, dove, coffin, kite, night, pall, wren, hen, psalm, bell, bull, air, a-sobbing, toll.*

As I came closer to the castle I spoke some of the lines out loud, just as I would when plotting one of my own books. Although all the other birds and creatures – the fly, the fish, the beetle, the owl, the rook, the lark, the linnet, the dove, the kite, the wren, the thrush, and the bull – knew that the sparrow had killed Cock Robin, none of them seemed to condemn the act. Instead, they all came together in a kind of theatrical performance of mourning, each taking a role. What if the same thing had happened here? Some of the guests – certainly Mr Peterson, the Frith-Stratton sisters, and most probably Miss Passerini – had received a letter inviting them to the lodge to witness the punishment of Robin Kinmuir.

Or at least they *said* they had received a letter. What if the whole thing was some kind of charade? Could the murder be staged to look like one thing when it was another altogether? Or instead of one murderer, could we have . . .?

Just then, as I was walking underneath an archway, I heard something shift above me. I looked up, and as I did so a large block of stone hurtled down towards me. I threw myself backwards. I felt a rush of air across my face as the piece of stone, spotted with yellow lichen, crashed into the ground by my feet, crushing a few wildflowers and spraying spots of dark soil over my skirt. Catching my breath, I struggled to my feet. My hands were stinging and it felt as if I had pulled a muscle in my back, but otherwise I was unhurt. I strained my neck to look up at the archway and, as I did so, I caught a quick movement, the mere glimpse of someone – a fragment of an arm – as they disappeared. I spun on my heels and ran as fast as I could in their direction.

'Stop!' I shouted.

Within a minute or so I was out of breath, but I followed the sound of footsteps and the rustle of ferns. With each renewed spurt of effort I kept hoping to catch sight of the person who, it seemed, had tried to kill me. The thought threatened to unsteady me, but the rush of adrenaline through my body spurred me on. I ran through the shell of the castle, passing the remains of what had been an elaborate staircase and through to what looked like an old chapel. There was no sign of divine worship here; the place of spiritual contemplation had been reduced to a few broken stones.

I stopped and listened for any sign of movement. All I could hear was the distant sound of gulls and the quick rise and fall of my own breath. But then I heard the gentle cascade of falling stones. I took another deep breath and set off running. I was convinced that if I turned the corner I would catch my would-be assailant. Then, as I ran over a pile of rocks covered over with a clutch of weeds, I tripped. I stretched out my hands to break my fall, but as I came crashing down I felt a sharp pain in my right wrist. Something warm and wet trickled down my cheek. I lay there for a few minutes as I recovered my breath and tried to isolate the pain. There was something wrong with my right hand. I wriggled my fingers and a shooting, stabbing sensation shot up my arm. I did it again. It was painful but possible to move my fingers. At least I would be able to write.

I sat up, feeling nauseous. I lifted my fingers to my scalp and brought them back into focus, enough to see that they were covered in a red sheen. I was bleeding from my head. I knew I was vulnerable. I listened for the sound of approaching footsteps. My eyes scanned the grounds of the ruined castle. Like a hunted animal my breathing was quick and shallow. I could easily be finished off here, my head crushed with a rock, my neck squeezed and strangled by a pair of strong and determined hands. I tried to stand but felt dizzy and my vision began to blur. But I had to move from this place. With legs that felt as if they were melting beneath me, I took one small step. I felt the metallic taste of blood on my lips. The periphery of my vision began to darken. I tried to steady myself, but it was no use. I fell back onto the ground as a cold shroud of darkness enveloped me.

Chapter Twenty-seven

I wasn't sure how long I lay there before I opened my eyes again. At first I saw a world of fragments. A patch of bare soil. A black rock. The etiolated stems of a few weeds. Then I remembered what had happened. Fear clutched at my throat. I tried to push myself up, but as I did so I heard the soft tread of footsteps. I couldn't speak. I dared not cry out for help in case I attracted the attention of the person who had tried to kill me. I tried to lie as still as a corpse.

The footsteps quickened. Someone was rushing towards me.

'Oh, my goodness, Mrs Christie!'

It was a man's voice. I tried to shrink away from the world, folding myself inwards as if to protect myself. But, of course, this child-like attempt at invisibility was no use.

'What happened to you?'

It was Mr Peterson. He knelt down by me and stretched out a hand, but I didn't take it. Even though I had only just recovered consciousness I remembered how he had suggested I take a walk up to the castle. And I knew that he blamed me for exposing the business of the letters.

'Let me help you get back to the lodge,' he said.

I did not answer him.

As he leant closer I felt his breath on my face. I began to tremble with fear, but I had to remain strong.

'Oh, my, you're bleeding,' he said. 'From a cut to your head.'

He took out a white handkerchief and delicately pressed it onto my forehead. 'Here, that should do it. Now, there's no need to panic. If you take my arm, I will make sure you get back safely to the lodge, where we can get you looked at. Did you fall?'

I nodded my head like a little girl. I looked into his face. His expression seemed to be one of genuine concern. But could I trust him? After all, he had been the first one on the scene. How did I know that he had not been waiting for me to awaken? Yet surely, if he had wanted to kill me, he could have me finished off as I lay there unconscious. All he would have had to do was take up another rock and smash it down hard on my head. I would have known nothing more about it. But here he was helping me to my feet. It was time to test his reactions.

'Don't be alarmed, but I think someone tried to kill me,' I said.

He looked at me as if I had uttered a sentence in a foreign language that he had not heard since a schoolboy.

'*What?*'

'Yes, here. In the castle. Under one of the archways. A block of stone came crashing down. I managed to throw myself out of its path just in time.'

'Are you sure it wasn't an accident?'

ANDREW WILSON

'I'm quite sure. Someone ran from the scene after it happened.'

'Did you see you who it was?'

'I'm not certain,' I said. 'Did you happen to see anyone?'

'No, I didn't, but we need to make the inspector aware of this.'

I looked at Mr Peterson in an imploring manner. 'Would you mind awfully if we kept this just between ourselves?'

'Why?'

'I don't want to cause a fuss,' I said.

'But if what you say is true, then your life is in danger. He may try again.'

I was struck by how he described my attacker as a man, not a woman.

'Well, that's what I thought too.'

This comment stopped him in his tracks. He released my arm for a moment and looked at me with surprise. 'But you can't be suggesting that you put yourself at risk? No, I'm afraid that would never do. I couldn't allow it. I'm going to have to tell the inspector about what you told me.'

'If I promise to tell the inspector myself will you in turn promise not to share what happened with any of the other guests?'

Mr Peterson thought for a moment. Then he nodded. 'But why would you want to keep it a secret?'

It was time to take another risk. 'If I may speak plainly, Mr Peterson?'

'Yes, please do.'

'I'm right in thinking that you and Miss Passerini have become close since you both arrived at the lodge?'

'Well, yes, we're on . . . friendly terms with one another.'

'And you wouldn't want anything to happen to her?'

'No, of course not.'

'And you don't think she is the one responsible for the murders in the house?'

'It's ridiculous to think she could be anything but innocent.'

'You see, I believe someone wants to frame Miss Passerini for the crimes.'

'And what evidence do you have for this?' he asked.

I couldn't tell him the truth as I did not know how far I could trust him. So I kept my response vague. 'As you suggest, she's not the type of person who could do such a thing,' I said. 'But if we are ever going to get to the bottom of this, and uncover who is the one behind the deaths of Mr Kinmuir and his aunt, then certain things may have to be kept back from the rest of the guests.'

Mr Peterson looked at me with a mix of surprise and respect. 'Yes, I quite understand now. Of course. And you think by doing this we might be able to clear Miss Passerini's name?'

'There's a great deal that needs to be done before we can do that. But yes, it's a start.'

'I can see how you write your novels now.'

'What do you mean?'

'You've got that kind of mind. You can see clearly into or through things. Oh, I'm not making myself clear. I'm not a very bookish or literary kind of man. I'm sure you can tell that. I've always been happier with columns of figures and the like. Goods coming in, goods going out. Import, export. Plus and minus. Those sorts of things.'

'Well, I take what you've said as a very high compliment indeed.'

Mr Peterson smiled, pleased with my response. 'And – as we're speaking plainly – I'm sorry for all that nonsense about the letters,' he said. 'You see, I didn't know how much you knew about them.'

'I understand. There's nothing to apologise for.'

Did I dare risk asking him more about Miss Passerini's secret? I decided against it, as to do so would open myself up to questions about the bad business deal between Robin Kinmuir and my father that I had invented.

We walked in silence down the track to the lodge, with Mr Peterson supporting me as I went. Certainly, he was gentle and attentive, holding my arm with just the right amount of pressure; there was nothing threatening or aggressive about him. But again I had to remind myself that this could be another performance. Perhaps he was hoping to ingratiate himself with me to find out just how much I knew. He could be using me, but then I suppose I was using him too, hoping to extract any nuggets of information that could help me piece together this dangerous puzzle.

Earlier that morning I had resolved to step away from the case. But now, as the pain throbbed through my head and the blood from the wound in my scalp began to dry in my hair, I realised that I could not do that. If someone had tried to kill me that meant I was getting somewhere. I was close. It would be foolish to retreat now. However, that did not mean that I would continue to work with Davison once this was over. Nothing would change my mind about that.

As we approached the open door to the lodge I saw

Davison standing in the hall, reading a letter that had arrived in the morning post. As he caught sight of me he rushed out. I watched his expression change from the mask of impersonal impartiality that he wore on most occasions to something else entirely. In just a moment his eyes registered a range of emotions – horror and shock soon followed by a dark, brooding look of guilt and then something else, something that could only be described as deep affection.

'Agatha, oh, my dear, what happened?' He tried to stop his voice from breaking.

'Nothing, just a little fall, up by the castle,' I replied. 'Mr Peterson found me and very kindly helped me back down.'

'But you're bleeding – from your head,' said Davison, looking from me to Mr Peterson and back again as he tried to assess the situation.

'I used my handkerchief to stem the bleeding. I think it's stopped now,' said Mr Peterson.

'I was very silly,' I said. 'I was looking out at the beauty of the sea loch and caught my foot on a piece of broken flagstone or an old root or something and came crashing down. I must have bumped my head as I fell.'

Davison looked with distrust at Mr Peterson.

'Thankfully, when I came to, Mr Peterson was right there,' I continued.

'You mean you were – you were out cold? Unconscious?'

'Yes, but only for a moment or so, I'm sure,' I said. I looked at Mr Peterson and nodded, a sign for him to tell his side of the story.

'I came across Mrs Christie lying on the ground,' said Mr

Peterson. 'Obviously, I did what any gentleman would do and accompanied her back to the house.'

'He's being far too modest,' I said. 'In fact, I don't know what I would have done without him.'

Davison knew there was more to the story. 'Well, I think we need to get you examined by Dr Fitzpatrick. He's just back from Mrs Kinmuir's post-mortem. In the meantime, let's get you up to bed.' He reached out for me and as he did so I felt the soft touch of fingers on my wrist. It was the touch of a friend, the dearest friend in the world.

I thanked Mr Peterson once more before Davison and I retreated upstairs, managing to escape to my room without anyone seeing us. As soon as the door was closed, Davison rushed towards me like a father intent on examining an injured child. He sat me down on the bed and checked the wound on my head.

Before he started asking me questions I told him I was sorry for what I had said while reading the notebook. It had been meant as a joke, nothing more. In turn, Davison apologised for the way he had reacted and for coming across as a prig. We laughed at our own stupidity, a form of necessary light relief before we got down to the darker matter in hand.

'So what really happened up there?' he asked as he sat down besides me.

'Someone made an attempt on my life,' I said.

All traces of humour melted from his face. 'How?'

'I was walking in the old castle's grounds when all of a sudden a block of stone came crashing down. I managed to push myself out of its path. As I did so I looked up and ... and caught a glimpse of someone running away.'

'Do you have any idea who it could have been?'

'I pursued them, but they were too quick for me. As I was running I fell and hit my head. As I said, when I came to, Mr Peterson was standing over me.'

'Do you think it could have been him?'

'That was my first thought. But if it *was* him he had plenty of opportunity to finish me off. I was an easy target.'

'Yes, I can see that. But who else could it have been? The only person we can rule out is Miss Passerini, who remains in custody in Portree. Did you get the impression that it was a man or a woman?'

'It could have been either,' I said. 'But it was someone who could run fast. As you know, I'm not much of a sprinter.'

'But why would they want to kill you? What is it they think you know?'

'That's what I've been trying to work out,' I said.

'Have you seen something or heard anything at all since you've been here that casts suspicion on one particular person?'

'I may have done, but it could have struck me as insignificant at the time.' I thought back over all the events that had occurred at Dallach Lodge since I arrived. As I did so I tried to tease out meaning from even the most seemingly banal encounters and trivial conversations. 'Let's assume that everyone has something to hide,' I said. 'We know – or we think we know – why Mr Peterson and the Frith-Strattons are here. Mrs Buchanan claims she never had a letter. But what about the others? Has Rufus Phillips got a hidden agenda? The servants? Simkins? And what about the cook? Even the doctor.'

'Fitzpatrick?'

'We have to assume the very worst of everyone, I'm afraid,' I said. As I uttered the words I was struck by how strange they sounded, as if they were being spoken by a character in one of my books. The image of Plato's cave came back to me and, for a moment, I felt so dizzy I was afraid I might pass out.

'You need to lie down,' said Davison.

'No, I'm sure I will be all right. Could I have a glass of water, please?'

Davison stood up, poured some water, and then went to open the window.

After taking a few sips and feeling the fresh air on my face, I felt a little better. 'We also need to find out about Miss Passerini's background and why she came to Skye,' I said, as I tried to breathe deeply. 'Do you think it would be possible for me to go and see her?'

'I would have thought the inspector would co-operate,' said Davison. 'There's no reason why he—'

Just then an almighty knocking shook the door. 'Mrs Christie! Are you in there?' Another loud knock. 'Mrs Christie!'

Davison walked across the room to open the door.

Mr Peterson stood there, looking desperate. 'Hello, Davison, Mrs Christie,' he said as he tried to compose himself. 'Inspector Hawkins has telephoned the house. It's awful. Just terrible news. Hawkins has charged Miss Passerini with murder.'

Chapter Twenty-eight

Mr Peterson's shock and grief soon turned into anger, anger directed at me. 'If it hadn't been for you, none of this would have happened,' he said. There was repressed rage in his voice and his eyes took on a desperate look. 'You had me fooled for a moment, back there up at the ruined castle. I pitied you. I thought you were another victim, lying prostrate on the ground. How could I have been so stupid?'

'Mr Peterson, what are you saying? Please consider yourself,' said Davison.

'Pretending that you had just been attacked!' He said the words with disgust, almost as if he had been forced to taste something foul. 'No wonder you didn't want to tell the inspector what had happened to you – because it was not true. And I fell for it! I actually began to trust you! But all the while you've been plotting and scheming, just like one of the killers in your books.'

'Peterson, pull yourself together,' said Davison in his best regimental voice. 'And close that blasted door!'

'Why should I close the door?' he replied. 'Unless you've

both got something to hide? What I want to know is what did Vivienne ever do to you? Why did you choose her to take the blame for all of this? Those things you said to the inspector to make him suspect her! I was there, I heard you. And then there are all the things I'm sure you must have said to him when I wasn't listening.'

'Mr Peterson, I can promise you that I sincerely regret saying anything that led the inspector to suspect Miss Passerini of the killings,' I said. 'In fact, I—'

But Peterson cut me off. 'You know what? I don't believe a word of what you say.'

'Please, Peterson,' said Davison. 'Have some decency.'

'Decency?' he replied, his voice rising. 'Neither of you know the meaning of the word.'

'If you would let me speak,' I said, barely managing to make myself heard above Mr Peterson's tirade. 'I was about to say that—'

'Why should I listen to anything you have to say?' He stopped talking for a moment and looked at me with distrust, if not downright hatred. 'After all, I know what you're both doing here.'

'I don't know what you mean,' I said, trying not to panic.

'You're one of *them*,' he said, spitting the last word out. 'Like my father, like Kinmuir.'

I tried to feign a look of astonishment. 'I'm at a loss to know what you're saying.'

'Bloody secret agents! Working for the same bunch of upper-class crooks who let my father be sacrificed.'

How did he know? Had he overheard us talking? Of course! He must have looked through the pockets of my

Burberry overcoat as I lay on the ground up there at the castle. I had been carrying a notebook with me, in which I had written down some details of the case, together with Davison's observations. He must have read my comments and worked out the rest for himself.

I tried to speak, so did Davison, but Mr Peterson shouted us down. 'I know how the SIS protects itself, how its members fool each other into thinking what they are doing is for the good of the country. But what about the good of the individuals? You don't worry about those, do you? Men like my father are just expendable to people like you. It makes me sick.'

Davison grasped Mr Peterson by his lapels and manhandled him into the room, slamming the door behind him.

'Why don't we talk about this in a civilised manner?' said Davison.

'I've got your attention now, haven't I?' cried Mr Peterson, emboldened with new-found confidence. 'Want to shut me up? Worried that your cover is about to be blown?'

How could we silence him? I suspected Davison was thinking the same thing, no doubt imagining violent scenarios including a quick bosh over the head or a scarf shoved into his mouth. But first I thought I should try another, more subtle tactic.

I moved over to him and whispered, 'Yes, you're right. Now, if you ever want to save the life of Miss Passerini I suggest you do what I say. Surely you don't want her to hang.'

The power of the last word silenced him and he looked astonished, almost as if I had injected a quick-acting potion into his system that made him listen.

'There is a killer in this house, one who has struck twice,' I continued, still in a whisper. 'And Miss Passerini – Vivienne – will be the next victim if you don't listen to what I have to say.'

I had his attention. 'Now, what I suggest is this. You come along quietly to Mr Davison's suite – it's a larger room, more comfortable than here – and we'll outline what we have discovered and what we can do to try to save Miss Passerini's life.'

'How do I know you're not just spinning one of your stories?' Mr Peterson asked. 'How do I know you're not lying?' There was a look of a young boy about him as he said this, as if he had been suddenly cast back to his childhood, a boy surrounded by a sea of adult faces, none of whom he could trust.

'If you'd let Mrs Christie explain I'm sure you'd believe her,' countered Davison. 'Now, why don't we retire to my room where we can have a ... more civil conversation?'

Mr Peterson looked from Davison to me, searching our faces for traces of deceit. Finally, after a moment's silent contemplation, he nodded his head. I retrieved my handbag and made sure I locked the door behind me before we filed into Davison's room. There was an air of ridiculous formality as Davison did his best to make Mr Peterson feel welcome. Davison himself was not quite sure what I was going to say. To be perfectly honest, I was far from certain myself. I knew I had to try to placate Mr Peterson. After all, he could be useful to me. But I did not know how much I could trust him. He might still be the one who had tried to kill me up there in the grounds of the ruined castle.

'Would you like a drink? There's whisky and water,' Davison said, as he gestured for Mr Peterson to sit in an armchair.

Mr Peterson refused, both the offer of refreshment and the seat. 'I think you'd better just say what you've got to say,' he replied, before he realised how blunt that sounded. 'I don't mean to be rude, but you must know I care very much for Miss Passerini's welfare and I can't stand the thought of her in that stinking, rotting cell in Portree.'

'Yes, I understand,' I said. 'And I know how much Miss Passerini's confinement must pain you. Now, I'll get straight to the point, as we do not have any time to waste. Yes, I am here on behalf of His Majesty's government, as is Mr Davison. And I must congratulate you on your ingenuity.'

Mr Peterson seemed pleased with his own cleverness and said, 'I know what you lot did to my father, disposing of him as if he were a piece of rubbish. And I won't have you do the same thing to Vivienne. I've seen the way you work. Sacrificial victims. Innocent people's lives ruined. All done in the name of King and Country. I won't have it, I tell you, I won't!'

'We know how much you value Miss Passerini's life and I can assure you that we do too,' I said. 'Which is why we are doing everything in our power to try to find out who is the real killer. You see, the person or persons behind this have been very clever – or I should say he or she believes they have been clever. But not quite clever enough.'

'What do you mean?'

'You must trust me, but I'm afraid I can't tell you everything at the moment,' I said with a confidence I did not feel. Indeed, there were great holes in my knowledge of what had happened at the lodge. I did not know whether I would be able to fill them in, but I was determined to try. 'I must admit I was suspicious of Miss Passerini mainly because she lied. Do you remember where she said she had recently returned from?'

'Yes, yes, I do. It was Berlin,' said Mr Peterson.

'That's right. But, according to the stamp in her passport, she had recently been not in Berlin but South America.'

Distrust crept back into his voice. 'But how do you know about the stamps in her passport?'

I had to think quickly. Although he knew my true purpose at Dallach Lodge, I did not want to tell him that I had stolen into the young woman's room in order to search through her possessions in case it made him even more angry. 'Oh, there was a silly mix-up on the day I arrived and Miss Passerini's passport – which she had deposited with Mr Kinmuir's office for safekeeping – was sent up to my room by mistake,' I said. 'Curiosity got the better of me and I opened it, I'm afraid. As I flicked through it I noticed the lovely stamps of those far-off countries that Miss Passerini had recently visited – Argentina, Venezuela and Uruguay. It was rather naughty of me to glance through it, but it was done entirely innocently. Of course I sent it back down to the butler with a note to say that it belonged to Miss Passerini.'

'So she could have brought back the curare from there,' said Mr Peterson. His face looked white. 'But why would she lie?'

'That's something we need to examine in greater detail,' I said.

'So that's why Hawkins thinks Miss Passerini might be guilty – because she's been to South America?'

'One of the reasons, yes, and I take responsibility for passing that information on to the inspector,' I said. 'But since then I have come across other things that have led me to question certain assumptions.'

'Such as?' he asked.

I looked at Davison. I could tell from the flicker of doubt that shadowed his grey eyes that he was willing me not to reveal much more. Although I had never been much of a poker player – my taste was for gentler games such as bridge and patience, rather like the late Mrs Kinmuir – there was an analogy here and I tried to keep my expression as blank as possible. I knew one should never put all of one's cards on the table until the very end of the game.

'I can't tell you much more because to do so would be to put you at risk,' I said.

'At risk?' Mr Peterson said with an unmistakable sneer. 'I don't think anyone will dare try anything with me.'

'You've forgotten that two people have been murdered in this house,' said Davison. 'And someone made an attempt on Mrs Christie's life too.'

'And Miss Passerini is in a cell in Portree, lined up and ready to be the next victim,' I added. 'If you want to try to stop that then you could help us. If you'd rather let the murderer get away with this – and kill Vivienne – in the process, then so be it. It's up to you.'

Mr Peterson considered this for a moment. Then he turned to me. 'How do I know I can trust you?'

'I'm afraid you can't be certain,' I said. I hoped my brutal honestly would convince him more than any elaborate parcel fashioned from silken words. 'You just have to do what you think is right, for yourself and for Miss Passerini.'

The conversation stood on a knife edge. If I had convinced him then there was a good chance that he would comply, at least for the short term. If I had not won his trust then there was a risk he would run out of the room and shout our real purpose to the rest of the house and our cover would be blown. My mouth felt dry and tasted sour. My heart beat with such an intensity I could almost hear the blood drumming through my brain.

Mr Peterson stood before us full of swagger. He looked at us not as two individuals but as symbols of everything he hated, a system that had taken his father away from him. And I knew then, in that instant, that we had lost.

'I'm sorry,' he said. 'I just don't believe you've got Miss Passerini's best interests at heart.'

As he turned from us and started to move towards the door I felt my breath being punched out of me. There was nothing left. As soon as our true identities were exposed, the murderer would win. We would have to leave the house and return to our lives, while Miss Passerini would go to the gallows, sentenced to die for a crime she did not commit. The defeat would represent not only a personal disappointment but a moral failure too. Evil was being allowed to triumph. The realisation made me feel weak and sick.

Just as Mr Peterson turned the handle on the door, Davison cleared his throat. 'Not so fast, Mr Peterson,' he said.

'I don't think there's anything you've got to say that requires my attention here,' Mr Peterson replied, opening the door.

'Or perhaps you'd rather I address you as Mr Kellaway?'

Mr Peterson did not move as Davison continued. 'Or should that be Mr Finlayson? Or Mr Houghton? Or what about Mr Yewtree? You have used so many names in the past.'

Mr Peterson turned and quickly shut the door. 'What's it to you?'

'It wouldn't mean anything to me were it not for the fact that we have something in common,' said Davison.

'We do?' Mr Peterson tried to remain calm, but there was something about the way his eyes darted about the room that indicated he was anything but calm. At that moment, whatever handsome qualities he once had seemed to melt away and he took on the look of a cornered rat.

'You may as well admit it, Peterson,' said Davison. 'You used to work for the SIS yourself.'

'How absurd!' said Mr Peterson, laughing. 'I may have used a few aliases in my past, that's all part of business. The import-export trade being what it is, from time to time one has to change—'

Davison took a letter out of his pocket. It must have been the one I had seen him reading when I returned to the lodge earlier that morning. 'I have here – written in code, of course – a list of all the missions you've worked on, together with the specific dates, and the number of men you killed during the course of your career. Quite impressive. It shows you have – or at least had – a certain talent for this particular sort of work.'

Mr Peterson did not respond.

'I wonder what your real intention was, though. With

your SIS training and very real knowledge, you certainly would have had access to poisons such as curare. And, of course, you did have a very real motive for murdering Robin Kinmuir. You blamed him for the death of your father, himself a SIS agent.'

'But you must know that's nonsense,' said Mr Peterson. 'Why would I tell you about the connection between my father and Kinmuir if I had actually killed him? That would have been foolhardy beyond belief.'

'You know as well as I do how bluff, double bluff and triple bluff work,' said Davison. 'Honesty can often act as a smokescreen to conceal a greater deception.'

'But you must know I am innocent,' said Mr Peterson.

'I'm afraid I don't know any such thing,' replied Davison. 'You had the motive and the means for the murder of Robin Kinmuir. What did you do? Did you steal into his rooms and smear a little of the curare on his shaving brush? It would have been easy to do. In and out. Kinmuir was none the wiser until he went out on his walk. And what about Mrs Kinmuir, the old lady? What did she know? Had Mr Kinmuir said something to her before his death that pointed to you as the killer? And it is interesting how you just happened to be up by the castle earlier today when Mrs Christie was attacked.'

'It's all nonsense – nonsense, I tell you!' shouted Mr Peterson. 'You're not going to pin this on me. I'd rather—'

'What? You'd rather Miss Passerini took the blame and is hanged for the crime?'

'No, I didn't say that. I just meant that—'

Davison did not let him finish his sentence. 'The records

here show that you seem to have a particular ability of snuffing out Bolsheviks, breaking up communist plots and that sort of thing. Yes, that would make very interesting reading for Miss Passerini.'

'You don't mean—'

'I don't mean what? That I won't tell Vivienne Passerini the truth about your past? Of course I will. What do you take me for? I'm sure if you were in my position that is exactly what you would do too.'

Mr Peterson remained silent as Davison continued. 'It's my supposition that Miss Passerini, of whom I am sure you are genuinely fond, will not take kindly to learning that you are, at worst, a murderer or, if not that, then at least a cad. Imagine if she discovered that you had come here so you could get close to her, that you pretended to make love to her just so you could learn more about her communist tendencies. I don't think such news would be conducive to the beginning of a romantic attachment, do you?'

Mr Peterson's face was ashen now. He must have realised that Davison had manoeuvred him into a corner. It took a while for him to speak; no doubt he was working out whether it was possible to use any information that he had gathered to gain an advantage over Davison.

Eventually acknowledging to himself that he had lost this particular round, he said, 'I can see that the situation does look bad, and I'm sure you know that I had nothing to do with those deaths. And neither did I come here hoping to spy on Miss Passerini. I'd hate it if she were to think that.' He swallowed hard, as if the words that followed were difficult for him to speak. 'But if there is anything I can do to prove to you that I was not involved, I am – well, I am willing to help.'

'It sounds like we can have, at last, a more reasonable discussion,' said Davison. 'Now, why don't you take a seat?'

Chapter Twenty-nine

The specks of dried blood from my head wound had turned the water pink. As Dr Fitzpatrick carefully washed the area around the gash I tried not to wince. The skin was still tender but, no doubt, over the course of the next few hours the swelling would begin to go down and at least I would be able to hide the injury under a hat. According to the doctor I would soon recover: there would be no permanent damage. I pleaded with Dr Fitzpatrick not to tell anyone about my injuries, which I said were the result of a fall. Everyone had enough to worry about, I said. Agreeing, he insisted that I rest and left me on the bed in my room.

As I thought about what had very nearly happened to me – my existence nearly snuffed out as easily as that of a snail on a hosta plant or a spider in the corner of a room – I felt overwhelmed by emotion. The thought of never seeing my daughter, Rosalind, again or my sister, Madge, upset me considerably. I would never again feel the fond touch of Max, so soon to be my husband. Instead of celebrating a wedding my friends would come together to mark my passing at a funeral. There would be no more travel, no more simple delights of long walks with my dog, Peter, no more sea swimming. I blinked back the tears. I could not afford to be sentimental. There was someone in the house who wanted me dead. And the only way to stop that person from murdering me was to solve the case.

I had to think logically. If someone wanted to kill me that meant they thought I knew or had seen something. But what? As I got up and dressed, I ran through everything that I had witnessed since arriving at Dallach Lodge. The accidental shooting of Robin Kinmuir by his nephew James. The awful grimace on the man's face, his hands grasping at that patch of heather as he fought for breath. Mrs Buchanan and that torn photograph. Vivienne Passerini's passport, stamped with the names of those countries in South America, and her lie about never having visited the continent. The scream of the girl servant as she discovered the body of old Mrs Kinmuir. The sight of the elderly lady's white blouse stained with blood. The playing cards scattered on the floor. The earring belonging to Vivienne Passerini that had been found on the floor by the victim's body. The paper knife – produced by Inspector Hawkins – which had been used to kill Mrs Kinmuir. And the blind woman's last words to me: '*Who killed Cock Robin? I, said the Sparrow, with my bow and arrow, I killed Cock Robin.*'

A moment before that, Mrs Kinmuir had said, '*L'ho visto morire*' – 'I saw him die'. Could she be referring to a murder in the past? I thought back to our conversation. My Italian was rudimentary, but I realised if the old lady had ended the word 'visto' with an 'a' instead of an 'o' then the subject of the sentence would not have been 'him' but 'her'. *L'ho vista morire* would translate 'I saw *her* die'. Could she have been referring to Catherine, the wife of Robin Kinmuir who had mysteriously disappeared all those years ago? Had she witnessed that death? Although Mrs Kinmuir probably could not have remembered what she had eaten for breakfast or which person had paid her a visit only moments before, perhaps she could have recalled something that had happened nearly fifteen years before.

I remembered the scene at dinner when I had related my conversation with old Mrs Kinmuir. Who had been there? James Kinmuir and Rufus Phillips. Mr Peterson. The Frith-Stratton sisters. Vivienne Passerini. Mrs Buchanan. Davison. And, hovering in the background, there had been Simkins, the butler.

Just then there was a gentle knock at my door. It was Davison. The inspector wanted to see all the guests in the library. He had some important news.

'Are you sure that you're feeling up to it?' asked Davison. 'I've just passed Dr Fitzpatrick on the stairs and he told me that you had to rest.'

'Nonsense,' I said. 'I'm feeling much better.' That was far from the truth, but I didn't want to make a fuss.

Nevertheless, Davison insisted on supporting me as we descended the stairs. There was something so comforting about feeling his strong arm holding on to me.

'Agatha, you do look awfully pale,' he said as we paused outside the library. 'I'm sure I can make an excuse for you, if you like.'

ANDREW WILSON

'Thank you, Davison,' I said, squeezing his hand. 'But, really, I'm well.' I smiled at him. 'Now let's see what the inspector has to tell us.'

As we entered the library Dr Fitzpatrick cast me a concerned look, but I reassured him with a smile. There was an air of expectation in the room and a look of slight impatience on the inspector's part as we took our seats; apparently we were the last to arrive.

'Thank you all for joining me,' he said somewhat brusquely. Hawkins had lost a great deal of respect for the group since the discovery of the business about the letters. 'As you will no doubt be aware, we have charged Miss Passerini with the murders of Robin Kinmuir and his aunt Mrs Veronica Kinmuir.'

'The bitch,' murmured Mrs Buchanan to herself.

'I realise that some of you came to the lodge for – well, for reasons particular to yourselves,' Hawkins continued, 'and while I don't condone your behaviour, I now know that none of you played a part in the murders. The crimes were done entirely by Miss Passerini and Miss Passerini alone must pay the price.'

'I hope she hangs for what she did,' interjected Mrs Buchanan, loudly so everyone could hear.

'I'm quite certain she will,' replied the inspector. 'After all, there is a good deal of evidence against her. We have the murder weapon that killed Mrs Kinmuir, the paper knife, and also Miss Passerini's earring that was found by the old lady's body. We have the fact that Miss Passerini lied to everyone here about her most recent travels, denying she had ever set foot on the continent of South America, which we know

242

to be the origin of the curare poison that killed Mr Kinmuir. And now we have discovered the motive.'

This was the one piece of the puzzle that had so far escaped me. I felt my heart begin to race as the inspector began to outline his case against the young woman.

'Before I get into the specifics, let me explain the wider context,' he said. 'You see, there is a great deal of bias when it comes to seeing women as murderers. We like to see them as caring, nurturing individuals who look after their menfolk and tend to their children. But you see, ladies and gentlemen, I've studied the annals of murder and I know that in some instances women can be just as ruthless and as cruel as men.'

He had the attention of the whole room and he addressed us as if he were a particularly gifted and articulate professor in a lecture hall full of devoted students.

'I'm sure you, Mrs Christie, are familiar with the case of Amelia Dyer?'

'Indeed,' I said, nodding my head gravely.

'For the benefit of the others, let me explain,' he said. 'Amelia Dyer was a nurse who was born Amelia Hobley in 1837, the daughter of a shoemaker in a village near Bristol. It was said that, as a girl, she grew to love poetry and literature, which is strange when you consider the monstrous things she did later, as an adult. You see, Amelia Dyer was responsible for the deaths of dozens of babies. It's difficult to know just how many she killed. Some say the number ran into the hundreds.'

'Babies?' cried May Frith-Stratton, her hand jumping up to cover her mouth.

'Yes, Amelia Dyer was what was known as a baby farmer,

taking in children for profit, infants who had been born ... illegitimately. But she did not want the bother of looking after the children. All she was interested in was the money. She killed the little mites by strangling them with white edging tape, the kind I believe is used in dressmaking.'

'I don't think I can bear any more. Inspector, please stop,' May pleaded. Her eyes look haunted.

But Hawkins continued. 'In 1896, after the discovery of a baby girl in the Thames near Reading, Mrs Dyer was arrested and charged with murder. At the Old Bailey it took the jury only four and a half minutes to find the woman guilty and, at the age of fifty-nine or sixty – the records are vague on that – she was hanged at Newgate Prison.'

'How awful,' said Mrs Buchanan.

'And then, before Mrs Dyer, there was the case of Mary Ann Cotton, who was convicted for poisoning her stepson,' intoned Hawkins. 'It is thought that she also murdered three husbands in order to profit from their insurance policies. Arsenic was her poison of choice, a poison which Mrs Christie here will know was often used by murderers because it went undetected unless tested – the symptoms of the poisoning were often mistaken for certain gastric problems. It is thought that she also murdered eleven out of her thirteen children.'

'I can't bear this,' said May Frith-Stratton, rising to her feet. 'Please excuse me.'

'As I said, I'm sorry to cause any upset among the ladies, but I do insist that you stay and listen to what I have to say,' said the inspector, raising his voice. 'Please, sit down.' There was a cruel tone to his manner now. Was this his way of getting revenge on the people who had come to the lodge with the sole purpose of witnessing the punishment meted out to Robin Kinmuir? 'Mrs Cotton, who was forty years old, was herself hanged at Durham jail in 1873.' He paused for dramatic effect and turned and looked at each one of us in the room. 'And, more recently, we have the famous case of Edith Thompson, who with her lover, Frederick Bywaters, was found guilty of the murder of her husband, Percy. She too—'

'I'm afraid that case was very different,' I interrupted. 'She should never have been found guilty. You see—'

Hawkins cut me off. 'The law is the law, Mrs Christie. There can be no arguing with it. The jury at the Old Bailey found Edith Thompson guilty, and the twenty-nine-year-old was hanged in Holloway prison in January 1923. It's as simple as that.'

'Yes, but there were certain pieces of evidence which—' The inspector did not let me finish my sentence.

'I mention these three cases of female murderers at random, but as I am sure you are aware there are many more. I know my criminal history, Mrs Christie.'

'I'm sure you do,' I said. 'But—'

'Which is why I'm certain that Miss Passerini will be found guilty and, after being found guilty, she will hang for her crimes,' he said.

Mrs Buchanan looked as satisfied and as pleased with herself as a dog which was within sniffing distance of a promised large bone.

'Of course, you want to know her motive,' said the inspector, pre-empting my next question.

The room was so quiet I could hear the sound of the breath of those guests closest to me.

'What I am going to describe to you now is not for the faint of heart, but it is a story that I must insist all of you listen to,' continued the inspector. 'After all, each of you here – apart from, I believe, Mrs Buchanan – came to this place hoping to see the punishment of one particular person: the late Mr Kinmuir.' So Hawkins believed Mrs Buchanan's denial. Either she was telling the truth, as she said, or she must have used all her skills of persuasion and performance to convince him of her innocence. 'And even though you did not do the deed yourselves – only Miss Passerini was responsible for the crime, or I should say crimes – you do bear some responsibility.'

The announcement was greeted by cries of alarm from the Frith-Stratton sisters and murmurs of disagreement on the part of Mr Peterson. Meanwhile, James Kinmuir, who stood away from the group by the window with his friend Rufus Phillips, looked on with approval. It seemed likely that he had had a conversation with Hawkins before entering the room. It was only natural that he wanted to make these people suffer for the base motives that had driven them to this island. He wanted the inspector to teach the guests a lesson, one they would never forget.

'Now, to get back to Miss Passerini,' said the inspector. 'Like each of you, she too had a connection to the late Mr Kinmuir. In her case, her need for revenge was, perhaps, the most pressing.' He paused for a moment, before he set forth the revelation that we were all waiting for. 'You see, Miss Passerini was the illegitimate daughter of Robin Kinmuir.'

A collective gasp echoed around the room. I felt a little light-headed as I tried to see how this new piece of information fitted into the larger picture.

'It is no surprise to learn that Mr Kinmuir had a number of intimate friendships and encounters with women other than his wife,' said Hawkins, glancing in the direction of Mrs Buchanan.

The actress had dropped her head and it was impossible to see the expression in her eyes. But from what I knew of her relationship with Mr Kinmuir I guessed that she would feel broken by the news. She was too much of a woman of the world not to know of Kinmuir's propensity for taking other lovers – she had been, after all, having an affair with a married man – but, even so, it must have been difficult to hear the truth of his infidelities. Eliza Buchanan accepted the need for Robin to have had a wife, but how would she feel knowing that he had had other mistresses, too? Had she known about this particular relationship – and the illegitimate child from that liaison? Could this have prompted her to turn to thoughts of murder? She had loved Robin Kinmuir, that much was clear, but I knew how easy it was for love to turn to hate. Indeed, weren't those two emotions really just extremes on the same spectrum?

'Miss Passerini was the offspring of an encounter Mr Kinmuir had had with a woman whose name we do not know,' continued Hawkins. 'Miss Passerini was born in 1909 in Italy, in Florence, and as a result the birth was not registered at Somerset House. Soon after the birth, however, it seems the mother died by her own hand.'

'How terrible,' said Mr Peterson.

'In turn, Miss Passerini was adopted by a very kind London couple, who were also quite wealthy. When I interviewed Miss Passerini in her cell in Portree, she told me that she discovered her true parentage when she turned twenty-one earlier this year.'

'But has she confessed to the crime?' I asked.

'No, of course she hasn't confessed,' said Hawkins, dismissively, as if this were not important. 'I wouldn't expect her to just yet. But give it time and I'm sure she will.'

'And what did she say about why she came here?' I persisted. 'To Skye.'

'She said that she had received a letter like the rest of you,' he replied. 'Calling her to Dallach Lodge to witness the punishment of Robin Kinmuir.'

'And you don't believe her?'

'Of course I don't believe her!' Hawkins snapped. 'It's clear that she was the one who wrote those letters to all of you. She blamed her mother's suicide on her father and, fuelled by hatred and revenge, she tried to find out who else had suffered because of him. And so, after doing some careful research, she lured a handful of strangers to the island with a prospect so delicious you could not refuse. A ringside seat to watch the humiliation of a man you all hated. Perhaps she thought she could get away with it. Perhaps she wanted to try to blame the murder of Mr Kinmuir on someone else. Unfortunately she wasn't as clever as she thought. Although she denies ever travelling to South America, her passport shows she was there quite recently. And while on that continent she must have acquired the curare with which she poisoned Mr Kinmuir, her father.'

'Aren't you forgetting something?' I asked.

Hawkins looked at me as if I were an annoying little midge that was about to settle on his skin and inflict a nasty bite.

'What do you mean?' he asked.

'Miss Passerini's name,' I said.

'Her name?'

'Yes, the Latin root. As I told you, *passer* means 'sparrow' in Latin. In the rhyme—'

'You don't expect me to listen to all that rot about that stupid nursery rhyme,' he said impatiently.

I tried to speak as calmly as possible, aware that Inspector Hawkins wanted to categorise me as an hysterical woman. 'If Miss Passerini was the one responsible for these murders, why would she advertise the fact? Her name gives her away.'

'Perhaps you're right,' he said.

Was he about to listen to what I had to say? My heartbeat increased as I steadied myself to explain my suspicions. But then, as soon as he started to speak, I realised that the inspector's theory blinded him to all other possibilities. My brief sense of elation turned to disappointment.

'Perhaps she wanted to be caught all along,' he said. 'I've known that to happen in cases before. Killers leaving clues so that they can be found. Arrest comes as something of a relief to them. In one case I believe there was a murderer responsible for the deaths of seven women who actually thanked the policeman who arrested him. I'm sorry, Mrs Christie, but I think it's best if you leave the solving of crimes to me.'

The guests were no doubt relieved that the inspector was turning on me rather than on them.

'Why don't you stick to writing about murder?' he added. 'That's where your real talents lie.'

The comment made me flush with suppressed rage. He knew that I couldn't say any more, as it would reveal the real reason why I had been sent with Davison to the lodge. And so I had to smile, ever so politely, and agree. As I did so I bit the inside of my cheek. I was sure I could taste blood.

Chapter Thirty

The word *blood* – or rather *bloody* – was on my lips too. As soon as Davison and I were alone again in his room I was spitting tacks.

'That b— infuriating man!' I shouted as I slammed the door behind me. 'Really! If I weren't, well, if I weren't as well brought up as I am then I would have something to say about him.'

'I'm sure you would, Agatha,' said Davison with an amused air.

'Did you hear what he said? That it's best if I leave the solving of crimes to him? What a —! And as for that patronising nonsense about how I should stick to writing about murder. Oh, it makes my blood boil just thinking about it.'

'I'm sure it does,' he said, smiling.

'But why didn't he listen to me? Doesn't he realise the significance of what I was telling him? And to think that I once believed he was an intelligent man! Did you notice I had to use every last ounce of self-control to stop myself from speaking my mind?'

'Indeed I did, and I was very impressed,' Davison said, with a sardonic grin spreading across his face.

'I don't see what's so amusing,' I said, somewhat peevishly. 'After all, this is life and death we're dealing with here. And the inspector's blinkered attitude could hasten Miss Passerini's journey to the gallows.'

'I know, and I'm sorry,' said Davison, clearing his throat. 'It's not a laughing matter, but I was just thrilled to see you so engaged.'

'It's a perfectly normal reaction,' I said.

'Of course it is, but I have been worried that you . . . well, that you'd lost interest in the case.'

So Davison had noticed my low spirits. He took a step towards me and smiled kindly, as if to welcome an old friend he hadn't seen in a while. 'I'm pleased to see you back in action, that's all,' he said. He became more serious. 'And if I upset you or caused you to feel any discomfort or unease, then I'm sorry.'

'Well, I did begin to think that I wasn't really up to the job,' I admitted.

'You're more than up to it.'

This seemed like the right time for me to tell Davison of my future plans: that I would see this case out, but after it was finished, then our time working together would be over. As I was formulating exactly how to express this, Davison took an envelope out of his pocket. He smiled mischievously as he did so.

'I've got something very interesting here,' he said. 'Do you remember we asked for information regarding any bodies that might have been discovered in or around Skye in 1916, when Catherine Kinmuir disappeared? Well, nothing came up on that score, but—'

'If that could just wait a moment, Davison,' I said.

'This could change everything.'

'Yes, but—'

'It sheds a whole new perspective on the case. Listen to this,' he said, unfolding the paper. 'It came from Hartford's office, along with the information about Mr Peterson. Do you remember we asked for background information on Fitzpatrick?'

'They have something on the doctor?'

'Oh, yes, they certainly do and it's good stuff,' he said with all the glee of a schoolboy. 'Not at all what we expected. It seems that he had enjoyed an intimate relationship with Robin Kinmuir's wife, Catherine.'

'Are you certain?'

'That's what the private detectives discovered and fed back to the office.'

'But weren't he and Kinmuir supposed to have been good friends?'

'I suppose that's never stopped anyone in the past.'

'No, you're right about that,' I admitted as I contemplated the breakdown of my own marriage. Although I had not been that close to Nancy Neele, the woman who was my husband's mistress, I had regarded her as a friendly acquaintance; she had even been to stay at our home. Now she was happily married to Archie and was soon to give birth. Discovering her pregnancy had felt like a dagger in the heart. How I envied Nancy for that. The image of her holding a baby, its warm breath on her cheek, made me feel sick with longing for another daughter, or a son, perhaps. Even though I was coming close to the end of my childbearing years, perhaps there was still time. But if I wanted another child I really would have to tell Davison of my intention to give up my work with the SIS. 'There's something I wanted to—'

Davison was having none of it – he was so carried away with the information that he had received that morning he would not let me speak. 'That's not all,' he said as his eyes scanned the letter, one that had been written in code. 'It seems as though Dr Fitzpatrick soon tired of Catherine and he embarked on a relationship with none other than – no, wait, can you guess?'

'No, no, I can't,' I replied.

'Eliza Buchanan!' he said, spreading out his hands as if he had just pulled off a particularly difficult magic trick.

'*What*? I don't understand. But she was in love with Robin Kinmuir.'

'She certainly was at one time, and that was confirmed by the detective who has found evidence of a love affair between them. But then Mrs Buchanan went on to have a relationship with the doctor. And so—'

'That letter that I took from Mrs Buchanan's room could have been from Dr Fitzpatrick.'

'Indeed,' replied Davison. 'And, of course, as a doctor he would have expert knowledge of poisons.'

My mind seemed to fire itself up and soon I was thinking at top speed. 'So you think that he and Mrs Buchanan could have killed Catherine? Perhaps Catherine became overly attached to Dr Fitzpatrick, perhaps obsessed by him. She could even have tried to blackmail Dr Fitzpatrick into staying with her. But how would Catherine have reacted when she discovered that she was being thrown over for another woman? Did she know that Eliza Buchanan had also had a love affair with her husband?'

'But if Dr Fitzpatrick and Mrs Buchanan were the ones who killed Robin Kinmuir, why do it now?' asked Davison.

'Perhaps Robin Kinmuir discovered a piece of evidence to show that Dr Fitzpatrick and Mrs Buchanan had killed Catherine?'

'And the letters sent to the other guests?'

'A classic ploy of misdirection,' I said, speaking of a device I had used in my novels. 'They could have been sent by Dr Fitzpatrick and Mrs Buchanan to put people off the scent. Or, more likely, they were hoping that by attracting Kinmuir's enemies to the lodge they could direct suspicion away from themselves. Everybody had a motive.'

'Well, it certainly seems to have worked,' said Davison.

'I know, the inspector seems so certain that Miss Passerini is guilty.'

Davison's eyes sparkled with delight. 'Talking of the inspector ...'

'What?'

Davison hesitated.

'Tell me, please,' I said. 'You know if there's one thing I cannot bear it is things being held back from me.'

'Very well,' he relented, looking down at another sheet of paper. 'Since I was in touch with Hartford's office, I thought it wise to enquire about Inspector Hawkins. And although it seems extraordinary that he too might have a motive for wanting Kinmuir dead, it indeed appears to be the case.'

'What kind of motive?'

'It seems that before Robin Kinmuir inherited this estate, it was the dwelling place of a number of tenant farmers. Kinmuir's father, like many other landowners in Scotland, made the decision to raise the rents on the local farms to something like three times what they had been. That hit families hard and forced them to leave the island. These Highland Clearances devastated communities, driving some as far as America and Australia. And, of course, it left a certain bitterness and hatred behind. Livelihoods were ruined, villages and communities were broken, children starved.'

'And one of those families was Hawkins's?'

'Yes, that's right. His grandfather was forced to leave Skye and settle on the mainland. His father lost a brother and a sister due to ill health and poor nutrition. Hawkins was brought up with a loathing of the Kinmuirs and everything they stood for.'

'So it's a case of the sins of the father being visited on the sons?'

'It certainly seems that way,' said Davison.

'So that could be the reason why Hawkins is so keen to fix the crime on Miss Passerini?'

'Indeed. And, as you know, as a policeman he would not only be above suspicion but he would also have the kind of mind which could plan a crime such as this.'

I tried to picture everything we knew about the murders, but the image in my mind was teeming with coloured boxes, overlapping circles and arrows which snaked from one person to the next. I would need to write it all down in my notebook. 'So, when it comes to suspects it seems we now have quite a few.'

'That's right, almost a castle full,' Davison replied, smiling before turning his attention to me. 'Now, what was it you wanted to talk to me about?'

The excitement I had felt during the last few minutes had melted away all my anxieties about my continued work with Davison. That conversation could wait.

'Oh, nothing important,' I said. 'At least, nothing as important as this.'

Chapter Thirty-one

It was going to be the last night at Dallach Lodge. James Kinmuir had resolved to put his personal feelings for the guests to one side and host a farewell dinner to thank Inspector Hawkins. No doubt he would be relieved to see the back of these people who had only travelled to Skye to see his uncle suffer, but his good breeding triumphed. What had happened at the lodge had been a tragedy, he said, and although he had been shocked by what had motivated the guests to come to Scotland, he understood that none of them were to blame for the deaths of his uncle and his great-aunt and that only Miss Passerini was truly guilty. He said he wished for them to leave with at least one positive memory of the place; he was certain that this was what Robin Kinmuir would have wanted. Soon the house would be cleared of its contents and the lodge put up for sale to pay his uncle's enormous debts.

The inspector, confident that he had found the murderer, had told us that although we were free to leave the hotel, we should stay on Skye until he gave permission to go.

Statements had to be checked and a few extra questions would no doubt need to be asked. The other guests said they would have liked to have been given leave to take the ferry back to the mainland, but at least it was a partial release.

The news was received with a collective sigh of relief. The lodge had come to be regarded by some as a prison and soon they would be free of it. All the horrors of the past week or so would be over and soon everyone could return to the normality of their own lives. Later, I had no doubt they would look back on this ghastly episode with incredulity. *Had they really been involved in such a thing? How had they endured it?* In addition, they would have to face the fact that they had been lured to the island by the thought of revenge. They had wanted to see Robin Kinmuir punished for what he had done. And he had been. He had been murdered, together with his aunt. Surely that knowledge would serve as a constant shadow, darkening their consciences for the rest of their days. But I believed one or more of the people in the house to be incapable of feeling guilt. He or she – or they – had plotted the whole thing. And it looked as though they were about to get away with it.

A sense of relief had replaced the funereal atmosphere that had filled the house. The inspector had the killer in custody. The guests were free to leave. A dinner party was being prepared. Yes, a wicked crime had been committed at the lodge, but life was moving on.

The ladies retired to their rooms to change for dinner – the Frith-Stratton sisters, who had forgotten their differences, were clucking like a pair of hens about which dresses and jewels they should wear – while Simon Peterson, James

Kinmuir and Rufus Phillips decided to take the dogs out for a walk before they too dressed for dinner. Dr Fitzpatrick said he was retiring to his room to catch up on his paperwork. Davison and I were left with the inspector, taking tea in the library. We had decided that the best course of action would be to try to lure Hawkins into a false sense of security.

'You must be thrilled to have caught the murderer,' said Davison.

'Thrilled is hardly the word,' replied Hawkins. 'Satisfied is more like it.'

'So it really does seem as though the evidence is strong enough to convict Miss Passerini?' I asked.

'Certainly, we have that classic trio – the means, the motive and the opportunity,' he replied. 'Miss Passerini is a botanist, with an expert knowledge of plants and their poisonous properties, and she had recently returned from South America, the source of the curare. And now we have uncovered her motive – her loathing of Mr Kinmuir resulting from the circumstances surrounding her own birth. On the morning of Robin Kinmuir's death she must have stolen into his room and smeared some curare onto his razor blade.'

'And of course, you found Miss Passerini's earring in the attic room,' I said.

'Yes, that's right,' he said. 'My only doubt was the motive behind that killing – *why* she decided to murder poor old Mrs Kinmuir.'

'What's your theory?' I asked.

'My only guess is that she has a loathing of the entire Kinmuir clan,' said the inspector. 'I believe that if we had not caught her then Mr James Kinmuir would have been next.'

Hawkins took a sip of tea as he looked out at the sea loch. 'Whether she would have used the curare again, or the paper knife which she had used to kill Mrs Kinmuir, or another method, is unclear. But I'm certain she would have made an attempt on James Kinmuir's life.'

'Did you inform Mr Kinmuir of this?' asked Davison.

'Of course,' replied Hawkins. 'He was shocked by the news, as anyone would be. Then that sense of shock and outrage turned to gratitude, which is why he has made me guest of honour at the dinner tonight.' The inspector looked more than a little embarrassed at this announcement. I got the impression that he was not, for the most part, an arrogant or proud man, but the cachet must have gone to his head. 'I don't mean to blow my own trumpet, but—'

'No, I quite understand,' said Davison. 'It was a first-rate investigation on your part. Absolutely perfect. I'm only sorry we couldn't do more to help.'

'I don't know,' said Hawkins. 'Mrs Christie here did provide some valuable leads. There was the tip-off about the passport, for one thing. And then that background information about the nursery rhyme. Yes, that really was very interesting. There's nothing like a little diversion in the midst of a brutal crime. Lifts one's spirits, don't you think?'

I felt like speaking my mind, but, of course, I smiled politely and let him continue.

'To be honest, I'm still trying to work out exactly what it was you were saying about the nursery rhyme,' he said. 'All that business about the Latin root of something or other.'

'I suppose it doesn't matter now, does it?' I said in a rather simpering manner. 'The case is more or less closed, isn't it?'

'Yes, I suppose it is,' said Hawkins. 'I've a few more reports to type up. And I'll still try to get a confession out of the woman, but I don't hold out much hope that she's going to crack now. She's a tough one, that Miss Passerini.'

I knew Hawkins's case against Miss Passerini was all wrong, particularly when it came to the all-important psychological aspect of the crime. If she was indeed the killer, motivated by hatred of the Kinmuirs and bearing the surname 'Sparrow', surely she would have confessed to the crime? No, the inspector's theory was flawed. But I didn't say anything about that.

'It's extraordinary how a crime can have its origins far back in time,' I said. 'What's that line from the Bible about the sins of the fathers being visited on the children to the third and fourth generation?'

I watched the inspector closely as I said this. But, apart from a slight twitch of the skin above his right eye, Hawkins remained impassive.

It was Davison's turn to speak. 'Yes, I once knew of a case where a feud took that long, yes, as long as three generations, before it resulted in murder.' Davison tried to talk casually, as if the story had only just come to mind. 'It was a falling-out between two families, where one family stole the other's land. Terrible bad blood between them, as you'd expect, but the resentment rumbled on for decades, until finally one of the members of the aggrieved family took it upon himself to shoot his counterpart in the opposing group. And just to think – the original offence had been carried out years before, by the men's great-grandfathers!'

'That's all very fascinating,' said the inspector, standing

up. 'And I would like to hear more about it, but I really must get going. As I said, there's some work I need to do before dinner.'

After Hawkins had left the room, Davison and I took care to talk about meaningless subjects such as the weather and our future travel plans, journeys that we knew we had no intention of taking. Davison then checked the door to make sure Hawkins was not listening before we began to discuss his behaviour.

'Cool as a cucumber,' said Davison. 'That's Hawkins.'

'Indeed,' I said. 'And it's difficult to know whether he realises that we know about his family's connection to the Kinmuirs.'

'If it was he who killed the two Kinmuirs then he's doing a very good job of covering it up,' said Davison.

'Next to murder, lying is easy,' I said.

Chapter Thirty-two

'Talking of lying,' said Davison, 'I think we need to have a word with Dr Fitzpatrick, don't you?'

'Yes, that's exactly what I was thinking,' I said. 'Now that he's alone in his room and doing his paperwork.'

I took Mrs Buchanan's letter from my handbag and the accompanying photograph and studied them. We talked about the best strategy to employ and the various ways in which the scene with the doctor might play itself out. As Davison walked ahead of me up the stairs and along the corridor towards the east wing of the house, I felt fear course through my body. My mouth was dry, my skin cold. If indeed Dr Fitzpatrick was a murderer he might well turn on us. He could have supplies of poison in his room. Yet Davison had assured me that he had a few tricks of his own.

At the door Davison turned to me and nodded. There was a confidence in his grey eyes that I sorely lacked. Was it too late to turn around and retreat to the relative safety of our rooms? Then Davison's hand stretched forwards and he knocked on the door.

'Dr Fitzpatrick?'

'Yes?' said the doctor's voice. 'What is it?'

'It's Davison here. I wondered if I could talk to you.'

A moment later the door opened and the doctor's jovial face beamed out at us. 'Of course,' he said. 'Oh, hello, Mrs Christie. Please, why don't you both come in? Forgive the mess on the desk. What with everything that has been going on I rather neglected my reports. Just trying to catch up.'

'Thank you,' said Davison as we stepped into the room.

I noticed that the doctor's breath smelt of alcohol. On the desk, by a mound of papers, was a large cut-glass tumbler of whisky.

'You both look rather serious,' he said. 'Please don't tell me there's been another murder. The death toll at Dallach Lodge is already high enough, don't you think?'

The joke fell flat.

'Sorry, that wasn't in the best of taste,' he said. 'Anyway, come in. I can only offer one of you a seat, I'm afraid. As you can see, I have one of the smallest rooms in the house. Not that I'm complaining, of course. Now what can I do for you?'

Davison cleared his throat. 'It's a slightly delicate matter relating to my cousin, Agatha.'

'Is something the matter, my dear?' he said, turning to me. Certainly, as he looked at me with his kind eyes, he appeared the very image of a caring doctor with a comforting bedside manner. 'How is your head? I hope you've had no more trouble since your nasty fall.'

'That's just it,' I said. 'I'm not sure whether it's due to the fall, but I have been experiencing a number of strange symptoms.'

ANDREW WILSON

'I'm sorry to hear that,' said Dr Fitzpatrick. 'Would you like me to take a look?'

'Yes, that would be very kind,' I said. I cast my eyes over the pile of paper on his desk. 'As long as I'm not disturbing you.'

'Not at all,' he said. 'Now, why don't we ask your cousin to leave us for a few minutes so that I—'

The idea of being alone with the doctor unsettled me. 'If you don't mind, I'd rather John stayed with me,' I said. 'It's just that, since the fall, I've been feeling rather fragile.' I brought out a handkerchief and started to twist it through my fingers.

'Of course,' said the doctor. 'It's understandable if, after all the terrible events that have happened, you're feeling a little on edge. Why don't you take a seat here,' he said, pointing to the chair by the desk.

That would never do; we needed to get to the notes on his desk without him seeing. I had to think quickly. 'Oh, John, it's happening again,' I said. I pretended to faint. 'It's the dizziness, it's come back.'

'Here,' said Dr Fitzpatrick as he took my arm. 'Mr Davison, if you could take your cousin's other arm. Why don't we move her over here?'

The two men gently guided me to the bed. 'If you could put your head between your knees,' said Dr Fitzpatrick as his hand touched the back of my neck. 'Yes, that's right, and now take some deep breaths. That should help. How often has she been suffering these dizzy spells?' he asked Davison.

'Every hour or so, I think,' said Davison. 'She also complains of strange patterns in front of her eyes. Flashing lights. And blinding headaches.'

'That's odd,' said Dr Fitzpatrick. 'When I first examined her she didn't say anything about these symptoms.'

'She didn't want to make a fuss,' said Davison. 'Even as a small girl she was taught that she should never complain. So the very fact that she is complaining about this, well, it must mean it's quite serious, don't you think?'

'Yes, I can see your point,' said the doctor. 'Let's have a look at her.'

He checked the wound on my head and the state of my wrist, nodding in satisfaction as he did so. Then he walked over to his desk, reached down for his medical bag, and took out his stethoscope.

'If I could ask you to loosen your blouse,' said Dr Fitzpatrick, as he returned to the bed.

I took a slight intake of breath as the doctor pressed the metal circle of his stethoscope onto my chest. I smelt the peaty aroma of malt whisky on his breath. As he listened to my heartbeat – a beat I knew to be racing – a concerned expression spread across his face.

'And now your pulse,' he said. He took my left arm and felt for the underside of my wrist. As he was taking my pulse, Davison began to edge his way closer to Dr Fitzpatrick's desk. I looked away and tried to concentrate on the tartan pattern of the blanket at the end of the bed. The thought that Davison might be discovered at any moment meant that my breaths were shallower and quicker than usual. As Davison reached out and took hold of a letter, I was aware of the doctor turning his head over his right shoulder. I felt panic flow through my body like a current of electricity.

'Yes, I can tell your heartbeat is higher than it should

be,' he said. 'Perhaps I should take your blood pressure. If it's high then that could manifest itself in bad headaches, tiredness and vision problems too. Now, where did I put that—'

Just at that moment, before the doctor had a full view of what was happening, Davison thrust a letter into his pocket.

'I think it's over on the desk,' he said as he moved away from me. 'Sorry for the mess. As I said, my paperwork has suffered since . . . since Robin was murdered.'

'That's understandable,' said Davison, whose expression hadn't changed. He looked as guileless and composed as ever. If only I could learn some of his techniques, I was sure I would be much better at this kind of subterfuge. When this was all over, I would ask him if he could teach me a few of his tricks. Then I remembered there would be no next time.

As Dr Fitzpatrick busied about with the blood pressure contraption, strapping the cuff around my arm and intoning about the possible causes of my symptoms, I told myself that I felt relieved that I had come to a decision about my future. I would be a married woman, as simple as that. Of course, I would carry on with my writing. I would need to in order to supplement Max's income; I knew that archaeologists were not paid a great deal. But soon I would be on honeymoon with Max in Venice. The thought of my husband-to-be made my body ache. What I wouldn't do to see his handsome face. I remembered the way he touched my cheek, my neck, my shoulder . . . I had to stop myself from thinking of him, otherwise it would drive me quite mad. But the idea that soon we would arrive in Venice! Yes, I would think of that instead.

I couldn't wait to see the sights of the floating city in the Adriatic. I recalled some of the images I had seen in books. The wine-dark lagoon. Santa Maria della Salute. The cemetery of Isola di San Michele; I had read that bodies were carried to the island on special funerary gondolas. And then there were museums like the Museo Correr and the Gallerie dell'Accademia, with its exquisite collection of paintings by those Renaissance masters which Max was so keen to see. I recited their names silently to myself: Bellini, Titian, Tintoretto, Giorgione . . .

'Mrs Christie? Mrs Christie?' The doctor's voice roused me from my reverie.

'Sorry, I must have been daydreaming,' I replied.

'Your blood pressure does seem to be a little on the high side, but not dangerously so,' said Dr Fitzpatrick. 'So what I would recommend is when you get home . . .'

Davison cleared his throat and took out the letter and photograph that I had stolen from Mrs Buchanan's room, together with the sample of handwriting that he had taken from Dr Fitzpatrick's desk. He had told me that our mission was simply to secure a document from Dr Fitzpatrick, handwriting which we could then compare to the stolen letter. *What was he doing?*

'Now, please don't agitate yourself, Mrs Christie,' said the doctor.

'I wonder if we could have a word?' Davison asked with the kind of polite air that a gentleman might use when soliciting a stranger for directions.

'Yes, I think she'll be all right in the long run,' said Fitzpatrick. 'Probably nerves. Not surprising, after everything that's gone on here. A terrible business, it really—'

At this he turned to see Davison standing in front of the desk, holding the letters.

'I'm not sure I understand,' said the doctor.

'Perhaps you'd like to sit down, doctor,' said Davison, gesturing to the chair by the desk. 'After all, we wouldn't want you to collapse from the shock.'

'What do you mean? I'm afraid I'm at a loss to know what—'

'Let me enlighten you,' said Davison.

I gave him a look of warning. *Did he really want to do this now?*

I watched the doctor's reaction as he realised exactly what Davison held in his hands. The strength seemed to seep out of his body and it took everything in his power to guide himself into the chair.

'I suspect you know what it is I've got here,' said Davison, brandishing the letter and photograph I had taken from Mrs Buchanan.

'It's not what you think,' said Dr Fitzpatrick.

'Isn't it? Well, perhaps you'd like to explain in that case.' There was a cruel edge to Davison's voice now. 'You see, to me this letter reads like a plan to commit a murder.'

Dr Fitzpatrick slumped forwards in the chair and held his bald head in his hands. He did not say anything for a while and the atmosphere in the room seemed to get heavier and more oppressive. The doctor sighed, looked up at us like a sick dog and opened his mouth to speak.

'In a way, this has come as something of a blessed relief,' he said, more to himself than to us. 'Yes, after all these years of dreading this moment, now it feels . . . well, it feels like I can finally be free.'

'Free?' I asked.

'Yes, free of *her*.'

'I don't understand,' said Davison. 'Who are you talking about?'

'Of that b—' he stopped himself. 'Eliza! I'm talking about Mrs Buchanan, of course.'

My brain tried to make sense of the fragments of information. What was he implying? That it was she who was responsible for the murders at Dallach Lodge? What kind of hold had she over him? Had she forced him to do the killing?

'Why don't you tell us from the beginning?' advised Davison in a quiet and reassuring voice. 'Get it off your chest.'

Dr Fitzpatrick blinked and gazed at us as if seeing us for the first time.

'Who the hell are you anyway?' he asked, steadying himself as he stood up. 'And what right do you have to go around like this, asking questions and taking things from my desk?'

What would Davison say? Would he tell him the truth?

'Dr Fitzpatrick, I am here at the behest of His Majesty's government,' said Davison. 'That is all you need to know.'

'I'm not standing for this, I'm going to tell the inspector that—'

'What? That you planned a murder years ago? The only question is did you go through with it? Exactly how did you kill Catherine Kinmuir?' There was no response. 'Now, I'd suggest you sit down. After all, this piece of evidence is unlikely to put you in a very good light, is it?' Davison held up the incriminating letter once more, an action which seemed to do the trick, as Dr Fitzpatrick slumped back into the chair. In a cold and dispassionate voice, Davison began to read from the letter. '"It's the only way ... I can't think of anything else ... I keep thinking of our life together when she is dead."' He paused for dramatic effect, and also to let the doctor reflect on the significance of the words. 'I'm right in thinking that this letter is written in your handwriting?'

'Yes, but how did you get hold of it?' asked Dr Fitzpatrick. 'She always said she kept it in a bank vault.'

'Perhaps this is a copy – but you wrote it to Mrs Buchanan?' Davison pressed.

'It's not what you think, you see—'

Davison cut him off. 'You once held strong feelings for Mrs Buchanan, feelings which perhaps you don't hold today?'

Dr Fitzpatrick nodded. His face was pale now, like the skin of a dead man. He reached out for his tumbler and swallowed the last dregs of whisky.

'It's over,' mumbled the doctor. 'Whatever I say, it makes no difference. I'm finished.'

'You may not be,' said Davison. 'I'm sure that if you tell us the truth then we can help you.'

There was no reply.

'Dr Fitzpatrick? What do you say?'

The doctor looked steadfastly in front of him, like a horse fitted with blinkers so that it could see no other way but directly ahead.

'And what of this photograph?' asked Davison.

'I'm not saying another word,' whispered Dr Fitzpatrick.

Davison cast me a quick glance. What did he expect me to do? He hadn't told me of his plan and I was not prepared. And so I had to think quickly.

I took a deep breath and shifted my position on the bed so that I sat a little closer to the doctor. The conversations I had had with Mrs Buchanan ran through my head. What was the best way to approach this? It was obvious that there was no love lost between him and the actress who had clearly once bewitched him. But what were his thoughts about Catherine?

'If I may speak plainly, Dr Fitzpatrick?' I began, trying to make my voice as soft and as gentle as possible. 'When we're in love – well, it's like we're under the influence of a kind of spell, don't you think? The world seems brighter somehow, the sky a keener shade of blue, the air fresher and more alive than ever. The only thing that matters is the person we love. All our attention is focused on that individual and we will do anything they ask of us. I'm sure you can cast your mind back to a time when you felt like that?'

The doctor's eyes began to moisten. It seemed my message was getting through to him.

'And if that person is as charismatic and as charming as Mrs Buchanan, well, then—'

'I wish I'd never set eyes on her,' he said.

I sensed that Davison was willing me to extract some kind of confession out of him, but I knew this could not be rushed. One wrong remark and he would clam up again.

'And then, once that person withdraws their love, well – and talking from my own experience – it can feel like being locked away in a cold, dark prison,' I said. 'A life lived in the shadows, with no prospect of warmth or light or joy.

But then another person comes along and the world seems brighter again.'

The doctor turned to me and seemed to understand my meaning. He nodded his head and was about to speak when Davison took a step towards the desk and banged his hand down on the surface, sending the papers scattering onto the floor.

'What the—' shouted Dr Fitzpatrick, rising from his seat.

'Davison!' I cried. 'Really. We were on the point of—'

'I don't care about any of that,' he replied. 'We haven't got time for sentiment. Look – two people have been murdered in this house. I know what you wrote in that letter, Dr Fitzpatrick. And it seems to me if you can plan one murder then you're certainly capable of planning another.'

'You can't believe that I would kill Robin? And old Mrs Kinmuir?'

'We have evidence here that suggests you wanted Robin's wife dead. You're not denying it?'

'No, but it wasn't like that,' the doctor replied. 'I've told you.'

'I'm afraid you've told us nothing,' said Davison. There was a hardness in his eyes now, one I hadn't seen before, an expression that frightened me. 'If you don't start to tell us what really happened then I'm going to have to share this letter with some of my close friends in the press. You've got a nice little number going on here, up on this island. But it's a closed community. Everyone knows one another. News travels fast. Imagine how fast it would travel if it became the subject of one of those Sunday newspaper spreads. A doctor who had an affair with his friend's wife. The same doctor who then stole his friend's mistress, the famous actress Eliza Buchanan. And if that weren't enough, this pillar of the community, this respectable gentleman then went on to plot a murder with the actress, the victim who happened to be—'

'Enough!' shouted Dr Fitzpatrick, choking back a sob. 'I can't bear it. I'll tell you the truth. I'll do anything you want. But please, please stop.'

Chapter Thirty-three

In the space of a few hours the house became a vision of light. Lamps blazed, dozens of candles flickered like fireflies in the night and the jewels worn by the women sparkled and glinted, brightening even the most pallid complexion. The diamond necklace that circled Mrs Buchanan's throat set off the dark beauty of her black silk gown. The Frith-Stratton sisters had chosen necklaces and bracelets fashioned from garnets, and as they moved the light cast miniature blood-red shadows onto the pale skin of their necks and wrists.

I wore the pearls and diamonds borrowed from my sister, which I paired with the trusty emerald-green evening dress, and even though Davison said I looked beautiful I did not feel like it. Murder was not good for the complexion, I thought to myself as I checked myself in the looking glass before going down to join the party. I wore a wide green hairband to cover the cut on my head and applied a little more powder over the bruising. The anxieties of the last few weeks seemed to have etched new lines onto my face, and I thought there was something of a haunted look about me.

I was desperate for a long, proper holiday and, once again, I dreamt of the time when I could enjoy my honeymoon with Max. As drinks were served in the drawing room I silently recited the words '*La Serenissima*' to myself and thought of Venice. The name conjured an image of a warm breeze playing over the Grand Canal, the waters lapping at the edge of St Mark's Square, a gondola floating across the lagoon.

I was distracted from these thoughts by a conversation taking place by the windows.

'It really is very kind of you to host this dinner, after . . . everything that's happened,' said Dr Fitzpatrick to James Kinmuir. The doctor was doing his best to behave normally, but our recent encounter with him had left him looking pale and distracted.

'It's the least I could do,' replied James. 'Now that the real culprit of these awful crimes has been caught – well, it's good to try to bring the whole thing to a close.'

'I couldn't agree more,' said the doctor, taking another swig of whisky. 'It's been dreadful. First to lose Robin like that and then poor Mrs Kinmuir.'

'I know,' said James. 'It was a terrible shock.'

'And how will you cope when you have to sell the house?' asked Dr Fitzpatrick. 'What will you do?'

James turned to his friend Rufus Phillips, who was standing by him like his shadow. 'Rufus has persuaded me to jack in my job at the school and travel to Italy.'

'But will you have the funds?'

James Kinmuir looked slightly taken aback by the directness of the doctor's question.

'Sorry to be so blunt – that was terribly rude of me,' said Dr Fitzpatrick. 'I've been a little out of sorts lately.'

'No, not at all,' said James. 'In fact, I've done the sums and it's cheaper than living here. I hope to get another teaching position out in Italy. Tutor to the dim son of a wealthy Englishman, that kind of thing.'

I thought I had better contribute to the conversation, rather than remain an awkward, solitary figure, and so I edged forwards, took a sip of my soda water, and said, 'Perhaps I will see you there.'

Again James seemed a little taken aback.

'In Italy, I mean. I'm off there on my honeymoon. Venice,' I'd explained. 'Where are you travelling to?'

'I'm not sure yet,' said James. 'It depends on when and where I get a position.'

'I see. And of course your great-aunt was such a lover of that country too. I remember Mrs Buchanan told me that.'

'Indeed she was,' said James, who looked down, no doubt to hide the tears that came into his eyes.

'It all seems so very different to Scotland,' I said, glancing out of the window at the moonlight reflected in the dark sea loch. 'I know there is an awful lot of water here, but just think – a floating city. The idea of Venice seems so magical, so unreal somehow.'

'I couldn't agree more,' said Rufus Phillips. 'I think it's my favourite place in the world.'

'If it's not too much trouble I would be so grateful if you could give me some advice about what to see and where to go,' I said.

'I'd be delighted,' he said, with a smile.

He launched into the splendours of Venice with boyish enthusiasm. There was talk of the glories of the Ca' d'Oro, the Scuola Grande di San Rocco and I Frari; spider crabs, courgette flowers, squid ink and dozens of ingredients I had never heard of, let alone tasted; passageways so narrow they never saw a ray of sunlight and hidden pockets of the city where few tourists ventured; and majestic Palladian villas situated on the Veneto which were so beautiful that they took one's breath away.

'Listening to you is like having a living Baedeker,' I said, a remark which made him laugh.

'It's good to hear the sound of laughter again in this house,' said the doctor. 'Everything has been so morbid, understandably so. But at least we can put all of it behind us now.'

He looked across the room to Eliza Buchanan, who had been trapped in conversation with the Frith-Stratton sisters.

'Excuse me.' He placed his empty glass down on the table, reached across to a tray of drinks and took two glasses of champagne, one for him and the other which he passed to Mrs Buchanan.

'Thank you, Jeremy,' she said. It was the first time I had heard her call him by his Christian name. The two turned away from the Frith-Strattons and started talking to one another, but in voices so low I couldn't make out their words.

Seeing that I was standing alone, Davison came over to join me.

'Look at this painting over here. I don't think I've looked at it properly before today.' Davison led me by the arm to an isolated spot on the opposite side of the room. As he pretended to study the landscape of the sublime Cuillin mountains, he lowered his voice. 'I think it's going to be an interesting evening. I think there's a chance we'll get to the truth.'

'Do you think Mr Peterson is comfortable with what he's got to do?' I whispered.

'No, I don't think he's comfortable at all, but he's got no choice,' Davison replied so that only I could hear. 'And he knows this is the last opportunity to try to save Vivienne Passerini from the gallows. After all, from tomorrow everyone will go their separate ways and the killer, or killers, will be able to melt away into the shadows.'

'It's terribly brave of him,' I said.

'Yes, it is, and I suppose it shows the real depth of feeling he has towards Miss Passerini.'

I looked across the drawing room and took in the scene. Simkins entered with another tray of drinks, which he served to the men in their evening dress and the women in their jewels and gowns. As the conversation bubbled away – the talk was of travel plans, former and future holidays and suchlike – it all looked so perfectly civilised, the very essence of respectability. Yet in the room there was at least one murderer, someone who had administered curare to Robin Kinmuir and who had then stabbed old Mrs Kinmuir in the back of the neck with a paper knife. Was it Mrs Buchanan, the actress who had had relationships with both the dead man and the doctor? Was it Dr Fitzpatrick himself, who, despite his protestations of innocence, could have had a hand in the disappearance, if not murder, of Robin Kinmuir's first wife? Was it Inspector Hawkins, who resented the fact that his ancestors had been forced from the land owned by the

Kinmuirs, and who had framed Vivienne Passerini for the crime? Or was it someone else entirely?

The room was heavy with secrets, poisoning the air like a toxic gas. But, after tonight was over, Davison and I were confident that some of these secrets would be exposed. The only danger was that another person might die in the process.

Chapter Thirty-four

Simkins sounded the gong calling us all to dinner. I held my handbag a little closer to me. Inside was everything I would need in order for me to complete my part in the forthcoming drama.

I stepped into the dining room. Again, the table was laid beautifully, with starched napkins, bone china so fine it was almost translucent and exquisite cut glass. The light from the candles danced off the fine silverware. I knew the opulence to be a façade – every fork and knife, every wine glass and candlestick would have to be sold to pay off Robin Kinmuir's debts. As I walked past portraits of people who were now long dead – ruddy-faced men in kilts, lairds surrounded by stags hunted to their deaths, ladies dressed in their finery – I wondered what these ancestors had witnessed in this room over the years.

I sat at the end of the long table, to the right of Simon Peterson. To his left was the ever-devoted Isabella Frith-Stratton who, now that Miss Passerini was in a cell in Portree, thought she might have a chance at winning the affections

of the handsome young man. Next to her sat Rufus Phillips
and then Davison. On the other side of the table, opposite
Davison, was James Kinmuir and then on his left were May
Frith-Stratton, Dr Fitzpatrick, Eliza Buchanan and Inspector
Hawkins, who sat opposite me.

As Simkins finished pouring the wine James Kinmuir
stood up and proposed a toast to thank the inspector for his
diligent work.

'Little did I think that evil would ever visit this house, but
this week it did,' he said. 'I won't talk any more about the
heinous crimes or . . .' He paused, no doubt thinking about
the reason why many around the table had descended on the
lodge. 'Only that had it not been for the investigative skills
of Inspector Hawkins, well, I'm not sure whether I would be
standing before you today. So you see, I have a great deal to
thank him for.' He raised his glass. 'To the inspector!'

I raised my glass of soda water as we all toasted the inspector, who smiled.

'I suppose it's not often that you see crimes of this nature
on the island,' I said to Hawkins.

'No, it's most unusual and illustrates a very determined
criminal mind,' he said.

'I'm sure it must mean promotion for you now. Where will
it be? Edinburgh? Glasgow?'

'I don't want to speak too soon, but I've always wanted to
try my hand in London.'

'I'm sure you would do very well there,' I said, even though
I was rather taken aback by the scale of Hawkins's ambitions.
'Scotland Yard could do with more men like you.'

'Thank you, Mrs Christie,' he said.

Mrs Buchanan, who had caught the tail end of our conversation, turned to the inspector and told him that when he was in London he simply must look her up. There was a sparkle in her eye, the kind that served as a preamble to flirtation. I knew that Eliza Buchanan was an expert seductress. Was the inspector going to be her next conquest?

'For my part, I cannot wait to get back to work,' she said. 'I've got a busy winter and spring ahead. Another season of Shakespeare. Another Lady Macbeth. Goneril. Tamora. Yes, good, juicy roles.'

I could have said something about the nature of those roles – namely that these women were all monsters – but instead I asked, 'Do you think you'll ever return to Skye?'

As I spoke I noticed that Dr Fitzpatrick turned his head slightly and seemed to lose interest in what May Frith-Stratton was saying to him.

'What do you mean?' asked Mrs Buchanan. 'That I might not return now that Robin is no longer here?'

'Yes, I wondered whether the island still held any attraction for you?'

Her reply was that of a politician. 'I still have friends here and Skye will always hold a very special place in my heart,' she said. She looked as though she wanted to add something, but Simkins was at her shoulder, offering her the first course of vegetable consommé. She nodded her head and the butler proceeded to serve her.

I noticed that Simkins's hands were shaking. Had he been drinking again? Just then, as he ladled some more of the clear, amber-coloured liquid into the bowl, a spot of it splashed onto Mrs Buchanan's gown.

'Can't you watch what you're doing, you fool!' hissed Mrs Buchanan with fire in her eyes. 'Really. This gown was made in Paris, of the finest silk.'

Simkins's gloved hand reached for a starched napkin that was draped over his arm, but as he approached her she brushed it aside. 'I'll do it myself,' she snapped, before she regulated the tone of her voice and began to speak in a more measured manner. 'If you would be so kind as to bring me a bowl of iced water.'

When Simkins left the room she turned to the inspector. 'I suspected he drank,' she said, 'but it's never been this bad. It really is intolerable. It's as if he doesn't care whether he keeps his job or not.'

Simkins had seemed confident enough about his future when I encountered him in the kitchens; indeed, a little too confident. Of course, that could have been the drink talking, but I suspected it was something else. When I found a quiet moment I planned to question him. But what of the cook, Mrs Baillie? And that poor girl, Rose Stewart, who had discovered the body of old Mrs Kinmuir? Would she get another position? The tea stain might be worked out of the carpet, but what of the stain on Rose's memory that lingered after she had discovered the body? That would be harder to erase. No doubt she would carry it with her throughout her life. I kept that thought in my mind as I opened my bag and took out a handkerchief. I pretended to use it to dab my eyes as I stole a look at Simon Peterson while he sipped a spoonful of consommé. From the opposite side of the table Dr Fitzpatrick watched Mr Peterson closely as he turned his head to talk to Isabella Frith-Stratton seated next to him.

I looked across the room to the clock. It was a quarter past eight.

Despite Mrs Buchanan's recent outburst, the room was full of laughter and smiles. Everyone now seemed relaxed and relatively happy, knowing that they could put the tragedies of the past week behind them. The guests were looking forward to leaving the lodge the next day. The light of the candles and the sparkle of the diamonds suggested an atmosphere of abundant joy. But all that was about to change in a moment.

'Is something the matter, Mrs Christie?' asked the inspector from across the table. He must have been watching me as I observed the rest of the group.

'No, nothing at all,' I said, lifting my handkerchief to my face once more. 'I felt something in my eye, but it's gone now.'

'I see,' said the inspector. 'And will you use any of the events of the past week in one of your future novels?'

'I don't think so,' I said. 'But if I do, I'll be certain to disguise it a great deal. Don't worry, I won't use you as a character.'

'I hope not!' he said, laughing. 'What, may I ask, are you working on at the moment?'

'I intend to have a little break from writing,' I said. 'I might try a short story or two, or sketch out a play, perhaps. But as for novels, I'm going to have a few months off.'

'Of course. You're about to be married, aren't you?'

'That's right,' I said. The thought of Max brought a slight blush to my cheek.

'Well, I hope you have a very happy life together,' he said. 'I know after I married – and, to be honest, I resisted for as long as possible – I felt like a different man. My wife, Lucy, she is the kind of—'

I knew why he had stopped. The look of alarm in the inspector's eyes told me that the sequence of events we had planned was about to begin.

Everything happened so fast. I turned to see Simon Peterson clutch a white napkin over his face. But it was no use. Vomit gushed from his mouth, the clear liquid leaking through the sides of the napkin and spraying onto the table.

'Oh, my goodness!' cried Isabella as a spot splashed onto her evening gown. But her love for Mr Peterson triumphed over her revulsion. 'Simon – are you all right?'

The table erupted as one, with each of the guests standing with such force that some of the chairs fell back onto the floor. Although I was used to the acidic stench from my nursing days, I knew that many could not bear the smell that had begun to fill the room. Mrs Buchanan clasped her napkin over her face in disgust. May Frith-Stratton looked as if she was about to faint. James Kinmuir gazed on the scene with horror. Dr Fitzpatrick rushed around the table to see what could be done.

'Perhaps it's food poisoning,' I said as I offered my napkin to Mr Peterson. 'I think we should get him upstairs.'

At this moment, Simkins arrived back in the dining room, bearing an enormous serving plate of roast beef. The sight that met him – the unruly table, the vomit-tainted cloth, the guests in uproar, the acrid smell – unsteadied him to such an extent that I feared he might drop the dish. But he rallied and managed to turn on his heels to take the food out again. He reappeared with a maid who was clutching some cloths and a bowl of water.

As the butler directed the girl to clear up the mess, Mrs Buchanan called over, 'Simkins, I think you have forgotten the iced water – for my dress.'

Simkins, quite rightly, ignored her.

'Honestly – this household,' murmured Mrs Buchanan. 'I've never seen anything like it and I've mixed in the most bohemian circles.'

James Kinmuir, who was clearly embarrassed by the whole scene, stepped forwards to try to take charge. 'I'm terribly sorry about this,' he said. 'Rufus, would you mind helping me? Mr Peterson, can you stand up?'

Mr Peterson began to ease himself out of his chair, but just as he was about to stand he seemed to lose all control. His body leant forwards and he fell straight onto the table, knocking off a plate and a glass which fell onto the floor. Isabella, standing by him, screamed.

'Simon! Simon!' she cried.

She reached out to him to see if he had hurt his face, but luckily it seemed he had only bruised himself. A moment later, he started to twitch like a fish wrenched out of water and it seemed he was on the point of drifting into unconsciousness.

'Doctor,' said Isabella. 'You must help him. Quick!'

May Frith-Stratton came over to comfort her sister. 'I'm sure it's just a case of food poisoning, as Mrs Christie suggests.'

Mr Peterson gripped his stomach as a wave of pain swept over him.

'I think he's been poisoned!' screamed Isabella. 'Something in his soup – or the wine.' She cast an accusatory glance in my direction. 'I was on Simon's left and I know I didn't do anything.' She left it at that, but the implication of her statement was clear: I was the one who had poisoned Mr Peterson.

'Oh, come now,' said the doctor. 'I know we've all had something of a shock and our nerves are shot to pieces, but really. I'm certain it's nothing but a case of food poisoning. Can you help me get him upstairs?'

Rufus Phillips and Davison came to Dr Fitzpatrick's aid, while James Kinmuir followed them out of the room. Isabella wanted to accompany them, but the doctor persuaded her that it would be for the best if she remained downstairs. He would examine the young man and report back shortly.

At the door, Kinmuir turned and apologised again. 'Hawkins, I'm sorry. This dinner was supposed to be in your honour and it's ended in a disaster.' His eyes sought out the butler. 'Simkins, would you set out some food and plates on the sideboard in the drawing room?' Then he addressed the guests. 'Perhaps you can all help yourselves there – if you're still in the mood for eating, that is.'

Of course, nobody had much of an appetite after what we had all witnessed, but we left the mess behind for the comfort of the drawing room. There, people made sympathetic noises about what could have caused poor Mr Peterson to have been taken ill. There was talk of shellfish: we had all feasted on giant langoustines only a day before, but none of us had suffered any ill effects.

'What I don't understand is why Mr Peterson didn't excuse himself from the table earlier?' said Mrs Buchanan. 'Surely he must have had some warning signs that he felt unwell.'

'Perhaps, the attack was so sudden, he was taken entirely unawares,' said the inspector.

'We'll have to ask the doctor if he's come across such a case before,' said Isabella, who was still suspicious of me. 'I must admit it strikes me as very odd. I do hope he feels better soon. I know he was very much looking forward to leaving this place, as I'm sure we all are.'

'It's such a nuisance that we can't yet leave the island immediately,' said Mrs Buchanan. 'Sorry, inspector, I forgot you were sitting there for a moment.'

'Don't mind me,' he said genially. 'Please, carry on.'

'Do we really have to remain here?' she asked.

'I'm afraid that would be for the best,' said Hawkins.

'We may try the hotel in Broadford,' said May Frith-Stratton. 'I've heard it's quite charming. And so handy for the steamer too.'

The thought of the two sisters staying at the hotel where I had left Rosalind, Carlo and Mary made me feel queasy.

'I think it depends very much on Mr Peterson's health,' Isabella replied. 'After all, we can't very well leave him if he's ill, can we?'

'Yes, perhaps it's best if we stay on at the lodge a little longer,' replied May. No doubt she wanted to eke out as much time with James Kinmuir as possible. Perhaps the young man's dire finances did not trouble her.

A short while later, Kinmuir, Phillips and Davison returned downstairs and helped themselves to drinks.

As soon as Isabella saw them she jumped up. 'How's Simon?' she asked. 'Is he feeling better? Please tell me he's improving.'

'I don't know what to say,' said Phillips. 'The poor chap is writhing around the bed like he's in a great deal of pain.'

'Oh, I must go to him,' she said, making for the door.

Mrs Buchanan stopped her. 'My dear, he won't thank you for it,' she said. 'He won't want you to see him in that kind of state. Do you understand what I'm saying?'

It took a moment or so before Isabella nodded her head. She asked the three men whether the doctor had given any indication of what might be wrong and wondered whether a cold compress should be sent up to Mr Peterson. She could not sit down but flitted about the room like a bird in a cage.

'I'm sure there's a perfectly reasonable explanation,' said James. 'Once he drinks some water, flushes whatever it is out of his system, I'll bet Peterson will be as right as rain.'

'Do you really think so?' asked Isabella. 'It's just that with everything else that has gone on here . . .'

'There is no need to worry yourself so,' said the inspector. 'The person behind the deaths at Dallach Lodge is locked away in Portree. She'll soon pay a heavy price for her crimes.' He nodded at James Kinmuir, who acknowledged the gesture with an inclination of his own head.

'Yes, you're right,' said Isabella, calming down. 'Sorry, it's all been such a terrible strain. Not as much as what you've had to go through, Mr Kinmuir. All the same I—'

'I understand,' said James, who looked as though he had finally forgiven Isabella Frith-Stratton and her sister and perhaps even the rest of us for coming to Dallach Lodge to watch the punishment of his uncle. If he had been short with me or had behaved oddly, I had to tell myself it was because he believed that I too had travelled to Skye for the same purpose. 'I'm sorry for any harsh words I might have spoken

ANDREW WILSON

in the heat of the moment. As you can imagine, finding out about those letters was a terrible shock.'

'I apologise for any distress I might have caused you,' I said to him. After all, I still had to play the part. 'If you need any help with anything – the funeral arrangements, the flowers and suchlike, do please tell me.'

'I think I can manage,' he said sharply. So perhaps he had not forgiven me for the part he believed I had played in all of this.

'That's extremely kind of you,' said Rufus Phillips, smiling warmly at me. 'I'm sure James appreciates your offer. Don't you, James?'

James Kinmuir forced himself to smile. 'Yes, yes, I do,' he muttered. 'Most kind.' But I knew that he did not mean it.

'I hope you don't mind me asking, but how do you feel about Miss Passerini now?' I asked.

'In what regard?' answered James.

'The person who killed your uncle and great-aunt was a relative of yours,' I said.

'As far as I'm concerned she's not related to me,' he replied. 'She has forfeited her right to be part of this family.'

Rufus stretched out and placed a hand on his friend's shoulder. The young man had such delicate hands and really quite graceful fingers. The hands of an artist.

'I wish she'd never come to this house,' said James. 'I wish she'd never been born.'

At that moment the door to the drawing room opened. Dr Fitzpatrick stood there sombre-faced, a messenger bearing bad news. The room went quiet as we all turned our heads in his direction, apart from Isabella Frith-Stratton, who rushed towards him.

'Please sit down, miss,' said the doctor. 'I'm sure it's for the best.' He took Isabella's hand and led her to a chair.

'What do you mean?' she cried.

'I'm not sure how to tell you all this,' said the doctor. 'But, from my preliminary examination, it seems as though Mr Peterson has been poisoned.'

'I knew it!' said Isabella. 'What did I tell you? Doctor, please tell me that Simon will be all right. He will recover?'

'It's difficult to know in cases such as these,' said Dr Fitzpatrick. 'He's a strong young man, but his system has been weakened. He's suffering from a range of symptoms. Stomach cramps, bloody . . . well, certain gastric problems. Dizziness and convulsions too.'

'I don't understand. You say he's been poisoned?' asked James Kinmuir. He looked as though the life had been sucked from him. No doubt he was thinking, *Please not another death, not in my house.*

'Yes, it looks like arsenic to me,' said the doctor.

The room went silent as the enormity of the statement sank in.

'But that means – that means that if Simon has been p-poisoned, then . . .' said Isabella Frith-Stratton, choking back the tears. 'Then Miss Passerini may not be . . . the murderer.' Her own words terrified her. She looked around the room. Her eyes, filled with tears and hatred, came to settle on me. She did not say anything, but her face told the whole story.

She thought I was the killer.

Chapter Thirty-five

'Now, let's not be hasty and jump to any conclusions,' said Inspector Hawkins. 'Even if Mr Peterson has been poisoned, that does not mean Miss Passerini is innocent of these crimes.'

His statement was immediately shouted down as several people spoke at once.

'I'll be damned,' said Rufus Phillips.

'It doesn't make sense,' cried Isabella.

'The murderer must be still in the house,' said May.

'I'm sure it's that awful butler,' said Mrs Buchanan. 'Always sneaking around. Did you see the way his hand was shaking at dinner? Spilt half the soup down my beautiful dress.'

'I thought all this was over,' said James Kinmuir as he slumped back into his chair. 'I'm not sure if I can bear it much longer.'

The inspector tried to take charge. 'Please calm yourselves,' he said, raising a hand as if he were a schoolmaster trying to quieten a room of unruly children. 'First of all, is anyone else feeling sick?'

May Frith-Stratton was the only one in the group who admitted to feeling nauseous, but after consultation with her sister she admitted that this was probably due to witnessing the unpleasant scene at dinner.

'Fitzpatrick,' asked the inspector, 'how certain are you that this is indeed a case of arsenical poisoning?'

'There are tests that will need to be done to confirm it, but all the symptoms seem to indicate ingestion of arsenic.'

'But I'm right in saying that the symptoms of arsenic poisoning are often similar to those of a stomach upset? We don't need to go into detail, not in front of the ladies, but—'

'They are similar, yes. But it's the severity of the symptoms, and the rather sudden way that Mr Peterson reacted, that makes me suspect arsenic.'

Hawkins was determined to make his point. 'So at this stage it's merely a *suspicion*, not a certainty?'

'If you put it like that, yes, but—'

'Well, let's keep an open mind, shall we?' said the inspector in a rather patronising manner. 'We will examine the soup and the wine and carry out some other tests that could take a few days. Once we have the results back, perhaps then we can decide whether it's a case of arsenical poisoning or a severe attack of gastritis.'

Dr Fitzpatrick did not take kindly to the inspector's tone of voice and, in turn, his response was sharp and to the point. 'Mr Peterson may not be around when the test results come back.'

'You don't mean that—'

'We need to get him to the hospital in Portree as quickly as possible. I'm afraid it's touch and go.'

Dr Fitzpatrick decided that the quickest way to get Mr Peterson to Portree would be to take him in his own car. He asked Davison, James Kinmuir and Rufus Phillips if they would help carry his patient down the stairs.

A few minutes later, Mr Peterson, with eyes closed and looking pale and near death, was brought down on a make-shift stretcher and placed in the back of Dr Fitzpatrick's car. The inspector, Rufus Phillips, James Kinmuir, Davison and I remained outside, looking up at the stars. Nobody spoke. All we could hear was the sound of the engine, the gentle water lapping at the side of the sea loch and the cry of a distant bird on the moor. As the car started to pull away, an odd noise came from the vehicle.

'That's strange,' said Davison.

'What's that?' asked the inspector.

They were both looking down at the car. Dr Fitzpatrick stuck his head out of the window and tried to move the car once more.

'There's something wrong with this damned car,' he said.

'We need some light here!' shouted James. 'Simkins!'

A moment later the butler ran out of the house with an oil lamp.

'Point it down here,' ordered Hawkins.

The butler shone the light onto the front tyre at the right-hand side of the car. The rubber had been slashed to ribbons.

'My God,' said Dr Fitzpatrick, as he got out of the car.

'Check the other tyres,' said Hawkins.

Each pocket of light told the same story: all four tyres had been punctured.

'When did you last use the car?' Davison asked Dr Fitzpatrick.

'It was yesterday, when I returned here after finishing Mrs Kinmuir's post-mortem.'

'And it was running well?' asked the inspector.

'Yes, of course,' said the doctor. 'Look – I haven't got much time. Peterson's life is at stake. Would you mind if I borrowed one of yours?'

'Be my guest,' said James. 'The easiest thing would be to bring it round and then we can lift Peterson from the back seat straight into the second car. I'll go with you.'

James led the doctor and the inspector to the side of the house, near the old stables, where the other cars were parked.

As Davison and I followed them at a safe distance, we breathed in the peaty, damp air.

I whispered, 'What do you think's going on?'

'I have my suspicions,' he said. 'I think the killer didn't want Fitzpatrick or Peterson to leave the house. And if I'm proved right, then ...'

Another cry came from the stable block. 'My car's been attacked too!' It was James Kinmuir.

We ran towards the three men and into a pool of light cast from an outside lamp. Hawkins, Kinmuir and Fitzpatrick looked like ghosts.

'Who would do such a thing?' asked James.

'Here, let's check the others,' said Hawkins.

The three men went from car to car, from tyre to tyre. Each of the vehicles had been damaged. Someone had taken a knife to the tyres, leaving them in shreds.

'It's impossible to drive any of these cars,' said the doctor.

'What am I going to do about Peterson? If I don't get him to a hospital then it's highly likely he will die. If there were still horses stabled here I could have used one of those . . .' He thought for a moment. 'I know – the boat. I could put him in that and take him to the next estate along, to the MacLeods. We could use their car to take him to Portree.'

We ran from the stables to the boathouse on the edge of the sea loch. But we were met by another scene of destruction. The bottom of the wooden boat had been smashed in.

'What on earth is going on?' cried James Kinmuir.

'Perhaps we can get someone to come here?' I suggested. 'An ambulance or at least another doctor?'

'I've a colleague in Portree who might be able to help,' said the doctor. 'But, as I say, we haven't got much time.'

We ran back to the house and the doctor immediately rushed to the telephone table. He picked up the receiver, placed it down again, and repeated this procedure a couple of times before he reached down behind the table and pulled up the wire.

'I don't believe it,' he said as he raised his hand to reveal that the wire had been cut.

James grabbed the telephone wire from the doctor's hand. 'Is this some kind of awful joke?'

'No, I don't think it is,' said the inspector, who was beginning to understand the enormity of his mistakes. All the carefully thought out deductions that he had assembled into a seemingly indestructible edifice began to crumble before his eyes. 'Dr Fitzpatrick, go and see to Mr Peterson. Davison, Kinmuir, Phillips – can you help to bring him back into the house? And don't leave him alone for a moment.'

The men did as he said. At that moment, Mrs Buchanan drifted down the stairs, closely followed by the Frith-Stratton sisters. The women had not been told about the slashed tyres on the car, nor about the telephone. But they demanded that they should all be allowed to leave. It was clear there was a killer on the loose. There had already been two murders and one poisoning resulting in near or certain death, and it was unreasonable that the women should spend another moment in the house.

'I know it's late, but I don't see why we can't leave,' said Mrs Buchanan. 'We may not be able to find anywhere to sleep, but I'd rather take my chances and lay my head down in the back of a car than risk my life by staying here.'

The Frith-Stratton sisters clucked in agreement.

'I don't think that will be— ' began the inspector.

'I don't see why not,' said the actress, using the force of personality and her well-practised performance skills to try to outwit the detective. 'After all, your own logic would seem to support my point of view. You said yourself, inspector, that you believe Miss Passerini is to blame for the original crimes. And you also said that you didn't believe that Mr Peterson had been poisoned. If you still stand by these two opinions then you yourself should not object to us going. I know you still want us to stay on the island, and of course I can understand that, but there really is no reason for us to remain in this damned place.'

'If you let me explain,' pleaded the inspector. 'You see, certain circumstances have come to light which mean that—'

'I don't want to stay in this house a moment longer,' said

Isabella. 'I want to go to Portree. To be near Simon. To watch over him. To make sure he gets the best care available.'

'I'm afraid that won't be possible,' said Hawkins, raising his hand to stop further objections. 'You see, Mr Peterson—'

And then the stretcher being carried by Kinmuir, Phillips and Davison, and bearing an unconscious Simon Peterson, appeared at the door, closely followed by the doctor.

'What the—' said Isabella, before she fell back onto the stairs. 'He's not . . .?'

'No, but he's not far off,' said the doctor. 'The cars have been sabotaged so we have to treat him here. Let's get him back upstairs, into his own bedroom. I can keep a close eye on him there. Mrs Christie? Did you say you were a nurse in the war?'

'Yes, that's right,' I said.

'Perhaps you wouldn't mind helping me?'

'Of course, doctor,' I said.

'No, not her,' said Isabella. 'Anyone but her.'

'I can assure you that Mrs Christie will do her utmost to help Mr Peterson pull through,' said the doctor.

But the assurance did nothing to convince Isabella Frith-Stratton.

'I still don't understand – what happened to the cars?' asked Mrs Buchanan. 'Inspector – please tell us what is going on.'

The inspector cleared his throat before he spoke. 'All the cars have had their tyres slashed. We thought about taking the boat out, but that too has been vandalised. We tried to telephone, but it seems the wire has been cut.'

'I must go and see my beautiful Rolls,' said Mrs Buchanan.

'Who would want to damage it? It was a gift from this director who, after my run of—'

'I'm sorry, Mrs Buchanan, but I think there are a few things more important than your precious car, even if it is a Rolls-Royce,' said the inspector.

'Well, I've never been spoken to—'

'You're not going out and neither is anybody else.' The inspector was taking control. He thought quickly as he ran through everything that needed to be done. 'Simkins, after I've checked that everyone is inside, lock the doors. Make sure the windows are secure, too. Mr Kinmuir, when you return from upstairs, tell me where the guns are kept and if there is a lock on the door. And if so, who might have keys to that room.'

A sense of panic was rising in the hall. Dr Fitzpatrick could not quite take in the inspector's words. Isabella Frith-Stratton was on the verge of a nervous collapse, while her sister looked like a frightened child. Mrs Buchanan raged with a silent fury. James Kinmuir, unsteady on his feet, struggled as he continued to hold the top end of the stretcher that bore Mr Peterson up the stairs, and it was obvious that his friend, now red in the face, and Davison were taking the majority of the weight at the bottom.

'There is no doubt about it,' said Hawkins. 'There's a murderer in our midst and tonight I am determined to catch him.'

And so, as the doors were locked, Dallach Lodge once more became a prison from which none of us could escape.

Chapter Thirty-six

'I don't like this,' whispered Davison to me when he returned to the hall after carrying Mr Peterson upstairs.

'Neither do I,' I said, making sure that nobody could hear our conversation. The inspector had gone down to the kitchens to try to explain the events to the servants, while the rest of the group were still discussing what had happened to the cars and the telephone wire. 'But thinking about it, the situation might well work to our advantage.'

'In what way?' Davison asked.

'I would assume that the killer, or killers, will be experiencing a great sense of panic now,' I explained. 'They won't quite know what is happening. We know that the poisoning of Mr Peterson was not part of their plan. It is in this state of mind that they are likely to make a mistake and that's how and when we'll catch them. Listen, I haven't got much time before I have to go to Mr Peterson's room to pretend to nurse him through the night. But we need to find Simkins and discover why he's been acting so queerly. One moment he's a bag of nerves and the next he's behaving in a very bullish manner, as if overly confident about his future.'

'You think he knows something about what's been going on?'

'I'm not sure, but I'd say so,' I said.

'He passed me on the stairs as we were carrying Peterson up to his room,' said Davison. 'Let's go up and see if we can find him.'

We slipped away and made our way up to the first floor. We checked the corridor and some of the open rooms before realising that Simkins must have gone up to the attic. We found him just as he was about to disappear into his own room.

'Excuse me, Simkins,' said Davison. 'I say, terrible business this, isn't it? I wonder if we could ask you a few questions?'

Davison's request was met by nothing but a shifty look. It was clear the butler thought he had fulfilled his duties for the night and no doubt he wanted to escape into his room where he could further indulge his love of drink.

'Perhaps we could have a quiet word with you?' I said.

'What's it about?'

His tone was offhand, bordering on the rude, but I chose to ignore his manner.

'You see, Simkins, I have been worrying about what will happen to some of the servants after the house is sold,' I began. 'I've been watching you closely and it can't have been easy dealing with everything that's gone on here at the lodge. But the long and short of it is, Mr Davison and I have been most impressed with how you've handled everything. You've remained calm and collected throughout. I wondered whether, well, whether you'd consider taking a position as a butler in my house?'

It was obvious that the question caught him off guard. Simkins looked astonished that anyone would offer him such a kindness.

'It's very nice of you, ma'am, indeed it is, but after I leave here I won't be seeking further employment.'

'You won't?' I asked.

'No, ma'am, indeed I won't,' he replied.

'But surely you're not old enough to retire?' asked Davison. 'And the small legacy left to you by the late Mr Kinmuir is hardly a fortune, that's if it ever gets paid to you.'

Simkins, now more rat-like than ever, was clearly in no mood to elaborate and tried to scuttle into his room.

'Just a moment,' said Davison. 'One other thing.'

'Yes, sir?' he said, sighing.

'Do you know anything about this business, anything that hasn't been told to the police?' asked Davison. 'About the murders?'

'What do you mean?' Simkins replied. 'I don't know a thing. And if that's all, then goodnight.'

Davison wedged his foot in the door just as Simkins was about to close it.

'What are you doing?' asked Simkins, clearly frightened now. He tried to force the door closed, but Davison's strength proved too great.

'Just trying to get to the bottom of your lies,' said Davison, pushing his way into the room.

'I'll be telling Mr Kinmuir about this, just you wait,' Simkins said.

'I hope you will, and while you're at it, you can tell him, and the inspector, everything else you know,' said Davison.

I stepped forwards, hoping to calm the situation and gain the butler's trust. 'You see, Simkins, as I said, I've admired your discretion and the way you've behaved during what must have been a very stressful time. But perhaps there are certain occasions when one's discretion and tact have to be put aside for the greater good. Do you understand what I'm saying?'

His eyes continued to look hostile and frightened.

'I don't doubt you're feeling rather alarmed by what Mr Davison is asking but please, if you do know anything – anything at all – about what's gone on here at the lodge, I beg you to share it with us.'

Again he remained silent. And so it was Davison's turn to use his particular method that he believed brought results. In a flash, he locked the door and pushed Simkins against the wall with a force that took the wind out of the man. He grabbed the butler's throat and began to press down hard on his neck.

'Be assured I can – and I will – get this information out of you,' whispered Davison into Simkins's ear. 'In whichever way I consider necessary.'

Simkins's face reddened as he gasped for breath. A horrible choking noise was coming from his throat and his eyes began to bulge. I was worried how far Davison would go in his search for the truth – surely he wouldn't kill the man? – and I was about to beg him to release the butler when he finally pushed him away in disgust. Simkins tried to steady himself, but he fell backwards onto the foot of his brass bed.

I went over to try to help him to his feet. 'I'm sorry about that, Simkins. Here …' I offered my hand, but the butler turned his face away from me as he pushed himself upwards using the frame of the bed. 'Listen, it's very important. I think I know what's been going on. The reason why you don't need another job is because you've come into a certain amount of money, isn't it? Or at least you believe you are soon going to do so.'

At this Simkins looked as shocked as if I had slapped him around the face.

'I'm right, aren't I?'

He said nothing and so I continued. 'I believe you know who the killer is and although I would rather not use the word blackmail – such an ugly word, don't you think – let's just say I think you've come to a mutual understanding with someone and certain financial benefits are due to come your way.'

'I don't know what you're talking about,' Simkins replied, straightening his shirt and tie.

'Simkins, don't play the fool with us,' said Davison. 'It's too dangerous a game.'

'The only dangerous thing around here is you,' said Simkins, feeling more certain of himself again. 'Who do you think you are, coming in here and behaving like that? It's not right, I tell you.'

'Simkins, I'm pleading with you,' I said. 'If you don't tell us what you know then you could be putting your life at risk.'

For a moment, a look of fear haunted his eyes before he dismissed my comment with a sneer and an unpleasant laugh. 'I think you've both lost your minds,' he said. 'And now I'd like you to leave my room.'

Davison ignored him and began to look around the butler's meagre quarters. He opened a small chest of drawers
and, as he searched through Simkins's belongings, began to
toss out the man's undergarments.

'Stop! You can't do that!' shouted Simkins.

'Agatha – look for anything that might be useful. Letters.
A diary,' said Davison.

As Simkins turned to try to stop me, Davison unearthed
two full whisky bottles in the bottom drawer, hidden away
among some clothes.

'This looks interesting,' said Davison, walking over to
the sink with one of the bottles. 'I hope you haven't taken to
pilfering these from your employer.'

Simkins moved towards Davison to try to stop him from
pouring his precious whisky down the sink while I searched
the room for anything of interest. By his bed I found a Latin
primer, inside of which were two sheets of paper covered
in handwriting. Perhaps these held a clue to the *passer* or
sparrow mystery. But as I snatched them up and placed them
inside my handbag Simkins turned and saw me.

'Give those back to me!' he demanded, his eyes full of
fury. He launched himself towards me. 'What do you think
you are doing?'

'What are you doing with a Latin primer?' I asked.

'Can't a man try to better himself?' said Simkins as he
reached out and grabbed my handbag.

'Leave her alone!' said Davison, who put the whisky bottles on top of the chest of drawers and came over to my aid.
'I say, Simkins, that's enough!'

But the butler had passed the point of no return. 'Coming

in here, accusing me of all sorts. Looking through my things, throwing them all about the place and trying to take my papers away.'

'It was simply a misunderstanding – here, let me find them,' I said, as I tried to hold on to my bag.

'Misunderstanding indeed!' he said, as he finally wrenched the bag from me. 'And there I was thinking that you were a nice lady offering me a job in your house. In truth, there was no job in your house, was there?'

'I'm sure we can come to some arrangement,' I said.

'Give Mrs Christie her handbag,' insisted Davison.

'Just as soon as I retrieve what is rightfully mine,' said Simkins as his fingers plunged into my bag. But instead of finding his sheets of paper or his primer he pulled out one of my notebooks.

'Please give me that,' I said, in as reasonable a voice as I could muster.

'Just a moment,' Simkins said. He opened the notebook and, as he began to read through it, smiled to himself. 'Now, this sheds a new light on proceedings, doesn't it?'

'You don't know what you're saying,' said Davison.

'Don't I just?' His eyes lit up with relish as he read what I had written about the case of Dallach Lodge. 'I know someone who will pay good money for this.'

'I'm sure you do,' I said. 'Now, Simkins, if you could please return that, I would be most grateful. We won't say any more about today and we can part on good terms.'

'I've always believed that expression – what is it? – *Fortune favours the brave*,' he said, fixing me with a nasty smile. 'I know, why don't we come to a compromise?'

I SAW HIM DIE

'Don't be so ridiculous,' said Davison. 'Now, I warn you, give the lady back her bag.'

'She can have it,' he said, as he let it drop to the floor.

'And the notebook?' I asked.

'I'm keeping hold of this,' he said. 'I'm sure it makes for very juicy reading all right.'

'Come on, man,' said Davison. 'You don't know what you're getting involved with here.'

'Don't I?' he replied. 'You'd be surprised. Once all this is over, I reckon I'll be set up for life.'

Davison lunged towards him and, with his right hand, punched him in the face, while with his left he grabbed the notebook. I heard a ripping sound as Simkins's fingers formed themselves into a claw around the paper. Davison took possession of the notebook, but a few pages, torn in half, remained in the butler's grip. At that moment, we heard someone calling up the stairs.

'Mrs Christie? Davison?' It was the inspector. 'Simkins? Where the hell are you?'

'We'd better go,' said Davison.

'And what about the room?' I asked.

'We've got no time to clear it up,' said Davison.

'And Simkins?'

'We'll have to leave him,' he said.

I bent down to try to retrieve the pages ripped from my notebook, but Simkins, his nose now bleeding, held them close to his chest. There was a knock at the door.

'Simkins?' the inspector called. 'Open the door!'

'Give me those pages,' I hissed.

Simkins returned my request with a look of pure hatred.

He was about to say something when the inspector knocked at the door again.

'What's going on in there?' he said.

The three of us looked at each other, frozen in a moment of nervousness, indecision and panic. I needed to draw upon my imagination to come up with a explanation for the situation. And I had seconds in which to do so.

'Inspector, thank goodness you've come ...' I said, going to open the door. 'If you could help us ... that would be most kind.'

Davison and Simkins looked slightly astonished, as if they were unsure about what I would say next. At that moment, so was I.

As he entered the room Hawkins was taken aback by its appearance, the contents of the drawers strewn across the floor, the whisky bottles and the state of Simkins's face. I looked at the scene through his eyes and an idea came to me.

'I'm afraid we came across a rather inebriated Simkins earlier,' I said. 'As you can see, it seems as though he's been having quite a time of it with the whisky bottle. I suppose it's the stress of all that's happened here, the poor man.'

'Yes, I can see that,' said Hawkins. 'I realise things have been difficult, but this won't do, Simkins. We need you to remain alert. God knows what's going to happen tonight. Your nose is bleeding. What did you do, man? Fall down drunk?'

Simkins nodded his head meekly.

'I'm thinking that it's probably best for James Kinmùir not to know about this,' Davison said. 'He's got enough to worry about at the moment.'

'Yes, you're probably right,' said Hawkins. 'But this must not happen again.' He looked around the room. 'Simkins, get your quarters into some kind of order. It's a disgrace.' He turned to us. 'Mrs Christie, Dr Fitzpatrick is looking for you. And Davison, if you could come with me, I want to ask your opinion about what tool might have been used to slash those car tyres.'

As we stepped out of the room Davison and I looked at one another with relief. Although Davison did his best to disguise it, there was also an element of fear in his eyes. Seeing his expression did nothing to calm my own nerves. But we had no choice. It was too late to turn back now.

Chapter Thirty-seven

After discussing the issue of the slashed car tyres with Davison, the inspector gave orders for everyone to go to bed and lock their doors. He would sit outside Mr Peterson's room while Dr Fitzpatrick and I would tend to the patient's needs. I would have liked to have been free to talk more to Davison and move around the house at will – indeed, I wanted to try to retrieve from Simkins's room those pages torn from my notebook – but it was essential to stick to our plan. Everyone at the lodge, including Inspector Hawkins, had to believe that Mr Peterson had been poisoned and was on the point of death. Only the doctor, Peterson, Davison and I were in on the plan.

Before being incarcerated in Mr Peterson's room for the night, the doctor and I made sure we had an ample supply of buckets, towels and water so that we could deal with the unpleasant effects of our patient's condition. The next morning I planned to take the buckets, covered with towels, and dispose of the contents in the nearby lavatory. Inside my handbag I had, of course, an abundant supply of other substances that could render a man unconscious, if not dead, in a matter of minutes. If Hawkins – or any other person – did try anything during the night I would be ready.

As I turned the key in the lock I gave a look of assurance first to Dr Fitzpatrick and then to Mr Peterson, who was lying in bed.

'You both did wonderfully,' I whispered. 'We can't talk much, because the inspector may be listening at the door.' I moved over towards the bed and asked Mr Peterson, 'Are you still feeling sick?'

He opened his eyes slightly and nodded his head. 'It was very noble of you to take that emetic, but its effects should soon start to wear off,' I said softly.

'Anything that can help Vivienne,' he said in a voice so slight that only I could hear. I held his hand as he closed his eyes once more.

I moved back towards the door and, in case anybody was listening, started to talk loudly to the doctor about the worries I had about Mr Peterson's condition. Dr Fitzpatrick, in turn, went along with the charade and outlined the man's symptoms and his poor prognosis before describing, in detail, how I should nurse him throughout the night. We talked at length about the Marsh test for detecting arsenic – named after the chemist James Marsh, who outlined his method in 1836 – and how one could use activated charcoal to treat the poison. At intervals we would stand up and slosh water from one bucket to the next and, occasionally, just as we were lapsing into silence, Mr Peterson would wake up and retch into a pan by his bed. Throughout the night we kept the window open to dispel the room's unpleasant odours.

I listened out for signs of disturbance in the house, but the hours of darkness seemed to pass without incident. I took advantage of the quiet to read through the pages I had taken from Simkins's room. It looked as though the butler had been trying to compose a blackmail letter. Certain sentences had been written down – 'If you do not do what I ask then there will be consequences for you' – before being reworked and reworded – 'Serious consequences will result from a failure to meet my demands.' But to whom had he been writing? I searched through the fragments of sentences for a clue, but there was no hint of a name.

I flicked through my notebook and saw the jagged edges of the missing pages wrenched out by Simkins. Fortunately, I didn't think I had written anything too revealing on them. I continued to read my observations about the case. I scribbled down a few random thoughts and used a series of arrows and question marks to help visualise the complex puzzle that lay before me. I wrote down the possible motives for each of my suspects. Once more, I studied the nursery rhyme of *Who Killed Cock Robin?* My mind went over the facts of the murders and how they fitted into the tale. I thought of all the different birds and creatures in the story. Cock Robin – that was the first victim, Robin Kinmuir. The sparrow was, by virtue of her name, Vivienne Passerini, the killer. Then there was the fly, who had witnessed the crime. That surely had to be old Mrs Kinmuir who, before her own murder, had said those words to me: *L'ho visto morire.* But she had been blind and could not see.

What was it that *I* could not see? I felt there was some-thing so obvious, just out of reach, sitting on the edge of my peripheral vision. I closed my eyes, making myself blind to the world. Darkness shrouded me. Faces loomed out of the gloom, a grotesque line-up of people who had come to Dallach Lodge. The Frith-Stratton sisters. Simon Peterson. Vivienne Passerini. All of them had said they had wanted to see Robin Kinmuir be punished and been drawn to Skye to witness his suffering. Mrs Buchanan. Dr Fitzpatrick. I had discovered they were bound by something that had happened in the past, relating to the death of Kinmuir's first wife, Catherine. Inspector Hawkins's family had a historic hatred of the Kinmuir clan. James Kinmuir, the man who had shot his uncle, would only inherit an enormous debt. Rufus Phillips had nothing in his past to connect him to the Kinmuirs other than his friendship with James. And then there was Simkins, who had more or less admitted he knew something of the murders.

I thought of Vivienne Passerini, locked up in that cell in Portree. Hawkins had her down as a cold-blooded killer. I was keen to clear her name, believing that she had been framed for the murders. But what if she was behind the crimes all along? Had she planted false evidence which would clear her? After all, if she stood trial and was then acquitted, she could never be found guilty of the murder again. What were the other possibilities? I ran through yet more permutations, but none seemed to make sense.

I desperately needed sleep but knew I could not risk it. I walked over to the open window to get some fresh air. In the distance, across the water from Skye, the dawn was breaking, sending delicate shards of pink light across the black mountains of the Knoydart Peninsula.

I went over to check on Mr Peterson. He opened his eyes and asked for a sip of water. The effects of the emetic were beginning to wear off, but he knew that he would have to play his designated role, that of a dead man, for some time yet. Soon, as we had agreed, Dr Fitzpatrick would announce to everyone in the house that, in the early hours of the morning, Mr Peterson had passed away. Of course, nobody – not even the inspector – would be allowed in to view the body. The doctor had his story ready. Dr Fitzpatrick would tell them that the corpse was in no fit state to be seen. In an effort to save Mr Peterson, he had had to perform a number of procedures which had left the body in a rather distressing condition. Also, he could not guarantee that anyone stepping into the room would be immune from picking up something nasty, possibly even a trace of the poison itself. Mr Peterson's death throes had been particularly violent and, if people really wanted to know, he could detail the unpleasant nature of the man's final moments.

I went over to Dr Fitzpatrick and placed my hand on his shoulder. The doctor woke up immediately and apologised for having fallen asleep.

'It's time,' I whispered. 'You need to tell everyone that there's been another murder.'

Chapter Thirty-eight

I opened the door to find the inspector's chair empty. The doctor followed me out of Simon's room and I locked the door behind us. The house was quiet and it seemed everyone was still sequestered in their quarters. I wondered what Davison had been doing during the hours of darkness.

Weak light started to creep through some of the east-facing windows of the house. Even though it was August there was something of a chill. I should have brought my shawl with me, I thought to myself, as a shiver played up my spine. I walked down the stairs, but there was no one there.

'Inspector?' Dr Fitzpatrick called out. 'Hawkins – where are you?'

One of the maids, up early to clean the rooms, appeared and told us that the inspector had left the house by the front entrance about ten minutes before. The two Labradors had followed him and Hawkins had said that he would take them for a quick walk. Since the death of their master, the dogs had been at a loss. They spent the day wandering around the house, whining, no doubt hoping to catch a glimpse of their master. But Robin Kinmuir was never coming back. The only time they seemed to perk up, their faces full of hope, was at breakfast when James Kinmuir would give them a piece of sausage meat from his plate. How I wished, as I peered into their sad black eyes, they could tell me what they had seen that day. They were dumb witnesses to the crime, full of knowledge but unable to communicate what they knew.

After I retrieved my coat from the hall I stepped out into the early morning air. Mist swirled around the sea loch and as I stood there, putting on my gabardine, I admired the beauty of the view. The next thing I knew I felt the skin on my neck begin to itch. An insect had bitten me. I recalled that fateful morning when a midge had played its part in the death of Robin Kinmuir. He had taken the top off a midge bite while he was shaving, and the curare on the razor blade had seeped into his bloodstream. Shortly afterwards while on his walk across the moors and after being accidentally shot by his nephew, he had collapsed and died. As I scratched the bite on my neck, I tried to recall who else had mentioned midges. Yes, that very first night I remembered the Frith-Stratton sisters talking about the problem. And one night at dinner, when we were discussing South America and its exotic snakes and spiders, Isabella had said, 'It's bad enough here with these midges. Even if I lived here, I don't suppose I would get used to them. The late Mr Kinmuir was a sufferer, I believe.'

The explanation could be a simple one – she was merely repeating something Kinmuir had said – but could this also be a clue that Isabella had played some part in his murder? After all, the person behind the crime – the one who had smeared the curare on that razor – would have had to have known that Robin Kinmuir had been bitten on the throat by a midge. The Frith-Strattons confessed that they had a motive – the ruination of their father by Robin Kinmuir. But was this the whole picture? Did that confession not mask another, darker story? For all their frumpiness and pathetic attempts to win romance where none existed, there was a strange blankness to the two sisters, particularly May. I thought back to some of my conversations with her and real-ised that she often said things not in a spontaneous manner but by rote, as if she had learnt her lines off by heart.

'Have you been bitten?' asked Dr Fitzpatrick as he saw me scratch my neck.

'Yes, but let's start walking – we need to find the inspec-tor,' I said, using my hand to fan away any other flying insects that might be lurking.

'Hawkins!' cried Dr Fitzpatrick.

'Over here,' answered the inspector.

We ran towards the sound of his voice and found Hawkins standing by the door to the old stable block. The dogs had been tied to a post, but there was a manic look in their eyes as they struggled to free themselves. When the inspector saw me, he raised a hand to indicate I should not proceed. He gestured for the doctor to enter the stable.

'I'm afraid to say that Peterson hasn't made it,' said Dr Fitzpatrick.

'Oh, damn,' said Hawkins.

'We did everything we could to save him, but it was no use,' said the doctor.

'I hope he died an agonising death,' said Hawkins. 'After what he did, he deserved to.'

'What do you mean?' I asked.

'Peterson was the one behind all of this, all the deaths,' said Hawkins. 'I would have liked to have seen him punished for his crimes, but at least it's over now.'

'I'm sorry, I don't understand,' I said.

'The answer's inside this stable and it's not something a lady should see.'

'What do you mean?' I asked. 'What's happened?'

'It's Simkins,' said Hawkins. 'He's hanged himself.'

Although Hawkins tried to stop me, I pushed my way into the stable. The space was dark and gloomy and faintly smelt still of the animals that had once been kept there. Hanging from one of the beams was the body of the butler. His face was bloated and ugly and his tongue lolled out of his mouth. I turned away, not needing to see any more. Simkins was an unpleasant man, no doubt a blackmailer. But he didn't deserve this.

'I was about to cut him down when I heard you calling,' said Hawkins. 'Here, Fitzpatrick, could you help?'

The two men cut the rope and laid Simkins on the ground, next to an empty whisky bottle.

'I found this on the floor near the body,' said the inspector, holding a sheet of paper. 'It's Simkins's suicide note.'

'What does it say?' I asked.

'Let me read it to you,' said Hawkins, clearing his throat.

It's all too much. I can't go on. I can't carry on living like this, knowing what I've done. I hope by poisoning Peterson I can bring an end to this living nightmare. I wish I had never set eyes on him. I should never have taken his money.

He told me that all he wanted to do was give Mr Kinmuir

a bit of a shock. He said that the stuff I was to put on his razor blade was just something to make his face swell up. He wanted the master to be made to look a fool in front of his guests. And he said he would pay me handsomely for it, a sum of two hundred pounds. I didn't know that what I had put on his razor would kill him.

'I tried to argue with Peterson. I told him I would go to the police. But he said that I was the one who had put that poison on the razor blade. And I would be the one who would hang for it. And so I kept quiet. But when he went on to kill old Mrs Kinmuir, I couldn't keep quiet any longer. What had she done to hurt him? But Peterson said he wanted to wipe out the whole lot of the Kinmuirs. He hated the family for what Robin Kinmuir had done to his father. He talked about something in the past in some foreign place that resulted in his father's death. And he said young Mr Kinmuir would be next.

'And then that nice Miss Passerini was arrested for the murders. Peterson pretended to love her, but he framed her for the crimes. He placed an earring belonging to Miss Passerini in Mrs Kinmuir's room and hid that paper knife, the one that had been used to stab the old lady in the back of the neck, among the young lady's things. That was a wicked thing to do. And I couldn't let Miss Passerini hang for a crime she never committed.

'And so I took the matter into my hands. I couldn't live with myself for what had happened. And I couldn't let Peterson commit another murder. I found the poison I put down for the rats and I slipped some of that into his food. I couldn't bear the thought of him being saved and so I slashed

the tyres of all the cars at the lodge, bashed in the bottom of the boat and cut the wire of the telephone.

'I hope he dies. I hope he rots in hell. He deserves to for what he did. And so do I.'

When Hawkins finished he looked up with an expression of finality. It seemed that the letter had explained everything. 'It certainly throws light on why Simkins was in such a state when I saw him with you and Mr Davison yesterday,' said the inspector. 'No wonder he was drinking. After poisoning Peterson, he must have known what he had to do. There was no turning back.'

'Indeed,' I said. 'He was in a very delicate frame of mind.'

'So I suppose this is an end to it, thank goodness,' said the inspector.

'It certainly seems like it,' said Dr Fitzpatrick, continuing to play his part well. 'I suppose the man's conscience got the better of him.'

'And Peterson certainly had me fooled, that's for sure,' said Hawkins. 'All that nonsense of him pretending to care for Miss Passerini when in truth he was framing her. And all for what? Something that had happened in the past.'

'I suppose Peterson must have gone insane,' said Dr Fitzpatrick. 'I've read about such cases.'

'Sins of the father and all that,' said Hawkins rather gloomily. 'Anyway, we can't stand around here. There's lots to do. Someone needs to walk to the nearest house and get a message to Portree. The bodies will have to be taken away. And, of course, Miss Passerini will be freed from her cell.' He paused as he acknowledged that had it not been for Simkins's actions against Peterson and his suicide note, Miss Passerini would probably have hanged. 'I'm going to have to issue a fulsome apology to that young lady. I hope she'll understand that I only went on what the evidence seemed to suggest.'

'I'm sure she'll come round to your point of view,' I said. 'But I suppose she has to come to terms with the greater pain of knowing that she was deceived by someone whom she thought cared for her – Simon Peterson.'

'Yes, that's going to be a hard blow to take,' said Hawkins, folding up Simkins's suicide note and placing it in the inside pocket of his jacket.

'If you wouldn't mind, inspector,' I said, 'could I have a quick look at what Simkins wrote?'

'Yes, of course,' he said, taking it out and passing it over to me.

The note was written in black ink on a sheet of thick, cream-coloured writing paper, probably taken from the desk in the library. I read through it once more. On the face of it, it all made perfect sense. Simkins's account explained the motives for the crimes and how everything fitted together. There were, of course, a few facts that the inspector could not be aware of – it was I who had administered the poison to Mr Peterson; but the poison was not arsenic, merely an emetic, something to make him sick; and, most importantly, Mr Peterson was very much alive.

The one thing that surprised me about the appearance of the note was that its style was messy, with some words trailing off into a scrawl and a most distinctive, curved capital letter 'I'. It was the opposite of Simkins's hand, which was, I knew, neat and tidy and ever so precise.

I had to do everything in my power to keep the surprise

from registering on my face. For the suicide note appeared as though it had been written by me.

'Anything the matter?' asked the inspector, as he untied the dogs and pulled them away from the stable block.

'No, nothing at all,' I said. 'A very sad state of affairs. But as you say, at least it's over now. And Simkins's confession has just come in time to save Miss Passerini's life. It would have been awful if she had hanged and become another of Mr Peterson's victims.'

Hawkins held his hand out for the letter. I hesitated sightly before giving it back. Even if Hawkins was the killer, there was no way he would destroy the suicide note because it cleared him of every last trace of guilt.

Whoever was behind the murders no doubt thought that the note – and that 'suicide' – was a masterstroke. But in fact, I was convinced that it would prove to be the killer's biggest mistake.

I ran through the sequence of events that had occurred at the lodge. At last, it was all beginning to make sense.

Chapter Thirty-nine

Just then we heard the sound of a car approaching the lodge. We rushed to the front of the house and saw Mr Glenelg, the solicitor, and his two assistants emerging from the vehicle. The lawyer who had read Robin Kinmuir's will had returned to undertake the inventory.

'I can't tell you how relieved I am you're here,' said the inspector as he greeted the lawyer. 'The phone line has been cut and the tyres on all the cars have been slashed.' Hawkins then gave his précis of the events of the night, ending with the revelation that Mr Peterson – the man the inspector believed to be behind all the murders – had been killed by his black-mailer, Simkins the butler.

The elderly Mr Glenelg listened to the account with a certain amount of dispassion, but even he, a man whose entire professional life had been spent in the law, was finding it difficult to contain his shock.

'So you mean there have been two *more* deaths?' asked the solicitor.

'Yes, that's right, but I'm pleased to say we can finally

draw a line under the whole sorry business,' said Hawkins. 'We have a suicide note from Simkins which explains everything.' The inspector related how Simkins had slashed the tyres on the cars, smashed the bottom of the boat and cut the telephone wire. 'I made a terrible mistake in arresting Miss Passerini and I need to ask you something. It's essential I take your car to get back to Portree. Not only do I need to oversee the release of Miss Passerini, but I also need to send an ambulance to retrieve the bodies.'

'My, what a night you've had,' said Mr Glenelg with understatement. 'Yes, of course you must take the car. I can start the inventory of the house with MacBrayne and Braes and we should be finished by the end of the day. You'll be back by then, I trust?'

Hawkins assured him that he would. 'And, while you're doing the inventory, could I ask you to avoid the stable block where Simkins hanged himself and the room on the first floor? Yes, that one there,' he said, pointing to the room at the front of the house which still had its window open. 'Peterson died in there. Once the bodies have been removed you can come back and check the rooms.'

'Very well,' said the solicitor.

The arrival of the car had drawn the other guests out of the lodge. As James came over to show Mr Glenelg and his two men into the house, the inspector took Kinmuir to one side, passed the dogs to him and informed him of the latest developments. First, he told him of Peterson's death in the night and then of Simkins's suicide and confession. Then, as Hawkins revealed to him that Peterson was the murderer and that he had been poisoned by Simkins, James's face went ashen.

'So this is well and truly over now?' asked Kinmuir.

'Yes, it seems so, sir,' answered the inspector.

'Well, thank you for your hard work,' said Kinmuir. 'The strain of living with all of . . . this, well, it has taken its toll on everyone and I'm glad that the person who killed my uncle and great-aunt has been identified. But I can't believe it was Peterson.'

'Shame he didn't hang for his crimes,' said Hawkins. 'That's my only regret. That and falsely accusing Miss Passerini, of course.'

'So the blaggard had the gall to show the young woman some affection and then frame her?' asked Kinmuir. 'I can't imagine what she will feel when she discovers the truth about him. And really, I can't get over Simkins's part in all of this. But at least he did the honourable thing, I suppose.'

James went over to the group by the door and told them about the horrific events of the night. By the time I joined them, Isabella was weeping into a handkerchief, mourning the loss of a man she adored but whom she now knew to be a murderer. Her sister was trying to comfort her, but the words were meaningless. Mrs Buchanan was telling Rufus Phillips of her suspicions about the butler – there was something unsettling about him, she said, hadn't she always said so? – but she was surprised that someone like Mr Peterson could be behind the crimes. I noticed that Davison was still absent. What was he up to?

I left the group and went inside the house to try to find him. By this time Glenelg and his men were in the drawing room, already busy with their notebooks and ledgers. I went upstairs and checked that the door to Mr Peterson's room was still locked – it was essential for everyone to believe that not only was he dead but that he was guilty of the murders – before making my way to Davison's quarters. I knocked gently on the door.

'Davison? It's Agatha.'

He opened the door and ushered me inside. His face was grave.

'What have you been doing?' I asked. 'So much has happened – Simkins is dead.'

'I know,' he said. 'I was listening at the open window. But tell me everything.'

'His body was found hanging in the stables,' I continued. 'It was another murder. By his body there was a suicide note, confessing to his part in the crimes and telling how Mr Peterson had duped him into placing the curare on Robin Kinmuir's razor blade. According to the note, Simkins couldn't live with himself any longer and so he poisoned Mr Peterson, the man behind the murders of Robin Kinmuir and old Mrs Kinmuir. But the interesting thing, in addition to the contents of the note, is the style of the letter itself.' I took a deep breath. 'You see, it was written in my handwriting.'

'Now, that is fascinating.' Davison's eyes lit up. 'Yes, I can see now it's all beginning to fit into place. And there's something I need to tell you, too. About what I saw last night.'

Chapter Forty

There was an atmosphere of liberation about the lodge. Most of the guests smiled to themselves as they put the finishing touches to their packing and discussed their final travel arrangements with one another, content in the knowledge that soon they would be leaving this house of death.

There were a number of people who did not look in such good spirits, however. In between bouts of weeping, Isabella insisted that she wanted to see Mr Peterson's body, a request that was refused by the doctor on the grounds that there was a danger of contamination. James Kinmuir watched with sadness as Mr Glenelg and his two men went around the house, noting down everything for their inventory: the silverware, the pictures on the walls, the furniture, carpets, glasses, bottles of wine and whisky, candlesticks, serving bowls, lamps, picture frames, and every other little worthless knick-knack. In an effort to cheer James up, Rufus Phillips suggested that they take the dogs for a quick walk. There was little point in witnessing the inventory – each valued family memento reduced to a mere scribble in a ledger – and surely they could do with a spot of fresh air. The two men disappeared, together with the Labradors, back up to the moor where Robin Kinmuir had died.

The inspector took Mr Glenelg's car and headed to Portree. After what Davison had witnessed, we were confident that Hawkins was not responsible for the deaths at Dallach Lodge. We had a good idea as to who was behind the murders, but we still needed a final piece of evidence. And so we began to plot, talking in Davison's room of how best to bring about a satisfactory conclusion. As we discussed the case, and how to force the identity of the killer out into the open, I was reminded of the thrill I felt when I was coming to the end of writing one of my novels. Indeed, the skills that I used to write my books – embedding certain clues into sentences so that they seemed almost invisible, working out the various strands of the plot so that they came together at the end, having an intuitive feel for the strengths and weaknesses of a particular personality – came to the fore now. Davison sat back as I held forth, discussing the possible options and possibilities. As I talked I felt anger driving me, anger at the loss of innocent life. Three people had been murdered – Robin Kinmuir, Veronica Kinmuir, the butler Simkins – there had been an attempt on my life and one woman might have gone to the gallows for crimes she had not committed. It was time for all that to end.

We later emerged from Davison's suite to join the other guests in the drawing room where tea was being served. Although we had gone without lunch, neither of us had much of an appetite. I stood back and watched as Rose Stewart, the maid who had found Mrs Kinmuir's body, began to pour the tea. Her hands shook as she lifted the teapot and handed around plates of bread and honey, sandwiches and cake. As Rose walked around the room serving the tea, asking if people wanted milk or sugar, I noticed that she looked like a frightened child. No doubt she had heard of Simkins's death, his suicide note, and the crimes and subsequent murder of Mr Peterson, so it was no surprise she looked so anxious. Murder, I knew, did not end with the arrest of a criminal. It continued to poison the lives of those affected by it for years afterwards.

'You can go, Rose,' said James, who had returned from his walk with Rufus. 'We can manage from now on.' He turned to the doctor. 'I'm just so relieved this awful business has finally come to an end. I must say you've done sterling work, Fitzpatrick. Can't have been easy for you, though.'

'No, not at all,' mumbled the doctor.

I could tell that he still felt uncomfortable lying about Mr Peterson.

'Just think,' said Mrs Buchanan, raising a china cup to her lips, 'we will all soon be free from this living nightmare. What a relief it will be to go back to our normal lives. I can get on with my rehearsals. I don't think the prospect of a few months in London ever looked so inviting. Do you know what time the inspector will return to the lodge?'

'I would think he will be here at any moment,' replied the doctor.

'And he'll come with a mechanic or someone who can replace the tyres on our cars?'

'Yes, I think that's his plan,' said the doctor.

I walked over to the table and took a slice of bread and

honey, even though I had no intention of eating it. I turned to Mrs Buchanan and asked, 'Do you intend to leave tonight?'

'Oh yes, just as soon as my Rolls is fixed,' she said. 'I'll probably stay a night in Kyleakin before I travel to the mainland tomorrow.'

At this moment, James Kinmuir and Rufus Phillips came to join us to pour themselves another cup of tea. Kinmuir stretched out his hand towards Mrs Buchanan and bowed his head.

'I know we've never been the best of friends, Mrs Buchanan, but I'd like to part on good terms, if we may?' he said.

Mrs Buchanan looked at him with an icy glare, an expression that could have frozen the heart of any man. But then, just as it seemed the temperature in the room was about to drop to Arctic levels, her face changed. She smiled, lifted her hand towards his and nodded her head in a silent gesture of acceptance.

'Thank you, that means a great deal to me,' said James. 'I know my uncle cared for you deeply and I wish only happiness and health for you.'

The actress did not say anything; she merely blinked, lowered her chin, and allowed herself to be honoured by the young gentlemen before eventually moving away. The scene should have been a touching one, but I knew that it was nothing more than a performance, a sham, like so much else that I had witnessed since I had first arrived at Dallach Lodge. Davison and I went to stand by the windows where I spent a minute or so studying the scene before me.

Here was a drawing room full of respectable people taking

afternoon tea. To an outsider it might appear a perfectly normal gathering. But the guests had endured a horrendous ten days at the lodge. Murder had visited the baronial house, leaving three people dead. But all that was over. The guests were making small talk, discussing their future plans, getting on with their lives. However, some people no longer had lives to enjoy. Robin Kinmuir. Mrs Kinmuir. Simkins, the butler. Robin Kinmuir was a difficult and promiscuous man, but did he deserve to be poisoned, dying among the heather on the moor like a wild animal? Mrs Kinmuir was an old woman who was blind and had lost her faculties. But no one had the right to snuff out her life. And in such a brutal way, too – a paper knife plunged into the back of her neck. And as for Simkins? He was a drunk and a nasty blackmailer, but did that merit such a grisly end? I remembered the gruesome sight that I had seen that morning. That swollen face. His tongue lolling from his mouth . . .

I shivered and drew my shawl around my shoulders.

'Are you cold?' asked Davison.

'Yes, I am, a little,' I said.

'I'll see if I can get one of the servants to light a fire,' he said as he cast me a knowing look, an expression of solidarity and resolve, and left the room. Those words were a signal that the final stages of our plan were about to be put into action.

A minute or so later, Rose Stewart returned to the drawing room and set about making up a fire. Although she must have done the task dozens of times, it was obvious she was finding it difficult. She misjudged the amount of paper and kindling and placed too heavy a log on the pile so that, when she tried to light it, the flames died out. She overcompensated by lighting more matches, but her hands were shaking so much that she dropped each one in the grate. After a number of attempts she cleared the whole thing out and began again, replacing the charred paper and kindling with fresh supplies, then successfully lit a couple of matches and the fire finally began to burn. I went over and thanked her and the girl nodded her head and made a hasty exit from the room. I was pleased that she would be out of the way when things turned nasty. The last thing she needed was to be forced to witness more violence.

As I stood by the fire, enjoying the comforting smell of woodsmoke and letting its gentle warmth caress my fingers, I heard the sound of car engines outside.

'It must be the inspector,' said Rufus Phillips, rushing to the window which looked out to the front of the house.

'And from the look of that van it seems as though our cars are about to get fixed,' said James Kinmuir.

'There's also an ambulance with a stretcher,' said Mrs Buchanan. 'The sooner that devil who did this is out of this house the better.'

'And oh – no, it can't be – but, yes, it is,' said May Frith-Stratton. 'It's Miss Passerini!'

I approached the window to see Vivienne Passerini being helped out of a car by the inspector. Her usual sallow complexion seemed bleached, yet as she walked towards the house she held herself with a certain dignity and composure.

'What on earth does one say to someone who has been falsely accused of murder?' asked Mrs Buchanan, who had been only too keen to believe that Miss Passerini was guilty. 'I do hope she doesn't cause a scene.'

But when Miss Passerini entered the drawing room, accompanied by Inspector Hawkins, she could not have been more stoic. It was obvious that she had suffered and would continue to suffer. Her feelings for Mr Peterson had been real and she would have to come to terms with the news that not only was he dead but that it had been he who had planned the murders at Dallach Lodge. In addition, she would by now have learnt that Peterson had also tried to frame her for the crimes. As she entered, part of me wanted to take her to one side and tell her the truth: that Mr Peterson was alive and was entirely innocent. Of course, I knew I could do no such thing.

'Would you like some tea, Miss Passerini?' asked the inspector. 'Please sit down and let me bring you some.' His tone was obsequious now. 'And what about some bread and honey, or some cake, perhaps?'

'Just a cup of tea, thank you,' she said flatly.

'As I said, I'm terribly sorry for what you've been through,' said the inspector.

Miss Passerini gave him a steely look, before she addressed us all. 'You may as well know that yes, I hated Mr Kinmuir for what he did, how he treated my mother, and I admit I came to this house to watch him suffer.'

She was about to say something else, but she stopped herself and took a vacant space on the sofa by the fire. It seemed as if the young woman had lost weight, but apart from that she seemed in good health. Yet there was a dullness to her emerald eyes, as if the spark of life had been extinguished. An awkward silence filled the room and people looked at everything – the flames of the fire, the pictures on the walls, their own hands or feet – rather than meet the gaze of Miss Passerini.

The silence was broken by Miss Passerini herself; after taking a sip of tea, she said, 'You know I don't believe it.'

'What don't you believe, my dear?' I asked.

'That Simon was behind all of this,' she replied. 'That he could ever do such a terrible thing.'

The inspector cleared his throat. 'I'm afraid, miss, that the evidence suggests quite the contrary. You see, Simkins's suicide note tells us that Peterson planned the whole thing. He is the one who must have sent those letters inviting you all here and I'm afraid to say that if Simkins had not intervened as he did, then you might have hanged. Indeed, if the butler had not taken the very drastic step of poisoning him, Peterson could well have made an attempt on James Kinmuir's life too. Such was his deep hatred of the Kinmuir family that—'

'I realise that it all fits in with the facts, but I still don't accept it,' she said.

'Why not?' asked the inspector.

'Simon's not the kind of man who would behave like that,' she said. 'Someone here must have tampered with my passport and I don't believe it was him. I know – I knew him and ...' Her voice trailed off. 'Sorry, I'm not making sense.' She fell silent.

Hawkins looked at his watch. 'If you'll all excuse me I will go and see to the ... well, I'll go and talk to the chaps who have come to take away the ...' His voice also faded away. 'Mr Kinmuir, everything will soon be dealt with, I promise.'

'Thank you, inspector,' said James Kinmuir. 'I appreciate all the work you've done here.'

I followed the inspector first out to the hallway and then out to the front of the house, where he was met by four uniformed ambulance men carrying two stretchers – one for Simkins, the other for Mr Peterson.

Hawkins spoke directly to the men in a clear voice, devoid of emotion or embarrassment now. Perhaps this was because the inspector had stepped away from the polite atmosphere of the drawing room and felt he could talk freely to fellow professionals, all of whom had witnessed terrible things in the course of their jobs. Or was it because he viewed both Simkins and Mr Peterson as murderers, men who deserved little sympathy? 'The first body is laid out in the stables, that's the hanging,' he said. 'And the second, he's upstairs in his room. He was the murderer, the one who was poisoned, so I'd take extra precautions when handling him.'

As two men manoeuvred past us with a stretcher in order to climb the stairs towards Mr Peterson's room, I asked Hawkins whether I could have a private word. I needed to slow down the proceedings and prevent the uniformed men from fetching Mr Peterson's body.

'Is it very urgent?' he asked. 'As you can see, I've rather got my hands full here.'

'I'm afraid it is,' I said. 'I was just thinking about Miss Passerini and her feelings. I wondered whether you might wait until the young woman is back in her room so she doesn't have to see the stretcher?'

It was obvious the thought had not occurred to him, but he dismissed it. 'I can see your point, but we haven't got time for sensitivities,' he said. 'We need to get the bodies back to Portree as soon as possible. Fitzpatrick will carry out the necessary post-mortems and then I can start on my report.'

'I wouldn't start writing your report straight away,' I said.

'What do you mean?'

'Well, it's just that the situation is a little more complicated than it seems.'

'I've said this before, Mrs Christie, but it's probably worth saying again,' Hawkins said. 'I am very grateful to you and Mr Davison for your help, but it's over now. I'm sorry I didn't listen to your defence of Miss Passerini. I was wrong about that. But the real murderer is dead. Now if you'll excuse me, I really must get on.' He turned to his colleagues. 'Right, follow me. The room you need is just at the top of these—'

But Hawkins never finished his sentence. His mouth dropped open and all colour drained from his face. He looked, as the familiar cliché goes, as if he had seen a ghost. At the top of the stairs stood Simon Peterson, flanked by Davison.

'What the—?' uttered Hawkins under his breath.

The two uniformed men bearing the stretcher backed away down the stairs, unsure what was going on.

'It can't be ... I thought that ...'

'As I said, inspector, the situation is rather more complex than it seems,' I said. But now was not the time for explanations; those would have to come later. Instead, we watched as Simon Peterson, still weak and shaken from the effects of the emetic, made his way down the stairs.

By the time he had reached the bottom the inspector had recovered his composure. 'Simon Peterson, I am arresting you for the murder of Mr Robin Kinmuir and Mrs Veronica Kin—'

'Don't be such a blockhead, Hawkins,' said Davison. 'Peterson's innocent. Surely you can see that?'

'How dare you talk to me like—' Hawkins said.

'Come into the drawing room and we'll explain,' said Davison. 'And you'll be able to catch your murderer.'

Hawkins turned to his uniformed colleagues. 'Stay outside the door and don't let anyone through,' he ordered. He walked up to Simon Peterson and frisked him to check whether he had a gun or a knife or any other kind of weapon hidden on his person. 'I've got no idea what this is all about,' the inspector said to him. 'But you're not going to pull the wool over my eyes so easily. The evidence shows that you are the one behind all of this, and at the moment that's what I believe.'

Davison tried to speak, but Hawkins raised his left hand and shouted him down with the words, 'I know your division, but I'm still the one in charge here.' With his right hand the inspector took a gun from his inside jacket pocket and pointed it at Simon Peterson. 'At the slightest provocation I will not hesitate to shoot.'

Chapter Forty-one

Simon Peterson's appearance in the drawing room provoked cries of astonishment from everyone, most particularly from Isabella Frith-Stratton. She jumped to her feet and was about to run to him, but her sister wisely stopped her. Instead, it was Miss Passerini who flew into his arms.

'Simon, Simon,' she whispered.

'Darling, are you all right?' asked Mr Peterson. 'You look exhausted.'

'Don't worry about me – what about you? I thought you were dead.'

'Well, at times I almost felt like it,' said Mr Peterson. 'You see, I—'

But Davison interrupted. 'I think it's best if you say as little as possible,' he said quietly. 'At least for the moment.'

'Yes, of course,' said Mr Peterson.

'If you could stand to one side, miss, I would be grateful,' said Hawkins.

Miss Passerini was reluctant to move away from the man she thought she had lost. 'I never believed any of the awful things they were saying about you,' she said, still clinging on to him. 'Not one word of it.'

Mr Peterson smiled as he gently detached Miss Passerini and, with some effort, took a couple of steps away from her.

'Doctor, can you explain this?' said James Kinmuir. 'You said this man was dead.'

Dr Fitzpatrick looked down and mumbled something about how he must have misread the signs.

'And, inspector, what is the meaning of bringing a murderer into the drawing room?' continued James. 'You did say, if I'm not mistaken, that Peterson intended to make me his next victim.'

'None of you need worry,' said Hawkins, raising his gun. The sight of the pistol produced another series of gasps. 'If he makes the slightest move he knows that I'll shoot him dead.'

'This is quite ridiculous,' said Mrs Buchanan. 'I've seen enough drama on the stage without witnessing any more here. I'm leaving.'

But as she made a move towards the door, Davison stood in front of it, blocking her path.

'If you'd be so kind as to step aside,' she said. The request may have been a polite one, but her eyes were full of fire.

Davison remained fixed to the spot.

'I don't know if you heard me, but I intend to leave this wretched place,' she said. 'My bags are packed and I'm sure my Rolls must be ready by now.'

'I'm afraid you are going to have to stay here,' said Davison.

'And what authority do you have to tell me what I can and can't do?' asked Mrs Buchanan. 'Really, you're just too tiresome for words. Now step aside.'

Davison lent forwards and whispered something in her ear. Whatever he said – something about his true identity as a secret intelligence officer, no doubt – stopped Mrs Buchanan in her tracks. She was desperate to save face, however, and said, 'Well, I can see your point. I will take my seat, yes, but let me tell you I am leaving here tonight, whatever happens.' She took longer than necessary to return to her place in an armchair near the front windows and retained her proud, regal composure as she sat down.

'Thank you, Mrs Buchanan,' said Davison before addressing the rest of the group. 'Now, you may all be wondering what's going on here. And you deserve an explanation. First, I must tell you that I didn't come to Dallach Lodge as a mere house guest. I came on behalf of His Majesty's government.'

Everyone spoke at once. 'So you're a—' said Vivienne Passerini.

'I don't believe it,' said May Frith-Stratton.

'How extraordinary,' said Rufus Phillips.

As Davison began to speak again the comments died away. 'Robin Kinmuir – who had, at one time, worked for a particular division of the Foreign Office – had reason to believe that someone wanted him dead. He had been sent a threatening note and so I was dispatched up here to protect him. On that score, I'm afraid I failed.'

'Indeed you did,' said Mrs Buchanan. 'In spectacular fashion.'

'Quite,' said Davison. 'And for that I must apologise.'

'In that case, why don't you arrest the man responsible – Simon Peterson?' said Mrs Buchanan. 'After all, he's standing right in front of you. I understand you have a suicide note from Simkins which outlines the details of the case.'

'Indeed we do,' said Davison.

'Well, I would have thought that settled it,' said Mrs Buchanan. 'Really, it's getting very frustrating. And some of us have appointments we must keep. The London stage is waiting for me.'

'I don't doubt it,' said Davison. 'But when it comes to Mr Peterson, I have to tell you all that he is not the guilty party.'

'Not the guilty party?' said James Kinmuir. 'But, inspector, I thought you said you had everything you needed to draw the case to a conclusion?'

The inspector was looking uncertain now and he no longer had his gun pointed at Mr Peterson. Perhaps he was beginning to work out the real nature of the killings for himself. 'Simkins's note did point to Peterson as the mastermind behind the murders,' said Hawkins, 'but what if Simkins's death was not a suicide?'

'Exactly,' said Davison. 'Simkins was just another victim here. He didn't hang himself. Rather, someone killed him and made it look as though he had taken his own life.'

'But what about the suicide note?' asked Rufus Phillips.

'Now, this is where it gets interesting,' said Davison. 'I'm going to pass you over to my colleague Mrs Christie, who will tell you a little more about that.'

'Mrs Christie?' said Mrs Buchanan, dismissively. 'Why would we want to listen to her? I mean she's just ... just a writer.'

'That may be so,' said Davison. 'But she has also played

an integral part in this investigation. So, please, Mrs Christie, if you could expand on what I've been saying?'

I was thankful that Davison had kept my role suitably vague. As I stepped forwards into the middle of the room, all eyes turned towards me, I felt the familiar prick and burning of my cheeks as I began to blush. I hated to be the centre of attention, but I owed it to the victims – to Robin Kinmuir, to old Mrs Kinmuir, even to Simkins himself – to explain the killings at Dallach Lodge and, as a result, bring about some sort of justice.

I took a deep breath and began. 'The case is very complex, but let me start with the suicide note found next to Simkins's body,' I said. 'We know that Simkins didn't write that note because it was not executed in his handwriting ... but my own.'

'What?' said Mrs Buchanan.

'I don't understand,' said James Kinmuir.

'If you could let Mrs Christie explain without interruptions, that would be best,' said Davison.

'Thank you,' I said. 'You see, the night before his death, the butler came into possession of a sample of my handwriting. He ripped some pages from my notebook and refused to return them to me. The killer must have seen these pages and subsequently copied my handwriting, believing it to be Simkins's own, in order to fashion the suicide note.'

'Which means ... the killer is still here,' said James Kinmuir. 'Among us.'

'Indeed,' I said.

'Oh, my Lord,' said May Frith-Stratton. 'I think I'm going to faint.'

The atmosphere in the room was so strained one could almost taste the tension.

Isabella Frith-Stratton spoke up. 'But if the fake suicide note was written in the hand of Mrs Christie, why aren't you simply arresting her for the crimes?'

'Yes, it's the kind of ploy she might use in one of her books, isn't it?' said her sister May. 'What's it called? A kind of bluff, or is it a double bluff. Is that the right term?'

'Now, let's not get carried away here,' said the inspector. He turned to address me. 'So I'm right in saying that the suicide note was written in your hand, but you didn't write it yourself?'

'Yes, that's right.'

'And why, may I ask, didn't you tell me this at the time, when you first saw the note?'

'Well, you see, it was vitally important for the killer to believe that they had got away with their plan,' I said.

It was obvious that I was getting on the inspector's nerves. He had been wrong not once but twice, and he was desperate to catch me out. 'So, Mrs Christie, would you care to tell us who in this room is the murderer?'

'Yes, of course,' I said. 'But to be strictly accurate, it was more than one person who was responsible for these murders.'

Chapter Forty-two

The revelation caused another wave of shock to reverberate around the room. I hesitated as I thought how best to explain everything.

'Of course, each of you came under suspicion at one point or another,' I continued.

The comment was met by outraged exclamations and yet more threats to leave the house immediately. Perhaps it was not the most tactful thing to say.

'I'm not listening to this nonsense,' said Mrs Buchanan, springing from her chair once more.

'Nobody is leaving this room until this is straightened out,' said the inspector. 'Nobody! Now, please, Mrs Buchanan, take your seat and let Mrs Christie speak.'

'Thank you, inspector,' I said. 'As you all know, Robin Kinmuir was found dead on the moor. The first suspect was his nephew and heir, James Kinmuir, who had accidentally shot him while he was out hunting for grouse with his friend Rufus Phillips. But he was dismissed as a suspect after it was revealed that Robin Kinmuir had not died from a gunshot wound but from curare, which had got into his system after his razor blade had been contaminated. Yes, it really was a quite horrible, gruesome and very painful death. It also came to light, through information supplied by the family solicitor, Mr Glenelg, that James Kinmuir would not inherit a penny. And so the two friends were cleared of any guilt.'

'Yes, and quite right too,' said May Frith-Stratton.

'Then came the murder of poor Mrs Kinmuir, stabbed in the back of the neck with a paper knife,' I said. 'A quite unforgivable crime. The old lady was almost blind, she was losing her faculties and she was murdered in her room at the top of the house, in a place where she should have felt safe.'

Quiet descended over the room as I continued to speak.

'Next we learnt that some of you in this room had been drawn to Dallach Lodge after being sent a letter inviting you to witness some kind of punishment to be inflicted on Robin Kinmuir,' I said. 'After all, many of you had good reason to hate Kinmuir. Isabella and May Frith-Stratton related how their father's business had been ruined as a result of Kinmuir's actions.'

'Surely you're not suggesting that we had anything to do with this?' snapped Isabella. 'And what about your own confession at the time? That you had come to the lodge because of what Kinmuir had done to your own father?'

'I'm afraid that was a little poetic licence on my part,' I said. 'I felt I needed to make up a story so as to gain your confidences. That might seem like treachery, but I hope you'll forgive me.'

'Well, if Mrs Christie can lie about that, how do we know she's not lying now?' Isabella continued. 'How do we know that she's not the one behind this wicked business?'

There was something I wanted to ask the two sisters, but despite Isabella's aggressive attitude I felt that it would be kinder to do so in private.

'*Please*, Miss Frith-Stratton,' said the inspector. 'Carry on, Mrs Christie.'

I nodded my head in recognition and continued. 'And then we learnt of Simon Peterson's grudge against Robin Kinmuir – he believed that Kinmuir was responsible for his father's death in Maastricht when serving as an agent during the war. Later, we discovered the reason why Miss Passerini was here as a guest – she is the illegitimate daughter of Robin Kinmuir and she blamed him for her mother's suicide. So, you see, all of you had a reason to take revenge on Mr Kinmuir.'

'Can I stop you for a moment?' asked the inspector. 'Not quite all of us. I certainly didn't receive one of these mysterious letters and I doubt whether Dr Fitzpatrick did either.'

'Well, this is where it gets interesting,' I said. 'Although you, Inspector Hawkins, may not have received a letter, you certainly had a reason for wanting Robin Kinmuir dead.'

'*What*?' he said. 'Now you really have lost your mind.'

'Am I not right in saying that your family was a victim of the clearances, that terrible time when tenant farmers on this land were evicted from their homes by the Kinmuirs?'

Hawkins looked stunned and started to say something, but I continued. 'And that your grandfather was forced to leave Skye? And he lost a brother and a sister to illness and poor nutrition? Indeed, you grew up to hate the Kinmuirs with a passion.'

'Inspector? Is this true?' asked James Kinmuir.

'Yes, but that was a very long time ago and I wouldn't do anything like you're suggesting,' he said. 'I'm an officer of the law.'

Hawkins's explanation failed to satisfy the group and everyone looked at him with suspicion in their eyes. The fact that he was brandishing a gun did nothing to allay people's fears.

'Turning to you, Dr Fitzpatrick,' I said. 'Your relationship with Mr Kinmuir was a complex one, wasn't it?'

'He was a good friend of many years,' said the doctor, shifting uncomfortably in his seat.

'But I am right in saying that you were more than good friends with his first wife, Catherine?'

'Yes, that's right,' said Dr Fitzpatrick, blushing.

'And you were also involved, at some stage, with Mrs Buchanan here?'

'This is too much!' said Mrs Buchanan. 'I'm not going to sit around while my name is bandied about like some cheap vaudeville show.'

I turned my attentions to the actress now. 'You managed to put on quite a performance,' I said. 'But it's time to tell the truth about—'

'I don't know what you mean,' she interrupted. 'This really is the most extraordinary behaviour. If you think I'm going to remain in this—'

I ignored her and continued. 'The disappearance of Catherine Kinmuir.'

I was sure my words must have had an impact on Mrs Buchanan, but she was such a skilled actress that she arranged her features into a perfect mask.

'There's no point denying it, Dr Fitzpatrick here told me everything,' I said.

For the very briefest of moments, Eliza Buchanan's defences collapsed. She flashed a desperate look at Dr Fitzpatrick, then she smiled. 'I don't know what you're talking about,' she said.

'Would you care to illuminate us, doctor?' I said.

Dr Fitzpatrick looked at me with all the pain and self-pity of a sick dog. 'Must I?'

I left the question unanswered. He knew from our talk that, at some point, he would have to tell the truth to the police. I felt sorry for him that this had to be done in front of an audience.

'Well, this would be back in—' he began.

'Don't you say another word!' hissed Mrs Buchanan. 'We had an agreement, Jeremy. You promised me!'

'Aye, and I'm afraid it's too late for all of that,' said Dr Fitzpatrick. 'She knows. They know.'

'Knows what?' asked the inspector.

'About the letter and how—'

'You don't know what you're talking about, you stupid man,' said Mrs Buchanan. 'The problem is you've always been weak. Weak then and weak now.'

'For God's sake, woman, can't you hear yourself!' shouted the doctor. Years of frustration and anger could be heard in his voice. 'No wonder you drive away every man who loves you.'

As Dr Fitzpatrick finished the sentence he looked surprised by the strength of his words. The comment stung Mrs Buchanan to the quick, and the carapace that she had so carefully constructed around herself began to crumble.

'Oh, Jeremy . . .' she said. She tried to speak, but she could say no more and her eyes filled with tears.

Yet I had seen Mrs Buchanan in action before, both on and off the stage. Were these tears real? How did I know whether she was sincere or whether she was drawing on her considerable skills as an actress?

'I'm sorry, Eliza, but it's best to tell them what you know,' said Dr Fitzpatrick.

'Yes, I can see you're right.' She appeared to compose herself. 'I'm afraid neither of us comes out of the story in a good light.'

She closed her eyes and began to declaim some lines of poetry.

> 'My love is as a fever, longing still
> For that which longer nurseth the disease . . .'

'Much as I'd like to stand around and listen to poetry all day, I think that we should get to the matter in hand,' said the inspector.

I could understand why she had chosen to quote the poem, Shakespeare's Sonnet 147, which ended with the lines, '*For I have sworn thee fair, and thought thee bright/Who art as black as hell, as dark as night.*' And, like the inspector, I had no time for veiled expressions and coded messages. It was time for the stark truth.

I took out the copy of the letter that I had taken from Mrs Buchanan's room and began to read. "'It's the only way. I can't think of anything else. I keep thinking of our life together when she is dead.'"

'Where did you get that?' asked Mrs Buchanan.

I answered her question with another question. 'Who wrote these words, Mrs Buchanan?'

'I did,' said the doctor. 'God knows I wish I hadn't, but she's been holding that damned letter over me all these years. Telling me that she kept the original in a bank vault.'

Mrs Buchanan looked astonished at the doctor's confession. He had already shared his secret with Davison and me, but now it was important that the rest of the group heard what he had to say.

'I wrote that letter to Eliza Buchanan in a moment of madness,' he said. 'Of course, I didn't mean it – I would never have hurt ...'

His voice trailed off.

'But when Robin Kinmuir's wife, Catherine, disappeared, Mrs Buchanan realised what she had in her possession,' I explained. 'She had some kind of evidence that could be made to look as though the doctor were the one responsible. You see, Catherine Kinmuir disappeared in 1916 and her body has never been found.'

'That's right, yes,' said Dr Fitzpatrick.

'So what happened?' asked the inspector. 'Are you suggesting Catherine Kinmuir was murdered? Is this what lies behind all these other killings?'

I looked to Mrs Buchanan for an answer. 'I think you can tell us the truth now, can't you, Mrs Buchanan?'

She looked at each of us in turn, almost as if she were assessing the quality of the audience before her. 'Oh, very well,' she said. 'Since Jeremy has confessed to his part in the matter then I may as well fill in the gaps. Some of you must have already guessed that Jeremy Fitzpatrick and I were lovers. But before that, I was the lover of Robin Kinmuir. And yes, Robin was married to Catherine at the time. But don't judge me so harshly – the oh-so-saintly Catherine Kinmuir and Dr Fitzpatrick were lovers too.'

'This is all very complicated, Mrs Buchanan,' said the inspector. 'Let me get this straight. While the late Mr Kinmuir was married to Catherine you embarked on a relationship with him. But Catherine Kinmuir was then the lover of Dr Fitzpatrick here.'

'Yes, that's what I just told you,' said Mrs Buchanan, casting a look at the inspector which clearly communicated her low opinion of him. 'Then, after that, Dr Fitzpatrick transferred his affections away from Catherine and towards me.'

'But it wasn't quite as simple as that, was it, Eliza?' said Dr Fitzpatrick. There was venom in his voice now. 'You've always wanted to be the most desired woman in the room, haven't you? Certainly, you had an alluring quality, but I didn't realise quite how dangerous you were.'

'Really!' exclaimed Mrs Buchanan, looking around the room for someone to come to her defence. But everybody remained silent. 'I don't have to remain here and be talked to like that.'

'What happened that night, the night my aunt disappeared?' asked James Kinmuir. 'Did you kill her?'

'Mrs Buchanan, at this moment I suspect you of being not

just as the murderer of Catherine Kinmuir but of three other people too,' said the inspector. 'So if you've got anything to say for yourself I suggest you tell us now.'

'What do you take me for?' she said. 'Of course I didn't murder Catherine! And I could never have killed Robin or dear old auntie.'

'So what do you know about what happened to them?' I asked.

'I drove Catherine to her death, that's what happened!' she snapped. Mrs Buchanan blinked a few times in quick succession, appearing astonished at the stark truth of her own statement. 'You may as well know it all. There's no point in hiding anything now. First, I took Robin away from her. Then, when I realised that Catherine was having a relationship with Jeremy Fitzpatrick, I lured him away from her too. It didn't take much doing. You know what men are like. And my charms were – well, let's say they were more considerable than Catherine's. But I didn't know what would happen. How could I?'

She took a deep breath and continued. 'That night, the night she disappeared, Catherine asked me to join her outside for some fresh air after dinner. She wanted to talk to me, she said. It started in a perfectly civilised manner as we walked through the gardens and ended up down by the banks of the loch. It was there that Catherine turned on me. She told me that she had discovered that Jeremy had switched his affections from her to me. She begged me to give him up. She wanted to divorce Robin and start a new life with Jeremy on the mainland, she said. But why should I give him up, I thought to myself. She was the one who was married. Both Jeremy and I were unattached, we had no ties. She kept going on about how much Jeremy loved her. That he would do anything for her. I'm afraid the argument turned quite unpleasant and I told her that Jeremy didn't love her; in fact, he wished she were dead. In the heat of the moment, I showed her the letter that Jeremy had written, in which he said those words: "It's the only way. I can't think of anything else. I keep thinking of our life together when she is dead." I left Catherine by the loch and came back inside the house. Of course, I didn't realise what she would do. But I assumed that she had walked into the loch that night and drowned herself and that the current must have carried her body out to sea.'

I looked over at Jeremy Fitzpatrick, whose eyes had filled with tears. He would have to live with his guilt for the rest of his life. Mrs Buchanan, meanwhile, did not seem to be in the least affected by the part she had played in Catherine Kinmuir's suicide.

'It was most unfortunate,' she said, now becoming more breezy in her manner, 'but I suppose, looking back, it was probably for the best. Catherine was a delicate soul – she'd never been quite herself since the death of her son Timothy in the war. She was too good for this world.'

Dr Fitzpatrick clenched his fists in an attempt to control his temper. Inspector Hawkins strode into the middle of the room, the gun still in his hand. 'And, Mrs Buchanan, how do we know you're telling the truth?' he demanded.

Mrs Buchanan opened her mouth to speak, but I raised my hand to silence her. 'Regarding the disappearance of Catherine Kinmuir we shall have to take Mrs Buchanan's word for it,' I said. 'But I can tell you that she is not the one responsible for the recent murders at Dallach Lodge.'

'Well, thank you for informing me of that, Mrs Christie,' said Mrs Buchanan in a sarcastic voice. 'I am grateful.'

Hawkins sighed in frustration. 'Let me go through this once more,' he said. 'If James Kinmuir, Rufus Phillips, Simon Peterson, Vivienne Passerini, Dr Fitzpatrick, May and Isabella Frith-Stratton and Mrs Buchanan are not guilty, then that means ... Well, it just leaves us with Mr Davison and you, Mrs Christie.'

As he raised his hand he pointed his gun at me. His fingers began to curl themselves around the trigger.

Fear threatened to silence me, but I had to speak. 'Inspector, if you had listened carefully to Mr Davison's observations and my own, the only people who were definitely not guilty of the murders at Dallach Lodge were Mr Peterson and Mrs Buchanan.'

'So, what are you saying?' asked the inspector. 'That the rest are guilty? That they planned the murders together? What – that they *all* did it?'

Chapter Forty-three

'I had at one time thought that this could be the case,' I said. 'As I have explained, each of them had a motive for wanting Robin Kinmuir dead.'

Hawkins lowered the gun and began to pace around the room like a confined animal. 'But you don't think that now?'

'No, I don't,' I said.

'So, who is the killer then?' barked Hawkins. 'Give us the names of the person or persons responsible for the recent murders at Dallach Lodge.'

'I will, but first I need to provide a little background information,' I said. 'I want to outline the context of the crime, and in particular the significance of *Who Killed Cock Robin*?'

'Not that blasted nursery rhyme again!' exclaimed the inspector.

'If you'd let Mrs Christie explain,' said Davison. 'It may sound unlikely, but it really does have some bearing on the case.'

'Thank you, Mr Davison,' I said.

'It might be helpful if I recite two verses from the rhyme,' I said.

> 'Who killed Cock Robin?
> I, said the Sparrow,
> With my bow and arrow,
> I killed Cock Robin.
>
> Who saw him die?
> I, said the Fly,
> With my little eye,
> I saw him die.'

'Really, I'm afraid I don't see the relevance of this,' said Isabella.

'And nor did I to begin with,' I said. 'Of course, when I first made a connection between the rhyme and the events at Dallach Lodge, I couldn't be sure of the significance. But, as time went on, it became clearer. Robin was Robin Kinmuir, who was killed by Miss Passerini, whose name '*passer*' means 'sparrow' in Latin. The fly was old Mrs Kinmuir, who told me that she had seen him die. But the problem was that not only was the old lady losing her faculties, but she was blind, too. Although her room was situated at the front of the house which looked out towards the moor where Robin Kinmuir had died, she couldn't have seen anything. That got me thinking. What if the rhyme was nothing but a distraction?'

'A distraction?' said James Kinmuir.

'Yes, like a smokescreen,' I said. 'It explained everything, and yet nothing.'

'I'm sorry, this is all rather cryptic,' said Mrs Buchanan.

'I know I'm probably not making myself understood,' I said. 'But I promise, if you bear with me, it should all become perfectly clear. You see, I believe the murderers planned this very much like a play. They thought their scheme was very clever and they almost succeeded. Their initial plan was to kill only Robin Kinmuir. But then I paid a visit to old Mrs Kinmuir and one day at dinner I repeated something she had said to me. "*L'ho visto morire*", which as you know translates from the Italian as "I saw him die". I thought that Mrs Kinmuir was referring to a line in the nursery rhyme, because immediately afterwards she said, "*Who saw him die? I, said the Fly, with my little eye, I saw him die.*"'

'And she wasn't?' asked the inspector.

'No, but I will come on to that,' I said. 'I didn't realise it at the time, but as soon as I repeated Mrs Kinmuir's words that night at dinner, I sealed her fate. There was someone at the table who knew exactly what she was referring to. Mrs Kinmuir would have to be got rid of and so they stabbed the old lady in the back of the neck with a paper knife, a weapon which was then placed among Miss Passerini's possessions so as to incriminate her further. Oh, yes, it was a very ingenious deception and the killers almost got away with it.'

'Who was there around the table that night?' asked the inspector.

'Well, let's see, there was Mr Davison and myself, together with the Frith-Stratton sisters, Mrs Buchanan, James Kinmuir, Rufus Phillips, Vivienne Passerini, Simon Peterson and, of course, Simkins, who served the food. Dr Fitzpatrick was not at the house that night as he was preparing his report on Robin Kinmuir's death, and you, inspector, had left the lodge for the day.'

Hawkins studied the faces of the assembled group for any traces of guilt before shaking his head in bafflement. 'So you're saying this hinges on something Mrs Kinmuir told you? Something in Italian?'

'Yes,' I said. 'There were so many hidden pieces to the puzzle and I only worked it out for certain last night. Unfortunately, I was too late to prevent Simkins's death. You see, the butler was blackmailing the murderers. He must have seen something suspicious, perhaps relating to the application of the curare to Robin Kinmuir's razor. They were also responsible for slashing the tyres because they couldn't risk Mr Peterson leaving the estate to seek treatment. After the murderers believed Mr Peterson had died and they realised that Miss Passerini would not be charged with the deaths, they needed to come up with another scheme. The killers wanted Simkins out of the way too, and they thought that if they could make everyone believe that he had killed Simon Peterson and then hanged himself, well, it was like killing two birds with one stone. But that was when they gave themselves away. By copying a scrap of paper that they had found in Simkins's room – written in my hand – they made a terrible mistake. I already had my suspicions as to the identities of the killers, but then Mr Davison here saw something last night which confirmed them.' I looked at Davison and nodded my head, signalling for him to step forwards. 'Would you be so kind, Mr Davison?'

'Of course,' he said. 'If you'll excuse me for a moment. There's a piece of evidence I'd like to show you.'

All eyes followed Davison as he walked across the drawing room and opened the door.

A few moments later, he came back in, carrying something under his arm, an object covered in sackcloth.

'What's that you've got there, Davison?' asked the inspector.

'Do you want to show them?' I asked.

'Very well,' said Davison as he slowly removed the sackcloth to reveal Rufus Phillips's painting of Robin Kinmuir. It was now in a frame with a hessian backing sealed across the rear of the canvas.

'What are you doing with that?' asked Rufus Phillips.

'All should become clear in just a moment,' I replied.

Davison carried the painting over to the fireplace and raised it so that everybody in the room could see it. The portrait was how I remembered it: sharp angles, blocks of colour and unsettling perspectives, but for all its modernity the composition was clearly a representation of Robin Kinmuir.

'Please tell us why you've brought this down for us to look at,' I said.

'I'm going to throw it in the fire,' said Davison.

'What?' exclaimed Rufus. 'You can't do that.'

Davison stepped towards the fire and was about to drop the picture into the flames, but Rufus was quick to respond.

'Just a minute,' he said politely. 'I know it might not be to everyone's taste, but—'

'It's not a matter of taste,' said Davison, moving the canvas nearer to the flames.

'Look here, Davison,' said James Kinmuir. 'I don't know what you're playing at, but this isn't funny.'

'Yes, what's this all about, Davison?' demanded the inspector. 'I thought you said you had a piece of evidence that would prove who the killers were?'

'Indeed we do,' I said, before turning back to my friend. 'Now, Mr Davison, please consign that portrait to the flames.'

'I said you can't do that!' shouted Rufus Phillips. All cordiality had gone from his voice now. 'It's my work. Give it back to me.'

'I don't know if you remember, Mr Phillips, but that first night, soon after I had arrived at the lodge, James Kinmuir told me that you didn't want to be paid for working on the portrait of his uncle,' I said.

'That's right,' said James Kinmuir, answering for his friend. 'Rufus was just pleased that my uncle agreed to sit for him. He said he had an interesting face.'

'And as such, the painting remains your property, Mr Phillips, something not entered into the inventory of the house with the rest of Mr Kinmuir's possessions,' I said.

'Well, yes, but I still don't understand what this is about.'

'You don't?' asked Davison. 'Let's find out then, shall we?'

As Davison moved to place the canvas into the flames Rufus Phillips jumped forwards and tried to stop him. The artist reached out and grabbed Davison's wrist.

'You don't want your work to be burnt to ashes, is that it?' asked Davison.

'Leave off, man, can't you see that the portrait has sentimental value to me?' said James Kinmuir. 'It's about the last image we have of my uncle.'

'So its value is nothing more than sentimental?' Davison asked.

'It matters to Rufus, of course, as he painted it, but I doubt anyone would buy it,' said Kinmuir. 'I mean, look at it, it's not even very good.'

'What are you getting at?' asked the inspector. 'You can't seriously expect me to believe that this portrait here has anything to do with the murders?'

'Mr Phillips, if you let go of my arm, I give you my word I won't damage your painting,' said Davison.

Rufus Phillips glared at Davison before he released his hand and moved away from the fireplace. Just as he did so, Davison whipped out a penknife from his inside jacket pocket and, with a quick cut, slashed open the hessian that had been fixed across the back of the picture.

'What the devil do you think you're doing?' demanded Phillips.

'I said I wouldn't damage the painting,' said Davison. 'But I am curious to discover something.'

A moment later Davison folded back the hessian and prised out a small rectangular panel that had been taped inside.

'Now, what's this we have here?' he asked.

He held another, much older painting, although its surface was so dark and dirty that from a distance it was difficult to make out its subject matter.

'Yes, I'd say Italian Renaissance,' said Davison, bringing the little painting closer to him so that he could study its detail. 'Probably Venetian.'

'How extraordinary,' said Phillips. 'I don't know how that can have got inside.'

ANDREW WILSON

'It's a crucifixion scene,' continued Davison. 'It needs a good clean, but it's a beautiful composition. The figures seem to loom out of the darkness and there's a mysterious quality about it, too.'

'I'm sorry to interrupt your lesson in art history,' said the inspector. 'But what has this to do with the murders?'

Davison turned to me. 'Perhaps you'd like to continue, Mrs Christie?'

'Very well,' I said. 'It's time to tell you all the names of the murderers of Robin Kinmuir, Mrs Veronica Kinmuir, and Simkins the butler ... They are Mr Rufus Phillips and Mr James Kinmuir.'

Chapter Forty-four

'Didn't I tell you that it was him,' said Mrs Buchanan, pointing at James Kinmuir. 'Right from the beginning. But nobody listened.'

'You must be out of your mind!' exclaimed James Kinmuir.

'Utter nonsense,' said Rufus Phillips. 'And you haven't got a shred of evidence to support such a ridiculous accusation.'

'But there, you see, you're wrong,' I said. 'First of all, though, I must finish the story of the rhyme because I believe that's where the idea for the murder plot started.'

'Murder based on an old nursery rhyme – it's preposterous!' said James Kinmuir. 'Really, Mrs Christie, I think you're going the way of old Auntie.'

'You can't dismiss me that easily, young man,' I said, feeling anger rising within me. 'And don't take the name of your great-aunt in vain. You should be utterly ashamed of what you did to her.' I took a deep breath, turned away from the two men and continued. 'Now, back to the rhyme. I suppose it must have started as a game between the two young friends, calling Robin Kinmuir "Cock Robin" behind his back and that sort of thing. After all, Robin Kinmuir had dyed his hair a rather garish shade of red. Perhaps the two friends also talked about how he resembled a red grouse. It was all very innocent, if not very polite, banter, the kind indulged in by young men such as these.

'But then, one day, when Rufus Phillips was visiting Dallach Lodge, he noticed one of the grime-covered paintings on the upstairs landing. Something about this little oil panel caught his eye. He turned it over and, yes, the inscription gave him an idea. No doubt we'll come back to that. Of course, I should have picked up on the clues much earlier – especially after I saw this portrait that Mr Phillips painted of Robin Kinmuir with his eyes missing. Robin Kinmuir was blind to what was before him – he had no knowledge of the provenance of the old crucifixion scene. I remember him saying that he did not have an eye for art. The painting was hiding in plain sight, you see. However, James knew that his uncle had a photographic memory and the two young men had to be careful. If he or Rufus had simply removed the painting then it might have alerted Robin Kinmuir to the nature – and value – of the work of art. And so they began to hatch a plan.'

'Honestly, you should hear yourself, Mrs Christie,' said James Kinmuir. 'I've lost count of the number of times you've used the words "perhaps" and "guess". This really is beyond belief.'

'You didn't have time to wait for your uncle to die – the doctor here pronounced him in good health. He could live for years,' I said, making an effort to keep my voice strong. 'But you wanted the money now. There was a problem, however. If Robin Kinmuir was murdered, and the painting was identified as being the work of one of the great artists of the Renaissance, a Giorgione, the finger of suspicion would point at you, Mr Kinmuir, because you were his heir.

'In addition, you were the only person close enough to your uncle who knew something of his dalliances and shady business deals. No doubt over the years he had entertained you with tales of his conquests, both in the bedroom and in the world of business. And, when you related those stories to Rufus Phillips, you came up with a scheme to entice his enemies to the lodge with the promise of watching him suffer. Oh, yes, it was a long time in the planning, but the rewards were high. And so you wrote letters to Simon Peterson, Vivienne Passerini and the Frith-Stratton sisters, inviting them to stay. You needed a number of suspects. To invite simply one stranger with a past grudge would have been too conspicuous. How you must have laughed when you realised that the Latin root of Miss Passerini's surname was '*passer*' – sparrow. She was the sparrow of the rhyme and, in your plan, she would be the one who would be framed for killing poor Cock Robin, your uncle, on the first day of the grouse season, the twelfth of August. Oh, the Glorious Twelfth – what an irony! It was almost too perfect for words.'

'If nothing else, I do admire your imagination, Mrs Christie,' said Rufus Phillips. 'But that's all this is – pure invention.'

I ignored him and carried on. 'Of course, I did have to ask myself if Vivienne Passerini was the sparrow of the rhyme – the real killer of Robin – would she really give herself away by virtue of her surname? I suppose you thought that the rhyme would serve as some sort of admission of guilt, the confession of someone who was clearly insane. And you would have enjoyed seeing Miss Passerini suffer as she protested her innocence. But that was your cruel streak at work, or rather, I should say, the combination of both of your twisted personalities. I wonder, if you had never met, whether either of you would have gone on to commit murder. But what is certain is that together you were lethal.'

'Have you quite finished?' asked James Kinmuir, looking at me with disdain.

'No, no, I haven't,' I said. 'We need to look at each of the deaths in turn. In fairness to you both, as I said, I believe you intended to commit only one murder – that of Robin Kinmuir. Your plan was a thorough and a detailed one, in which you would confess to the murder before being cleared of it. You warned Mr Kinmuir of his imminent demise in a series of anonymous letters, another symptom of your sadistic natures.

'The arrival of Mr Davison and myself at Dallach Lodge must have unsettled you, especially when Mr Davison took it upon himself to sleep in a camp bed in Robin Kinmuir's dressing room. But of course you realised that it would be impossible for Mr Davison to watch your uncle every minute of the day, especially when he was bathing and so on. At some point you managed to slip into your uncle's room and smear the curare on his razor, knowing that he had already been bothered by a midge bite on his throat.

'You also knew that each morning he took a walk with his beloved dogs. They were a key to the murder, one you didn't think anyone would pick up on. That morning, the morning of Mr Kinmuir's death, I paid a visit to see the cook, Mrs

Baillie, who told me that James Kinmuir had recently got into the habit of taking sausages away with him from breakfast. I remember too how you fed the dogs straight from the table. I think that morning you left a trail of sausage meat across the moor, knowing that would lead the dogs and, in turn, Mr Kinmuir towards you. As your uncle ran after the Labradors, you shot him, but you were careful not to kill him. What did you do then? After all, you didn't know exactly how long it would be before the curare began to take effect. Did you go over and stand there by your uncle and wait for him to die? Did you look into his eyes as he took his last breath?'

'I hope you're writing all this down, inspector, as I intend to bring a case of slander against this woman,' said James Kinmuir. 'The next time I see you, Mrs Christie, will be in court. Come on, Rufus. We're leaving.'

'I've taken it all down, Mr Kinmuir, and neither you nor Mr Phillips are going anywhere,' said Hawkins. 'Now, carry on, Mrs Christie.'

'Thank you, inspector,' I said. 'The next murder was that of old Mrs Kinmuir on the eighteenth of August and, as I said, that was unforgivable. You had to kill her because of something she told me during my chat with her. The following day, on the nineteenth of August, one of you, I'm not sure whether it was you, Mr Phillips, or you, Mr Kinmuir, made an attempt on my life up by the old derelict castle. You were worried that I was getting too close to finding out the truth and so you tried to silence me by hurling a rock down on my head. Luckily, I managed to jump out of the way and I was found by Mr Peterson.

'And now to your final murder – that of Simkins, who

was blackmailing you, I believe because he had seen you enter Robin Kinmuir's room and tamper with his razor. You were running out of time – you knew Mr Glenelg and his men were coming to take the inventory of the house – and so you did something desperate. In order to fake Simkins's suicide note, you stole what you believed to be a sample of his handwriting from his room. Your first mistake was not to double-check that it was his writing. The second was to forge the handwriting you found so accurately that even its creator – myself – could scarcely tell the difference between the original sample and the forged copy. You see, those pages were from my notebook, pages which Simkins had ripped from it. Only an artist of the first order – someone like you, Mr Phillips – could execute such a forgery. No doubt you employed the same artistic skills when it came to forging Miss Passerini's passport, which seemed to show that she had recently visited South America. Talking of South America, I believe one of you must have visited that continent recently in order to purchase the curare. My guess is that it was you, Mr Phillips. On your return I think you cut out the pages in your passport and then, very cleverly, you spliced them into Miss Passerini's documents.'

I looked at Rufus Phillips, whose eyes now blazed with hatred. 'But none of this is proof, it's just … just conjecture,' he said.

'Perhaps,' I said. 'But what Mr Davison saw last night certainly isn't. In fact, what he witnessed proves beyond the shadow of a doubt that you are both guilty.'

'You see, Mr Phillips and Mr Kinmuir, unbeknownst to you, I saw you take this small picture down from the wall and replace it with another,' said Davison. 'I followed you up to the studio room in the attic, where I overheard you talking about your plan. There you untacked the back of the portrait of Robin Kinmuir, slipped the panel inside and tacked up the cover again. I even overheard you name the artist – Giorgione – and boast about the value of—'

But before Davison could finish his sentence, Rufus Phillips grabbed hold of my arm and pulled me towards him, forcing me to drop my handbag. In a flash, he whipped out a razor from his pocket, flicked it open with one hand and positioned the blade an inch away from my throat. Davison and Inspector Hawkins rushed towards him, the inspector brandishing his gun, but Phillips threatened to press the sharp metal edge hard against my skin. The taste of fear soured my mouth.

'Step away,' said Phillips. 'All of you, get away from me.'

'Rufus, stop!' shouted James Kinmuir. 'Don't you see they haven't got anything on us, they're bluffing.'

Panic overcame Rufus Phillips and he looked like an animal that had been hunted and cornered. He realised that his actions had betrayed him, that he had reached the point of no return. 'The blade is covered in curare,' he said, spitting the words out. 'One cut, even if it's not a deep one, will be fatal.'

'Phillips – put that razor down now!' ordered Hawkins, aiming his gun directly at him. At this moment, two uniformed officers stormed into the room.

'Tell them to get out now!' shouted Phillips. 'If they don't, she's a dead woman.'

Hawkins gestured for the men to leave.

'And I'll only put it down when I'm outside the house, in a car, with that painting by my side,' said Phillips. 'If you shoot, I will make sure I cut deep into Mrs Christie's skin, even if it's the last thing I do.'

'Don't be so damned stupid, Rufus,' said James Kinmuir. 'Can't you see, it's over now.'

'No, it's not!' Phillips protested as droplets of spittle exploded from his mouth. 'It can't be, not after everything we've put into it. After all *I've* done. I can't go back to that life, painting portraits of the rich and grand for next to nothing. Constantly having an empty stomach, living in a cold, damp attic. The artistic life is all very well, but when you're not born with money it's no fun. But what's the point of it all if we don't take the painting, James?'

'It's too late now, can't you see that?' insisted his friend.

Phillips bent my arm backwards, sending an icicle of pain stabbing through my shoulder blades.

'I wish I'd killed her up there by the castle,' Phillips said. So it *had* been him.

'Davison, give me that painting,' he demanded. 'Now!'

Davison looked at the Renaissance panel in his hand for a moment, almost as if he were trying to see beneath the dark surface to its hidden beauty, before he gently reached out and allowed Phillips to snatch it from him.

'You go first, James,' Phillips told his friend. 'Just walk out of the door. If your car is not ready to drive then we can take one of the others, or a van.'

James Kinmuir looked at Rufus as though his friend were speaking a foreign tongue and remained fixed to the spot, unsure about what to do.

'If any of you try to stop me or James from leaving the house then I will not hesitate to use this on you,' said Phillips as he held up the razor in the air.

The sight of the blade, its deadly silver sheen reflecting the flames of the fire, brought me to my senses. I realised that since Phillips had grabbed me I had fallen into a state of shock, unable to respond in any way. I felt weak and nauseous, but if I didn't do something I had no doubt that Phillips would kill me.

I readied myself for action.

'You do know that the painting's a fake, don't you?' I said. 'Your friend James here substituted the real work for this forgery soon after we arrived at the house.'

The words hit Phillips like a bullet. His face drained of colour and he looked like he was going to collapse.

'I d-don't believe you,' he said.

'Don't listen to her, Rufus, she's lying,' said James Kinmuir.

'I'm afraid Mrs Christie is right,' said Davison. 'The real Giorgione is stashed upstairs, hidden away in James Kinmuir's bedroom. So you see, everything you've done – the murders of Robin Kinmuir, of old Mrs Kinmuir, of Simkins – has been for nothing.'

'It's not true,' said Kinmuir. 'You just said that—'

'It's a very good copy though, isn't it,' said Davison. 'And clever of you to spot the original, Mr Phillips. I congratulate you, you must have quite an eye. No doubt you thought that your plan would net you hundreds of thousands of pounds. You told everyone here that after leaving Dallach Lodge you planned to travel to Italy and I suppose you thought of taking this small panel with you and selling it to a wealthy collector. Neither of you would ever need to work again. Both of you would be rich beyond your wildest dreams, even after the substantial debts on Dallach Lodge had been paid off. After all, there are so few genuine Giorgiones in existence. But you didn't count on your friend here betraying you.'

'They're making all this up, Rufus,' said Kinmuir. 'Surely you can see that. They've already contradicted themselves when they said that—'

'So your dreams of a better life are over now,' said Davison. 'It's time to put the razor down and release Mrs Christie.'

'That's right, Phillips,' said the inspector, jabbing his gun in the direction of the artist once more. 'There's nothing left for you now – you need to give yourself up.'

'I would never do that to you, Rufus, you must know that,' James Kinmuir assured him. 'They're trying to set us against one another.'

I felt the artist's quickened breath on my neck and could discern the acrid smell of fear emanating from his skin. People behaved unpredictably in such a state. There was no telling how he might react. And perhaps he didn't know himself.

What he did now would make the difference between life and death, his and my own. A quick slash with the razor and my existence would be snuffed out. I thought of how much I had risked to bring the killers to justice. I thought of the possibility of not seeing my daughter, Rosalind, again. My chance of happiness with Max – the man who was due to be my husband – would disappear. And I would be no more. My memories, my experiences, all gone. And what would I leave behind? A few novels and a clutch of entertaining short stories. People might talk fondly of me for a while, but then I would slip away from their minds, melting into the mists of the past.

No, I was not ready for that.

In my handbag at my feet there was something that I could use to drug Phillips. But would I be able to reach the bag, open it, and inject him with the drug before he took a quick swipe at me with the blade? I knew the chances of my survival were low, but I had to fight back. What other option did I have? I took a deep breath and was about to launch myself forwards when I felt Phillips's grip on me loosen. I turned my head to see his eyes full of fury, pure and black.

'It was *my* idea,' shouted Phillips at his friend. 'Without me you wouldn't have known about the Giorgione. There was only one person in this house who knew and that was the old lady.'

'Calm down, Rufus,' said Kinmuir. 'I told you, it's not true. You can go and search my bedroom if you like. That's the original oil there, the one you're holding. And how would I have got hold of such a perfect copy?'

But Phillips could not see the logic behind such a statement. 'You said that we would never have to worry again, that we could live out the rest of our lives in style,' said Phillips. 'And there you were, planning to double-cross me from the beginning.' He laughed then, a harsh, sardonic laugh that brought tears to his eyes. 'To think – I actually thought you were the nicer one of us. The mild-mannered schoolmaster whose family had fallen on hard times. A handsome chap, if a little on the dim side. You were amazed when I told you the name of the artist who painted this.' He held up the panel. 'To you it was simply one of those little pictures that clutter the upstairs landing. Nothing special. You didn't realise it had been painted by the Venetian master Giorgione and could be worth – well, it was priceless. And then, when I came up with the plan to kill your uncle, you said that I was a genius. But in truth I was being manipulated from day one.' The anger that had clouded his face cleared and, in just a few brief moments, he looked at his friend with a range of emotions that veered from longing to regret through pain and disappointment. 'Well, who's the fool now?'

At that exact moment, Phillips pushed me to one side and threw the Giorgione into the fire.

I looked up to see that both Davison and Hawkins were pointing their guns directly at Rufus, ready to fire.

'Don't shoot him!' I shouted. Justice needed to done.

I watched, mesmerised, as the flames began to consume the corners of the wooden panel, blackening the already dark picture. James Kinmuir rushed across the room, a look of desperation in his eyes.

'What the bloody hell do you think you're doing?' he said to Phillips.

Kinmuir grabbed a pair of brass tongs and wrenched the painting from the fire but, as he did so, Phillips struck out with the razor, slashing him across the stomach. At first Kinmuir looked only mildly surprised, but then he screamed in pain as he understood what had been done to him and registered the seriousness of the injury. He stared at the small panel, which was still alight, and let it and the brass tongs fall by his feet. His hands grasped his belly in an effort to stem the bleeding, but the thick red liquid oozed out between his fingers, staining his shirt and trousers so that it looked as though he were wearing a bloody apron.

'Watch out!' shouted Davison, as he looked down at the burning painting.

Davison tried to stamp out the flames which were beginning to lick at the corner of the Persian rug, but with each kick the fire only seemed to grow. A moment later the flames caught the tassels at the bottom of the red velvet curtains and a second or so after that the whole window became a terrifying spectacle of fire.

'Get everyone out of here!' screamed Davison. His words were unnecessary; everyone apart from myself, Davison, the inspector, Rufus Phillips and the seriously injured James Kinmuir had rushed out of the room.

'Agatha – you too! Go now!' said Davison. 'We'll take care of Phillips and Kinmuir.'

He must have read the concerned expression on my face – what exactly did he mean by 'take care'? – because he added, 'Don't worry. We'll make sure someone stands trial for all of this.'

'Very well,' I said as I began to cough from the thick acrid smoke that was beginning to fill the room.

But, as I turned to pick up my handbag, I felt a hand encircle my left wrist.

'Where do you think you're going?' said Phillips, holding up the bloodied razor and kicking my bag away from me.

I should have let the men shoot him.

The fire had started to take full possession of the room now, rippling across the wood panelling, licking its way around the cornices and consuming the edges of the furniture.

The air was blackening, making it difficult to breathe.

I tried to wrench my wrist away from Phillips, but he tightened his grip, digging his bony fingers deep into my flesh. His eyes – once almost girlish in their prettiness – had taken on an empty, hollow quality that frightened me. It was as if he knew he had nothing left to lose now.

'Let her go!' ordered Davison, pointing his gun at Phillips again.

The inspector trained his gun on the artist as well.

'There's no way out of this,' Davison warned.

The fire encircled me now, crackling and fizzing with a manic intensity. I felt the heat of the flames burn my face and the smoke filling my throat. Phillips shunted me towards him so that I stood in front of him, functioning as a kind of shield. He knew that if Davison or Hawkins were to shoot they ran a high risk of killing me too.

'What – what is it you want?' I managed to ask, as the smoke began to choke me.

'I want to see you die,' whispered Phillips.

Davison and Hawkins tried shifting their positions to see if they could take Phillips by surprise or have a clear aim at his back or shoulder, but with each step he outmanoeuvred them. He held me closer to him so that I felt his breath against my ear. It was the embrace of a lover, but here that lover was death itself. I tried to struggle – if I could just reach my handbag I might stand a chance – but with each attempt to break free he held me more tightly.

'Why did you have to ruin it?' Phillips asked. 'You know you made it so much worse. If you'd never come here, there would only have been one death – Robin's. If you'd never come, the old lady would still be alive. How does that make you feel? Don't you think you should share the burden of guilt?'

I thought of that night at dinner when I had casually related the details of my conversation with Mrs Kinmuir. I remembered the melancholy which had shadowed James Kinmuir's face when I declaimed the *Cock Robin* rhyme.

I tried to answer Phillips, but the smoke was too much for me.

'Move away from her,' shouted Hawkins. 'Move or I'll shoot.'

I heard the click of a trigger and then a moment later an explosion deafened me.

'You hit the fireplace,' said Davison. 'Don't do it again, Hawkins, it's too risky.'

'But, if we do nothing, he's going to kill her.' Hawkins was coughing so hard that it sounded as though he might fetch up his lungs. 'In fact, if we don't get out, all of us are going to die in here.'

He reached out to try to encourage Davison to leave with him then staggered to the door. Something cracked above him – a beam or the joists in the room over us – and then a piece of the ceiling crashed down, narrowly missing him.

'Davison – get out while you can!' the inspector shouted before he disappeared through the door.

'Don't worry, Agatha – I'm not leaving you,' Davison called out.

Again I tried to talk, but the burning sensation in my throat had silenced me.

Phillips brought up the razor and pressed its blade to my

cheek once more. The feel of the cold metal as it touched my hot face came as something of a relief.

'So, what will it be?' asked Phillips. 'How do you want to die?'

How would I die? Would it be death by inhaling too much smoke, after which the fire would consume my body? Or would Phillips snuff out my life with a quick slash of the poisoned blade across my throat?

I tried to make out Davison's form through the smoke, but his figure looked as insubstantial as a ghost. Was he taking a step towards the door? Was he going to abandon me after all? There was no point in him sacrificing his life.

I coughed, managed to clear my throat and rasped out the words, 'Just end it – end it now.'

But as I finished the sentence, Phillips let out an almighty scream. He pushed me from him and fell down by the burning Persian carpet.

'Agatha – quick – over here!' Davison cried out, his form coming out of the gloom. 'Take my hand.'

His fingers closed around mine and at that moment I had never felt so grateful for the touch of another human being.

As Davison pulled me towards him I glanced down to see Rufus Phillips gripping the bottom of his leg in agony. Kinmuir's eyes looked at me through the smoke before they settled on the brass tongs which now lay by Phillips's legs. James had taken them, held them in the fire and then pressed the hot metal hard onto his friend's ankle. Phillips began to move with a fury, thrashing out at anything near him. I felt his hand grip my ankle, but Davison wrenched me forward.

The sound of destruction was all around us now. It seemed as if the room, indeed the whole house, were groaning in pain. Glass shattered, ceilings sounded like they were collapsing, furniture was splintering.

'Here, put this over your mouth and eyes,' said Davison, handing me a piece of cloth.

As he guided me through the blackness, I felt the flames singe my skin. I smelt my hair burning. I couldn't breathe. I heard the crack of a staircase, an implosion rather than an explosion, a scream, or rather screams, and then nothing. I felt hands on me and a splash of water on my face. I removed the cloth from my mouth and took in great gulps of air. I felt a coolness on my face, a spray of drizzle on my skin.

Davison was by my side, administering to me like a nurse with her charge.

'Agatha, Agatha – are you all right?' he asked.

I nodded, still unable to speak, but behind Davison's head I saw Dallach Lodge completely engulfed by fire. The flames were so fierce and bright that they lit up the dark ruins of the castle on the ridge above.

Davison must have read the panicked expression in my eyes because he said, 'Don't worry – all the guests and servants are out of the house, apart from Phillips and Kinmuir, that is.' He placed his hand on my shoulder and brushed some ash from my hair. 'It's over, Agatha. And you're safe.'

Chapter Forty-five

The house burnt throughout the evening, sending great clouds of black smoke up into the sky and causing the air to turn a sickly, unnatural shade of pink. All of us watched from a safe spot down by the banks of the sea loch as the windows exploded, masonry collapsed and the roof seemed to melt away into itself before it sent huge billows of dust and dark matter into the air. The noise was terrifying, that of an enormous beast in its death throes.

'*Resurgere ex cineribus*,' muttered Davison to himself.

'What was that?' I asked.

'The family motto of the Kinmuirs,' he replied. 'Do you remember that first day at dinner when Robin Kinmuir told us about the history of the ruined castle? But I don't think anyone will rise out of the ashes from this, do you?'

'No,' I said as I stood transfixed by the awful spectacle before me. 'Phillips and Kinmuir might not have been the only victims. Both of us could have died in there.'

'Yes, I realise that,' said Davison.

'It was stupid of us – stupid of me – to risk so much,' I said, looking down at my dirty hands and blackened dress.

'Perhaps, but what you did was very brave, very brave indeed,' he said. He paused and looked at me as if trying to read my thoughts. 'If you feel you can no longer carry on your association with the intelligence service I would understand. After all, what happened here was just awful, ghastly.'

So he had guessed my feelings.

'And you've done more, much more, than I or anyone from the department could ever have expected. My only hope, if you decide to sever ties with us, is that we can part as friends.'

I looked at him, tears forming in my eyes. 'Of course, friends always,' I said. 'After all, you were the one who dragged me out of there. You saved my life.'

'Well, it's what any gentleman would do,' he said, forcing a smile to keep his own emotions in check.

'There's one other thing I'd like you to do for me,' I said.

'Yes, anything, you know that,' he said.

'John, would you do me the honour of coming to my wedding? I know you must be terribly busy, but it would mean the world to me.' I had risked so much during my days at Dallach Lodge. But now all that was over. Before long I would be a married woman. The idea that I would soon be reunited with Max and Rosalind filled me with joy. 'I meant to ask you before now, but it never seemed like the right time, what with everything going on here. You *will* come, won't you?'

The question seemed to take him a little by surprise. 'Agatha ... I would be delighted.' He coughed and wiped his face with his sleeve as he became aware that the Frith-Stratton sisters were walking over to join us.

I smiled and kissed him softly on the cheek. We stood for a moment, saying nothing as we looked into one another's eyes. What we had experienced at Dallach Lodge – what we had survived – would bind us together for the rest of our lives.

The arrival of the sisters shattered the tender moment between us. 'Oh, my dear,' said May, beginning to fuss around me.

'Look at the state of you,' said Isabella. 'Here, take my handkerchief.'

'Thank you,' I said, wiping the taste of ash and soot from my lips.

'I'm sorry for accusing you earlier,' said Isabella, taking my hand. 'Whatever must you think of us?'

'Don't be silly,' I said. Although I doubted it had anything to do with the investigation, I had a sense that something had been kept from me by the Frith-Stratton sisters. I wasn't certain how to ask the question. It turned out I didn't need to.

'There's something you want to know, I can tell,' said May. 'Is it about my baby?'

Isabella cast a warning look at May, but her sister ignored it. 'It's too late for any more secrets, sister. And I don't mind telling Mrs Christie, not after what she's been through – she nearly perished in there.'

Davison stepped away from us as May took a deep breath and began. 'You see, I was once married – Bill was a lovely man, but he died in the war,' she said. 'He left me a parting gift, a baby. But when my little girl, Lily, was one year old she caught a cold, which turned into a fever and then pneumonia. The doctor tried to save her, but it was no good.'

May struggled to control her emotions. Her lips trembled and her eyes filled with tears. I remembered how upset she had been when the inspector talked about Amelia Dyer and the murders of those babies in her care. Now she turned away and looked into the distance, across the sea loch, as she continued with her story. 'It all proved too much for me and, for a while, I had to go … into an institution.'

'May, you don't need to say all this, not now,' said Isabella.

But May ignored her and carried on. 'If it hadn't been for dear Isabella's care, I doubt I would have made it out of the asylum,' she said, taking her sister's hands. 'I thought I would die in there. The screams – such terrible screams. And then there were some other things I saw, such awful things.' Her face became haunted by memories of the past and she started to cry like a little girl. 'I'm sorry,' she said as her sister placed her arm around her. 'I'm sorry.'

So I had been right: the strange blankness about the two sisters could be explained by the shared secret and May's sense of shame regarding her time in an asylum. And what of the writing of the romantic novels? I didn't want to ask any more – Inspector Hawkins was walking over to join us – but I suspected it was Isabella who bore the greater share of the work.

'I hope I'm not interrupting anything, Mrs Christie?' asked the inspector.

'No, not at all,' I said, forcing a smile.

He raised his hand and gestured for Davison to come closer. 'I don't know whether you and Mr Davison would be happy to answer a few questions?' he added. 'It's just that there are some things I need to get straight in my head. We can leave it until later if you like, or if you'd rather come to the station in Portree?'

ANDREW WILSON

'No, now will do as well as any time,' I said. Davison agreed.

'Thank you,' he said. 'It's a shame no one will stand trial for all of this and a great deal of evidence will no doubt have been lost in the fire.' Hawkins looked once more at the burning building and shook his head. 'But I suppose death comes as the end for men like Phillips and Kinmuir, whether it's the gallows or a fire.'

'Indeed,' I said.

'Now, as for the painting by this Italian artist . . . ?'

'Yes, Giorgione,' said Davison. 'After I overhead Kinmuir and Phillips talking in the attic room, I came down to the library to do some research. I found some books about art history belonging to old Mrs Kinmuir. One volume about the Italian Renaissance told me that the artist was born Giorgio Barbarelli da Castelfranco around 1477 or 1478. Scholars don't know that much about him other than that he started quite young with commissions to paint the portraits of powerful men such as the Doge Agostino Barbarigo and that he was famous for works such as *The Three Philosophers* and *The Tempest*. He's known for the mysterious nature of his paintings and the fact that there are so few of them in existence. So to find an undocumented one . . . well, as you can imagine, its value would be tremendous.'

'And the original was upstairs in Kinmuir's room?' asked Hawkins.

'No, I'm afraid not,' I said. 'That was just an invention on my part to try to cause a schism between the two friends.'

'So you let a painting worth – what? – hundreds of thousands of pounds be consigned to the flames?'

'Yes, I'm afraid we did,' I said. 'You see, Mr Davison and I, well, we discussed all the possible outcomes and we came to the conclusion that this was the best one. We thought that bringing these two men to justice was worth more than any work of art — even such a rare one as this. You see, evil cannot be seen to triumph. And what those two men did was evil, especially framing an innocent young woman – Miss Passerini – for the crimes and murdering poor old Mrs Kinmuir in that way.'

At the mention of her name Miss Passerini came over to join us, accompanied by Simon Peterson. It was clear he would never want to leave her side again.

'Talking of the old lady, I wanted to ask you something,' said Hawkins.

'Yes?' I replied.

'I still don't quite understand the full significance of those Italian words that Mrs Kinmuir said to you during your talk with her – that you in turn repeated to the group that night at dinner.'

By now we had been joined by Mrs Buchanan and Dr Fitzpatrick, and everyone was eager to find out the missing answers to the puzzle.

'The words must have come back to her in her dotage,' I said. 'As we know, when people are losing their faculties, they may not remember anything about what they have just done – who they saw that morning, what they had for breakfast and so on. But sometimes they can recall quite clearly conversations they had with people going back years. And the two young men didn't know what else the old lady might say.

'That day when I went to see Mrs Kinmuir, in the midst of reciting some of the verses from *The Grand Old Duke of York*, she had said, "Oh yes, it was a grand tour all right." At the time the words meant nothing to me as I thought she had been referring to the nursery rhyme. But of course, I realised later she must have been talking about one of her relatives going on the Grand Tour, in the days when young men from good families travelled to France, Switzerland and Italy to study and collect art. I suppose that is how the Giorgione came to be in the family. Mrs Kinmuir clearly knew of the painting's existence but had not told her nephew or anyone else in the family about it because I believe at one point there had been a falling-out between them. Robin related something of this to me the first night I was here. I suspect the source of that problem was Mrs Kinmuir's disapproval of her nephew's treatment of his first wife. And, by the time Mrs Kinmuir came to live here at Dallach Lodge, she had lost her faculties. Yes, a very sad state of affairs.'

I looked at Davison, who, with a slight nod, gave me permission to relate something he in turn had told me.

'So you see, a small, seemingly insignificant painting drove two men to commit murder,' I said. 'You probably didn't have a chance to study the picture, and even if you had done so you might not have been able to see much because its surface was very aged and dirty. It was of a crucifixion scene, with someone, possibly Saint John the Evangelist, gazing up at Christ in his last moments. On the back of the canvas there was an inscription, very faint, but Mr Davison made it out.'

I took a breath, realising that everyone had turned to me to hear the very last clue. 'That inscription was the title of the painting, "*L'ho visto morire*" . . . or *I Saw Him Die*.'

The Facts

- In August 1930, Agatha Christie travelled to Skye with her daughter, Rosalind; her secretary, Carlo Fisher; and Carlo's sister, Mary. They registered to stay at the Broadford Hotel. 'I found Skye lovely,' Christie wrote in her autobiography. 'I did sometimes wish it wouldn't rain every day, though it was only a fine misty rain which did not really count.'

- On 11 September 1930, Agatha married the archaeologist Max Mallowan, whom she had met in Ur, Iraq, earlier that year. They married in the Memorial Chapel of St Cuthbert's Church, Edinburgh. Agatha worried that Max was far too young for her and, on their wedding certificate, both of them lied about their ages — she gave her age as 37, while his was recorded as 31. In fact, Agatha was 40 and Max was 26. 'I had had so much publicity, and been caused so much misery by it, that I wanted things kept as quiet as possible,' Christie wrote in her autobiography.

- Many details about the Secret Intelligence Service mentioned in *I Saw Him Die* are true, including information about Sir Paul Dukes (https://en.wikipedia.org/wiki/Paul_Dukes) and Sir Mansfield Smith-Cumming (*The Quest for C: Mansfield Cumming and the Founding of the Secret Service* by Alan Judd, HarperCollins). According to an article in the *Independent*, 'Cumming was so pleased to discover that semen made a good invisible ink that his agents adopted the motto: "Every man his own stylo".' ('The spymaster who was stranger than fiction', Piers Brendon, *Independent*, 29 October 1999). For more details, read Keith Jeffery's excellent book *MI6: The History of the Secret Intelligence Service, 1909–1949* (Bloomsbury).

- Agatha Christie wrote a number of novels whose titles echo popular nursery rhymes, including *And Then There Were None* (1939); *One, Two, Buckle My Shoe* (1940); *Five Little Pigs* (1942); *Crooked House* (1949); *A Pocket Full of Rye* (1953) and *Hickory Dickory Dock* (1955). Her long-running play *The Mousetrap*, which opened in London's West End in 1952, started life as a BBC radio play *Three Blind Mice* which she wrote for Queen Mary's eightieth birthday celebrations in May 1947. Keen-eyed readers might spot allusions to these and other works in *I Saw Him Die*.

- Agatha Christie is still the bestselling novelist of all time.

Acknowledgements

I would like to thank my fabulous agent and friend, Clare Alexander, as well as the whole team at Aitken Alexander Associates, in particular Lisa Baker, Lesley Thorne, Steph Adam, Anna Watkins, Monica MacSwan and Amy St Johnston.

At Simon & Schuster in the UK I would like to acknowledge Ian Chapman and my fantastic editor, Suzanne Baboneau, both of whom have supported me throughout the writing of this series. In addition I would like to thank Bec Farrell, Judith Long, UK copy editor Sally Partington, Justine Gold, and the marketing department, the brilliant Jess Barratt, Harriett Collins, and everyone in publicity, Gill Richardson, Claire Bennett, Richard Hawton, Rhys Thomas, and the super-enthusiastic sales team. The cover was the work of the talented Mark Smith and was designed by Pip Watkins.

In the US I would like to thank the wonderful staff at Atria, particularly my editor Peter Borland, as well as Sean Delone and Stephanie Mendoza.

Thanks too to all the Agatha fans, scholars and academics who have embraced the series, particularly Dr John Curran, Mike Linane, Dr Jamie Bernthal, Scott Wallace Baker, Tina Hodgkinson, Emily and Audrey at The Year of Agatha blog, and many more.

Lastly, I would like to thank all my family and friends and Marcus Field.